D1030933

The Fairy Ring

THE FAIRY RING

EDITED BY

**KATE DOUGLAS WIGGIN and
NORA ARCHIBALD SMITH**

ILLUSTRATED BY ELIZABETH MacKINSTRY

DOUBLEDAY & COMPANY, INC.
GARDEN CITY 1956 NEW YORK

PRINTED IN THE UNITED STATES OF AMERICA

Messrs. McClure, Phillips & Company wish to make acknowledgment of their indebtedness to the following publishers:

Little, Brown & Company, for permission to use "Blanche and Vermilion" and "Prince Desire and Princess Mignonette" from Old-Fashioned Fairy Tales;

A. Wessells Company, for permission to use the story of "The Clever Prince" from Fairy Tales from Afar;

American Book Company, for permission to use "Drakesbill and His Friends" from Fairy Tales and Fables;

University Publishing Company, for permission to use "The Troll's Hammer" from Fairy Life;

Harper & Brothers, for permission to use "The Fair One with Golden Locks," "The White Cat," "Prince Cherry," and "The Frog Prince" from Miss Mulock's Fairy Book, and "Yvon and Finette," "The Twelve Months," and "The Story of Coquerico" from Laboulaye's Fairy Tales of all Nations;

G. P. Putnam's Sons, for permission to use "History of Tom Thumb" and "Tattercoats" from Joseph Jacobs's English Fairy Tales; "Munachar and Manachar" from Joseph Jacobs's Celtic Fairy Tales, and "Master Tobacco," "Mother Roundabout's Daughter," and "The Sheep and the Pig" from Dasent's Tales from the Fjeld;

F. A. Stokes Company, for permission to use "Lars, My Lad," and "Twigmuntus and Cowbelliantus" from Fairy Tales from the Swedish;

Longmans, Green & Company, for permission to use the following stories: "The Yellow Dwarf," "The Many-Furred

[v]

Creature," "Spindle, Shuttle, and Needle," "Princess and the Glass Hill," "The Golden Crab," "The Magic Ring," "Snow-white and Rose-red," "Graciosa and Percinet," "The Iron Stove," "The Good Little Mouse," and "The Three Feathers" from the Andrew Lang Fairy Books.

We also wish to express our thanks to Mr. Seumas Mac-Manus, for permission to use "The Bee, the Harp, and the Bum-Clock," "The Long Leather Bag," and "The Widow's Daughter" from his books, Donegal Fairy Tales *and* In Chimney Corners, *published by us.*

CONTENTS

SCANDINAVIAN

ENGLISH

FRENCH

[vii]

CONTENTS

CONTENTS

CONTENTS

ILLUSTRATIONS

ILLUSTRATIONS

Throned on a grassy knoll, I watch
  The elfin host come trooping by,
And hear the whir of fairy wings,
  The goblin voices, shrill and high.
Behind them glides a magic train
  Of Kings and Princes, armor-clad,
And serving as their squires bold
  Boots, Ashiepattle, Cinderlad.
With silken rustle, flash of gem,
  Queen and Czaritsa sweep along,
While red-capped Troll and rainbow Sprite
  Peep out amid the enchanted throng.

> *Ting-ling, ting-ling, how sweet the ring,*
>   *Like golden bells, of fairy laughter;*
> *Rap-tap, rap-tap, how sharp the clap*
>   *Of fairy footfalls following after!*

Where witch-grass grows and fern-seed lies,
  A Fairy Ring is dimly seen ;
And there a glitt'ring host is met
  To dance upon the moonlit green.
Riquet, the Tufted, lightly turns
  The Fair One with the Golden Hair ;
And Prince Desire and Mignonette
  Form yet another graceful pair.
Tall as a tower stands Galifron;
  The Desert Fay, with snakes bedight,
First pirouettes with him and then
  With wee Tom Thumb, King Arthur's Knight.

> *Ting-ling, ting-ling, how sweet the ring,*
>   *Like golden bells, of fairy laughter;*
> *Rap-tap, rap-tap, how sharp the clap*
>   *Of fairy footfalls following after!*

Sweet, unseen harpers harp and sing,
  Faint elfin horns the air repeat ;
Rapunzel shakes her shining braids,
  The White Cat trips with velvet feet.
Rose-red, Snow-white, the faithful Bear,
  Cross hands with gallant Percinet;
While Tattercoats, in turn, salutes
  Yvon, the Fearless, and Finette.
—But hark ! the cock begins to crow ;
  The darkness turns to day, and, look!
The fairy dancers whirl within
  The crimson covers of this book!

NORA ARCHIBALD SMITH

INTRODUCTION

"THERE was once upon a time a king who had a garden; in that garden was an apple tree, and on that apple tree grew a golden apple every year."

These stories are the golden apples that grew on the tree in the king's garden; grew and grew and grew as the golden years went by; and being apples of gold they could never wither nor shrink nor change, so that they are as beautiful and precious for you to pluck to-day as when first they ripened long, long ago.

Perhaps you do not care for the sort of golden apples that grew in the king's garden; perhaps you prefer plain russets or green pippins? Well, these are not to be despised, for they also are wholesome food for growing boys and girls; but unless you can taste the flavor and feel the magic that lies in the golden apples of the king's garden you will lose one of the joys of youth.

No one can help respecting apples (or stories) that gleam as brightly to-day as they did hundreds and thousands of years ago, when first the tiny blossoms ripened into precious fruit.

> "Should you ask me whence these stories,
> Whence these legends and traditions
> With the odors of the forest,
> With the dew and damp of meadows?"—

I can say only that the people were telling fairy tales in Egypt, in Joseph's time, more than three thousand years ago; and that grand old Homer told them in the famous "Odyssey," with its witches and giants, its cap of darkness, and shoes of swiftness. Old nurses and village crones have repeated them by

[xv]

INTRODUCTION

the fireside and in the chimney corner; shepherds and cow-herds have recounted them by the brookside, until the children of the world have all learned them by heart, bequeathing them, generation after generation, as a priceless legacy to their own children. Nor must you fancy that they have been told in your own tongue only. Long, long before the art of printing was known, men and women of all nations recited these and similar tales to one another, never thinking that the day would come when they would be regarded as the peculiar property of youth and childhood. There is not a country in Europe, Asia, Africa, Australia, or the islands of the sea where fairy stories of one sort or another have not been current since the dawn of speech; and to make this Fairy Ring of sixty-odd tales the editors have read and sifted as many hundreds. You will miss Cinderella, Red Riding Hood, Jack and the Beanstalk, Toads and Diamonds, Puss in Boots, Blue-beard, Beauty and the Beast, and other favorites, but these have been omitted because they can be easily found in half a dozen volumes already on your shelves, and we preferred to give you in their stead stories less well known and hackneyed.

The so-called Household Tales, such as Drakesbill, The Little Good Mouse, and The Grateful Cobra go back to the times when men thought of animals as their friends and brothers, and in the fireside stories of that period the central figures were often wise and powerful beasts, beasts that had language, assumed human form, and protected as well as served mankind. Frogs, fishes, birds, wolves, cobras, cats, one and all win our sympathy, admiration, and respect as we read of their deeds of prowess, their sagacious counsel, their superhuman power of overcoming obstacles and rescuing from danger or death the golden-haired princess, the unhappy queen mother, or the intrepid but unfortunate prince.

The giants and ogres and witches in the fairy stories need not greatly affright even the youngest readers. For the most part they overreach themselves in ill-doing and are quite at the mercy (as they properly should be) of the brave and virtuous knight or the clever little princess.

INTRODUCTION

If you chance to be an elder brother or sister it may surprise and distress you to find that all the grace, courage, wit, and beauty, as well as most of the good fortune, are vested in the youngest member of the household. The fairy-tale family has customs of its own when it comes to the distribution of vices and virtues, and the elder sons and daughters are likely to be haughty, selfish, and cruel, while the younger ones are as enchantingly beautiful as they are marvelously amiable. The malevolent stepmother still further complicates the domestic situation, and she is so wicked and malicious that if it were not for the dear and delightful one in your own household, or the equally lovable one next door, you might think step-mothers worse than ogres or witches. I cannot account for this prejudice, except that perhaps the ideal of mother love and mother goodness has always been so high in the world that the slightest deviation from it has been held up to scorn. As for the superhuman youngest son and daughter, perhaps they are used only to show us that the least and humblest things and persons are capable of becoming the mightiest and most powerful.

Wiseacres (and people who have no love for golden apples) say that in many of these tales "The greater the rogue the better his fortune"; but the Grimm brothers, most famous and most faithful of fairy-tale collectors, reply that the right user of these narratives "will find no evil therein, but, as an old proverb has it, merely a witness of his own heart. Children point at the stars without fear, while others, as the popular superstition goes, thereby offend the angels."

The moment you have plucked a golden apple from the magic tree in the king's garden (which phrase, being interpreted, means whenever you begin one of the tales in this book) you will say farewell to time and space as readily as if you had put on a wishing cap, or a pair of seven league boots, or had blown an elfin pipe to call the fairy host. It matters not when anything happened. It is "Once upon a time," or "A long time ago." As to just where, that is quite as uncertain and unimportant, for we all feel familiar with

INTRODUCTION

the fairy-tale landscape, which has delightful features all its own, and easily recognizable. The house is always in the heart of a deep, deep wood like the one " amidst the forest darkly green" where Snowwhite lived with the dwarfs. You know the Well at the World's End whence arose the Frog Prince; the Glass Mountain that Cinderlad climbed, first in his copper, then in his silver, then in his golden armor; the enchanted castle where the White Cat dwelt; the sea over which Faithful John sailed with the Princess of the Golden Roof.

In the story of The Spindle, the Shuttle, and the Needle, the prince has just galloped past the cottage in the wood where the maiden is turning her wheel, when the spindle leaps out of her hand to follow him on his way—leaps and dances and pursues him along the woodland path, the golden thread dragging behind. Then the prince turns (fairy princes always turn at the right time), sees the magic spindle, and, led by the shimmering thread, finds his way back to the lovely princess, the sweetest, loveliest, thriftiest, most bewitching little princess in the whole world, and a princess he might never have found had it not been for the kind offices of the spindle, shuttle, and needle.

This book is the magic spindle; the stories that were golden apples have melted into a golden thread, a train of bright images that will lead you into a radiant country where no one ever grows old; where, when the prince finds and loves the princess, he marries her and they are happy ever after; where the obstacles of life melt under the touch of comprehending kindness; where menacing clouds of misfortune are blown away by gay good will; and where wicked little trolls are invariably defeated by wise simpletons.

We feel that we can do anything when we journey in this enchanting country. Come, then, let us mount and be off; we can ride fast and far, for imagination is the gayest and fleetest of steeds. Let us climb the gilded linden tree and capture the Golden Bird. Let us plunge into the heart of the Briar Wood where the Rose o' the World lies sleeping. Let us break the spell that holds all her court in drowsy slumber, and then,

[xviii]

INTRODUCTION

coming out into the sunshine, mount and ride again into the forest. As we pass the Fairy Tree on the edge of the glade we will pluck a Merry Leaf, for this, when tucked away in belt or pouch, will give us a glad heart and a laughing eye all the day long. We shall meet ogres, no doubt, and the more the merrier, for, like Finette, we have but to cry "Abracadabra!" to defeat not ogres only, but wicked bailiffs, stewards, seneschals, witch hags, and even the impossibly vicious stepmother! Cormoran and Blunderbore will quail before us, for our magic weapons, like those of Cornish Jack, will be all-powerful. Then, flushed with triumph we will mount the back of the North Wind and search for the castle that lies East o' the Sun and West o' the Moon. Daylight will fade, the stars come out, the fire burn low on the hearth, playmates' voices sound unheeded. We shall still sit in the corner of the window seat with the red-covered volume on our knees; for hours ago the magic spindle wrought its spell, and we have been following the golden thread that leads from this work-a-day world into fairyland.

KATE DOUGLAS WIGGIN

East o' the Sun and West o' the Moon

ONCE on a time there was a poor husbandman who had so
many children that he hadn't much of either food or
clothing to give them. Pretty children they all were,
but the prettiest was the youngest daughter, who was so lovely
that there was no end to all her loveliness.

So one day—'twas on a Thursday evening, late at the fall
of the year, the weather was so wild and rough outside, and
it was so cruelly dark, and rain fell and wind blew till the
walls of the cottage shook again—there they all sat round the
fire, busy with this thing and that. But just then, all at once,
something gave three taps on the windowpane. Then the
father went out to see what was the matter, and when he got
out of doors, what should he see but a great big white bear!

"Good evening to you," said the White Bear.

"The same to you," said the man.

"Will you give me your youngest daughter? If you will,
I'll make you as rich as you are now poor," said the Bear.

Well, the man would not be at all sorry to be rich, but still
he thought he must have a bit of a talk with his daughter first,
so he went in and told them how there was a great white bear
waiting outside, who had given his word to make them rich
if he could only have the youngest daughter.

The lassie said "No" outright. Nothing could get her to
say anything else. So the man went out and settled it with
the White Bear that he should come again the next Thursday
evening and get an answer.

Meantime, he talked his daughter over, and kept on telling
her of all the riches they would get, and how well off she

[3]

would be herself; and so at last she thought better of it, and washed and mended her rags, made herself as smart as she could, and was ready to start.

Next Thursday evening came the White Bear to fetch her, and she got upon his back with her bundle, and off they went.

So, when they had gone a bit of the way, the White Bear said:

"Are you afraid?"

No, she wasn't.

"Well, mind and hold tight to my shaggy coat, and then there's nothing to fear," said the White Bear.

So she rode a long, long way, until they came to a very steep hill. There, on the face of it, the White Bear gave a knock, and a door opened, and they came into a castle where there were many rooms, all lit up, rooms gleaming with silver and gold, and there, too, was a table ready laid, and it was all as grand as grand could be.

Then the White Bear gave her a silver bell, and when she wanted anything she had only to ring it and she would get it at once.

Well, after she had eaten and drunk, and evening wore on, she got sleepy after her journey, and thought she would like to go to bed. So she rang the bell, and she had scarce taken hold of it before she came into a chamber where there was a bed made, as fair and white as anyone could wish to sleep in, with silken pillows and curtains and gold fringe.

She slept quite soundly until morning; then she found her breakfast waiting in a pretty room. When she had eaten it, the girl made up her mind to take a walk around, in order to find out if there were any other people there besides herself.

But she saw nobody but an old woman, whom she took to be a witch, and as the dame beckoned to her, the girl went at once.

"Little girl," said the Witch, "if you'll promise not to say a word to anybody, I'll tell you the secret about this place."

Of course, the girl promised at once, so the old dame said:

"In this house there lives a White Bear, but you must know

[4]

that he is only a White Bear in the daytime. Every night he throws off his beast shape and becomes a man, for he is under the spell of a wicked fairy. Now, be sure and not mention this to anybody, or misfortune will come," and with these words she disappeared.

So things went on happily for some time, but at last the girl began to grow sad and sorrowful, for she went about all day alone, and she longed to go home to see her father and mother and brothers and sisters.

"Well, well," said the Bear, "perhaps there's a cure for all this sorrow. But you must promise me one thing. When you go home, you mustn't talk about me, except when they are all present, or, if you do, you will bring bad luck to both of us."

So one Sunday the White Bear came and said now they would set off to see her father and mother.

Well, off they started, she sitting on his back, and they went far and long. At last they came to a grand house, and there her brothers and sisters were running about out of doors at play, and everything was so pretty 'twas a joy to see.

"This is where your father and mother live now," said the White Bear; "but don't forget what I told you, or you'll make us both unlucky."

No—bless her!—she'd not forget, and when they reached the house the White Bear turned right about and left her.

Then, when she went in to see her father and mother, there was such joy there was no end to it. None of them could thank her enough for all the good fortune she had brought them.

They had everything they wished, as fine as could be, and they all wanted to know how she got on and where she lived.

Well, she said it was very good to live where she did, and she had all she wished. What she said besides I don't know, but I don't believe any of them had the right end of the stick, or that they got much out of her.

But after dinner her sister called her outside the room, and asked all manner of questions about the White Bear—whether he was cross, and whether she ever set eyes on him, and such like—and the end of it all was that she told her sister the story of how the White Bear was under a spell.

But the other girl wouldn't listen to the story, for she said it couldn't be true, and this made the youngest daughter very angry.

In the evening the White Bear came and fetched her away, and when they had gone a bit of the way he asked her whether she had done as he had told her and refused to speak about him.

Then she confessed that she had spoken a few words to her sister about him, and the Bear was very angry, for he said she would surely bring bad luck to them both.

When they reached home, she remembered how her sister had refused to believe the story about the White Bear, so in the night, when she knew that the Bear was fast asleep, she stole out of bed, lighted her candle, and crept into his room. Yes, there he lay fast asleep, but instead of being a White Bear, he was the handsomest Prince you ever saw. She gave such a start that she dropped three spots of hot tallow from the candle on to his pillow, so she ran off in a great fright.

Next morning the White Bear said to her: " I fear you have found out my secret, for I saw the drops of tallow on my pillow this morning, and now I know that you spoke to your sister about me. If you had only kept quiet for a whole year, then I should have become a man for always, and I should have made you my wife at once. But now all ties are snapped between us, and I must go away to a big castle which stands East o' the sun and West o' the moon, and there, too, lives a Princess with a nose three ells long, and she's the wife I must have now."

The girl wept, and took it ill, but there was no help for it, go he must.

Then she asked if she mightn't go with him.

No! she mightn't.

" Tell me the way, then," she said, " and I'll search you out; that, surely, I may get leave to do."

Yes; she might do that, but there was no way to the place.

THE FAIRY RING

It lay East o' the sun and West o' the moon, and thither she'd never find her way.

So next morning, when she woke, both Prince and castle were gone, and there she lay on a little green patch, in the midst of the thick, gloomy wood, and by her side lay the same bundle of rags that she had brought with her from her old home.

So when she had rubbed the sleep from her eyes, and wept till she was tired, she set out on her way and walked many, many days, till she came to a lofty crag. Under it sat an old hag, who played with a golden apple, which she tossed about. The lassie asked her if she knew the way to the Prince who lived in the castle that lay East o' the sun and West o' the moon, and who was to marry a Princess with a nose three ells long.

"How did you come to know about him?" said the old hag; "but maybe you are the lassie who ought to have had him?"

Yes, she was.

"So, so, it's you, is it?" said the old hag. "Well, all I know about him is that he lives in the castle that lies East o' the sun and West o' the moon, and thither you'll come, late or never; but still you may have the loan of my horse, and on him you can ride to my next neighbor. Maybe she'll be able to tell you what you want to know; and when you get there, just give the horse a switch under the left ear, and beg him to be off home; and stay, you may take this golden apple with you."

So she got upon the horse and rode a long, long time, till she came to another crag, under which sat another old hag, with a golden carding-comb in her hand. The lassie asked her if she knew the way to the castle that lay East o' the sun and West o' the moon, and she answered, like the first old hag, that she knew nothing about it, except that it was East o' the sun and West o' the moon.

"And thither you'll come, late or never; but you shall have the loan of my horse to go to my next neighbor; maybe she'll tell you all about it; and when you get there, just switch the horse under the left ear and beg him to be off home."

And this old hag gave her the golden carding-comb; it might be she'd find some use for it, she said. So the lassie got up on the horse and rode far, far away, and had a weary time; and so at last she came to another great crag, under which sat another old hag, spinning with a golden spinning wheel. The lassie asked her, too, if she knew the way to the Prince and where the castle was that lay East o' the sun and West o' the moon. So it was the same thing over again.

"Maybe it's you who ought to have had the Prince?" said the old hag.

Yes, it was.

But, she, too, didn't know the way a bit better than the other two. East o' the sun and West o' the moon she knew it was; that was all.

"And thither you'll come, late or never; but I'll lend you my horse, and then I think you'd best ride to the East Wind and ask him; maybe he knows those parts and can blow you thither. But when you get to him, you need only give the horse a switch under the left ear, and he'll trot home of himself."

And so, too, she gave the lassie the golden spinning wheel. "Maybe you'll find a use for it," said the old hag.

Then on she rode a great many weary days before she got to the East Wind's house; but at last she did reach it, and then she asked the East Wind if he could tell her the way to the Prince who dwelt East o' the sun and West o' the moon. Yes, the East Wind had often heard about them, both the Prince and the castle, but he couldn't tell her the way, for he'd never blown so far.

"But, if you will, I'll go with you to my brother, the West Wind; maybe he's been there, for he's much stronger. So, if you will just jump on my back, I'll carry you thither."

Yes, she got on his back, and I should just think they went swiftly along.

So, when they reached there, they went into the West

Wind's house, and the East Wind said the lassie he had brought was the one that ought to have married the Prince who lived in the castle East o' the sun and West o' the moon, and that she had set out to seek him. He then said how he had come with her, and would be glad to know if the West Wind knew how to get to the castle.

"Nay," said the West Wind, "for I've never blown so far; but, if you will, I'll go with you to our brother, the South Wind, for he's much stronger than either of us, and he has flapped his wings both far and wide. Maybe he'll tell you; so you can get on my back and I'll carry you to him."

Yes, she got on his back, and so they traveled to the South Wind, and they weren't so very long on the way, I should think.

When they reached there, the West Wind asked him if he could tell them the way to the castle that lay East o' the sun and West o' the moon, for this was the lassie who ought to have married the Prince who lived there.

"You don't say so! That's she, is it?" said the South Wind. "Well, I've blustered about in most places in my time, but so far I have never blown; but, if you will, I'll take you to my brother, the North Wind; he is the oldest and strongest of all of us. If he doesn't know where to find the place, you will never find anybody to tell you where it is. You can get on my back and I'll carry you thither."

Yes, she got on his back, and away he went from his house at a very high rate, and this time, too, she wasn't long on her way.

When they got to the North Wind's house, he was so wild and cross that the puffs came from quite a long way off.

"WHAT DO YOU WANT?" he roared out to them, in such a voice that it made them both shiver.

"Well," said the South Wind, "you needn't talk like that, for here I am, your brother, the South Wind, and here is the lassie who ought to have had the Prince who dwells at the castle that lies East o' the sun and West o' the moon,

THE FAIRY RING

and now she wants to know if you were ever there, and can tell her the way, for she would be so glad to find it again."

"YES! I KNOW WELL ENOUGH WHERE IT IS," said the North Wind. "Once in my life I blew an aspen leaf there, but I was so tired that I couldn't blow another puff for days after. But if you really wish to go there, and aren't afraid to trust yourself to me, I'll take you on my back and blow you thither."

Yes! with all her heart. She must and would get thither, if it were possible in any way; and as for fear, however madly he went, she wouldn't be at all afraid.

"Very well, then," said the North Wind. "But you must sleep here to-night, for we must have the whole day before us if we are to get thither at all."

Early next morning the North Wind woke her, and puffed himself up, and blew himself out, and made himself so stout and big 'twas fearful to look at him; so off they went, up through the air, as if they would never stop till they came to the world's end.

Down below there was such a storm, it threw down long tracts of wood and many houses, and when it swept over the great sea, ships foundered by hundreds.

So they tore on and on—nobody can believe how far they went—and all the while they still went over the sea, and the North Wind got more and more weary, and so out of breath he could scarce get out a puff. His wings drooped and drooped, till at last he sank so low that the crests of the waves dashed over his heels.

"Are you afraid?" asked the North Wind.

No, she wasn't.

But they weren't very far from land, and the North Wind had still so much strength in him that he managed to throw her upon the shore under the windows of the castle which lay East o' the sun and West o' the moon; but then he was so weak and worn out that he had to stay there and rest for many days before he was fit to return home.

Next morning the lassie sat down under the castle window

[10]

THE LASSIE RIDING OVER THE SEA ON THE BACK OF THE NORTH WIND

and began to play with the golden apple; and the first person she saw was Long-nose, who was to marry the Prince.

"What do you want for your golden apple, lassie?" said Long-nose; and she threw up the window.

"It's not for sale, for gold or money," said the lassie.

"If it's not for sale for gold or money, what is it that you will sell it for?" said the Princess. "You may name your own price for it."

"Well, if you will let me speak a few words alone with the Prince who lives in the castle, I will give you the apple," she answered.

Yes, she might; that could be done. So the Princess got the golden apple, and the lassie was shown into the Prince's room. But when she got inside she found that the Prince was fast asleep, and although she shook him and called him loudly, it was no use, for she couldn't wake him, so she had to go away again.

Next day she sat down under the castle window again, and began to card with her golden carding-comb; and the same thing happened. The Princess asked what she wanted for it; and she said it wasn't for sale for either gold or money, but that if she might have a few words alone with the Prince, the Princess should have the comb.

So she was taken up to the Prince's room, and again she found him fast asleep; and although she wept and shook him for quite a long time she couldn't get life into him.

So the next morning the lassie sat down under the castle window and began to spin with her golden spinning wheel; and that, too, the Princess with the long nose wanted to have.

So she threw up the window and asked what the lassie wanted for it; and the girl said, as she had said twice before, that if she might have a few words alone with the Prince the Princess might have the wheel, and welcome.

Yes, she might do that; and the lassie was shown again into the Prince's room. This time he was wide awake, and he was very pleased indeed to see her.

"Ah!" said the Prince, "you've just come in the nick of

[11]

time, for to-morrow is to be our wedding day; but now I won't
have Long-nose, and you are the bride for me. I'll just say
that I want to find out what my wife is fit for, and then I'll
beg her to wash the pillow slip which has on it the three spots
of tallow. She will be sure to say 'Yes'; but when she tries
to get out the spots she'll soon find that it is not possible,
for she is a troll, like all the rest of her family, and it is not
possible for a troll to get rid of the marks. Then I'll say that
I won't have any other bride than she who can wash out the
spots of tallow, and I'll call you in to do it."

The wedding was to take place next day, so just before
the ceremony the Prince said:

"First of all, I'd just like to see what my bride is fit
for."

"Yes," said the mother, "I'm quite willing."

"Well, I have a pillow slip which, somehow or other, has got
some spots of grease on it, and I have sworn never to take any
bride but the woman who is able to wash them out for me. If
she can't do that, she is not worth having."

Well, that was no great thing, they said, so they agreed;
and she with the long nose began to wash away as hard as
ever she could; but the more she rubbed and scrubbed the
bigger the spots grew.

"Ah!" said the old hag, her mother, "you can't wash; let
me try."

But she hadn't long taken the job in hand before it got
far worse than ever; and with all her rubbing, wringing, and
scrubbing, the spots grew bigger and blacker and darker and
uglier.

Then all the other trolls began to wash; but the longer it
lasted the blacker and uglier it grew, until at last it looked
as though it had been up the chimney.

"Ah!" said the Prince, "you are none of you worth a
straw; you can't wash. Why, there outside sits a beggar
lassie, and I'll be bound she knows how to wash better than
the whole lot of you."

So he shouted to the lassie to come in, and in she came.

THE FAIRY RING

"Can you wash this clean, lassie?" said he.

"I don't know, but I think I can."

And almost before she had taken it and dipped it in the water, it was white as driven snow, and whiter still.

"Yes, you are the lassie for me," said the Prince.

At that the old hag flew in such a rage that she burst on the spot, and the Princess with the long nose after her; and then the whole pack of trolls did the same.

As for the Prince and Princess, they had a grand wedding, and lived happily at the castle East o' the sun and West o' the moon until the end of their days.

The Golden Lantern, Golden Goat, and Golden Cloak

THERE was once a poor widow who had three sons. The two elder went out to work for their living and while at home they were of little use, as they seldom did as their mother wished, whatever she might say to them. But the youngest lad always remained at home, and helped the old widow in her daily occupations. Hence he was much beloved by his mother, but disliked by his brothers, who in mockery gave him the nickname of *Pinkel*.

One day the old widow said to her sons: "You must all go abroad in the world, and seek your fortunes while you can. I am no longer able to feed you here at home, now that you are grown up." The lads answered that they wished for nothing better, since it was contrary to their mother's will that they should remain at home. They then prepared for their departure, and set out on their journey; but, after wandering about from place to place, were unable to procure any employment.

After journeying thus for a long time, they came, late one evening, to a vast lake. Far out in the water there was an

[13]

island, on which there appeared a strong light, as of fire. The lads stopped on shore observing the wondrous light, and thence concluded that there must be human beings in the place. As it was now dark, and the brothers knew not where to find a shelter for the night, they resolved on taking a boat that lay among the reeds, and rowing over to the island to beg a lodging. With this view they placed themselves in the boat and rowed across. On approaching the island they perceived a little hut standing at the water's edge; on reaching which they discovered that the bright light that shone over the neighborhood proceeded from a golden lantern that stood at the door of the hut. In the yard without, a large goat was wandering about, with golden horns, to which small bells were fastened, that gave forth a pleasing sound whenever the animal moved. The brothers wondered much at all this, but most of all at the old crone, who with her daughter inhabited the hut. The crone was both old and ugly, but was sumptuously clad in a pelisse or cloak, worked so artificially with golden threads that it glittered like burnished gold in every hem. The lads saw now very clearly that they had come to no ordinary human being, but to a troll.

After some deliberation the brothers entered, and saw the crone standing by the fireplace, and stirring with a ladle in a large pot that was boiling on the hearth. They told their story and prayed to be allowed to pass the night there; but the crone answered *No!* at the same time directing them to a royal palace, which lay on the other side of the lake. While speaking she kept looking intently on the youngest boy, as he was standing and casting his eyes over everything in the hut. The crone said to him: "What is thy name, my boy?" The lad answered smartly: "I am called Pinkel." The Troll then said: "Thy brothers can go their way, but thou shalt stay here; for thou appearest to me very crafty, and my mind tells me that I have no good to expect from thee if thou shouldst stay long at the King's palace." Pinkel now humbly begged to be allowed to accompany his brothers, and promised never to cause the crone harm or annoyance. At length he also

THE TROLL'S HUT, THE LANTERN, AND THE GOAT WITH THE GOLDEN HORNS

had leave to depart; after which the brothers hastened to the boat, not a little glad that all three had escaped so well in this adventure.

Toward the morning they arrived at a royal palace, larger and more magnificent than anything they had ever seen before. They entered and begged for employment. The eldest two were received as helpers in the royal stables, and the youngest was taken as page to the King's young son; and, being a sprightly, intelligent lad, he soon won the good will of everyone, and rose from day to day in the King's favor. At this his brothers were sorely nettled, not enduring that he should be preferred to themselves. At length they consulted together how they might compass the fall of their young brother, in the belief that afterwards they should prosper better than before.

They therefore presented themselves one day before the King, and gave him an exaggerated account of the beautiful lantern that shed light over both land and water, adding that it ill beseemed a king to lack so precious a jewel. On hearing this the King's attention was excited, and he asked: "Where is this lantern to be found, and who can procure it for me?" The brothers answered: "No one can do that unless it be our brother Pinkel. He knows best where the lantern is to be found." The King was now filled with a desire to obtain the golden lantern about which he had heard tell, and commanded the youth to be called. When Pinkel came, the King said: "If thou canst procure me the golden lantern that shines over land and water I will make thee the chief man in my whole court." The youth promised to do his best to execute his lord's behest, and the King praised him for his willingness; but the brothers rejoiced at heart; for they well knew it was a perilous undertaking, which could hardly terminate favorably.

Pinkel now prepared a little boat, and, unaccompanied by anyone, rowed over to the island inhabited by the Troll-crone. When he arrived it was already evening, and the crone was busied in boiling porridge for supper, as was her custom. The youth creeping softly up to the roof cast from time to time a handful of salt through the chimney, so that it fell down into the pot that was boiling on the hearth. When the porridge was ready, and the crone had begun to eat, she could not conceive what had made it so salt and bitter. She was out of humor, and chided her daughter, thinking that she had put too much salt into the porridge; but let her dilute the porridge as she might, it could not be eaten, so salt and bitter was it. She then ordered her daughter to go to the well, that was just at the foot of the hill, and fetch water, in order to prepare fresh porridge. The maiden answered: " How can I go to the well? It is so dark out of doors that I cannot find the way over the hill." " Then take my gold lantern," said the crone, peevishly. The girl took the beautiful gold lantern accordingly, and hastened away to fetch the water. But as she stooped to lift the pail, Pinkel, who was on the watch, seized her by the feet, and cast her headlong into the water. He then took the golden lantern, and betook himself in all haste to his boat.

In the meantime the crone was wondering why her daughter stayed out so long, and, at the same moment, chancing to look through the window she saw the light gleaming far out on the water. At this sight she was sorely vexed, and hurrying down to the shore, cried aloud: " Is that thou, Pinkel? " The youth answered: " Yes, dear mother, it is I." The Troll continued: " Art thou not a great knave? " The lad answered: " Yes, dear mother, I am so." The crone now began to lament and complain, saying: " Ah! what a fool was I to let thee go from me; I might have been sure thou wouldst play me some trick. If thou ever comest hither again, thou shalt not escape." And so the matter rested for that time.

Pinkel now returned to the King's palace, and became the chief person at court, as the King had promised. But when the brothers were informed what complete success he had had in his adventure, they became yet more envious and embittered than before, and often consulted together how they might accomplish the fall of their young brother, and gain the King's favor for themselves.

Both brothers went, therefore, a second time before the King, and began relating at full length about the beautiful goat that had horns of the purest gold, from which little gold bells were suspended, which gave forth a pleasing sound whenever the animal moved. They added that it ill became so rich a king to lack so costly a treasure. On hearing their story, the King was greatly excited, and said: " Where is this goat to be found, and who can procure it for me? " The brothers answered: " That no one can do, unless it be our brother Pinkel; for he knows best where the goat is to be found." The King then felt a strong desire to possess the goat with the golden horns, and therefore commanded the youth to appear before him. When Pinkel came, the King said: " Thy brothers have been telling me of a beautiful goat with horns of the purest gold, and little bells fastened to the horns, which ring whenever the animal moves. Now it is my will that thou go and procure for me this goat. If thou art successful I will make thee lord over a third part of my kingdom." The youth having listened to this speech, promised to execute his lord's commission, if only fortune would befriend him. The King then praised his readiness, and the brothers were glad at heart, believing that Pinkel would not escape this time so well as the first.

Pinkel now made the necessary preparations and rowed to the island where the Troll-wife dwelt. When he reached it, evening was already advanced, and it was dark, so that no one could be aware of his coming, the golden lantern being no longer there, but shedding its light in the royal palace. The youth now deliberated with himself how to get the golden goat; but the task was no easy one; for the animal lay every night in the crone's hut. At length it occurred to his mind that there was one method which might probably prove successful, though, nevertheless, sufficiently difficult to carry into effect.

At night, when it was time for the crone and her daughter to go to bed, the girl went as usual to bolt the door. But Pinkel was just outside on the watch, and had placed a piece of wood behind the door, so that it would not shut close. The girl stood for a long time trying to lock it, but to no purpose. On perceiving this the crone thought there was something out of order, and called out that the door might very well remain unlocked for the night; as soon as it was daylight they could ascertain what was wanting. The girl then left the door ajar and laid herself down to sleep. When the night was a little more advanced, and the crone and her daughter were snug in deep repose, the youth stole softly into the hut, and approached the goat where he lay stretched out on the hearth. Pinkel now stuffed wool into all the golden bells, lest their sound might betray him; then seizing the goat, he bore it off to his boat. When he had reached the middle of the lake, he took the wool out of the goat's ears, and the animal moved so that the bells rang aloud. At the sound the crone awoke, ran down to the water, and cried in an angry tone: "Is that thou, Pinkel?" The youth answered: "Yes, dear mother, it is." the crone said: "Hast thou stolen my golden goat?" The youth answered: "Yes, dear mother, I have." The Troll continued: "Art thou not a big knave?" Pinkel returned for answer: "Yes, I am so, dear mother." Now the beldam began to whine and complain, saying: "Ah! what a simpleton was I for letting thee slip away from me. I well knew thou wouldst play me some trick. But if thou comest hither ever again, thou shalt never go hence."

Pinkel now returned to the King's court and obtained the government of a third part of the kingdom, as the King had promised. But when the brothers heard how the enterprise had succeeded, and also saw the beautiful lantern and the goat with golden horns, which were regarded by everyone as great wonders, they became still more hostile and embittered than ever. They could think of nothing but how they might accomplish his destruction.

They went, therefore, one day again before the king, to whom they gave a most elaborate description of the Troll-crone's fur cloak that shone like the brightest gold and was worked with golden threads in every seam. The brothers said it was more befitting a queen than a Troll to possess such a treasure, and added that that alone was wanting to the King's good fortune. When the King heard all this he became very thoughtful, and said: " Where is this cloak to be found, and who can procure it for me?" The brothers answered: " No one can do that except our brother Pinkel; for he knows best where the golden cloak is to be found." The King was thereupon seized with an ardent longing to possess the golden cloak, and commanded the youth to be called before him. When Pinkel came, the King said: "I have long been aware that thou hast an affection for my young daughter; and thy brothers have been telling me of a beautiful fur cloak which shines with the reddest gold in every seam. It is, therefore, my will that thou go and procure for me this cloak. If thou art successful, thou shalt be my son-in-law, and after me shalt inherit the kingdom." When the youth heard this he was glad beyond measure, and promised either to win the young maiden or perish in the attempt. The King thereupon praised his readiness; but the brothers were delighted in their false hearts, and trusted that the enterprise would prove their brother's destruction.

Pinkel then betook himself to his boat and crossed over to the island inhabited by the Troll-crone. On the way he anxiously deliberated with himself how he might get possession of the crone's golden cloak; but it appeared to him not very likely that his undertaking would prove successful, seeing that the Troll always wore the cloak upon her. So after having concerted divers plans, one more hazardous than another, it occurred to him that he would try one method which might perhaps succeed, although it was bold and rash.

In pursuance of his scheme he bound a bag under his clothes, and walked with trembling step and humble demeanor into the beldam's hut. On perceiving him, the Troll cast on him a savage glance, and said: " Pinkel, is that thou?" The youth answered: " Yes, dear mother, it is." The crone was overjoyed, and said: " Although thou art come voluntarily into my power, thou canst not surely hope to escape again

[19]

from here, after having played me so many tricks." She then took a large knife and prepared to make an end of poor Pinkel; but the youth, seeing her design, appeared sorely terrified, and said: "If I must needs die, I think I might be allowed to choose the manner of my death. I would rather eat myself to death with milk porridge, than be killed with a knife." The crone thought to herself that the youth had made a bad choice, and therefore promised to comply with his wish. She then set a huge pot on the fire, in which she put a large quantity of porridge. When the mess was ready, she placed it before Pinkel that he might eat, who for every spoon-ful of porridge that he put into his mouth, poured two into the bag that was tied under his clothes. At length the crone began to wonder how Pinkel could contrive to swallow such a quantity; but just at the same moment the youth, making a show of being sick to death, sank down from his seat as if he were dead, and unobserved cut a hole in the bag, so that the porridge ran over the floor.

The crone, thinking that Pinkel had burst with the quantity of porridge he had eaten, was not a little glad, clapped her hands together, and ran off to look for her daughter, who was gone to the well. But as the weather was wet and stormy, she first took off her beautiful fur cloak and laid it aside in the hut. Before she could have proceeded far, the youth came to life again, and springing up like lightning seized on the golden cloak, and ran off at the top of his speed.

Shortly after, the crone perceived Pinkel as he was rowing in his little boat. On seeing him alive again, and observing the golden cloak glittering on the surface of the water, she was angry beyond all conception, and ran far out on the strand, crying: "Is that thou, Pinkel?" The youth answered: "Yes, it is I, dear mother." The crone said: "Hast thou taken my beautiful golden cloak?" Pinkel responded: "Yes, dear mother, I have." The Troll continued: "Art thou not a great knave?" The youth replied: "Yes, I am so, dear mother." The old witch was now almost beside herself, and began to whine and lament, and said: "Ah! how silly was it of me to let chee slip away. I was well assured thou wouldst play me many wicked tricks." They then parted from each other.

The Troll-wife now returned to her hut, and Pinkel crossed the water, and arrived safely at the King's palace; there he delivered the golden cloak, of which everyone said that a more sumptuous garment was never seen nor heard of. The King honorably kept his word with the youth, and gave him his young daughter to wife. Pinkel afterwards lived happy and content to the end of his days; but his brothers were and continued to be helpers in the stable as long as they lived.

Mother Roundabout's Daughter

ONCE on a time there was a goody who had a son, and he was so lazy and slow he would never turn his hand to anything that was useful; but singing and dancing he was very fond of; and so he danced and sang as long as it was day, and sometimes even some way on in the night. The longer this lasted, the harder it was for the goody; the boy grew, and meat he must have without stint, and more and more was spent in clothing as he grew bigger and bigger, and it was soon worn out, I should think; for he danced and sprang about both in wood and field.

At last the goody thought it too bad; so she told the lad that now he must begin to turn his hand to work and live steadily, or else there was nothing before both of them but starving to death. But that the lad had no mind to do. He said he would far rather woo Mother Roundabout's daughter; for if he could only get her, he would be able to live well and softly all his days, and sing and dance, and never do one stroke of work.

When his mother heard this she, too, thought it would be a very fine thing; and so she fitted out the lad as well as she could, that he might look tidy when he reached Mother Roundabout's house; and so he set off on his way.

Now when he got out of doors the sun shone warm and bright; but it had rained the night before, so that the ways were soft and miry and all the bog holes stood full of water. The lad took a short cut to Mother Roundabout's, and he sang and jumped, as was ever his wont; but just as he sprang and leaped he came to a bog hole, and over it lay a little bridge, and from the bridge he had to make a spring across a hole on to a tuft of grass, that he might not dirty his shoes. But *plump*, it went all at once, and just as he put his foot on the tuft it gave way under him, and there was no stopping till he found himself in a nasty, deep, dark hole. At first he could see nothing, but when he had been there a while he had a glimpse of a rat, that came wiggle-waggle up to him with a bunch of keys at the tip of her tail.

"What! you here, my boy?" said the rat. "Thank you kindly for coming to me. I have waited long for you. You come, of course, to woo me, and you are eager at it, I can very well see; but you must have patience yet a while, for I shall have a great dower. I am not ready for my wedding just yet, but I'll do my best that it shall be as soon as ever I can."

When she had said that, she brought out ever so many eggshells, with all sorts of bits and scraps, such as rats are wont to eat, and set them before him, and said:

"Now, you must sit down and eat; I am sure you must be both tired and hungry."

But the lad thought he had no liking for such food.

"If I were only well away from this, above ground again," he thought to himself, but he said nothing out loud.

"Now, I dare say you'd be glad to go home again," said the rat. "I know your heart is set on this wedding, and I'll make all the haste I can; and you must take with you this linen thread, and when you get up above you must not look round, but go straight home, and on the way you mus . mind and say nothing but

'Short before, and long back,
Short before, and long back';"

[22]

THE FAIRY RING

and as she said this she put the linen thread into his hand.

"Heaven be praised!" said the lad, when he got above ground. "Thither I'll never come again, if I can help it."

But he still had the thread in his hand, and he sprang and sang as he was wont; but even though he thought no more of the rat hole, he had got his tongue into the tune, and so he sang,

"Short before, and long back,
Short before, and long back."

So when he got back home into the porch he turned round, and there lay many, many hundred ells of the whitest linen, so fine that the handiest weaving girl could not have woven it finer.

"Mother! mother! come out," he cried and roared.

Out came the goody in a bustle, and asked whatever was the matter; but when she saw the linen woof, which stretched as far back as she could see and a bit besides, she couldn't believe her eyes, till the lad told her how it had all happened. And when she had heard it, and tried the woof between her fingers, she grew so glad that she, too, began to dance and sing.

So she took the linen and cut it out, and sewed shirts out of it both for herself and her son, and the rest she took into the town and sold, and got money for it. And now they both lived well and happily a while; but when the money was all gone, the goody had no more food in the house, and so she told her son he really must now begin to go to work, and live like the rest of the world, else there was nothing for it but starving for them both.

But the lad had more mind to go to Mother Roundabout and woo her daughter. Well, the goody thought that a very fine thing, for now he had good clothes on his back, and he was not such a bad-looking fellow either. So she made him smart, and fitted him out as well as she could; and he took out his new shoes and brushed them till they were as bright as glass, and when he had done that, off he went.

[23]

But all happened just as it did before. When he got out of doors the sun shone warm and bright; but it had rained overnight, so that it was soft and miry, and all the bog holes were full of water. The lad took the short cut to Mother Roundabout, and he sang and sprang as he was ever wont. Now he took another way than the one he went before; but just as he leaped and jumped, he got upon the bridge over the moor again, and from it he had to jump over a bog hole on to a turf that he might not soil his shoes. But *plump* it went, and down it went under him, and there was no stopping till he found himself in a nasty, deep, dark hole. At first he could see nothing; but when he had been there a while he caught a glimpse of a rat with a bunch of keys at the tip of her tail, who came wiggle-waggle up to him.

"What! you here, my boy?" said the rat. "That was nice of you to wish to see me so soon again. You are very eager, that I can see; but you really must wait a while, for there is still something wanting to my dower, though the next time you come, it shall be all right."

When she had said this she set before him all kinds of scraps and bits in eggshells, such as rats eat and like; but the lad thought it all looked like meat that had been already eaten once, and he wasn't hungry, he said; and all the time he thought, "If I could only once get above ground, well out of this hole." But he said nothing out loud.

So after a while the rat said:

"I dare say now you would be glad to get home again; but I'll hasten on the wedding as fast as ever I can. And now you must take with you this thread of wool; and when you come above ground you must not look round, but go straight home, and all the way you must mind and say nothing but

'Short before, and long back,
Short before, and long back';"

and as she said that she gave him a thread of wool in his hand.

"Heaven be praised!" said the lad, "that I got away. Thither I'll never go again, if I can help it"; and so he sang and jumped as he was wont. As for the rat hole, he thought no more about it; but as he had got his tongue into tune he sang,

> "Short before, and long back,
> Short before, and long back";

and so he kept on the whole way home.

When he had got into the yard at home again he turned and looked behind him, and there lay the finest cloth, more than many hundred ells; aye, almost above half a mile long, and so fine that no town dandy could have had finer cloth to his coat.

"Mother! mother! come out!" cried the lad.

So the goody came out of doors, and clapped her hands, and was almost ready to swoon for joy when she saw all that lovely cloth; and then he had to tell her how he had got it, and how it had all happened from first to last. Then they had a fine time of it, you may fancy. The lad got new clothes of the finest sort, and the goody went off to the town and sold the cloth by little and little, and made heaps of money. Then she decked out her cottage, and looked as smart in her old days as though she had been born a lady. So they lived well and happily; but at last that money came to an end too, and so the day came when the goody had no more food in the house, and then she told her son he really must turn his hand to work, and live like the rest of the world, else there was nothing but starvation staring both of them in the face.

But the lad thought it far better to go to Mother Roundabout and woo her daughter. This time the goody thought so too, and said not a word against it; for now he had new clothes of the finest kind, and he looked so well, she thought it quite out of the question that anyone could say "No" to so smart a lad. So she smartened him up, and made him as tidy as she could; and he himself brought out his new shoes, and rubbed them till they shone so he could see his face in them, and when he had done that, off he went.

This time he did not take the short cut, but made a great bend, for down to the rats he would not go if he could help it, he was so tired of all that wiggle-waggle and that everlasting bridal gossip. As for the weather and the ways, they were just as they had been twice before. The sun shone, so that it was dazzling on the pools and bog holes, and the lad sang and sprang as he was wont; but just as he sang and jumped, before he knew where he was, he was on the very same bridge across the bog again. So he tried to jump from the bridge over a bog hole on to a tuft that he might not dirty his bright shoes. *Plump* it went, and it gave way with him, and there was no stopping till he was down in the same nasty, deep, dark hole again. At first he was glad, for he could see nothing; but when he had been there a while he had a glimpse of the ugly rat, and loath he was to see her with the bunch of keys at the end of her tail.

"Good day, my boy!" said the rat; "you are heartily welcome again, for I see you can't bear to be any longer without me. Thank you, thank you kindly; but now everything is ready for the wedding, and we shall set off to church at once."

"Something dreadful is going to happen," thought the lad, but he said nothing out loud.

Then the rat whistled, and there came swarming out such a lot of small rats and mice of all the holes and crannies, and six big rats came harnessed to a frying pan; two mice got up behind as footmen, and two got up before and drove; some, too, got into the pan, and the rat with the bunch of keys at her tail took her seat among them. Then she said to the lad:

"The road is a little narrow here, so you must be good enough to walk by the side of the carriage, my darling boy till it gets broader, and then you shall have leave to sit up in the carriage alongside of me."

[26]

THE FAIRY RING

"Very fine that will be, I dare say," thought the lad. "If I were only well above ground, I'd run away from the whole pack of you." That was what he thought, but he said nothing out loud.

So he followed them as well as he could; sometimes he had to creep on all fours, and sometimes he had to stoop and bend his back as well, for the road was low and narrow in places; but when it got broader he went on in front, and looked about him how he might best give them the slip and run away. But as he went forward he heard a clear, sweet voice behind him, which said:

"Now the road is good. Come, my dear, and get up into the carriage."

The lad turned round in a trice, and had near lost both nose and ears. There stood the grandest carriage, with six white horses to it, and in the carriage sat a maiden as bright and lovely as the sun, and round her sat others who were as pretty and soft as stars. They were a princess and her playfellows, who had been bewitched all together. But now they were free because he had come down to them, and never said a word against them.

"Come now," said the princess. So the lad stepped up into the carriage, and they drove to church; and when they drove from church again the princess said: "Now we will drive first to my house, and then we'll send to fetch your mother."

"That is all very well," thought the lad, for he still said nothing, even now; but, for all that, he thought it would be better to go home to his mother than down into that nasty rat hole. But just as he thought that, they came to a grand castle; into it they turned, and there they were to dwell. And so a grand carriage with six horses was sent to fetch the goody, and when it came back they set to work at the wedding feast. It lasted fourteen days, and maybe they are still at it. So let us all make haste; perhaps we, too, may come in time to drink the bridegroom's health and dance with the bride.

The Bear and Skrattel

ONE Christmas Day, the King of Norway sat in the great hall of his palace, holding a feast. "Here's a health," said he, "to our brother the King of Denmark! What present shall we send our royal brother as a pledge of our good will, this Christmas-time?" "Send him, please your majesty," said the Norseman Gunter, who was the King's chief huntsman, "one of our fine white bears, that his liegemen may show their little ones what sort of kittens we play with." "Well said, Gunter!" cried the King; "but how shall we find a bear that will travel so long a journey willingly, and will know how to behave himself to our worthy brother when he reaches him?" "Please your majesty," said Gunter, "I have a glorious fellow, as white as snow, that I caught when he was a cub; he will follow me wherever I go, play with my children, stand on his hind legs, and behave himself as well as any gentleman ought to do. He is at your service, and I will myself take him wherever you choose."

So the King was well pleased, and ordered Gunter to set off at once with master Bruin: "Start with the morning's dawn," said he, "and make the best of your way."

The Norseman went home to his house in the forest; and early next morning he waked master Bruin, put the King's collar round his neck, and away they went over rocks and valleys, lakes and seas, the nearest road to the court of the King of Denmark. When they arrived there, the King was away on a journey, and Gunter and his fellow-traveler set out to follow. It was bright weather, the sun shone, and the birds sang, as they journeyed merrily on, day after day, over hill and over dale, till they came within a day's journey of where the King was.

All that afternoon they traveled through a gloomy, dark forest; but toward evening the wind began to whistle through the trees, and the clouds began to gather and threaten a stormy night. The road, too, was very rough, and it was not

THE FAIRY RING

easy to tell which was more tired, Bruin or his master. What made the matter worse was that they had found no inn that day by the roadside, and their provisions had fallen short, so that they had no very pleasant prospect before them for the night. "A pretty affair this!" said Gunter. "I am likely to be charmingly off here in the woods, with an empty stomach, a damp bed, and a bear for my bedfellow."

While the Norseman was turning this over in his mind, the wind blew harder and harder, and the clouds grew darker and darker: the bear shook his ears, and his master looked at his wits' end, when to his great joy a woodman came whistling along out of the woods, by the side of his horse dragging a load of fagots. As soon as he came up Gunter stopped him, and begged hard for a night's lodging for himself and his countryman.

The woodman seemed hearty and good-natured enough, and was quite ready to find shelter for the huntsman; but as to the bear, he had never seen such a beast before in his life, and would have nothing to do with him on any terms. The huntsman begged hard for his friend, and told how he was bringing him as a present to the King of Denmark; and how he was the most good-natured, best-behaved animal in the world, though he must allow that he was by no means one of the handsomest.

The woodman, however, was not to be moved. His wife, he was sure, would not like such a guest, and who could say what he might take it into his head to do? Besides, he should lose his dog and his cat, his ducks and his geese; for they would all run away for fright, whether the bear was disposed to be friends with them or not.

"Good night, master huntsman!" said he; "if you and old shaggy-back there cannot part, I am afraid you must e'en stay where you are, though you will have a sad night of it, no doubt." Then he cracked his whip, whistled up his horse, and set off once more on his way homeward.

The huntsman grumbled, and Bruin grunted, as they followed slowly after; when to their great joy they saw the wood-

[29]

man, before he had gone many yards, pull up his horse once more and turn round. "Stay, stay!" said he; "I think I can tell you of a better plan than sleeping in a ditch. I know where you may find shelter, if you will run the risk of a little trouble from an unlucky imp that has taken up its abode in my old house down the hill yonder. You must know, friend, that till last winter I lived in yon snug little house that you will see at the foot of the hill if you come this way. Everything went smoothly on with us till one unlucky night, when the storm blew as it seems likely to do to-night, some spiteful guest took it into his head to pay us a visit; and there have ever since been such noises, clattering, and scampering up stairs and down, from midnight till the cock crows in the morning, that at last we were fairly driven out of house and home. What he is like no one knows; for we never saw him or anything belonging to him, except a little crooked high-heeled shoe, that he left one night in the pantry. But though we have not seen him, we know he has a hand or a paw as heavy as lead; for when it pleases him to lay it upon anyone, down he goes as if the blacksmith's hammer had hit him. There is no end of his monkey tricks. If the linen is hung out to dry, he cuts the line. If he wants a cup of ale, he leaves the tap running. If the fowls are shut up, he lets them loose. He puts the pig into the garden, rides upon the cows, and turns the horses into the hay yard; and several times he nearly burned the house down, by leaving a candle alight among the fagots. And then he is sometimes so nimble and active that when he is once in motion, nothing stands still around him. Dishes and plates—pots and pans—dance about, clattering, making the most horrible music, and breaking each other to pieces; and sometimes, when the whim takes him, the chairs and tables seem as if they were alive, and dancing a hornpipe, or playing battledore and shuttlecock together. Even the stones and beams of the house seem rattling against one another; and it is of no use putting things in order, for the first freak the imp took would turn everything upside down again.

"My wife and I bore such a lodger as long as we could,

out at length we were fairly beaten; and as he seemed to have taken up his abode in the house, we thought it best to give up to him what he wanted; and the little rascal knew what we were about when we were moving, and seemed afraid we should not go soon enough. So he helped us off; for on the morning we were to start, as we were going to put our goods upon the wagon, there it stood before the door ready loaded; and when we started we heard a loud laugh, and a little sharp voice cried out of the window, 'Good-by, neighbors!' So now he has our old house all to himself to play his gambols in, whenever he likes to sleep within doors; and we have built ourselves a snug cottage on the other side of the hill, where we live as well as we can, though we have no great room to make merry in. Now if you, and your ugly friend there, like to run the hazard of taking up your quarters in the elf's house, pray do! Yonder is the road. He may not be at home to-night."

"We will try our luck," said Gunter. "Anything is better to my mind than sleeping out of doors such a night as this. Your troublesome neighbor will perhaps think so, too, and we may have to fight for our lodging; but never mind, Bruin is rather an awkward hand to quarrel with, and the goblin may perhaps find a worse welcome from him than your house dog could give him. He will at any rate let him know what a bear's hug is; for I dare say he has not been far enough north to know much about it yet."

Then the woodman gave Gunter a fagot to make his fire with, and wished him a good night. He and the bear soon found their way to the deserted house, and no one being at home they walked into the kitchen and made a capital fire.

"Lack-a-day!" said the Norseman; "I forgot one thing —I ought to have asked that good man for some supper; I have nothing left but some dry bread. However, this is better than sleeping in the woods. We must make the most of what we have, keep ourselves warm, and get to bed as soon as we can." So after eating up all their crusts, and drinking some water from the well close by, the huntsman wrapped himself up close in his cloak, and lay down in the snuggest corner he could find. Bruin rolled himself up in the corner of the wide fireplace, and both were fast asleep, the fire out, and everything quiet within doors long before midnight.

Just as the clock struck twelve the storm began to get louder—the wind blew—a slight noise within the room wakened the huntsman, and all on a sudden in popped a little ugly skrattel, scarce three spans high, with a hump on his back, a face like a dried pippin, a nose like a ripe mulberry, and an eye that had lost its neighbor. He had high-heeled shoes and a pointed red cap; and came dragging after him a nice fat kid, ready skinned and fit for roasting. "A rough night this," grumbled the goblin to himself; " but, thanks to that booby woodman, I've a house to myself. And now for a hot supper and a glass of good ale till the cock crows."

No sooner said than done. The skrattel busied himself about, here and there; presently the fire blazed up, the kid was put on the spit and turned merrily round. A keg of ale made its appearance from a closet, the cloth was laid, and the kid was soon dished up for eating. Then the little imp, in the joy of his heart, rubbed his hands, tossed up his red cap, danced before the hearth, and sang his song:

> "Oh! 'tis weary enough abroad to ride,
>   In the shivery midnight blast;
> And 'tis dreary enough alone to bide,
>   Hungry and cold,
>   On the wintry wold,
>   Where the drifting snow falls fast.
>
> "But 'tis cheery enough to revel by night,
>   In the crackling fagot's light;
> 'Tis merry enough to have and to hold
>   The savory roast,
>   And the nut-brown toast,
>   With jolly good ale and old."

The huntsman lay snug all this time, sometimes quaking. in dread of getting into trouble, and sometimes licking his lips

THE FAIRY RING

at the savory supper before him, and half in the mind to fight for it with the imp. However, he kept himself quiet in his corner; till all of a sudden the little man's eye wandered from his cheering ale cup to Bruin's carcass, as he lay rolled up like a ball fast asleep in the chimney corner.

The imp turned round sharp in an instant, and crept softly nearer and nearer to where Bruin lay, looking at him very closely, and not able to make out what in the world he was. "One of the family, I suppose!" said he to himself. But just then Bruin gave his ears a shake, and showed a little of his shaggy muzzle. "Oh, ho!" said the imp, "that's all, is it? But what a large one! Where could he come from, and how came he here? What shall I do? Shall I let him alone or drive him out? Perhaps he may do me some mischief, and I am not afraid of mice or rats. So here goes! I have driven all the rest of the live stock out of the house, and why should I be afraid of sending this brute after them?"

With that the elf walked softly to the corner of the room, and taking up the spit, stole back on tiptoe till he got quite close to the bear; then raising up his weapon, down came a rattling thump across Bruin's mazard, that sounded as hollow as a drum. The bear raised himself slowly up, snorted, shook his head, then scratched it, opened first one eye, then the other, took a turn across the room, and grinned at his enemy; who, somewhat alarmed, ran back a few paces and stood with the spit in his hand, foreseeing a rough attack. And it soon came, for the bear, rearing himself up, walked leisurely forward, and putting out one of his paws caught hold of the spit, jerked it out of the goblin's hand, and sent it spinning to the other end of the kitchen.

And now began a fierce battle. This way and that way flew tables and chairs, pots and pans. The elf was one moment on the bear's back, lugging his ears and pommeling him with blows that might have felled an ox. In the next, the bear would throw him up in the air, and treat him as he came down with a hug that would make the little imp squall. Then up he would jump upon one of the beams out of Bruin's reach,

[33]

and soon, watching his chance, would be down astride upon his back.

Meantime Gunter had become sadly frightened, and seeing the oven door open, crept in for shelter from the fray, and lay there quaking for fear. The struggle went on thus a long time, without its seeming at all clear who would get the better—biting, scratching, hugging, clawing, roaring, and growling, till the whole house rang. The elf, however, seemed to grow weaker and weaker. The rivals stood for a moment as if to get breath, and the bear was getting ready for a fierce attack when, all in a moment, the skrattel dashed his red cap right in his eye, and while Bruin was smarting with the blow and trying to recover his sight, darted to the door, and was out of sight in a moment, though the wind blew, the rain pattered, and the storm raged in a merciless manner.

"Well done! Bravo, Bruin!" cried the huntsman, as he crawled out of the oven and ran and bolted the door. "Thou hast combed his locks rarely; and as for thine own ears, they are rather the worse for pulling. But come, let us make the best of the good cheer our friend has left us!" So saying, they fell to and ate a hearty supper. The huntsman, wishing the skrattel a good night and pleasant dreams in a cup of his sparkling ale, laid himself down and slept till morning; and Bruin tried to do the same, as well as his aching bones would let him.

In the morning the huntsman made ready to set out on his way, and had not got far from the door before he met the woodman, who was eager to hear how he had passed the night. Then Gunter told him how he had been awakened, what sort of creature the elf was, and how he and Bruin had fought it out. "Let us hope," said he, "you will now be well rid of the gentleman. I suspect he will not come where he is likely to get any more of Bruin's hugs; and thus you will be well paid for your entertainment of us, which, to tell the truth, was none of the best, for if your ugly little tenant had not brought his supper with him, we should have had but empty stomachs this morning."

THE FAIRY RING

The huntsman and his fellow-traveler journeyed on, and let us hope they reached the King of Denmark safe and sound; but, to tell the truth, I know nothing more of that part of the story.

The woodman, meantime, went to his work, and did not fail to watch at night to see whether the skrattel came, or whether he was thoroughly frightened out of his old haunt by the bear, or whatever he might take the beast to be that had handled him as he never was handled before. But three nights passed over, and no traces being seen or heard of him, the woodman began to think of moving back to his old house.

On the fourth day he was out at his work in the forest, and as he was taking shelter under a tree from a cold storm of sleet and rain that passed over, he heard a little cracked voice singing, or rather croaking in a mournful tone. So he crept along quietly, and peeped over some bushes, and there sat the very same figure that the huntsman had described to him. The goblin was sitting without any hat or cap on his head, with a woe-begone face, and with his jacket torn into shreds, and his leg scratched and smeared with blood, as if he had been creeping through a bramble bush. The woodman listened quietly to his song, and it ran as before:

> "Oh! 'tis weary enough abroad to ride,
> In the shivery midnight blast;
> And 'tis dreary enough alone to bide,
> Hungry and cold,
> On the wintry wold,
> Where the drifting snow falls fast."

"Sing us the other verse, man!" cried the woodman, for he could not help cracking a joke on his old enemy, who he saw was sadly in the dumps at the loss of his good cheer and the shelter against the bad weather. But the instant his voice was heard the little imp jumped up, stamped with rage, and was out of sight in the twinkling of an eye.

The woodman finished his work and was going home in the evening, whistling by his horse's side, when all of a sudden he saw, standing on a high bank by the wayside, the very same little imp, looking as grim and sulky as before. "Hark ye, bumpkin?" cried the skrattel; "canst thou hear, fellow? Is thy great cat alive, and at home still?" "My cat?" said the woodman. "Thy great white cat, man!" thundered out the little imp. "Oh, my cat!" said the woodman, at last recollecting himself. "Oh, yes, to be sure! alive and well, I thank you; very happy, I'm sure, to see you and all friends whenever you will do us the favor to call. And hark ye, friend! as you seem to be so fond of my great cat, you may like to know that she had five kittens last night." "Five kittens?" muttered the elf. "Yes," replied the woodman, "five of the most beautiful white kits you ever saw—so like the old cat, it would do your heart good to see the whole family—such soft, gentle paws—such delicate whiskers—such pretty little mouths!" "Five kittens?" muttered, or rather shrieked out, the imp again. "Yes, to be sure!" said the woodman; "five kittens! Do look in to-night, about twelve o'clock—the time, you know, that you used to come and see us. The old cat will be so glad to show them to you, and we shall be so happy to see you once more. But where can you have been all this time?"

"I come? Not I, indeed!" shrieked the skrattel. "What do I want with the little wretches? Did not I see the mother once? Keep your kittens to yourself. I must be off—this is no place for me. Five kittens! So there are six of them now! Good-by to you, you'll see me no more; so bad luck to your ugly cat and your beggarly house!" "And bad luck to you, Mr. Crookback!" cried the woodman, as he threw him the red cap he had left behind in his battle with Bruin. "Keep clear of my cat, and let us hear no more of your pranks, and be hanged to you!"

So now that he knew his troublesome guest had taken his leave, the woodman soon moved back all his goods, and his wife and children into their snug old house. And there they lived happily, for the elf never came to see them any more; and the woodman every day after dinner drank, "Long life to the King of Norway," for sending the cat that cleared his house of vermin.

THE FAIRY RING

The Golden Bird

*T*HERE was once upon a time a king who had a garden; in that garden there was an apple tree, and on that apple tree there grew a golden apple every year; but when the time came to pluck the apple it was gone, and no one knew who took it or what became of it; but gone it was.

The King had three sons, and one day he told them that he who could bring him the apple or get hold of the thief, should have the kingdom after him, no matter whether he was the eldest, the second, or the youngest son.

The eldest set out first and sat down under the tree to keep watch for the thief. Soon after dark a golden bird came flying, and the light from it was so strong and dazzling that it could be seen a long way off. When the Prince saw the bird and the dazzling light he became so frightened that he dared not stay any longer, but rushed indoors as fast as he could.

Next morning the apple was gone; the Prince had then, however, recovered his courage and began to get ready for his journey and wanted to set off to find the bird. The King fitted him out in grand style and spared neither money nor fine raiment. When the Prince had gone a bit on the way he became hungry, opened his scrip and sat down to his breakfast by the roadside. A fox then came out of the wood and sat down and looked at him.

" Do give me a little to eat," said the fox.

" I'll give you some powder and shot," said the Prince; " my food I shall want myself; nobody can tell how far and how long I may have to travel," said he.

" Just so," said the fox, and so he went back into the wood again.

When the Prince had finished his meal and rested awhile he set out on his way again. After a long time he came to a big city, and in that city there was an inn, where there was always joy and never any sorrow; he thought that would be a nice place to stop at, and so he remained. And there was such dancing and drinking and joy and merry-making that he forgot the bird and his father and his journey and the whole kingdom.

Away he was and away he stopped.

The next year the second prince was to watch for the thief in the garden; he also sat down under the tree when the apple began to ripen. But one night, all of a sudden, the golden bird came flying, shining like the sun, and the Prince became so afraid that he took to his heels and ran indoors as fast as he could.

In the morning the apple was gone, but the Prince had then recovered his courage and wanted to set out and find the bird. He began to get ready and the King fitted him out in grand style and spared neither money nor fine raiment. But the same thing happened to him as to his brother; when he had got a bit on the way he became hungry, opened his scrip and sat down to his breakfast by the roadside. A fox then came out from the pine wood and sat down and looked at him.

"Do give me a little to eat," said the fox.

"I'll give you some powder and shot," said the Prince; "my food I shall want myself; nobody can tell how far and how long I may have to travel," said he.

"Just so," said the fox, and so he went back into the wood again.

When the Prince had finished his meal and rested awhile, he set out on his way again. After a long time he came to the same city and the same inn, where there was always joy and never any sorrow; and there he also thought it would be nice to stop, and the first he met was his brother, and so he remained. The brother had been leading a gay and reckless life and had scarcely any clothes left on his back; but now he began afresh, and there was such dancing and drinking and joy and merriment that the second prince also forgot the bird and his father and his journey and the whole kingdom. Away he was and away he stopped.

When the time came for the apple to ripen again the youngest prince was to go into the garden and watch for the thief. He took a companion with him who was to help him up into the tree, and to pass away the time so that he should not fall asleep. All of a sudden they saw a bright light, as if from the sun; every feather of the bird could be seen long before it came to the tree. The Prince climbed up into the tree and at the same time the golden bird swooped down and took the apple; the Prince tried to seize the bird, but he only caught a feather out of its tail.

So he went to the King's bedroom, and as he came in with the feather, it became as light as day.

He also wanted to try if he could find his brothers and catch the bird, for he had been so near to it that he had got a feather from its tail and would know it again anywhere, he said.

Well, the King went and pondered long whether he should let him go, for he thought the youngest would not fare any better than the two eldest, who ought to have more knowledge of the world, and he was afraid he should lose him also. But the Prince begged so earnestly that at last he got permission to go.

He then began to get ready and the King fitted him out in grand style, both with clothes and money, and so he set off.

When he had traveled for some time he became hungry and took his scrip and sat down to have his breakfast, but just as he was in the midst of it a fox came out of the wood and sat down close by his side and looked at him.

"Do give me a little to eat," said the fox.

"I shall want the food myself," said the Prince, "for I cannot tell how far I shall have to travel, but I have enough to give you a little."

THE FAIRY RING

When the fox had got the piece of meat he asked the Prince where he was going.

Yes, that he would tell him.

"If you will listen to me, I will help you, and you will have good luck," said the fox.

The Prince promised he would, and so they set off together. They traveled a while till they came to the same city and the same inn, where there was always joy, but no sorrow.

"I must keep outside here; the dogs are rather a nuisance," said the fox, and so he told the Prince where his brothers were to be found and what they were doing; "and if you go in there you will not get any further either," said he.

The Prince promised he would not go in there, and gave him his hand on it, and so each went his way. But when the Prince came to the inn and heard the noise and merriment going on he felt he must go in; there was no help for it, and when he met his brothers there was such rejoicing that he forgot both the fox and the journey and the bird and his father. But when he had been there awhile the fox came—he had ventured into the city after all—and opened the door a little and made a sign to the Prince, saying that now they must be off. So the Prince bethought himself, and they went their way.

When they had traveled awhile they saw a big mountain far away. The fox said:

"Three hundred miles at the back of that mountain there is a gilded linden tree with golden leaves, and in that tree sits the golden bird from which you took the feather."

Thither they traveled together. When the Prince was going to catch the bird the fox gave him some bright feathers which he was to wave in his hands, and so attract the bird, which would then fly down and sit on his hand.

But the fox said he must not touch the linden tree, for inside it was a big troll who owned it, and if the Prince

[40]

touched only the smallest twig the troll would come out and kill him on the spot.

No, he would not touch it, said the Prince; but when he had got the bird on his hand he thought he must have a twig of the tree; there was no help for it, it was so bright and beautiful. So he took a tiny little sprig, but the same moment the troll came out.

"Who is that stealing my tree and my bird?" roared the troll, and he was so angry that he spurted sparks of fire.

"Thieves believe that all men steal," said the Prince; "but only those get hanged who do not steal properly," said he.

The troll said that made no difference, and was going to kill him, but the Prince begged him to spare his life.

"Well," said the troll, "if you can bring me back the horse which my nearest neighbor has taken from me you will get off with your life."

"Where shall I find it, then?" said the Prince.

"Oh, he lives three hundred miles at the back of that big blue mountain against the horizon yonder," said the troll.

The Prince promised he would do his best. But when he came back to the fox he found him in rather a bad temper.

"Now you have got yourself into trouble," said the fox; "if you had listened to me we could have been on our way home by this," said he.

So they had to make a fresh start, for the Prince had pledged his word, and his life depended on his finding the horse.

At last they got there, but as the Prince was going to take the horse the fox said:

"When you come into the stable you will find all sorts of bridles hanging on the wall, both of gold and silver; you must not touch them, for then the troll will come and kill you; you must take the ugliest and shabbiest you see."

Yes, the Prince promised he would; but when he came into the stable he thought it was quite unreasonable not to take a fine bridle, for there were plenty of them, and so he took the brightest he could find. It was as bright as gold, but just then the troll came and was so angry that sparks flew from him.

"Who is that stealing my horse and my bridle?" he shrieked.

"Thieves believe that all men steal," said the Prince; "but only those get hanged who do not steal properly," said he.

"Well, that makes no difference. I'll kill you on the spot," shouted the troll.

But the Prince begged him to spare his life.

"Well," said the troll, "if you can bring me back the fair damsel which my nearest neighbor has taken from me I will spare you."

"Whereabouts does he live, then?" asked the Prince.

"Oh, he lives three hundred miles at the back of that big blue mountain against the horizon yonder," said the troll.

The Prince promised he would fetch the damsel, and was allowed to go, and so he escaped with his life.

But when he came out you may imagine how angry the fox was.

"Now you've got yourself into trouble again," said he; "if you had listened to me we could have been on our way home long ago. I almost think I will not go with you any further."

But the Prince begged and prayed and promised he would never do anything else but what the fox told him, if he would only remain with him. At last the fox gave in, and they became firm friends again; so they set off once more and came at last to where the fair damsel was.

"Well," said the fox, "I have your promise, but I dare not let you in to the troll, after all; this time I must go myself." So he went in, and after a while he came out with the damsel, and so they went back the same way they had come.

When they got to the troll who had the horse they took both the horse and the brightest bridle; and when they got to the troll who had the linden tree and the bird, they took both the tree and the bird and started off with them.

When they had got a bit on the way they came to a field of rye, and the fox then said:

"I hear a thundering noise; you had better go on ahead; I will remain here awhile," he said. He then plaited himself a gown of rye straw, in which he looked like a preacher. All at once the three trolls came rushing along, hoping to overtake the Prince.

"Have you seen anyone passing here with a fair damsel, a horse with a golden bridle, a golden bird, and a gilded linden tree?" they shouted to the fox as he stood there preaching.

"Well, I've heard from my grandmother's grandmother that something of the kind passed this way, but that was in the good old times, when my grandmother's grandmother baked halfpenny cakes and gave back the halfpenny."

Then all the trolls burst out laughing: "Ha, ha, ha!" they laughed and held on to one another.

"If we have slept so long we may as well turn our noses homeward, and go to sleep again," they said, and so they went back the way they came.

The fox then set off after the Prince, but when they came to the city where the inn and his brothers were, he said:

"I dare not go through the town on account of the dogs; I must go my own way just above here, but you must take good care your brothers do not get hold of you."

But when the Prince came into the city he thought it would be too bad if he did not look in upon his brothers and have a word with them, and so he tarried there for a while.

When the brothers saw him they came out and took the damsel, and the horse, and the bird, and the linden tree, and everything from him, and they put him in a barrel, and threw him into the sea; and so they set off home to the King's palace, with the damsel, and the horse, and the bird, and the linden tree, and everything. But the damsel would not speak, and she became pale and wretched to look upon; the horse got so thin and miserable that it could hardly hang together; the bird became silent and shone no more, and the linden tree withered.

In the meantime the fox was sneaking about outside the city where the inn and the merriment were, and was waiting for the Prince and the damsel, and wondering why they did not return.

He went hither and thither, waiting and watching for them, and at last he came down to the shore, and when he saw the barrel, which was lying out at sea drifting, he shouted: "Why are you drifting about there, you empty barrel?"

"Oh, it is I," said the Prince in the barrel.

The fox then swam out to sea as fast as he could, got hold of the barrel, and towed it to land; then he began to gnaw the hoops, and when he had got some off the barrel, he said to the Prince: "Stamp and kick."

The Prince stamped and kicked till all the staves flew about, and out he jumped from the barrel.

So they went together to the King's palace, and when they got there the damsel regained her beauty and began to talk, the horse became so fat and sleek that every hair glistened; the light shone from the bird and it began to sing; the linden tree began to blossom and its leaves to sparkle, and the damsel said, "He is the one who has saved us."

They planted the linden tree in the garden, and the youngest prince was to marry the princess, for such the damsel really was; but the two eldest brothers were put each in a barrel and rolled down a high mountain.

Then they began to prepare for the wedding, but the fox first asked the Prince to put him on the block and cut his head off, and although the Prince both prayed and cried,

there was no help for it; he would have to do it. But as he cut the head off, the fox turned into a handsome prince, and he was the brother of the princess, whom they had rescued from the troll.

So the wedding came off and everything was so grand and splendid, that the news of the festivities reached all the way here.

The Doll in the Grass

ONCE upon a time there was a King who had twelve sons. When they were grown up he told them they must go out into the world and find themselves wives, who must all be able to spin and weave and make a shirt in one day, else he would not have them for daughters-in-law. He gave each of his sons a horse and a new suit of armor, and so they set out in the world to look for wives.

When they had traveled a bit on the way they said they would not take Ashiepattle with them, for he was good for nothing Ashiepattle must stop behind; there was no help for it. He did not know what he should do or which way he should turn; he became so sad that he got off the horse and sat down on the grass and began to cry.

When he had sat a while, one of the tussocks among the grass began to move, and out of it came a small white figure; as it came nearer Ashiepattle saw that it was a beautiful little girl, but she was so tiny, so very, very tiny.

She went up to him and asked him if he would come below and pay a visit to the doll in the grass.

Yes, that he would; and so he did. When he came down below, the doll in the grass was sitting in a chair, dressed very finely and looking still more beautiful. She asked Ashiepattle where he was going and what was his errand.

He told her they were twelve brothers, and that the King had given them each a horse and a suit of armor, and told them to go out in the world and find themselves wives, but they must all be able to spin and weave and make a shirt in a day.

"If you can do that and will become my wife, I will not travel any farther," said Ashiepattle to the doll in the grass.

Yes, that she would, and she set to work at once to get the shirt spun, woven, and made; but it was so tiny, so very, very tiny, no bigger than—so!

Ashiepattle then returned home, taking the shirt with him; but when he brought it out he felt very shy because it was so small. But the King said he could have her for all that, and you can imagine how happy and joyful Ashiepattle became.

The road did not seem long to him as he set out to fetch his little sweetheart. When he came to the doll in the grass he wanted her to sit with him on his horse; but no, that she wouldn't; she said she would sit and drive in a silver spoon, and she had two small white horses which would draw her. So they set out, he on his horse and she in the silver spoon; and the horses which drew her were two small white mice.

Ashiepattle always kept to one side of the road, for he was so afraid he should ride over her; she was so very, very tiny.

When they had traveled a bit on the way they came to a large lake; there Ashiepattle's horse took fright and shied over to the other side of the road, and upset the spoon, so that the doll in the grass fell into the water. Ashiepattle became very sad, for he did not know how he should get her out again; but after a while a merman brought her up. But now she had become just as big as any other grown-up being and was much more beautiful than she was before. So he placed her in front of him on the horse and rode home.

When Ashiepattle got there all his brothers had also returned, each with a sweetheart; but they were so ugly and ill-favored and bad-tempered that they had come to blows with their sweethearts on their way home. On their heads they had hats which were painted with tar and soot, and this had run from their hats down their faces, so that they were still uglier and more ill-favored to behold.

When the brothers saw Ashiepattle's sweetheart they all be-

"SHE SAID SHE WOULD SIT AND DRIVE IN A SILVER SPOON"

came envious of him, but the King was so pleased with Ashiepattle and his sweetheart that he drove all the others away,
and so Ashiepattle was married to the doll in the grass; and
afterwards they lived happy and comfortable for a long, long
while; and if they re not dead, they must be still alive.

The Princess on the Glass Hill

ONCE upon a time there was a man who had a meadow
which lay on the side of a mountain, and in the meadow
there was a barn in which he stored hay. But there
had not been much hay in the barn for the last two years, for
every St. John's eve, when the grass was in the height of its
vigor, it was all eaten clean up, just as if a whole flock of
sheep had gnawed it down to the ground during the night.
This happened once and it happened twice, but then the man
got tired of losing his crop, and said to his sons—he had
three of them, and the third was called Cinderlad—that one
of them must go and sleep in the barn on St. John's night,
for it was absurd to let the grass be eaten up again, blade and
stalk, as it had been the last two years, and the one who went
to watch must keep a sharp lookout, the man said.

The eldest was quite willing to go to the meadow. He
would watch the grass, he said, and he would do it so well
that neither man nor beast, nor even the devil himself, should
have any of it. So when evening came he went to the barn
and lay down to sleep; but when night was drawing near there
was such a rumbling and such an earthquake that the walls
and roof shook again, and the lad jumped up and took to his
heels as fast as he could, and never even looked back, and the
barn remained empty that year just as it had been for the
last two.

Next St. John's eve the man again said he could not go
on in this way losing all the grass in the outlying field year
after year, and that one of his sons must just go there and

watch it, and watch well, too. So the next oldest son was willing to show what he could do. He went to the barn and lay down to sleep, as his brother had done; but when night was drawing near there was a great rumbling, and then an earthquake, which was even worse than that on the former St. John's night; and when the youth heard it he was terrified, and went off, running as if for a wager.

The year after it was Cinderlad's turn, but when he made ready to go the others laughed at him and mocked him. "Well, you are just the right one to watch the hay, you who have never learned anything but how to sit among the ashes and bake yourself!" said they. Cinderlad did not trouble himself about what they said, but when evening drew near rambled away to the outlying field. When he got there he went into the barn and lay down, but in about an hour's time the rumbling and creaking began, and it was frightful to hear it. "Well, if it gets no worse than that I can manage to stand it," thought Cinderlad. In a little time the creaking began again, and the earth quaked so that all the hay flew about the boy. "Oh! if it gets no worse than that I can manage to stand it," thought Cinderlad. But then came a third rumbling and a third earthquake, so violent that the boy thought the walls and roof had fallen down; but when that was over everything suddenly grew as still as death around him. "I am pretty sure that it will come again," thought Cinderlad; but no, it did not. Everything was quiet and everything stayed quiet, and when he had lain still a short time he heard something that sounded as if a horse were standing chewing just outside the barn door. He stole away to the door, which was ajar, to see what was there, and a horse was standing eating. It was so big and fat and fine a horse that Cinderlad had never seen one like it before, and a saddle and bridle lay upon it, and a complete suit of armor for a knight, and everything was of copper and so bright that it shone again. "Ha! ha! it is thou who eatest up our hay, then," thought the boy; "but I will stop that." So he made haste and took out his steel for striking fire and threw it over the horse, and then it had no power to stir from the spot, and became so tame that the boy could do what he liked with it. So he mounted it and rode away to a place which no one knew of but himself, and there he tied it up. When he went home again his brothers laughed and asked how he had got on.

"You didn't lie long in the barn, if even you have been so far as the field!" said they.

"I lay in the barn till the sun rose, but I saw nothing and heard nothing, not I," said the boy. "Heaven knows what there was to make you two so frightened."

"Well, we shall soon see whether you have watched the meadow or not," answered the brothers; but when they got there the grass was all standing just as long and as thick as it had been the night before.

The next St. John's eve it was the same thing once again. Neither of the two brothers dared to go to the outlying field to watch the crop, but Cinderlad went, and everything happened exactly the same as on the previous St. John's eve. First there was a rumbling and an earthquake, and then there was another, and then a third; but all three earthquakes were much, very much more violent than they had been the year before. Then everything became still as death again, and the boy heard something chewing outside the barn door, so he stole as softly as he could to the door, which was slightly ajar, and again there was a horse standing close by the wall of the house, eating and chewing, and it was far larger and fatter than the first horse, and it had a saddle on its back, and a bridle was on it, too, and a full suit of armor for a knight, all of bright silver, and as beautiful as anyone could wish to see. "Ho! ho!" thought the boy, "is it thou who eatest up our hay in the night? But I will put a stop to that." So he took out his steel for striking fire and threw it over the horse's mane, and the beast stood there as quiet as a lamb. Then the boy rode this horse, too, away to the place where he kept the other, and then went home again.

"I suppose you will tell us that you have watched well again this time." said the brothers.

"Well, so I have," said Cinderlad. So they went there again, and there the grass was, standing as high and as thick as it had been before; but that did not make them any kinder to Cinderlad.

When the third St. John's night came, neither of the two elder brothers dared to lie in the outlying barn to watch the grass, for they had been so heartily frightened the night that they had slept there that they could not get over it; but Cinderlad dared to go, and everything happened just the same as on the two former nights. There were three earthquakes, each worse than the other, and the last flung the boy from one wall of the barn to the other, but then everything suddenly became still as death. When he had lain quietly a short time he heard something chewing outside the barn door. Then he once more stole to the door, which was slightly ajar, and behold! a horse was standing just outside it, which was much larger and fatter than the two others he had caught. "Ho! ho! it is thou, then, who art eating up our hay this time," thought the boy; "but I will put a stop to that." So he pulled out his steel for striking fire and threw it over the horse, and it stood as still as if it had been nailed to the field, and the boy could do just what he liked with it. Then he mounted it and rode away to the place where he had the two others, and then he went home again. Then the two brothers mocked him just as they had done before, and told him that they could see that he must have watched the grass very carefully that night, for he looked just as if he were walking in his sleep; but Cinderlad did not trouble himself about that, but just bade them go to the field and see. They did go, and this time, too, the grass was standing, looking as fine and as thick as ever.

The King of the country in which Cinderlad's father dwelt had a daughter whom he would give to no one who could not ride up to the top of the glass hill, for there was a high, high hill of glass, slippery as ice, and it was close to the King's palace. Upon the very top of this the King's daughter was to sit with three golden apples in her lap, and the man who could ride up and take the three golden apples should marry her and have half the kingdom. The King had this proclaimed in every church in the whole kingdom, and in many other kingdoms, too. The Princess was very beautiful, and all who saw her fell violently in love with her, even in spite of themselves. So it is needless to say that all the princes and knights were eager to win her and half the kingdom besides, and that for this cause they came riding thither from the very end of the world, dressed so splendidly that their raiments gleamed in the sunshine, and riding on horses which seemed to dance as they went, and there was not one of these princes who did not think that he was sure to win the Princess.

When the day appointed by the King had come, there was such a host of knights and princes under the glass hill that they seemed to swarm, and everyone who could walk or even creep was there, too, to see who won the King's daughter. Cinderlad's two brothers were there, but they would not hear of letting him go with them, for he was so dirty and black with sleeping and grubbing among the ashes that they said everyone would laugh at them if they were seen in the company of such an oaf.

"Well, then, I will go all alone by myself," said Cinderlad.

When the two brothers got to the glass hill all the princes and knights were trying to ride up it, and their horses were in a foam; but it was all in vain, for no sooner did the horses set foot upon the hill than down they slipped, and there was not one which could get even so much as a couple of yards up. Nor was that strange, for the hill was as smooth as glass windowpanes and as steep as the side of a house. But they were all eager to win the King's daughter and half the kingdom, so they rode and they slipped, and thus it went on. At length all the horses were so tired that they could do no more and so hot that the foam dropped from them, and the riders were forced to give up the attempt.

The King was just thinking that he would cause it to be proclaimed that the riding should begin afresh on the follow-

ing day, when perhaps it might go better, when suddenly a
knight came riding up on so fine a horse that no one had ever
seen the like of it before, and the knight had armor of copper, and his bridle was of copper, too, and all his accouter-
ments were so bright that they shone again. The other knights
all called out to him that he might just as well spare himself
the trouble of trying to ride up the glass hill, for it was of
no use to try; but he did not heed them, and rode straight off
to it and went up as if it were nothing at all. Thus he rode
for a long way—it may have been a third part of the way
up—but when he had got so far he turned his horse round
and rode down again. But the Princess thought that she had
never yet seen so handsome a knight, and while he was riding
up she was sitting thinking, "Oh, how I hope he may be able
to come up to the top!" And when she saw that he was turning his horse back she threw one of the golden apples down
after him, and it rolled into his shoe. But when he had come
down from off the hill he rode away, and that so fast that no
one knew what had become of him.

So all the princes and knights were bidden to present themselves before the King that night, so that he who had ridden
so far up the glass hill might show the golden apple which
the king's daughter had thrown down. But no one had anything to show. One knight presented himself after the other,
and none could show the apple.

At night, too, Cinderlad's brothers came home again and
had a long story to tell about the riding up the glass hill. At
first, they said, there was not one who was able to get even
so much as one step up, but then came a knight who had
armor of copper and a bridle of copper, and his armor and
trappings were so bright that they shone to a great distance,
and it was something like a sight to see him riding. He rode
one third of the way up the glass hill, and he could easily
have ridden the whole of it if he had liked; but he had turned
back, for he had made up his mind that that was enough for
once. "Oh! I should have liked to see him too, that I should,"
said Cinderlad, who was as usual sitting by the chimney among

JUST AS CINDERLAD TURNED HIS HORSE AROUND, THE PRINCESS THREW
THE GOLDEN APPLE

the cinders. "You, indeed!" said the brothers. "You look as if you were fit to be among such great lords, dirty creature that you are to sit there!"

Next day the brothers were for setting out again, and this time, too, Cinderlad begged them to let him go with them and see who rode; but no, they said he was not fit to do that, for he was much too ugly and dirty. "Well, well, then I will go all alone by myself," said Cinderlad. So the brothers went to the glass hill, and all the princes and knights began to ride again, and this time they had taken care to rough the shoes of their horses; but that did not help them. They rode and they slipped as they had done the day before, and not one of them could even get so far as a yard up the hill. When they had tired out their horses, so that they could do no more, they again had to stop altogether. But just as the King was thinking that it would be well to proclaim that the riding should take place next day for the last time, so that they might have one more chance, he suddenly bethought himself that it would be well to wait a little longer to see if the knight in copper armor would come on this day too. But nothing was to be seen of him.

Just as they were still looking for him, however, came a knight riding on a steed that was much, much finer than that which the knight in copper armor had ridden, and this knight had silver armor and a silver saddle and bridle, and all were so bright that they shone and glistened when he was a long way off. Again the other knights called to him, and said that he might just as well give up the attempt to ride up the glass hill, for it was useless to try; but the knight paid no heed to that, but rode straight away to the glass hill, and went still farther up than the knight in copper armor had gone; but when he had ridden two thirds of the way up he turned his horse round and rode down again. The Princess liked this knight still better than she had liked the other, and sat longing that he might be able to get up above, and when she saw him turning back she threw the second apple after him, and it rolled into his shoe, and as soon as he had got down the

glass hill he rode away so fast that no one could see what had
become of him.

In the evening, when everyone was to appear before the
King and Princess, in order that he who had the golden apple
might show it, one knight went in after the other, but none
of them had a golden apple to show.

At night the two brothers went home as they had done the
night before, and told how things had gone, and how everyone had ridden, but no-one had been able to get up the hill.
"But last of all," they said, "came one in silver armor, and
he had a silver bridle on his horse and a silver saddle, and oh,
but he could ride! He took his horse two thirds of the way
up the hill, but then he turned back. He was a fine fellow,"
said the brothers, "and the Princess threw the second golden
apple to him!"

"Oh, how I should have liked to see him too!" said
Cinderlad.

"Oh, indeed! He was a little brighter than the ashes that
you sit grubbing among, you dirty, black creature!" said the
brothers.

On the third day everything went just as on the former
days. Cinderlad wanted to go with them to look at the riding,
but the two brothers would not have him in their company,
and when they got to the glass hill there was no one who
could ride even so far as a yard up it, and everyone waited
for the knight in silver armor, but he was neither to be seen
nor heard of. At last, after a long time, came a knight riding
upon a horse that was such a fine one its equal had never yet
been seen. The knight had golden armor and the horse a
golden saddle and bridle, and these were all so bright that they
shone and dazzled everyone, even while the knight was still at
a great distance. The other princes and knights were not able
even to call to tell him how useless it was to try to ascend the
hill, so amazed were they at the sight of his magnificence. He
rode straight away to the glass hill, and galloped up it as if
it were no hill at all, so that the Princess had not even time
to wish that he might get up the whole way. As soon as he

had ridden to the top he took the third golden apple from the lap of the Princess, and then turned his horse about and rode down again, and vanished from their sight before anyone was able to say a word to him.

When the two brothers came home again at night they had much to tell of how the riding had gone off that day, and at last they told about the knight in the golden armor too. "He was a fine fellow, that was! Such another splendid knight is not to be found on earth!" said the brothers.

"Oh, how I should have liked to see him too!" said Cinderlad.

"Well, he shone nearly as brightly as the coal-heaps that thou art always lying raking among, dirty black creature that thou art!" said the brothers.

Next day all the knights and princes were to appear before the King and the Princess—it had been too late for them to do it the night before—in order that he who had the golden apple might produce it. They all went in turn, first princes and then knights, but none of them had a golden apple.

"But somebody must have it," said the King, "for with our own eyes we all saw a man ride up and take it." So he commanded that everyone in the kingdom should come to the palace and see if he could show the apple. And one after the other they all came, but no one had the golden apple, and after a long, long time Cinderlad's two brothers came likewise. They were the last of all, so the King inquired of them if there was no one else in the kingdom left to come.

"Oh, yes, we have a brother," said the two, "but he never got the golden apple! He never left the cinder-heap on any of the three days."

"Never mind that," said the King. "As everyone else has come to the palace, let him come too."

So Cinderlad was forced to go to the King's palace.

"Hast thou the golden apple?" asked the King.

"Yes, here is the first, and here is the second, and here is the third too," said Cinderlad, and he took all the three apples out of his pocket, and with that threw off his sooty rags and appeared there before them in his bright golden armor, which gleamed as he stood.

"Thou shalt have my daughter and the half of my kingdom, and thou hast well earned both!" said the King. So there was a wedding, and Cinderlad got the King's daughter, and everyone made merry at the wedding, for all of them could make merry, though they could not ride up the glass hill, and if they have not left off their merry-making they must be at it still.

The Ram and the Pig who went into the Woods to Live by Themselves

THERE was once upon a time a ram, who was being fattened up for killing. He had therefore plenty to eat, and he soon became round and fat with all the good things he got. One day the dairymaid came and gave him some more food.

"You must eat, Ram," she said; "you'll not be long here now, for to-morrow we are going to kill you."

"There's an old saying that no one should sneer at old women's advice, and that advice and physic can be had for everything except death," thought the Ram to himself; "but perhaps I might manage to escape it this time."

And so he went on eating till he was full, and when he was quite satisfied he ran his horns against the door, burst it open, and set off to the neighboring farm. There he made straight for the pigsty, to look for a pig with whom he had struck up an acquaintance on the common, since when they had always been good friends and got on well together.

"Good day, and thanks for your kindness last time we met," said the Ram to the Pig.

"Good day, and thanks to you," said the Pig.

"Do you know why they make you so comfortable, and why they feed you and look after you so well?" said the Ram.

[56]

"No," said the Pig.

"There are many mouths to feed on this farm, you must know," said the Ram; "they are going to kill you and eat you."

"Are they?" said the Pig. "Well, much good may it do them!"

"If you are of the same mind as I, we will go into the woods and build a house and live by ourselves; there is nothing like having a home of your own, you know," said the Ram.

Yes, the Pig was quite willing. "It's nice to be in fine company," said he, and off they started.

When they had got a bit on the way they met a goose.

"Good day, my good people, and thanks for your kindness last time we met," said the Goose. "Where are you off to?"

"Good day, and thanks to you," said the Ram. "We had it altogether too comfortable at our place, so we are off to the woods to live by ourselves. In your own house you are your own master, you know," said he.

"Well, I'm very comfortable where I am," said the Goose; "but why shouldn't I join you? Good company makes the day shorter," said she.

"But neither hut nor house can be built by gabbling and quacking," said the Pig. "What do you think you can do?"

"Good counsel and skill may do as much as a giant's will," said the Goose. "I can pluck moss and stuff it into the crevices, so that the house will be warm and comfortable."

Well, she might come with them, thought the Pig, for he liked the place to be warm and cozy.

When they had gone a bit on the way—the Goose was not getting along very fast—they met a hare, who came scampering out of the wood.

"Good day, my good people, and thanks for your kindness the last time we met," said the Hare. "How far are you going to-day?" said he.

"Good day, and thanks to you," said the Ram; "we had it altogether too comfortable at our place, so we are off to the woods to build a house and live by ourselves. When you have tried both East and West, you'll find that a home of your own is, after all, the best," said he.

"Well, I have, of course, a home in every bush," said the Hare; "but I have often said to myself in the winter that if I lived till the summer I would build a house, so I have a good mind to go with you and build one after all," said he.

"Well, if the worst comes to the worst, we might take you with us to frighten the dogs away," said the Pig, "for you couldn't help us to build the house, I should say."

"There is always something for willing hands to do in this world," said the Hare. "I have teeth to gnaw pegs with, and I have paws to knock them into the walls, so I'll do very well for a carpenter; for 'good tools make good work,' as the man said, when he skinned his mare with an auger," said the Hare.

Well, he might come along with them and help to build the house; there could be no harm in that.

When they had got a bit farther on the way they met a cock.

"Good day, my good people, and thanks for your kindness last time we met," said the Cock; "where are you all going to-day?" he said.

"Good day, and thanks to you," said the Ram; "we had it altogether too comfortable at our place, so we are off to the woods to build a house and live by ourselves. 'For unless at home you bake, you'll lose both fuel and cake,'" said he.

"Well, I am comfortable enough where I am," said the Cock, "but it's better to have your own roost than to sit on a stranger's perch and crow; and that cock is best off who has a home of his own," said he. "If I could join such fine company as yours, I, too, would like to go to the woods and build a house."

"Well, flapping and crowing is all very well for noise, but it won't cut joists," said the Pig. "You can't help us to build a house," he said.

"It is not well to live in a house where there is neither dog nor cock," said the Cock; "I am early to rise and early to crow."

"Yes, 'early to rise makes one wealthy and wise,' so let

him come with us!" said the Pig. (He was always the heaviest sleeper.) "Sleep is a big thief, and steals half one's life," he said.

So they all set off to the woods and built the house. The Pig felled the trees and the Ram dragged them home; the Hare was the carpenter, and gnawed pegs and hammered them into walls and roof; the Goose plucked moss and stuffed it into the crevices between the logs; the Cock crew and took care that they did not oversleep themselves in the mornings, and when the house was ready and the roof covered with birch bark and thatched with turf, they could at least live by themselves, and they were all both happy and contented.

"It's pleasant to travel both East and West, but home is, after all, the best," said the Ram.

But a bit farther into the wood two wolves had their lair, and when they saw that a new house had been built hard by they wanted to know what sort of folks they had got for neighbors. For they thought, "a good neighbor is better than a brother in a foreign land, and it is better to live among good neighbors than to be known far and wide."

So one of them made it his business to call there and ask for a light for his pipe. The moment he came inside the door the Ram rushed at him, and gave him such a butt with his horns that the wolf fell on his head into the hearth; the Pig snapped and bit, the Goose nipped and pecked, the Cock flew up on a rafter and began to crow and cackle, and the Hare became so frightened that he scampered and jumped around, both high and low, and knocked and scrambled about from one corner of the room to the other.

At last the Wolf managed to get out of the house.

"Well, to know one's neighbors is to add to one's wisdom," said the Wolf who was waiting outside; "I suppose you had a grand reception, since you stayed so long. But what about the light? I don't see either pipe or smoke," said he.

"Yes, that was a nice light I got, and a nice lot of people they were," said he who had been inside. "Such treatment I never met with before, but 'as you make your bed so you must lie,' and 'an unexpected guest must put up with what he gets,'" said the Wolf. "No sooner was I inside the door than the shoemaker threw his last at me, and I fell on my head in the middle of the forge; there sat two smiths, blowing bellows and pinching and snipping bits of flesh off me with red-hot tongs and pincers; the hunter rushed about the room looking for his gun, but, as luck would have it, he couldn't find it. And up on the rafters sat some one beating his arms about and shouting: 'Let's hook him! let's hook him! Sling him up! sling him up!' and if he had only got hold of me I should never have come out alive."

The Troll's Hammer

WHEN a great famine prevails in a country even the rich suffer. Hard, indeed, must the lot of the poor peasant be at such a time.

During a famine a poor peasant, unable to support all his family, told his eldest son, Niels, that he would have to go out in the world and provide for himself.

Niels left home and went out to seek his fortune. As the evening of the first day drew on, he found himself in a dense forest, and fearing lest the wild beasts might do him harm during the night, he climbed into a tree. Hardly had he reached his perch, when he saw a little man running toward the tree. He was hunchbacked, and had crooked legs, a long beard, and wore on his head a red cap. He was pursued by a wolf, which attacked him just under the tree in which Niels was sitting. The little man began to scream; he bit and scratched, and defended himself as well as he could. But the wolf was the stronger, and would have torn the little fellow to pieces if Niels had not sprung down from the tree. As soon as the wolf saw that he had two to contend with, he fled back into the forest.

The troll then said to Niels:

THE FAIRY RING

"Thou hast preserved my life and done me a good service; in return I will also give thee something that will be of use. See! here is a hammer with which thou shalt be able to do smith's work that no one shall be able to equal." When the troll had spoken these words, he sank into the ground and disappeared.

The next day the boy wandered on until he came to the neighborhood of the royal palace, and here he engaged himself to a smith.

Now it just happened that a few days before a thief had broken into the King's treasury and stolen a large bag of money. All the smiths in the city were therefore sent for to the palace, and the King promised that he who could make the best lock should be appointed court locksmith, and have a handsome reward into the bargain. The lock had to be finished in eight days, and so constructed that it could not be picked by anyone.

When the smith, with whom Niels lived, returned home and related this, the boy thought he should like to try whether his hammer really possessed those qualities which the troll had said. He therefore begged his master to allow him to make a lock, and promised that it should be finished by the appointed time. Although the smith had no great opinion of the boy's abilities, he permitted the trial.

Niels then requested a separate workshop, locked himself in, and began hammering the iron. One day went, and then another, and the master began to be curious; but Niels let no one come into his shop, and the smith was obliged to remain outside, and peep through the keyhole. The work, however, succeeded far better than the boy himself had expected; and, without his really knowing how it came to pass, the lock was finished on the evening of the third day.

The following morning he went down to his master and asked for some money. "Yesterday I worked hard," said Niels, "and to-day I will enjoy myself."

He went out of the city, and did not return to the workshop till late in the evening. The next day and the next he did the same, and so through the rest of the week.

His master was very angry at this, and threatened to turn him away unless he finished his work at the appointed time. But Niels told him to rest easy, and engaged that his lock should be the best.

When the day arrived, Niels brought his work forth, and carried it up to the palace. His lock was so ingenious and so delicately made, that it far excelled all the others. Niels's master was acknowledged as the most skillful, and he received the promised office and reward.

The smith was delighted, but he took good care not to confess to anyone who it was that had made the curious lock. He received one job after another from the King, and let Niels do them all.

In the meantime the report spread from place to place of the wonderful lock the King had got for his treasury. Travelers came from a distance to see it, and a foreign King came among them. When he had examined the work a long time he said that the man who had made such a lock deserved to be honored and respected.

" But however good a smith he may be," added the foreign King, " I have his master at home."

He continued boasting in this manner, till at length the two kings made a wager as to which smith could execute the most skillful piece of workmanship. The smiths were sent for, and the two kings determined that each smith should make a knife.

The smith related to Niels what had passed, and desired him to try whether he could make as good a knife as the lock he had made. Niels promised to do so, although his last work had not brought him much. The smith was in truth a mean man, and treated Niels so niggardly that sometimes he had not enough to eat and drink.

One day, as he was out buying steel to make the knife, he met a man from his own village, and, in the course of conversation, Niels learned that his father was in great want and misery. Then he asked his master for some money, but this was the answer: "You shall not have a shilling until you have made the knife."

Thereupon Niels shut himself up in the workshop for a whole day, and, as on the former occasion, the knife was made without his knowing how it had happened.

When the day arrived on which the work was to be exhibited, Niels dressed himself in his best clothes, and went with his master up to the palace where the two kings were expecting them.

The strange smith first showed his knife. It was so beautiful, and so curiously wrought, that it was a pleasure to look at; it was, moreover, so sharp and well-tempered that it would cut through a millstone as easily as through a cheese. Niels's knife, on the contrary, looked very poor and common.

The King already began to think he had lost his wager, and spoke harshly to the master-smith, when his boy begged leave to examine the stranger's knife a little more closely.

After having looked at it for some time, he said: "This is a beautiful piece of workmanship which you have made, and shame on those who would say otherwise; but my master is, nevertheless, your superior, as you shall soon experience."

Saying this, he took the stranger's knife and split it lengthwise from point to handle with his own knife as easily as one splits a twig of willow. The kings could scarcely believe their eyes, and the consequence was that Niels's master was declared the victor.

When Niels asked for payment, the master refused to give him anything, although knowing full well that the poor boy only wanted the money to help his father. Upon this Niels grew angry, went to the King, and told who it was that had made both the lock and the knife. The master was then called, but he denied everything, and accused Niels of being an idle boy, whom he had taken into service out of charity and compassion.

"We shall soon find out the truth of this story," said the

King, who sided with the master. " Since thou sayest it is thou who hast made this wonderful knife, and thy master says it is he who has done it, I will adjudge each of you to make a sword for me within eight days. He who can make the most perfect one shall be my master-smith; but he who loses shall forfeit his life."

Niels was well satisfied with this agreement. He went home, packed up all his things, and bade his master farewell. The smith would gladly have made all good again, but Neils appeared not to understand him, and went his way. He engaged with another master, and began cheerfully to work on the sword.

When the appointed day arrived, both Niels and his former master met at the palace, and the master produced a sword of the most beautiful workmanship that anyone could wish to see. It was inlaid with gold and set with precious stones. The King was greatly delighted with it.

" Now, little Niels," said he, " what dost thou say to this sword? "

" It is not so badly made as one might expect from such a bungler," said the boy.

" Canst thou show anything like it? " asked the King.

" I believe I can," answered Niels.

" Well, where is thy sword? " said the King.

" In my waistcoat pocket," replied Niels.

Hereupon there was a general laugh which was increased when they saw the boy take a little packet out of his waistcoat pocket. Niels opened the paper in which the blade was rolled up like a watch-spring. " Here is my work," said he. " Will you just cut the thread, master? "

The smith did it willingly, and in a moment the blade straightened out and struck him in the face.

Niels took out of his other pocket a hilt of gold and screwed it fast to the blade; then he presented the sword to the King; and all present were obliged to confess that they never before had seen such matchless workmanship.

Niels was declared the victor, and the master was obliged

to acknowledge that the boy had made both the lock and the knife.

The King in his indignation would have had the master put to death if the boy had not begged for mercy on the culprit.

Niels received a handsome reward from the King, and from that day all the work from the palace was intrusted to him. He took his old father to reside with him, and lived in comfort and happiness till his death.

The Clever Prince

ONCE upon a time there was a youthful Prince who was so wonderfully handsome that no one had ever seen his like; and he knew this, and was very glad of it. And everybody said that he was as clever as he was handsome, and that no one could be compared to him. Of this he was quite convinced, and he made a solemn vow that he would never take any woman to wife unless she was as handsome and nearly as clever as he was himself. If he could find such a paragon he would marry her. There were many beautiful maidens in the land, but they were not the cleverest. There were also many maidens who were clever enough, but they were not the fairest. This much is certain, the Prince found no girl who combined in her person half enough good looks and wit to suit him. He was now of an age when he and his father the King, and their faithful subjects, were all of opinion that he ought to get married; but, as we have seen, because of the vow he had made, there was not a maiden in the land to whom he could pay his addresses.

So he determined to journey to other countries, and to travel *incognito* and unattended. He wanted to see things for himself, and to have no one with him who could reveal anything about him. He traveled far and wide, from one land to another, but it fared with him abroad as it had fared with him at home; he could find no girl beautiful or clever enough for him, much less could he find one who could lay claim to the possession of both these attributes. So once more he felt his quest for a worthy bride had proved vain, and turned his face homeward.

One day he was riding through a wood. He rode and rode, still he could not get to the end of the forest. Noonday came, and the evening came, and still he was in the wood, and still could see no way out of it. He had completely lost his way; he had no idea where he was, nor where he was going, nor where he should find shelter for the night and food and rest for himself and his horse. And they were both tired out. At last he saw a small cloud of blue smoke rising amid the green trees, and riding toward it he soon came to a little cottage, very poor and mean-looking. But he was glad enough, for here at least he should find somebody. He got off his horse and knocked at the door. A poor old man opened it, and a poor old woman also came forward. They appeared very much astonished to see such a fine, handsome young knight. The Prince, after wishing them good evening, said that he had lost his way, and that he had been riding through the wood all day long without coming to a dwelling of any kind, and now he begged them to give him shelter for the night. At first they said they were not the sort of people to receive such grand gentlefolk. It was easy to see they wanted to get rid of him; but when he told them that neither he nor his horse could hold out any longer, so greatly did they need rest and a night's lodging, the old couple had not the heart to refuse, so they agreed to take him in if he would put up with what they could offer him. His first care was for his horse. Stable there was none, but there was a bit of a shed for the old people's cow. As it was summer time the cow was out to grass, so the Prince put his horse up in the shed, and gave him a drink of water and a bundle of hay, to the great content of the poor, tired beast. Then he went into the cottage, which consisted of one little room, which was both dark and low. He sat down on a wooden bench and began to talk to the old people. Did they live here all alone in the wild wood? Yes, the old folk said, they did. There was nobody else in the house, and there was no other house for miles and miles around. They got on as best they could, and managed to make a living out of their goat and their cow.

Then the Prince had his supper, the best the house could afford—a crust of dry bread and a bowl of milk. The old folk then fetched a wisp of straw and spread it out on the floor, intending to lie upon it—they had but one bed, and they meant to give it up to their grand guest. But the Prince would not hear of such a thing; they should sleep in their own bed, and he would lie on the bundle of straw that was spread upon the floor. So it was arranged as he wished, and they all three retired to rest. It was quite a different sort of couch from the one he was accustomed to, but he was thoroughly tired out, so he soon fell asleep, and he dreamt of all the beautiful maidens who were not clever enough, and of all the clever maidens who were not beautiful enough, and so he slept sweetly till the day began to dawn.

Then he awoke, and stiff enough he was in all his limbs from lying on so hard a bed; twist and turn as he might, he could not get to sleep again. Presently he heard something stirring in the little loft overhead. It might be rats or mice, or perhaps a cat. Yes, it was certainly a cat. But a little while after he heard a whirring sound, exactly like a spinning wheel. Then he heard singing. That could not be the cat, nor was it the song of the birds out in the wood; no, it was a woman's sweet voice keeping time with the whirring of the wheel. So sweet a song he had never heard before. He sprang to his feet, rubbed his eyes, pricked up his ears, and at the same moment the old folk got up too. The Prince at once asked them who it was up there in the loft that had begun spinning and singing at break of day. All was quite quiet again overhead now, and the old people persisted, as they had done the previous night, that there was no one in the house but themselves.

"Nay," said the Prince, "it is no use trying to make me believe that. I prefer believing what I have heard with my own ears. And you may as well tell me the plain truth, for I am determined to learn it, one way or another."

So then the old man made a clean breast of it. The Prince was quite right, there was somebody else in the house—it was their daughter, in her little room up in the loft. They were so afraid lest some one should see her and want to take her away from them; for, indeed, they would miss her sadly, old and feeble as they were; she earned a few pence by her spinning and weaving. Who else was there to take care of them? Soon they would be no longer able to look after themselves.

Well, the Prince said he had heard her, and now he wanted to see her. He was no man-eater, nor woman-eater either, so far as he knew; therefore they might surely let him see the maiden. So the old man had to go and call her, and she came running down, tripping along, clad in mean attire, so blithe and fresh and fair. When she saw the handsome young man, she blushed rosy red, and the Prince was thunderstruck as he looked on her. Never had he seen anything half so lovely as she was! He was utterly at a loss what to say or do. In all his travels he had seen no one to be compared with her. This poor peasant's daughter was far more beautiful than all the princesses and grand ladies he had ever met at home or abroad. He could not picture to himself anything more lovely. But a poor beggar-maid, such as she was, he might not even dream of making his wife. So he turned resolutely away, and at once bestirred himself, getting his horse ready to start, and would not so much as allow himself to look at her again. But when he was in the saddle, just setting off, as he nodded good-by to the old folk, to whom he had given a broad gold piece for his night's lodging, and who now were bowing and scraping before him, he could not help giving a side glance to where she stood gazing at him with lovely, wondering eyes. And now, of course, he was obliged to lift his hat and bow "farewell"; and as she returned his greeting with downcast eyes, and bowed and blushing face, the Prince felt as if his heart were in his mouth. The lovely eyes looked up once more as he galloped off, and they followed him till he was out of sight. And not only did they follow him thus far, but long after he had left both house and wood far behind those beautiful eyes still haunted him. And as he rode along he said to himself:

"Yes, she is beautiful, and more than beautiful enough for me; but I also vowed that she whom I marry must be as clever, or nearly as clever, as I am, and that, of course, she cannot be."

He marked well where the little cottage stood, and soon he reached a road he knew well, for the wild wood lay on the very border of his own land. He rode straight home to his father's castle, and told him he had not yet found anyone who could be considered his equal.

The old King was much vexed on hearing this, but he was so certain of his son's exceeding cleverness that he had no doubt matters were exactly as the Prince represented. He had but one wish, to see his son married before closing his eyes forever, and he had such faith in his son that he knew the Prince's choice of a wife would be a wise one.

So now the Prince was at home once more, surrounded by all the good things imaginable, and yet he knew not one moment's content. Dainty food failed to tempt his appetite, no sweet sleep came to him on his downy couch. His thoughts were always with the fair young maiden who dwelt in the wild wood. He thought of her early and late, and whether he would or not.

At last he said to himself: "There must be an end of this."

He called to mind his vow that the loveliest and cleverest girl should be his bride, and so in order to be rid of all thought of her he determined to convince himself that although the peasant's daughter might be beautiful enough, yet she was far from being clever enough for him. So he wrote a letter to her, enclosing two skeins of silk, and bidding her weave for him with them a pair of bed curtains. He sent off a royal courier at once, bidding him bring back an immediate answer. The messenger returned the same evening with a letter from the woodland maiden, and in the letter lay two tiny splinters of wood. The maiden had written that if out of these bits of wood he would make her a loom she would weave him the curtains he had ordered.

After this the Prince could no longer doubt that she was quite as clever as he was, and now he felt bound to perform the vow that he had made, which was just what he most wished to do. So he rode forth with all his royal train to the cottage in the wild wood; and he told the old people that he had come to woo their daughter for his bride—if she were willing. And she was willing. The old folk were very down-hearted at parting from their child, but they did not wish to stand in the way of her happiness, so they gave their consent. Then the court ladies clad the bride in scarlet and silk attire, and adorned her with gold and jewels. And she had ladies-in-waiting and coaches and carriages and all sorts of splendor, and the wedding was celebrated with joy and great magnificence.

"Lars, my Lad!"

THERE was once a Prince or a Duke, or something of that sort, but at any rate he belonged to a very grand family, and he would not stop at home. So he traveled all over the world, and wherever he went he was well liked, and was received in the best and gayest families, for he had no end of money. He made friends and acquaintances, as you may imagine, wherever he went, for he who has a well-filled trough is sure to fall in with pigs who want to have their fill. But he went on spending his money until he came to want, and at last his purse became so empty that he had not even a farthing left. And now there was an end to all his friends as well, for they behaved like the pigs; when the trough was empty and he had no more to give them, they began to grunt and grin, and then they ran away in all directions. There he stood alone with a long face. Everybody had been so willing to help him to get rid of his money, but nobody would help him without it; and so there was nothing for it but to trudge home and beg for crusts on the way.

So late one evening he came to a great forest. He did not know where he should find a shelter for the night, but he went on looking and searching till he caught sight of an old tumble-down hut, which stood in the middle of some bushes. It was not exactly good enough for such a fine cavalier, but when you cannot get what you want you must take what you can get. And, since there was no help for it, he went into the hut. Not a living soul was to be seen; there was not even a stool to sit upon, but alongside the wall stood a big chest. What could there be inside that chest? If only there were some bits of moldy bread in it! How nice they would taste! For, you must know, he had not had a single bit of food the whole day, and he was so hungry and his stomach so empty that it groaned with pain. He lifted the lid. But inside the chest there was another chest, and inside that chest there was another; and so it went on, each one smaller than the other, until they became quite tiny boxes. The more there were the harder he worked away, for there must be something very fine inside, he thought, since it was so well hidden.

At last he came to a tiny, little box, and in this box lay a bit of paper—and that was all he got for his trouble! It was very annoying, of course, but then he discovered there was something written on the paper, and when he looked at it he was just able to spell it out, although at first it looked somewhat difficult.

" Lars, my lad! "

As he pronounced these words something answered right in his ear:

" What are master's orders? "

He looked round, but he saw nobody. This was very funny, he thought, and so he read out the words once more:

"Lars, my lad!"

And the answer came as before:

"What are master's orders?"

But he did not see anybody this time either.

"If there is anybody about who hears what I say, then be kind enough to bring me something to eat," he said. And the next moment there stood a table laid out with all the best things one could think of. He set to work to eat and drink, and had a proper meal. He had never enjoyed himself so much in all his life, he thought.

When he had eaten all he could get down, he began to feel sleepy, and so he took out the paper again:

"Lars, my lad!"

"What are master's orders?"

"Well, you have given me food and drink, and now you must get me a bed to sleep in as well. But I want a really fine bed," he said, for you must know he was a little more bold now that his hunger was stayed. Well, there it stood, a bed so fine and dainty that even the King himself might covet it. Now this was all very well in its way, but when once you are well off you wish for still more, and he had no sooner got into bed than he began to think that the room was altogether too wretched for such a grand bed. So he took out the paper again:

"Lars, my lad!"

"What are master's orders?"

"Since you are able to get me such food and such a bed here in the midst of the wild forest, I suppose you can manage to get me a better room, for you see I am accustomed to sleep in a palace, with golden mirrors and draped walls and ornaments and comforts of all kinds," he said. Well, he had no sooner spoken the words than he found himself lying in the grandest chamber anybody had ever seen.

Now he was comfortable, he thought, and felt quite satisfied as he turned his face to the wall and closed his eyes.

But that was not all the grandeur; for when he woke up in the morning and looked round, he saw it was a big palace he had been sleeping in. One room led into the other, and wherever he went the place was full of all sorts of finery and luxuries, both on the walls and on the ceilings, and they glittered so much when the sun shone on them that he had to shade his eyes with his hand, so strong was the glare of gold and silver wherever he turned. He then happened to look out of the window. Good gracious! How grand it was! There was something else than pine forests and juniper bushes to look at, for there was the finest garden anyone could wish for, with splendid trees and roses of all kinds. But he could not see a single human being, or even a cat; and that, you know, was rather lonely, for otherwise he had everything so grand and had been set up as his own master again.

So he took out the bit of paper:

"Lars, my lad!"

"What are master's orders?"

"Well, now you have given me food and bed and a palace to live in, I intend to remain here, for I like the place," he said, "yet I don't like to live quite by myself. I must have both lads and lasses whom I may order about to wait upon me," he said.

And there they were. There came servants and stewards and scullery maids and chambermaids of all sorts, and some came bowing and some curtseying. So now the Duke thought he was really satisfied.

But now it happened that there was a large palace on the other side of the forest, and there the King lived who owned the forest, and the great, big fields around it. As he was walking up and down in his room he happened to look out through the window and saw the new palace, where the golden weathercocks were swinging to and fro on the roof in the sunlight, dazzling his eyes.

"This is very strange," he thought; and so he called his courtiers. They came rushing in, and began bowing and scraping.

THE FAIRY RING

"Do you see the palace over there?" said the King.

They opened their eyes and began to stare.

Yes, of course, they saw it.

"Who is it that has dared to build such a palace on my grounds?" said the King.

They bowed, and they scraped with their feet, but they did not know anything about it.

The King then called his generals and captains.

They came, stood at attention and presented arms.

"Be gone, soldiers and troopers," said the King, "and pull down the palace over there, and hang him who has built it; and don't lose any time about it!"

Well, they set off in great haste to arm themselves, and away they went. The drummers beat the skins of their drums, and the trumpeters blew their trumpets, and the other musicians played and blew as best they could, so that the Duke heard them long before he could see them. But he had heard that kind of noise before, and knew what it meant, so he took out his scrap of paper:

"Lars, my lad!"

"What are master's orders?"

"There are soldiers coming here," he said, "and now you must provide me with soldiers and horses, that I may have double as many as those over in the wood, and with sabers and pistols, and guns and cannons with all that belongs to them; but be quick about it."

And no time was lost; for when the Duke looked out, he saw an immense number of soldiers, who were drawn up around the palace.

When the King's men arrived, they came to a sudden halt and dared not advance. But the Duke was not afraid; he went straight up to the Colonel of the King's soldiers and asked him what he wanted.

The Colonel told him his errand.

"It's of no use," said the Duke. "You see how many men I have; and if the King will listen to me, we shall become good friends, and I will help him against his enemies,

and in such a way that it will be heard of far and wide,"
he said.

The Colonel was of the same opinion, and the Duke then
invited him and all his soldiers inside the palace, and the
men had more than one glass to drink and plenty of everything to eat as well.

But while they were eating and drinking they began
talking; and the Duke then got to hear that the King had
a daughter who was his only child, and was so wonderfully
fair and beautiful that no one had ever seen her like before.
And the more the King's soldiers ate and drank the more
they thought she would suit the Duke for a wife.

And they went on talking so long that the Duke at last
began to be of the same opinion. "The worst of it," said
the soldiers, "is that she is just as proud as she is beautiful, and will never look at a man."

But the Duke laughed at this. "If that's all," said the
Duke, "there's sure to be a remedy for that complaint."

When the soldiers had eaten and drunk as much as they
could find room for, they shouted "Hurrah!" so that it
echoed among the hills, and then they set out homeward.
But, as you may imagine, they did not walk exactly in parade
order, for they were rather unsteady about the knees, and
many of them did not carry their guns in regulation manner.
The Duke asked them to greet the King from him. He
would call on him the following day, he said.

When the Duke was alone again, he began to think of
the Princess, and to wonder if she were as beautiful and
fair as they had made her out to be. He would like to
make sure of it; and as so many strange things had happened that day it might not be impossible to find that
out as well, he thought.

"Lars, my lad!"

"What are master's orders?"

"Well, now you must bring me the King's daughter as
soon as she has gone to sleep," he said; "but she must not
be awakened either on the way here or back. Do you hear

[75]

that?" he said. And before long the Princess was lying on the bed. She slept so soundly and looked so wonderfully beautiful as she lay there. Yes, she was as sweet as sugar, I can tell you.

The Duke walked round about her, but she was just as beautiful from whatever point of view he looked at her.

The more he looked the more he liked her.

"Lars, my lad!"

"What are master's orders?"

"You must now carry the Princess home," he said, "for now I know how she looks, and to-morrow I will ask for her hand," he said.

Next morning the King looked out of the window. "I suppose I shall not be troubled with the sight of that palace any more," he thought. But, zounds! There it stood just as on the day before, and the sun shone so brightly on the roof, and the weathercocks dazzled his eyes.

He now became furious, and called all his men.

They came quicker than usual.

The courtiers bowed and scraped, and the soldiers stood at attention and presented arms.

"Do you see the palace there?" screamed the King.

They stretched their necks, and stared and gaped.

Yes, of course, that they did.

"Have I not ordered you to pull down the palace and hang the builder?" he said.

Yes, they could not deny that; but then the Colonel himself stepped forward and reported what had happened and how many soldiers the Duke had, and how wonderfully grand the palace was.

And next he told him what the Duke had said, and how he had asked him to give his greetings to the King, and all that sort of thing.

The King felt quite confused, and had to put his crown on the table and scratch his head. He could not understand all this, although he was a king; for he could take his oath it had all been built in a single night; and if the Duke were not the evil one himself, he must in any case have done it by magic.

While he sat there pondering, the Princess came into the room.

"Good morning to you, father!" she said. "Just fancy, I had such a strange and beautiful dream last night!" she said.

"What did you dream then, my girl?" said the King.

"I dreamed I was in the new palace over yonder, and that I saw a Duke there, so fine and handsome that I could never have imagined the like; and now I want to get married, father," she said.

"Do you want to get married?—you, who never cared to look at a man! That's very strange!" said the King.

"That may be," said the Princess; "but it's different now, and I want to get married, and it's the Duke I want," she said.

The King was quite beside himself, so frightened did he become of the Duke.

But all of a sudden he heard a terrible noise of drums and trumpets and instruments of all kinds; and then came a message that the Duke had just arrived with a large company, all of whom were so grandly dressed that gold and silver glistened in every fold. The King put on his crown and his coronation robes, and then went out on the steps to receive them. And the Princess was not slow to follow him.

The Duke bowed most graciously, and the King of course did likewise, and when they had talked awhile about their affairs and their grandeur they became the best of friends. A great banquet was then prepared, and the Duke was placed next to the Princess at the table. What they talked about is not easy to tell, but the Duke spoke so well for himself that the Princess could not very well say "No" to anything he said, and then he went up to the King and asked for her hand. The King could not exactly say "No" either, for he could very well see that the Duke was a person with whom it was best to be on friendly terms; but give his sanction there and then, he could not very well do that either. He wanted to see the Duke's palace first, and find out about the state of affairs over there, as you may understand.

So it was arranged that he should visit the Duke and take the Princess with him to see his palace; and with this they parted company.

When the Duke returned home, Lars became busier than ever, for there was so much to attend to. But he set to work and strove hard; and when the King and his daughter arrived everything was so magnificent and splendid that no words can describe it. They went through all the rooms and looked about, and they found everything as it should be, and even still more splendid, thought the King, and so he was quite pleased.

The wedding then took place, and that in grand style; and on the Duke's arrival home with his bride he, too, gave a great feast, and then there was an end to the festivities.

Some time passed by, and one evening the Duke heard these words:

" Are you satisfied now? "

It was Lars, as you may guess, but the Duke could not see him.

" Well, I ought to be," said the Duke. " You have provided me with everything I have," he said.

" Yes, but what have I got in return? " asked Lars.

" Nothing," said the Duke; " but, bless me, what could I have given you, who are not of flesh and blood, and whom I cannot see either? " he said. " But if there is anything I can do for you, tell me what it is, and I shall do it."

" Well, I should like to ask you for that little scrap of paper which you found in the chest," said Lars.

" Nothing else? " said the Duke. " If such a trifle can help you, I can easily do without it, for now I begin to know the words by heart," he said.

Lars thanked the Duke, and asked him to put the paper

on the chair in front of the bed when he retired to rest, and he would be sure to fetch it during the night.

The Duke did as he was told; and so he and the Princess lay down and went to sleep.

But early in the morning the Duke awoke and felt so cold that his teeth chattered, and when he had got his eyes quite open he found he was quite naked and had not even as much as a thread on his back; and instead of the grand bed and the beautiful bedroom, and the magnificent palace, he lay on the big chest in the old tumble-down hut.

He began to shout:

"Lars, my lad!" But he got no answer. He shouted once more:

"Lars, my lad!" But he got no answer this time either. So he shouted all he could:

"Lars, my lad!" But it was all in vain.

Now he began to understand how matters stood. When Lars had got the scrap of paper he was freed from service at the same time, and now he had taken everything with him. But there was no help for it. There stood the Duke in the old hut quite naked; and as for the Princess she was not much better off, although she had her clothes on, for she had got them from her father, so Lars had no power over them.

The Duke had now to tell the Princess everything, and ask her to leave him. He would have to manage as best he could, he said. But she would not hear of it. She well remembered what the parson had said when he married them, and she would never, never leave him, she said.

In the meantime the King in his palace had also awakened, and when he looked out of the window he did not see any sign whatever of the other palace where his daughter and son-in-law lived. He became uneasy, as you may imagine, and called his courtiers.

They came in, and began to bow and scrape.

"Do you see the palace over yonder behind the forest?" he asked.

They stretched their necks and stared with all their might. No, they did not see it.

"Where has it gone to, then?" asked the King.

Well, really they did not know.

It was not long before the King set out with all his court through the forest; and when he arrived at the place where the palace with the beautiful gardens should have been, he could not see anything but heather and juniper bushes and firs. But then he discovered the old tumble-down hut, which stood there among the bushes. He entered the hut and—mercy on us!—what a sight met his eyes! There stood his son-in-law, quite naked, and his daughter, who had not very many clothes on either, and who was crying and moaning.

"Dear, dear! what does all this mean?" said the King: but he did not get any answer, for the Duke would rather have died than tell him.

The King did his utmost to get him to speak; but in spite of all the King's promises and threats the Duke remained obstinate and would not utter a word.

The King then became angry—and no wonder, for now he could see that this grand Duke was not what he pretended to be, and so he ordered the Duke to be hanged, and that without any loss of time. The Princess begged and prayed for mercy; but neither prayers nor tears were of any help now; for an impostor he was, and as an impostor he should die, said the King.

And so it had to be. They erected a gallows, and placed the rope round the Duke's neck. But while they were getting the gallows ready, the Princess got hold of the hangman, and gave both him and his assistant some money, that they should so manage the hanging of the Duke that he should not lose his life, and in the night they were to cut him down, so that he and the Princess might then flee the country. And that's how the matter was arranged.

In the meantime they had strung up the Duke, and the King and his court and all the people went their way.

THE FAIRY RING

The Duke was now in great straits. He had, however, plenty of time to reflect how foolish he had been in not saving some of the crumbs when he was living in plenty, and how unpardonably stupid he had been in letting Lars have the scrap of paper. This vexed him more than all. If only he had it again, he thought, they should see he had been gaining some sense in return for all he had lost. But it is of little use snarling if you haven't got any teeth. "Ah, well, well!" he sighed, and so he dangled his legs, which was really all he could do.

The day passed slowly and tediously for him, and he was not at all displeased when he saw the sun setting behind the forest. But just before it disappeared he heard a fearful shouting, and when he looked down the hill, he saw seven cartloads of worn-out shoes, and on the top of the hindmost cart he saw a little old man in gray clothes and with a red pointed cap on his head. His face was like that of the worst scarecrow, and the rest of him was not very handsome either.

He drove straight up to the gallows, and when he arrived right under it he stopped and looked up at the Duke, and then burst out laughing, the ugly old fellow!

"How stupid you were!" he said; "but what should the fool do with his stupidity if he did not make use of it?" And then he laughed again. "Yes, there you are hanging now, and here am I carting away all the shoes I have worn out for your whims. I wonder if you can read what is written on this bit of paper, and if you recognize it?" he said with an ugly laugh, holding up the paper before the Duke's eyes.

But all who hang are not dead, and this time it was Lars who was befooled.

The Duke made a clutch, and snatched the paper from him.

"Lars, my lad!"

"What are master's orders?"

"Well, you must cut me down from the gallows and put

the palace and all the rest in its place again, exactly as it was before, and when the night has set in you must bring back the Princess."

All went merrily as in a dance, and before long every-thing was in its place, just as it was when Lars took him-self off.

When the King awoke the next morning he looked out of the window, as was his custom, and there stood the palace again, with the weathercocks glittering so beautifully in the sunshine. He called his courtiers, and they came and began to bow and scrape.

They stretched their necks as far as they could, and stared and gaped.

"Do you see the palace over there?" said the King.

Yes, of course, they did.

The King then sent for the Princess, but she was not to be found. He then went out to see if his son-in-law was still hanging on the gallows, but neither son-in-law nor gal-lows was to be seen.

He had to lift off his crown and scratch his head. But that did not improve matters; he could not make head or tail of either one thing or the other. He set off at once with all his court through the forest, and when he came to the place where the palace should stand, there it stood sure enough. The gardens and the roses were exactly as they used to be, and the Duke's people were to be seen everywhere among the trees. His son-in-law and his daugh-ter received him on the steps, dressed in their finest clothes.

"Well, I never saw the like of this," said the King to himself; he could scarcely believe his own eyes, so won-derful did it all seem to him.

"God's peace be with you, father, and welcome here!" said the Duke.

The King stood staring at him.

"Are you my son-in-law?" he asked.

"Well, I suppose I am," said the Duke. "Who else should I be?"

"Did I not order you to be hanged yesterday like any common thief?" said the King.

"I think you must have been bewitched on the way," said the Duke, with a laugh. "Do you think I am the man to let myself be hanged? Or is there anyone here who dares to believe it?" he said, and looked so fiercely at the courtiers that they felt as if they were being pierced through and through.

They bowed and scraped and cringed before him.

Who could believe such a thing? Was it at all likely?

"Well, if there is anyone who dares to say the King could have wished me such evil, let him speak out," said the Duke, and fixed his eyes upon them still more fiercely than before.

They went on bowing and scraping and cringing.

How could anyone dare to say such a thing? No, they had more sense than that, they should hope.

The King did not know what to believe, for when he looked at the Duke he thought he never could have wished him such evil; but still he was not quite convinced.

"Did I not come here yesterday, and was not the whole palace gone, and was there not an old hut in its place? And did not I go into that hut, and did not you stand stark naked right before my eyes?" he asked.

"I wonder the King can talk so," said the Duke. "I think the trolls must have bewitched your eyes in the forest and made you quite crazy; or what do you think?" he said, and turned round to the courtiers.

They bowed and bowed till their backs were bent double, and agreed with everything he said, there could be no mistake about that. The King rubbed his eyes, and looked round about him.

"I suppose it is as you say. then," he said to the Duke, "and it is well I have got back my proper sight and have come to my senses again. For it would have been a sin and a shame if I had let you be hanged," he said; and so he was happy again, and nobody thought any more about the matter.

"Once bitten, twice shy," as the proverb says; and the Duke now took upon himself to manage and look after most of his affairs, so that it was seldom Lars had to wear out his shoes. The King soon gave the Duke half the kingdom into the bargain; so he had now plenty to do, and people said they would have to search a long time to find his equal in wise and just ruling.

Then one day Lars came to the Duke, looking very little better than the first time he had seen him; but he was, of course, more humble, and did not dare to giggle and make grimaces.

"You do not want my help any longer, now," he said; "for although I did wear out my shoes at first, I am now unable to wear out a single pair, and my feet will soon be covered all over with moss. So I thought I might now get my leave of absence, he said.

The Duke quite agreed with him. "I have tried to spare you, and I almost think I could do without you," he said. "But the palace and all the rest I do not want to lose, for such a clever builder as you I shall never get again; nor do I ever want to adorn the gallows again, as you can well understand; so I cannot give you back the paper on any account," he said.

"Well, as long as you have got it, I need not fear," said Lars; "but if anybody else should get hold of it there will be nothing but running and trudging about again, and that's what I want to avoid; for when one has been tramping about for a thousand years, as I have done, one begins to get tired of it," he said.

But they went on talking, and at last they agreed that the Duke should put the paper in the box, and then bury it seven ells under the ground, under a stone fixed in the earth. They then gave mutual thanks for the time they had spent in each other's company, and so they parted.

The Duke carried out his part of the agreement, for he

was not likely to want to change it. He lived happy and contented with the Princess, and they had both sons and daughters. When the King died, he got the whole of the kingdom, and you may guess he was none the worse off for that; and there no doubt he still lives and reigns, if he is not dead.

But as for that box with the scrap of paper in it, there are many who are still running about looking for it.

Twigmuntus, Cowbelliantus, Perchnosius

ONCE upon a time there was a king who was so very learned that no parson in the whole world could surpass him; in fact, he was so learned that ordinary folks could hardly understand what he said, nor could he understand them either. But in order to have some one to talk with he procured seven wise professors, who were not quite so learned as himself, but who were just able to interpret his learned sayings so that people could apprehend them, and who could twist and turn about the talk of ordinary folk so that it became sufficiently learned and complicated for the King to understand it.

The King had no son, but he had a daughter, and in order that she should be happily married, and the country governed according to the fundamental principles of his learning, he issued an edict that he who was so learned as to put the King and his professors to silence should have his daughter and half the kingdom there and then. But anyone who attempted the task and did not succeed should lose his head for having dared to exchange words with the King.

That was no joke; but the Princess was so fair and beautiful that it was no joke to gaze at her either. And the King did not keep her caged up, for anyone who wished could see her.

There came princes and counts and barons and parsons and doctors and learned persons from all quarters of the world; and no sooner did they see the Princess than they one

[85]

and all wanted to try their luck. But, however learned they were, their learning never proved sufficient, and everyone of them lost his head.

Over in a corner of the kingdom there lived a farmer who had a son. This lad was not stupid; he was quick of apprehension and sharp-witted, and he was not afraid of anything.

When the King's edict came to this out-of-the-way place, and the parson had read it from the pulpit, the lad wanted to try his luck. "He who nothing risks, nothing wins," thought the lad; and so he went to the parson and told him that if he would give him lessons in the evenings, he would work for this worship in the daytime, but he wanted to become so learned that he could try a bout with the King and his professors.

"Whoever means to compete with them must be able to do something more than munch bread," said the parson.

"That may be," said the lad; "but I'll try my luck."

The parson thought, of course, that he was mad; but when he could get such a clever hand to work for him only for his keep, he thought he could not very well say no; and so the lad got what he wanted.

He worked for the parson in the daytime, and the parson read with him in the evening; and in this way they went on for some time, but at last the lad grew tired of his books.

"I am not going to sit here and read and grind away, and lose what few wits I have," he said; "and it won't be of much help either, for if you are lucky things will come right of themselves, and if you are not lucky you'll never make a silk purse out of a sow's ear."

And with this he pitched the books on the shelf and went his way.

All at once he came to a large forest, where the trees and the bushes were so thick that it was with difficulty he could get along. While he was thus pushing his way through, he began wondering what he should say when he came to the king's palace, and how best he could make use of the learning he had picked up from the parson. All of a sudden the twig of a tree struck him across his mouth, so that his teeth rattled.

"That is Twigmuntus," he said.

A little while after he came to a meadow where a cow was standing bellowing so furiously that it almost deafened him.

"That is Cowbelliantus," he said.

He then came to a river; but as there was neither bridge nor planks across it, he had to put his clothes on his head and swim across.

While he was swimming a perch came and bit him on the nose.

"That is Perchnosius," he said.

At last he came to the King's palace, where things did not look at all pleasant, for there were men's heads stuck on long stakes round about, and they grinned so horribly that they were enough to frighten anyone out of his wits. But the lad was not easily frightened.

"God's peace!" he said, and raised his cap. "There you stick and grin at me; but who knows if I may not be keeping you company before the day is over, and be grinning with you at others? But if I happen to be alive, you shall not stick there any longer gaping at people," he said.

So he went up to the palace and knocked at the gate.

The guard came out and asked what he wanted.

"I have come to try my luck with the Princess," said the lad.

"You?" said the guard, "well, you're a likely one, you are! Have you lost your senses? There have been princes and counts and barons and parsons and doctors and learned persons here, and all of them have had to pay with their heads for that pleasure; and yet you think you'll succeed!" he said.

"I should say it is no concern of yours," said the lad; "just open the gate, and you'll see one who's not afraid of anything."

But the guard would not let him in.

"Do as I tell you," said the lad, "or there'll be a fine to-do!"

But the guard would not.

The lad then seized him by the collar and flung him against the wall so that it creaked; and then he walked straight in to the King, who sat in his parlor with his seven professors about him. Their faces were long and thin, and they looked like puny, sickly persons about to die. They were sitting with their heads on one side, meditating and staring at the floor.

Then one of them, who looked up, asked the lad in ordinary language: "Who are you?"

"A suitor," said the lad.

"Do you want to try for the Princess's hand?"

"Well, that's about it!" said the lad.

"Have you lost your wits? There have been princes and counts and barons and parsons and doctors and learned persons here, and all of them have gone headless away; so you had better turn about and get away while your head is on your shoulders," he said.

"Don't trouble yourself on that account, but rather think of the head on your own shoulders," said the lad. "You look after yours, and I'll take care of mine! So just begin and let me hear how much wit you have got, for I don't think you look so very clever," he said.

The first professor then began a long harangue of gibberish; and when he had finished the second went on; and then the third; and in this way they continued till at length it was the turn of the seventh. The lad did not understand a single word of it all, but he didn't lose courage for all that. He only nodded his approval to all of it.

When the last had finished his harangue he asked:

"Can you reply to that?"

"That's easy enough," said the lad. "Why, when I was in my cradle and in my go-cart I could twist my mouth about and prate and jabber like you," he said. "But since you are so terribly learned, I'll put a question to you, and that shall not be a long one:

"Twigmuntus, Cowbelliantus, Perchnosius? Can you give me an answer to that?"

And now you should have seen how they stretched their

necks and strained their ears. They put on their spectacles and began to look into their books and turn over the leaves.

But while they were searching and meditating, the lad put his hands in his trousers pockets, and looked so frank and fearless that they could not help admiring him, and wondering that one who was so young could be so learned and yet look just like other people.

"Well, how are you getting on?" said the lad. "Cannot all your learning help you to open your mouths, so that I can have an answer to my question?" he said.

Then they began to ponder and meditate, and then they glanced at the ceiling, and then they stared at the walls, and then they fixed their eyes upon the floor. But they could not give him any answer, nor could the King himself, although he was much more learned than all the others together. They had to give it up, and the lad got the Princess and half the kingdom. This he ruled in his own way, and if it did not fare better, it did not fare worse for him than for the King with all his fundamental principles.

Master Tobacco

ONCE upon a time there was a poor woman who went about begging with her son; for at home she had neither a morsel to eat nor a stick to burn. First she tried the country, and went from parish to parish; but it was poor work, and so she came into the town. There she went about from house to house for a while, and at last she came to the Lord Mayor. He was both open-hearted and open-handed, and he was married to the daughter of the richest merchant in the town, and they had one little daughter. As they had no more children, you may fancy she was sugar and spice and all that's nice, and in a word there was nothing too good for her. This little girl soon came to know the beggar boy as he went about with his mother; and as the Lord Mayor was a wise man, as soon as he saw what friends the two were, he took the boy into his house that he might be his daughter's playmate. Yes, they played and read and went to school together, and never had so much as one quarrel.

One day the Lady Mayoress stood at the window, and watched the children as they were trudging off to school. There had been a shower of rain, and the street was flooded, and she saw how the boy first carried the basket with their dinner over the stream, and then he went back and lifted the little girl over, and when he set her down he gave her a kiss.

When the Lady Mayoress saw this, she got very angry. "To think of such a ragamuffin kissing our daughter—we who are the best people in the place!" That was what she said. Her husband did his best to stop her tongue. "No one knew," he said, "how children would turn out in life, or what might befall his own. The boy was a clever, handy lad, and often and often a great tree sprang from a slender plant."

But no! it was all the same, whatever he said and whichever way he put it. The Lady Mayoress held her own, and said beggars on horseback always rode their cattle to death, and that no one had ever heard of a silk purse being made out of a sow's ear; adding, that a penny would never turn into a shilling, even though it glittered like a guinea. The end of it all was that the poor lad was turned out of the house, and had to pack up his rags and be off.

When the Lord Mayor saw there was no help for it, he sent him away with a trader who had come thither with a ship, and he was to be cabin boy on board her. He told his wife he had sold the boy for a roll of tobacco.

But before he went the Lord Mayor's daughter broke her ring into two bits and gave the boy one bit, that it might be a token to know him by if they ever met again; and so the ship sailed away, and the lad came to a town, far, far off in the world, and to that town a priest had just come who was so good a preacher that everyone went to church to hear him, and the crew of the ship went with the rest the Sunday after

"AND WHEN HE SET HER DOWN HE GAVE HER A KISS"

"AND WHEN HE SET HER DOWN HE GAVE HER A KISS."

to hear the sermon. As for the lad, he was left behind to mind the ship and to cook the dinner. So while he was hard at work he heard some one calling out across the water on an island. So he took the boat and rowed across, and there he saw an old hag, who called and roared.

"Aye," she said, "you have come at last! Here have I stood a hundred years calling and bawling, and thinking how I should ever get over this water; but no one has ever heard or heeded but you, and you shall be well paid if you will put me over to the other side."

So the lad had to row her to her sister's house, who lived on a hill on the other side close by; and when they got there, she told him to beg for the old tablecloth which lay on the dresser. Yes! he would beg for it; and when the old witch who lived there knew that he had helped her sister over the water, she said he might have whatever he chose to ask.

"Oh," said the boy, "then I won't have anything else than that old tablecloth on the dresser yonder."

"Oh," said the old witch, "that you never asked out of your own wits."

"Now I must be off," said the lad, "to cook the Sunday dinner for the church-goers."

"Never mind that," said the first old hag; "it will cook itself while you are away. Stop with me, and I will pay you better still. Here have I stood and called and bawled for a hundred years, but no one has ever heeded me but you."

The end was he had to go with her to another sister, and when he got there the old hag said he was to be sure and ask for the old sword, which was such that he could put it into his pocket and it became a knife, and when he drew it out it was a long sword again. One edge was black and the other white, and if he smote with the black edge everything fell dead, and if with the white everything came to life again. So when they came over, and the second old witch heard how he had helped her sister across, she said he might have anything he chose to ask for her fare.

"Oh," said the lad, "then I will have nothing else but that old sword which hangs up over the cupboard."

"That you never asked out of your own wits," said the old witch; but for all that he got the sword.

Then the old hag said again: "Come on with me to my third sister. Here have I stood and called and bawled for a hundred years, and no one has heeded me but you. Come on to my third sister, and you shall have better pay still."

So he went with her, and on the way she told him he was to ask for the old hymn book; and that was such a book that when anyone was sick and the nurse sang one of the hymns, the sickness passed away, and they were well again. Well! when they got across, and the third old witch heard he had helped her sister across, she said he was to have whatever he chose to ask for his fare.

"Oh," said the lad, "then I won't have anything else but granny's old hymn book."

"That," said the old hag, "you never asked out of your own wits."

When he got back to the ship the crew were still at church, so he tried his tablecloth, and spread just a little bit of it out, for he wanted to see what good it was before he laid it on the table. Yes! in a trice it was covered with good food and strong drink, enough and to spare. So he just took a little snack, and then he gave the ship's dog as much as it could eat.

When the church-goers came on board, the captain said: "Wherever did you get all that food for the dog? Why, he's as round as a sausage, and as lazy as a snail."

"Oh, if you must know," said the lad, "I gave him the bones."

"Good boy," said the captain, "to think of the dog."

So he spread out the cloth, and at once the whole table was covered all over with such brave meat and drink as they had never before seen in all their born days.

Now when the boy was again alone with the dog, he wanted to try the sword, so he smote at the dog with the black edge, and it fell dead on the deck; but when he turned the blade and smote with the white edge the dog came to life again and wagged his tail and fawned on his playmate. But the book— that he could not get tried just then.

Then they sailed well and far till a storm overtook them which lasted many days, so they lay to and drove till they were quite out of their course, and could not tell where they were. At last the wind fell, and then they came to a country far, far off that none of them knew; but they could easily see there was great grief there, as well there might be, for the King's daughter was a leper. The King came down to the shore, and asked was there anyone on board who could cure her and make her well again.

"No, there was not." That was what they all said who were on deck.

"Is there no one else on board the ship than those I see?" asked the King.

"Yes; there's a little beggar boy."

"Well," said the King, "let him come on deck."

So when he came and heard what the King wanted, he said he thought he might cure her; and then the captain got so wroth and mad with rage that he ran round and round like a squirrel in a cage, for he thought the boy was only putting himself forward to do something in which he was sure to fail, and he told the King not to listen to such childish chatter.

But the King only said that wit came as children grew, and that there was the making of a man in every bairn. The boy had said he could do it, and he might as well try. After all, there were many who had tried and failed before him. So he took him home to his daughter, and the lad sang a hymn once. Then the Princess could lift her arm. Once again he sang it, and she could sit up in bed. And when he had sung it thrice, the King's daughter was as well as you and I are.

The King was so glad he wanted to give him half his king dom and the princess to wife.

"Yes," said the lad, "land and power are fine things to have half of," and was very grateful; "but as for the Princess, he was betrothed to another," he said, " and he could not take her to wife."

So he stayed there awhile and got half the kingdom; and when he had not been very long there, war broke out, and the lad went out to battle with the rest, and you may fancy he did not spare the black edge of his sword. The enemy's soldiers fell before him like flies, and the King won the day. But when they had conquered, he turned the white edge, and they all rose up alive and became the King's soldiers, who had granted them their lives. But then there were so many of them that they were badly off for food, though the King wished to send them away full, both of meat and drink. So the lad had to bring out his tablecloth, and then there was not a man that lacked anything.

Now when he had lived a little longer with the King, he began to long to see the Lord Mayor's daughter. So he fitted out four ships of war and set sail; and when he came off the town where the Lord Mayor lived, he fired off his cannon like thunder, till half the panes of glass in the town were shivered. On board those ships everything was as grand as in a King's palace; and as for himself, he had gold on every seam of his coat, so fine he was. It was not long before the Lord Mayor came down to the shore and asked if the foreign lord would not be so good as to come up and dine with him. " Yes, he would go," he said; and so he went up to the Mansion House where the Lord Mayor lived, and there he took his seat between the Lady Mayoress and her daughter.

So as they sat there in the greatest state, and ate and drank and were merry, he threw the half of the ring into the daughter's glass, and no one saw it; but she was not slow to find out what he meant, and excused herself from the feast and went out and fitted his half to her half. Her mother saw there was something in the wind and hurried after her as fast as she could.

" Do you know who that is in there, mother? " said the daughter.

" No! " said the Lady Mayoress.

"He whom papa sold for a roll of tobacco," said the daughter.

At these words the Lady Mayoress fainted and fell down flat on the floor.

In a little while the Lord Mayor came out to see what was the matter, and when he heard how things stood he was almost as uneasy as his wife.

"There is nothing to make a fuss about," said Master Tobacco. "I have only come to claim the little girl I kissed as we were going to school."

But to the Lady Mayoress he said:

"You should never despise the children of the poor and needy, for none can tell how they may turn out; since there is the making of a man in every child of man, and wit and wisdom come with growth and strength."

The History of Tom Thumb

IN the days of the great Prince Arthur there lived a mighty magician, called Merlin, the most learned and skillful enchanter the world has ever seen.

This famous magician, who could take any form he pleased, was traveling about as a poor beggar, and being very tired, he stopped at the cottage of a plowman to rest himself, and asked for some food.

The countryman bade him welcome, and his wife, who was a very good-hearted woman, soon brought him some milk in a wooden bowl, and some coarse brown bread on a platter.

Merlin was much pleased with the kindness of the plowman and his wife; but he could not help noticing that though everything was neat and comfortable in the cottage, they both seemed to be very unhappy. He therefore asked them why they were so melancholy, and learned that they were miserable because they had no children.

The poor woman said, with tears in her eyes: "I should be

the happiest creature in the world if I had a son; although he was no bigger than my husband's thumb, I would be satisfied."

Merlin was so much amused with the idea of a boy no bigger than a man's thumb that he determined to grant the poor woman's wish. Accordingly, in a short time after, the plowman's wife had a son, who, wonderful to relate, was not a bit bigger than his father's thumb!

The queen of the fairies, wishing to see the little fellow, came in at the window while the mother was sitting up in the bed admiring him. The queen kissed the child, and, giving it the name of Tom Thumb, sent for some of the fairies, who dressed her little godson according to her orders:

> An oak-leaf hat he had for his crown;
> His shirt of web by spiders spun,
> With jacket wove of thistle's down.
> His trousers were of feathers done;
> His stockings, of apple-rind, they tie
> With eyelash from his mother's eye;
> His shoes were made of mouse's skin,
> Tann'd with the downy hair within.

Tom never grew any larger than his father's thumb, which was only of ordinary size; but as he got older he became very cunning and full of tricks. When he was old enough to play with the boys, and had lost all his own cherry stones, he used to creep into the bags of his playfellows, fill his pockets, and, getting out without their noticing him, would again join in the game.

One day, however, as he was coming out of a bag of cherry stones, where he had been stealing as usual, the boy to whom it belonged chanced to see him. "Ah, ah! my little Tommy," said the boy, "so I have caught you stealing my cherry stones at last, and you shall be rewarded for your thievish tricks." On saying this, he drew the string tight round his neck, and gave the bag such a hearty shake that poor little Tom's legs, thighs, and body were sadly bruised.

He roared loud with pain, and begged to be let out, promising never to steal again.

A short time afterwards his mother was making a batter-pudding, and Tom, being very anxious to see how it was made, climbed up to the edge of the bowl; but his foot slipped, and he plumped over head and ears into the batter, without his mother noticing him, who stirred him into the pudding-bag, and put him in the pot to boil.

The batter filled Tom's mouth and prevented him from crying; but, on feeling the hot water, he kicked and struggled so much in the pot that his mother thought that the pudding was bewitched, and, pulling it out of the pot, she threw it outside the door. A poor tinker, who was passing by, lifted up the pudding, and, then putting it into his budget, walked off. As Tom had now got his mouth cleared of the batter, he then began to cry aloud, which so frightened the tinker that he flung down the pudding and ran away. The pudding being broken to pieces by the fall, Tom crept out, covered all over with the batter, and walked home. His mother, who was very sorry to see her darling in such a woeful state, put him into a teacup and soon washed off the batter; after which she kissed him, and laid him in bed.

Soon after the adventure of the pudding, Tom's mother went to milk her cow in the meadow, and she took him along with her. As the wind was very high, for fear of being blown away, she tied him to a thistle with a piece of fine thread. The cow soon observed Tom's oak-leaf hat, and liking the appearance of it, took poor Tom and the thistle at one mouthful. While the cow was chewing the thistle, Tom was afraid of her great teeth, which threatened to crush him in pieces, and he roared out as loud as he could: " Mother, mother! "

" Where are you, Tommy, my dear Tommy? " said his mother.

" Here, mother," replied he, " in the red cow's mouth."

His mother began to cry and wring her hands; but the cow, surprised at the odd noise in her throat, opened her mouth and let Tom drop out. Fortunately his mother caught him in her apron as he was falling to the ground, or he would have been dreadfully hurt. She then put Tom in her bosom and ran home with him.

Tom's father made him a whip of a barley straw to drive the cattle with, and having one day gone into the fields, Tom slipped a foot and rolled into the furrow. A raven, which was flying over, picked him up, and flew with him over the sea, and there dropped him.

A large fish swallowed Tom the moment he fell into the sea, which was soon after caught and bought for the table of King Arthur. When they opened the fish in order to cook it, everyone was astonished at finding such a little boy, and Tom was quite delighted at being free again. They carried him to the King, who made Tom his dwarf, and he soon grew a great favorite at court; for by his tricks and gambols he not only amused the King and Queen, but also all the Knights of the Round Table.

It is said that when the King rode out on horseback he often took Tom along with him, and if a shower came on he used to creep into his majesty's waistcoat pocket, where he slept till the rain was over.

King Arthur one day asked Tom about his parents, wishing to know if they were as small as he was, and whether they were well off. Tom told the King that his father and mother were as tall as anybody about the court, but in rather poor circumstances. On hearing this the King carried Tom to his treasury, the place where he kept all his money, and told him to take as much money as he could carry home to his parents, which made the poor little fellow caper with joy. Tom went immediately to procure a purse, which was made of a water bubble, and then returned to the treasury, where he received a silver threepenny-piece to put into it.

Our little hero had some difficulty in lifting the burden upon his back; but he at last succeeded in getting it placed to his mind, and set forward on his journey. However, without meeting with any accident, and after resting himself more than a hundred times by the way, in two days and two nights he reached his father's house in safety.

Tom had traveled forty-eight hours with a huge silver-piece on his back, and was almost tired to death, when his mother ran out to meet him, and carried him into the house. But he soon returned to court.

As Tom's clothes had suffered much in the batter-pudding and the inside of the fish, his majesty ordered him a new suit of clothes and to be mounted as a knight on a mouse.

> Of butterfly's wings his shirt was made,
>   His boots of chicken's hide;
> And by a nimble fairy blade,
> Well learnèd in the tailoring trade,
>   His clothing was supplied.
>   A needle dangled by his side;
> A dapper mouse he used to ride,
> Thus strutted Tom in stately pride!

It was certainly very diverting to see Tom in this dress and mounted on the mouse as he rode out a-hunting with the King and nobility, who were all ready to expire with laughter at Tom and his fine prancing charger.

The King was so charmed with his address that he ordered a little chair to be made, in order that Tom might sit upon his table, and also a palace of gold, a span high, with a door an inch wide, to live in. He also gave him a coach, drawn by six small mice.

The Queen was so enraged at the honors conferred on Sir Thomas that she resolved to ruin him, and told the King that the little knight had been saucy to her.

The King sent for Tom in great haste, but being fully aware of the danger of royal anger, he crept into an empty snail shell, where he lay for a long time, until he was almost starved with hunger; but at last he ventured to peep out, and seeing a fine large butterfly on the ground near the place of his concealment, he got close to it, and jumping astride on it was carried up into the air. The butterfly flew with him from tree to tree and from field to field, and at last returned to the court, where the King and nobility all strove to catch him; but at last poor Tom fell from his seat into a watering pot, in which he was almost drowned.

When the Queen saw him she was in a rage, and said he should be beheaded; and he was again put into a mouse trap until the time of his execution.

However, a cat, observing something alive in the trap, patted it about till the wires broke, and set Thomas at liberty.

The King received Tom again into favor, which he did not live to enjoy, for a large spider one day attacked him; and although he drew his sword and fought well, yet the spider's poisonous breath at last overcame him.

> He fell dead on the ground where he stood,
> And the spider suck'd every drop of his blood.

King Arthur and his whole court were so sorry at the loss of their little favorite that they went into mourning and raised a fine white marble monument over his grave with the following epitaph:

> Here lies Tom Thumb, King Arthur's knight,
> Who died by a spider's cruel bite.
> He was well known in Arthur's court,
> Where he afforded gallant sport;
> He rode a tilt and tournament,
> And on a mouse a-hunting went.
> Alive he filled the court with mirth;
> His death to sorrow soon gave birth.
> Wipe, wipe your eyes, and shake your head
> And cry,—Alas! Tom Thumb is dead!

THE FAIRY RING

Tattercoats

IN a great palace by the sea there once dwelt a very rich
old lord who had neither wife nor children living, only
one little granddaughter, whose face he had never seen
in all her life. He hated her bitterly, because at her birth his
favorite daughter died; and when the old nurse brought him
the baby he swore that it might live or die as it liked, but he
would never look on its face as long as it lived.

So he turned his back and sat by his window looking out
over the sea, and weeping great tears for his lost daughter,
till his white hair and beard grew down over his shoulders and
twined round his chair and crept into the chinks of the floor,
and his tears, dropping on to the window ledge, wore a channel
through the stone and ran away in a little river to the great
sea. And meanwhile his granddaughter grew up with no one
to care for her or clothe her; only the old nurse, when no one
was by, would sometimes give her a dish of scraps from the
kitchen or a torn petticoat from the rag bag; while the other
servants of the palace would drive her from the house with
blows and mocking words, calling her "Tattercoats," and
pointing at her bare feet and shoulders, till she ran away crying, to hide among the bushes.

And so she grew up, with little to eat or wear, spending
her days in the fields and lanes, with only the gooseherd for
a companion, who would play to her so merrily on his little
pipe when she was hungry or cold or tired that she forgot all
her troubles, and fell to dancing, with his flock of noisy geese
for partners.

But one day people told each other that the King was traveling through the land, and in the town near by was to give a
great ball to all the lords and ladies of the country, when the
Prince, his only son, was to choose a wife.

One of the royal invitations was brought to the palace
by the sea, and the servants carried it up to the old lord
who still sat by his window, wrapped in his long white

hair and weeping into the little river that was fed by his tears.

But when he heard the King's command he dried his eyes and bade them bring shears to cut him loose, for his hair had bound him a fast prisoner and he could not move. And then he sent them for rich clothes and jewels, which he put on; and he ordered them to saddle the white horse with gold and silk that he might ride to meet the King.

Meanwhile Tattercoats had heard of the great doings in the town, and she sat by the kitchen door weeping because she could not go to see them. And when the old nurse heard her crying she went to the lord of the palace, and begged him to take his granddaughter with him to the King's ball.

But he only frowned and told her to be silent, while the servants laughed and said: "Tattercoats is happy in her rags, playing with the gooseherd; let her be—it is all she is fit for."

A second, and then a third time, the old nurse begged him to let the girl go with him, but she was answered only by black looks and fierce words, till she was driven from the room by the jeering servants with blows and mocking words.

Weeping over her ill success, the old nurse went to look for Tattercoats; but the girl had been turned from the door by the cook, and had run away to tell her friend the gooseherd how unhappy she was because she could not go to the King's ball.

But when the gooseherd had listened to her story he bade her cheer up, and proposed that they should go together into the town to see the King and all the fine things; and when she looked sorrowfully down at her rags and bare feet he played a note or two upon his pipe, so gay and merry that she forgot all about her tears and her troubles, and, before she well knew, the herdboy had taken her by the hand, and she and he, and the geese before them, were dancing down the road toward the town.

Before they had gone very far a handsome young man, splendidly dressed, rode up and stopped to ask the way to the castle where the King was staying; and when he found that

TATTERCOATS FORGOT ALL HER TROUBLES AND FELL TO DANCING

INTENDING BRIDE AT THE THRESHOLD AND FEEDS THE SWANS.

they too were going thither, he got off his horse and walked beside them along the road.

The herdboy pulled out his pipe and played a low, sweet tune, and the stranger looked again and again at Tattercoats' lovely face, till he fell deeply in love with her and begged her to marry him.

But she only laughed and shook her golden head.

"You would be finely put to shame if you had a goosegirl for your wife!" said she; "go and ask one of the great ladies you will see to-night at the King's ball, and do not flout poor Tattercoats."

But the more she refused him the sweeter the pipe played and the deeper the young man fell in love, till at last he begged her, as a proof of his sincerity, to come that night at twelve to the King's ball, just as she was, with the herdboy and his geese, and in her torn petticoat and bare feet, and he would dance with her before the King and the lords and ladies, and present her to them all as his dear and honored bride.

So when night came, and the hall in the castle was full of light and music, and the lords and ladies were dancing before the King, just as the clock struck twelve, Tattercoats and the herdboy, followed by his flock of noisy geese, entered at the great doors and walked straight up the ballroom, while on either side the ladies whispered, the lords laughed, and the King, seated at the far end, stared in amazement.

But as they came in front of the throne Tattercoats' lover rose from beside the King and came to meet her. Taking her by the hand, he kissed her thrice before them all, and turned to the King.

"Father," he said, for it was the Prince himself, "I have made my choice, and here is my bride, the loveliest girl in all the land, and the sweetest as well!"

Before he had finished speaking the herdboy put his pipe to his lips and played a few low notes that sounded like a bird singing far off in the woods; and as he played, Tattercoats' rags were changed to shining robes sewn with glittering jewels, a golden crown lay upon her golden hair, and the flock of geese behind her became a crowd of dainty pages bearing her long train.

And, as the King rose to greet her as his daughter, the trumpets sounded loudly in honor of the new Princess, and the people outside in the street said to each other:

"Ah, now the Prince has chosen for his wife the loveliest girl in all the land!"

But the gooseherd was never seen again, and no one knew what became of him; while the old lord went home once more to his palace by the sea, for he could not stay at court when he had sworn never to look on his granddaughter's face.

So there he still sits by his window, if you could only see him, as you some day may, weeping more bitterly than ever, as he looks out over the sea.

History of Jack the Giant-Killer

*I*N the reign of the famous King Arthur there lived in Cornwall a lad named Jack, who was a boy of a bold temper and took delight in hearing or reading of conjurers, giants, and fairies, and used to listen eagerly to the deeds of the Knights of King Arthur's Round Table.

In those days there lived on St. Michael's Mount, off Cornwall, a huge giant, eighteen feet high and nine feet round, and whose fierce and savage looks were the terror of all who beheld him.

He dwelt in a gloomy cavern on the top of the mountain, and used to wade over to the mainland in search of prey, when he would throw half a dozen oxen upon his back, tie three times as many sheep and hogs around his waist, and march back to his own abode.

The giant had done this for many years, when Jack resolved to destroy him.

Jack took a horn, a shovel, a pickax, his armor, and a dark lantern, and one winter's evening he went to the mount.

There he dug a pit twenty-two feet deep and twenty broad. He covered the top over so as to make it look like solid ground. He then blew such a tantivy that the giant awoke and came out of his den, with a cry: "You saucy villain, you shall pay for this! I'll broil you for my breakfast!"

He had just finished, when, taking one step farther, he tumbled headlong into the pit, and Jack struck him a blow on the head with his pickax that killed him. Jack then returned home to cheer his friends with the news.

Another giant, called Blunderbore, vowed to be revenged on Jack if ever he should have him in his power. This giant kept an enchanted castle in the midst of a lonely wood, and some time after the death of Cormoran, Jack was passing through a wood, and being weary sat down and went to sleep.

The giant, passing by and seeing Jack, carried him to his castle, where he locked him up in a large room, the floor of which was covered with the bodies, skulls, and bones of men and women.

Soon after the giant went to fetch his brother, who was likewise a giant, to take a meal off his flesh, and Jack saw with terror through the bars of his prison the two giants approaching.

Jack, perceiving in one corner of the room a strong cord, took courage, and making a slipknot at each end, he threw them over their heads and tied it to the window bars; he then pulled till he had choked them. When they were black in the face he slid down the rope and quickly disposed of them.

Jack next took a great bunch of keys from the pocket of Blunderbore and went into the castle again. He made a strict search through all the rooms, and in one of them found three ladies tied up by the hair of their heads and almost starved to death. They told him that their husbands had been killed by the giants, who had then condemned them to be starved to death, because they would not eat the flesh of the captives he brought in.

"Ladies," said Jack, "I have put an end to the monster

and his wicked brother, and I give you this castle and all
the riches it contains, to make some amends for the dreadful pains you have felt." He then very politely gave them
the keys of the castle and went farther on his journey to
Wales.

As Jack had but little money he went on as fast as possible. At length he came to a handsome house. Jack
knocked at the door, when there came forth a Welsh giant.
Jack said he was a traveler who had lost his way, on which
the giant made him welcome and let him into a room where
there was a good bed to sleep in.

Jack took off his clothes quickly, but though he was weary
he could not go to sleep. Soon after this he heard the
giant walking backward and forward in the next room and
saying to himself:

> "Though here you lodge with me this night,
>   You shall not see the morning light;
>   My club shall dash your brains out quite."

"Say you so?" thought Jack. "Are these your tricks
upon travelers? But I hope to prove as cunning as you
are." Then, getting out of bed, he groped about the room,
and at last found a large thick billet of wood. He laid it
in his own place in the bed and then hid himself in a dark
corner of the room.

The giant, about midnight, entered the apartment, and
with his bludgeon struck many blows on the bed, in the
very place where Jack had laid the log; and then he went
back to his own room, thinking he had broken all Jack's
bones.

Early in the morning Jack put a bold face upon the
matter and walked into the giant's room to thank him for his
lodging. The giant started when he saw him and began
to stammer out: "Oh, dear me! Is it you? Pray how did
you sleep last night? Did you hear or see anything in the
dead of the night?"

"Nothing worth speaking of," said Jack carelessly. "A

rat, I believe, gave me three or four slaps with its tail and disturbed me a little, but I soon went to sleep again."

The giant wondered more and more at this, yet he did not answer a word, but went to bring two great bowls of hasty pudding for their breakfast. Jack wanted to make the giant believe that he could eat as much as himself, so he contrived to button a leathern bag inside his coat and slip the hasty pudding into this bag, while he seemed to put it into his mouth.

When breakfast was over he said to the giant: "Now I will show you a fine trick. I can cure all wounds with a touch. I could cut off my head in one minute and the next put it sound again on my shoulders. You shall see an example." He then took hold of the knife, ripped up the leathern bag, and all the hasty pudding tumbled out upon the floor.

"Ods splutter hur nails!" cried the Welsh giant, who was ashamed to be outdone by such a little fellow as Jack, "hur can do that hurself." So he snatched up the knife, plunged it into his own stomach, and in a moment dropped down dead.

Jack, having hitherto been successful in all his undertakings, resolved not to be idle in future. He therefore furnished himself with a horse, a cap of knowledge, a sword of sharpness, shoes of swiftness, and an invisible coat, the better to perform the wonderful enterprises that lay before him.

He traveled over high hills, and on the third day he came to a large and spacious forest through which his road lay. Scarcely had he entered the forest when he beheld a monstrous giant dragging along by the hair of their heads a handsome knight and his lady. Jack alighted from his horse, and tying him to an oak tree, put on his invisible coat, under which he carried his sword of sharpness.

When he came up to the giant he made several strokes at him, but could not reach his body, though he wounded his thighs in several places; and at length putting both hands to his sword and aiming with all his might, he cut off both his legs. Then Jack, setting his foot upon the giant's neck, plunged his sword into the great body, when the monster gave a groan and expired.

The knight and his lady thanked Jack for their deliverance and invited him to their house, to receive a proper reward for his services. "No," said Jack, "I cannot be easy till I find out this monster's habitation." So taking the knight's directions, he mounted his horse and soon after came in sight of another giant, who was sitting on a block of timber waiting for his brother's return.

Jack alighted from his horse and, putting on his invisible coat, approached and aimed a blow at the giant's head, but missing his aim he only cut off his nose. On this the giant seized his club and laid about him most unmercifully.

"Nay," said Jack, "if this be the case I'd better dispatch you!" So jumping upon the block he stabbed him in the back, when he dropped down dead.

Jack then proceeded on his journey and traveled over hills and dales, till arriving at the foot of a high mountain he knocked at the door of a lonely house, when an old man let him in.

When Jack was seated, the hermit thus addressed him: "My son, on the top of this mountain is an enchanted castle, kept by the giant Galligantus and a vile magician. I lament the fate of a duke's daughter, whom they seized as she was walking in her father's garden and brought hither transformed into a deer."

Jack promised that in the morning, at the risk of his life, he would break the enchantment, and after a sound sleep he arose early, put on his invisible coat, and made ready for the attempt.

When he had climbed to the top of the mountain he saw two fiery griffins, but he passed between them without the least fear of danger, for they could not see him because of his invisible coat. On the castle gate he found a golden trumpet, under which were written these lines:

"THE GIANT AND THE CONJURER NOW KNEW THAT THEIR WICKED COURSE WAS AT AN END"

THE FAIRY RING

"Whoever can this trumpet blow
Shall cause the giant's overthrow."

As soon as Jack had read this he seized the trumpet and blew a shrill blast, which made the gates fly open and the very castle itself tremble.

The giant and the conjurer now knew that their wicked course was at an end, and they stood biting their thumbs and shaking with fear. Jack, with his sword of sharpness, soon killed the giant, and the magician was then carried away by a whirlwind; and every knight and beautiful lady who had been changed into birds and beasts returned to their proper shapes. The castle vanished away like smoke, and the head of the giant Galligantus was then sent to King Arthur.

The knights and ladies rested that night at the old man's hermitage, and next day they set out for the court. Jack then went up to the King and gave his majesty an account of all his fierce battles.

Jack's fame had now spread through the whole country, and at the King's desire the duke gave him his daughter in marriage, to the joy of all his kingdom. After this the King gave him a large estate, on which he and his lady lived the rest of their days in joy and contentment.

Yvon and Finette

A TALE OF BRITTANY

I

ONCE upon a time there lived in Brittany a noble lord, who was called the Baron Kerver. His manor house was the most beautiful in the province. It was a great Gothic castle, with a groined roof and walls, covered with carving, that looked at a distance like a vine climbing over an arbor. On the first floor six stained glass balcony windows looked out on each side toward the rising and the setting sun. In the morning when the Baron, mounted on his dun mare, went forth into the forest, followed by his tall greyhounds, he saw at each window one of his daughters, with prayer book in hand, praying for the house of Kerver, and who, with their fair curls, blue eyes, and clasped hands, might have been taken for six madonnas in an azure niche. At evening when the sun declined and the Baron returned homeward, after riding round his domains, he perceived from afar, in the windows looking toward the west, six sons, with dark locks and eagle gaze, the hope and pride of the family, who might have been taken for six sculptured knights at the portal of a church. For ten leagues round all who wished to quote a happy father and a powerful lord named the Baron Kerver.

The castle had but twelve windows, and the Baron had thirteen children. The last, the one that had no place, was a handsome boy of sixteen by the name of Yvon. As usual, he was the best beloved. In the morning at his departure, and at evening on his return, the Baron always found Yvon waiting on the threshold to embrace him. With his fair hair falling to his waist, his graceful figure, his willful air, and his bold bearing, Yvon was beloved by all the Bretons. At twelve years of age he had bravely attacked and killed a wolf with an ax, which had won him the name of *Fearless*. He deserved the title, for never was there a bolder heart.

One day, when the Baron had stayed at home, and was amusing himself by breaking a lance with his squire, Yvon entered the armory in a traveling dress, and, bending one knee to the ground:

"My lord and father," said he to the Baron, "I come to ask your blessing. The house of Kerver is rich in knights, and has no need of a child; it is time for me to go to seek my fortune. I wish to go to distant countries to try my strength, and to make myself a name."

"You are right, Fearless," replied the Baron, more moved than he wished to appear. "I will not keep you back; I have no right to do so; but you are very young, my child; perhaps it would be better for you to stay another year with us."

"I am sixteen, my father; at that age you had already fought one of the proudest lords of the country. I have not forgotten that our arms are a unicorn ripping up a lion, and our motto, "Onward!" I do not wish the Kervers to blush for their last child."

Yvon received his father's blessing, shook hands with his brothers, embraced his sisters, bade adieu to all the weeping vassals, and set out with a light heart.

Nothing stopped him on his way. A river appeared, he swam it; a mountain, he climbed it; a forest, he made his way through it with the sun for a guide. "On—the Kerver!" he cried, whenever he met with an obstacle, and went straight forward in spite of everything.

For three years he had been roaming over the world in search of adventures, sometimes conquering, sometimes conquered, always bold and gay, when he received an offer to go to fight the heathen of Norway. To kill unbelievers and to conquer a kingdom was a double pleasure. Yvon enlisted twelve brave comrades, freighted a ship, and hoisted from the mainmast a blue standard, with the unicorn and motto of the Kervers.

The sea was calm, the wind fair, and the night serene. Yvon, stretched on the deck, watched the stars, and sought the one which cast its trembling light on his father's castle. All at once the vessel struck upon a rock; a terrible crash was heard; the sails fell like tinder; and an enormous wave burst over the deck, and swept away everything upon it.

"On—the Kerver!" cried Yvon, as soon as his head appeared above the water; and he began to swim as tranquilly as if he had been bathing in the lake of the old castle. Happily the moon was rising. Yvon saw, at a little distance, a black speck among the silvery waves—it was land. He approached it, not without difficulty, and finally succeeded in gaining a foothold. Dripping wet, exhausted with fatigue, and out of breath, he dragged himself on the sand; then, without more anxiety, said his prayers, and went to sleep.

II

IN the morning, on awaking, Yvon tried to discover in what country he had been cast. He saw in the distance a house as large as a church, with windows fifty feet in height. He walked a whole day before reaching it, and at last found himself in front of an immense door, with a knocker so heavy that it was impossible for a man to lift it.

Yvon took a great stone and began to knock. " Come in," cried a voice, that sounded like the roar of a bull. At the same instant the door opened, and the little Breton found himself in the presence of a giant not less than forty feet in height.

" What is your name, and what do you want here?" said the giant, taking up Yvon between his thumb and finger, and lifting him from the ground so as to see him better.

" My name is Fearless, and I am seeking my fortune," answered Yvon, looking at the monster with an air of defiance.

" Well, brave Fearless, your fortune is made," said the giant, in a mocking tone. " I am in need of a servant, and I will give you the place. You can go to work directly. This is the time for leading my sheep to the pasture; you may clean the stable while I am gone. I shall give you nothing else to do," added he, bursting into a laugh. " You see that I am a good master. Do your task, and, above all things, don't prowl about the house, or it will cost you your life."

" Certainly I have a good master; the work is not hard," thought Yvon, when the giant was gone. " I have plenty of time to sweep the stable. What shall I do meanwhile to amuse myself? Shall I look about the house? Since I am forbidden to do so, it must be because there is something to see."

He entered the first room, and saw a large fireplace, in which a great pot was hanging, suspended from a hook. The pot was boiling, but there was no fire on the hearth.

" What does this mean?" thought Yvon; " there is some

mystery here." He cut off a lock of his hair, dipped it into the pot, and took it out all coated with copper.

"Oh, oh!" cried he, "this is a new kind of soup; anybody that swallows it must have an iron-clad stomach."

He went into the next room; there also a pot was suspended from a hook, and boiling without fire. Yvon dipped a lock of hair into it, and took it out all coated with silver.

"The broth is not so rich as this in the Kerver kitchen," thought he, "but it may have a better taste."

Upon this, he entered the third room. There also a pot was suspended from a hook, and boiling without fire. Yvon dipped a lock of hair into it, and took it out all coated with gold. It shone so brightly that it might have been mistaken for a sunbeam.

"Good!" cried he. "In our country the old women have a saying, 'Everything gets worse and worse'; here it is just the contrary, everything gets better and better. What shall I find in the fourth room, I wonder—diamond soup?"

He pushed open the door, and saw something rarer than precious stones. This was a young woman of such marvelous beauty that Yvon, dazzled, fell on his knees at the sight.

"Unfortunate youth!" cried she, in a trembling voice, "what are you doing here?"

"I belong to the house," answered Yvon; "the giant took me into his service this morning."

"His service!" repeated the young girl. "May Heaven preserve you from it!"

"Why so?" said Yvon. "I have a good master; the work is not hard. The stable once swept, my task is finished."

"Yes, and how will you set to work to sweep it?" asked the lady. "If you sweep it in the usual way, for every forkful of dung that you throw out of the door, ten will come in at the window. But I will tell you what to do. Turn the fork and sweep with the handle, and the dung will instantly fly out of itself."

"I will obey," said Yvon; upon which he sat down by the young girl and began to talk with her. She was the daughter of a fairy, whom the wretched giant had made his slave. Friendship soon springs up between companions in misfortune. Before the end of the day, Finette (for that was the lady's name) and Yvon had already promised to belong to each other, if they could escape from their abominable master. The difficulty was to find the means.

Time passes quickly in this kind of talk. Evening was approaching when Finette sent away her new friend, advising him to sweep the stable before the giant came home.

Yvon took down the fork and attempted to use it as he had seen it done at his father's castle. He soon had enough of it. In less than a second there was so much dung in the stable that the poor boy knew not which way to turn. He did as Finette had bid him; he turned the fork and swept with the handle, when behold! in the twinkling of an eye, the stable was as clean as if no cattle had ever entered it.

The task finished, Yvon seated himself on a bench before the door of the house. As soon as he saw the giant coming, he lolled back in his seat, crossed his legs, and began to sing one of his native airs.

" Have you cleaned the stable?" asked the giant, with a frown.

" Everything is ready, master," answered Yvon, without troubling himself to move.

" I am going to see for myself," howled the giant. He entered the stable grumbling, found everything in order, and came out furious.

" You have seen my Finette," cried he; " this trick did not come from your own head! "

" What is myfinette?" asked Yvon, opening his mouth and shutting his eyes. " Is it one of the animals that you have in this country? Show it to me, master."

" Hold your tongue, fool," replied the giant; " you will see her sooner than you will want to."

The next morning the giant gathered his sheep together to lead them to the pasture; but, before setting out, he ordered Yvon to go in the course of the day in search of his horse, which was turned out to graze on the mountain. "After that," said he, bursting into a laugh, "you can rest all day long. You see that I am a good master. Do your task; and, above all things, don't prowl about the house, or I will cut off your head."

Yvon winked his eye as the giant left. "Yes, you are a good master," said he between his teeth. "I understand your tricks; but, in spite of your threats, I shall go into the house, and talk with your Finette. It remains to be seen whether she will not be more mine than yours."

He ran to the young girl's room. "Hurrah!" cried he; "I have nothing to do all day but to go to the mountain after a horse."

"Very well," said Finette; "how will you set to work to ride him?"

"A fine question," returned Yvon. "As if it were a difficult thing to ride a horse! I fancy that I have ridden worse ones than this."

"It is not so easy as you think," replied Finette; "but I will tell you what to do. Take the bit that hangs behind the stable door, and, when the animal rushes toward you breathing fire and smoke from his nostrils, force it straight between his teeth; he will instantly become as gentle as a lamb, and you can do what you please with him."

"I will obey," said Yvon; upon which he sat down by the side of Finette, and began to talk with her. They talked of everything; but, however far their fancy strayed, they always came back to the point that they were promised to each other, and that they must escape from the giant. Time passes quickly in this kind of talk. The evening drew nigh. Yvon had forgotten the horse and the mountain, and Finette was obliged to send him away, advising him to bring back the animal before his master's arrival.

Yvon took down the bit that was hidden behind the stable door, and hastened to the mountain, when lo! a horse almost as large as an elephant rushed toward him at full gallop, breathing fire and smoke from his nostrils. Yvon firmly awaited the huge animal, and, the moment he opened his enormous jaws, thrust between them the bit; when lo! the horse instantly became as gentle as a lamb. Yvon made him kneel down, sprang on his back, and tranquilly returned home.

His task finished, Yvon seated himself on the bench before the door of the house. As soon as he saw the giant coming, he lolled back in his seat, crossed his legs, and began to sing one of his native airs.

"Have you brought back the horse?" asked the giant with a frown.

"Yes, master," answered Yvon, without taking the trouble to move. "He is a fine animal, and does you credit. He is gentle, well trained, and as quiet as a lamb. He is feeding yonder in the stable."

"I am going to see for myself!" howled the giant. He entered the stable grumbling, found everything in order, and came out furious.

"You have seen my Finette," said he; "this trick did not come from your own head."

"Oh, master," returned Yvon, opening his mouth and shutting his eyes, "it is the same story over again. What is this myfinette? Once for all, show me this monster."

"Hold your tongue, fool," returned the giant; "you will see her sooner than you will want to."

The third day at dawn the giant gathered his sheep together to lead them to the pasture; but, before setting out, he said to Yvon:

"To-day you must go to the bottomless pit to collect my rent. After that," continued he, bursting into a laugh, "you may rest all day long. You see that I am a good master."

"A good master, so be it," murmured Yvon, "but the task is none the less hard. I will go and see my Finette, as the giant says; I have great need of her help to get through to-day's business."

When Finette had learned what was the task of the day, "Well," said she, "how will you go to work to do it?"

"I don't know," said Yvon sadly; "I have never been to

the bottomless pit, and, even if I knew the way there, I should not know what to ask for. Tell me what to do."

"Do you see that great rock yonder?" said Finette; "that is one of the gates of the bottomless pit. Take this stick, knock three times on the stone, and a demon will come out all streaming with flames, who will ask you how much you want. Take care to answer, 'No more than I can carry.'"

"I will obey," said Yvon; upon which he took a seat by the side of Finette, and began to talk with her. He would have been there till this time if the young girl had not sent him to the great rock, when the evening drew nigh, to execute the giant's commands.

On reaching the spot pointed out to him, Yvon found a great block of granite. He struck it three times with the stick, when lo! the rock opened, and a demon came forth all streaming with flames.

"What do you want?" he cried.

"I have come for the giant's rent," answered Yvon calmly.

"How much do you want?"

"I never want any more than I can carry," replied the Breton.

"It is well for you that you do not," returned the man in flames. "Enter this cavern, and you will find what you want."

Yvon entered, and opened his eyes wide. Everywhere he saw nothing but gold, silver, diamonds, carbuncles, and emeralds. They were as numerous as the sands on the seashore. The young Kerver filled a sack, threw it across his shoulder, and tranquilly returned home.

His task finished, our Breton seated himself on the bench before the door of the house. As soon as he saw the giant coming, he lolled back in his seat, crossed his legs, and began to sing one of his native airs.

"Have you been to the bottomless pit to collect my rent?" asked the giant, with a frown.

"Yes, master," answered Yvon, without taking the trouble

to stir. "The sack is there right before your eyes; you can count it."

"I am going to see for myself!" howled the giant. He untied the strings of the sack, which was so full that the gold and silver rolled in all directions.

"You have seen my Finette," he cried; "this trick did not come from your own head."

"Don't you know but one song," said Yvon, opening his mouth and shutting his eyes. "It is the old story, myfinette, myfinette. Once for all, show me this thing."

"Well, well," roared the giant with fury, "wait till to-morrow, and you shall make her acquaintance!"

"Thank you, master," said Yvon. "It is very good of you; but I see from your face that you are laughing at me."

III

THE next morning the giant went out without giving Yvon any orders, which troubled Finette. At noon he returned without his flock, complaining of the heat and fatigue, and said to the young girl:

"You will find a child, my servant, at the door. Cut his throat, put him into the great pot to boil, and call me when the broth is ready." Saying this he stretched himself on the bed to take a nap, and was soon snoring so loud that it seemed like thunder shaking the mountains.

Finette prepared a log of wood, took a large knife, and called Yvon. She pricked his little finger; three drops of blood fell on the log.

"That is enough," said Finette; "now help me to fill the pot."

They threw into it all that they could find—old clothes, old shoes, old carpets, and everything else. Finette then took Yvon by the hand, and led him through the three antechambers, where she ran in a mold three bullets of gold, two bullets of silver, and one bullet of copper, after which they quitted the house and ran toward the sea.

"*On—the Kerver!*" cried Yvon, as soon as he saw himself in the country. "Explain yourself, dear Finette; what farce are we playing now?"

"Let us run—let us run!" she cried; "if we do not quit this wretched island before night, it is all over with us."

"*On—the Kerver!*" replied Yvon laughing, "and down with the giant!"

When he had snored a full hour, the giant stretched his limbs, half opened one eye, and cried, "Is it ready?"

"It is just beginning to boil," answered the first drop of blood on the log.

The giant turned over, and snored louder than ever for an hour or two longer. Then he stretched his limbs, half opened one eye, and cried out, "Do you hear me? Is it almost ready?"

"It is half done," answered the second drop of blood on the log.

The giant turned over, and slept an hour longer. Then he yawned, stretched his great limbs, and cried out impatiently, "Isn't it ready yet?"

"It is ready now," answered the third drop of blood on the log.

The giant sat up in bed, rubbed his eyes, and looked around to see who had spoken; but it was in vain to look; he saw nobody.

"Finette!" howled he, "why isn't the table set?"

There was no answer. The giant, furious, sprang out of bed, seized a ladle, which looked like a caldron with a pitchfork for a handle, and plunged it into the pot to taste the soup.

"Finette!" howled he, "you haven't salted it. What sort of a soup is this? I see neither meat nor vegetables."

No; but, in return, he saw his carpet, which had not quite all boiled to pieces. At this sight he fell into such a fit of rage that he could not keep his feet.

"Villains!" said he, "you have played a fine trick on me; but you shall pay for it!"

He rushed out with a stick in his hand, and strode along at such a rate that in a quarter of an hour he discovered the two fugitives still far from the seashore. He uttered such a cry of joy that the earth shook for twelve leagues around.

Finette stopped, trembling. Yvon clasped her to his heart.

"*On—the Kerver!*" said he; "the sea is not far off; we shall be there before our enemy."

"Here he is! here he is!" cried Finette, pointing to the giant not a hundred yards off; "we are lost if this charm does not save us."

She took the copper bullet and threw it on the ground, saying:

"Copper bullet, save us, pray,
Stop the giant on his way."

And behold, the earth cracked apart with a terrific noise, and an enormous fissure, a bottomless pit, stopped the giant just as he was stretching out his hand to seize his prey.

"Let us fly!" cried Finette, grasping the arm of Yvon, who was gazing at the giant with a swaggering air, defying him to come on.

The giant ran backward and forward along the abyss like a bear in his cage, seeking a passage everywhere and finding none; then, with a furious jerk, he tore up an immense oak by the roots, and flung it across the gap. The branches of the oak nearly crushed the children as it fell. The giant seated himself astride the huge tree, which bent under his weight, and crept slowly along, suspended between heaven and earth, entangled as he was among the branches. When he reached the other side, Yvon and Finette were already on the shore, with the sea rolling before them.

Alas! there was neither bark nor ship. The fugitives were lost. Yvon, always brave, picked up stones to attack the giant, and to sell his life dearly. Finette, trembling with fear, threw one of the silver bullets into the sea, saying:

"Silver bullet, bright and pliant,
Save us from this frightful giant."

[120]

Scarcely had she spoken the magic words when a beautiful ship rose from the waves like a swan spreading its white wings. Yvon and Finette plunged into the sea; a rope was thrown them by an invisible hand; and when the furious giant reached the shore, the ship was receding rapidly at full sail, leaving behind it a long furrow of shining foam.

Giants do not like the water. This fact is certified to by old Homer, who knew Polyphemus; and the same observation will be found in all natural histories worthy of the name. Finette's master resembled Polyphemus. He roared with rage when he saw his slaves about to escape him. He ran hesitatingly along the shore; he flung huge masses of rock after the vessel, which happily fell by the side of it, and only made great black holes in the water; and, finally, mad with anger he plunged head foremost into the sea, and began to swim after the ship with frightful speed. At each stroke he advanced forty feet, blowing like a whale, and like a whale cleaving the waves. By degrees he gained on his enemies; one more effort would bring him within reach of the rudder, and already he was stretching out his arm to seize it, when Finette threw the second silver bullet into the sea, and cried, in tears:

> "Silver bullet, bright and pliant,
> Save us from this frightful giant."

Suddenly from the midst of the foam darted forth a gigantic swordfish, with a sword at least twenty feet in length. It rushed straight toward the giant, who scarcely had time to dive, chased him under the water, pursued him on the top of the waves, followed him closely whichever way he turned, and forced him to flee as fast as he could to his island, where he finally landed with the greatest difficulty, and fell upon the shore dripping, worn out, and conquered.

"*On—the Kerver!*" cried Yvon, "we are saved!"

"Not yet," said Finette, trembling. "The giant has a witch for a godmother, I fear that she will revenge on me the insult offered to her godson. My art tells me, my dear

THE FAIRY RING

Yvon, that if you quit me a single instant until you give me your name in the chapel of the Kervers, I have everything to dread."

"By the unicorn of my ancestors," cried Yvon, "you have the heart of a hare and not of a hero! Am I not here? Am I going to abandon you? Do you believe that Providence has saved us from the fangs of that monster to wreck us in port?"

He laughed so gayly that Finette laughed in turn at the terror that had seized her.

IV

THE rest of the voyage passed off admirably. An invisible hand seemed to impel the ship onward. Twenty days after their departure the boat landed Yvon and Finette near Kerver Castle. Once on shore, Yvon turned to thank the crew. No one was there. Both boat and ship had vanished under the waves, leaving no trace behind but a gull on the wing.

Yvon recognized the spot where he had so often gathered shells and chased the crabs to their holes when a child. Half an hour's walk would bring him in sight of the towers of the old castle. His heart beat; he looked tenderly at Finette, and saw, for the first time, that her dress was fantastic and unworthy of a woman about to enter the noble house of Kerver.

"My dear child," said he, "the Baron, my father, is a noble lord, accustomed to be treated with respect. I cannot introduce you to him in this gypsy dress; neither is it fitting that you should enter our great castle on foot like a peasant. Wait for me a few moments, and I will bring you a horse and one of my sister's dresses. I wish you to be received like a lady of high degree. I wish my father himself to meet you on your arrival, and hold it an honor to give you his hand."

"Yvon, Yvon!" cried Finette, "do not quit me, I beg you. Once returned to your castle, I know that you will forget me."

"Forget you!" exclaimed Yvon. "If anyone else were to offer me such an insult, I would teach him with my sword to

"HE FLUNG HUGE MASSES OF ROCK AFTER THE VESSEL"

THE FAIRY RING

suspect a Kerver. Forget you, my Finette! you do not know the fidelity of a Breton."

That the Bretons are faithful, no one doubts; but that they are still more headstrong is a justice that none will deny them. It was useless for poor Finette to plead in her most loving tones; she was forced to yield. She resigned herself with a heavy heart, and said to Yvon:

" Go without me, then, to your castle, but only stay long enough to speak to your friends; then go straight to the stable, and return as soon as possible. You will be surrounded by people; act as if you saw no one, and, above all, do not eat or drink anything whatever. Should you take only a glass of water, evil would come upon us both."

Yvon promised and swore all that Finette asked, but he smiled in his heart at this feminine weakness. He was sure of himself; and he thought with pride how different a Breton was from those fickle Frenchmen, whose words, they say, are borne away by the first breath of the wind.

On entering the old castle he could scarcely recognize its dark walls. All the windows were festooned with leaves and flowers within and without; the courtyard was strewn with fragrant grass; on one side were spread tables groaning under their weight; on the other, musicians, mounted on casks, were playing merry airs. The vassals, dressed in their holiday attire, were singing and dancing, and dancing and singing. It was a day of great rejoicing at the castle. The Baron himself was smiling. It is true that he had just married his fifth daughter to the Knight of Kervalec. This marriage added another quartering to the illustrious escutcheon of the Kervers.

Yvon, recognized and welcomed by all the crowd, was instantly surrounded by his relatives, who embraced him and shook him by the hand. Where had he been? Where did he come from? Had he conquered a kingdom, a duchy, or a barony? Had he brought the bride the jewels of some queen? Had the fairies protected him? How many rivals had he overthrown? All these questions were showered upon

[123]

him without reply. Yvon respectfully kissed his father's hand, hastened to his sisters' chamber, took two of their finest dresses, went to the stable, saddled a pony, mounted a beautiful Spanish jennet, and was about to quit the castle, when he found his relatives, friends, squires, and vassals all standing in his way, their glasses in their hands, ready to drink their young lord's health and his safe return.

Yvon gracefully thanked them, bowed, and made his way by degrees through the crowd, when, just as he was about to cross the drawbridge, a fair-haired lady, with a haughty and disdainful air, a stranger to him, a sister of the bridegroom, perhaps, approached him, holding a pomegranate in her hand.

"My handsome knight," said she, with a singular smile, "you surely will not refuse a lady's first request. Taste this pomegranate, I entreat you. If you are neither hungry nor thirsty after so long a journey, I suppose at least that you have not forgotten the laws of politeness."

Yvon dared not refuse this appeal. He was very wrong. Scarcely had he tasted the pomegranate when he looked round him like a man waking from a dream.

"What am I doing on this horse?" thought he. "What means this pony that I am leading? Is not my place in my father's house at my sister's wedding? Why should I quit the castle?"

He threw the bridle to one of the grooms, leaped lightly to the ground, and offered his hand to the fair-haired lady, who accepted him as her attendant on the spot, and gave him her bouquet to hold as a special mark of favor.

Before the evening was over there was another betrothed couple in the castle. Yvon had pledged his faith to the unknown lady, and Finette was forgotten.

V

Poor Finette, seated on the seashore, waited all day long for Yvon, but Yvon did not come. The sun was setting in the fiery waves, when Finette rose, sighing, and took the way to the castle in her turn. She had not walked long in a steep road, bordered with thorn trees in blossom, when she found herself in front of a wretched hut, at the door of which stood an old woman about to milk her cow. Finette approached her, and, making a low courtesy, begged a shelter for the night.

The old woman looked at the stranger from head to foot. With her buskins trimmed with fur, her full red petticoat, her blue jacket edged with jet, and her diadem, Finette looked more like an Egyptian princess than a Christian. The old woman frowned, and, shaking her fist in the face of the poor forsaken girl, " Begone, witch! " she cried; " there is no room for you in this honest house."

" My good mother," said Finette, " give me only a corner of the stable."

" Oh," said the old woman, laughing, and showing the only tooth she had left, which projected from her mouth like a bear's tusk, " so you want a corner of the stable, do you! Well, you shall have it, if you will fill my milk pail with gold."

" It is a bargain," said Finette quietly. She opened a leather purse which she wore at her belt, took from it a golden bullet, and threw it into the milk pail, saying:

> " Golden bullet, precious treasure,
> Save me, if it be thy pleasure."

And behold! the pieces of gold began to dance about in the pail; they rose higher and higher, flapping about like fish in a net, while the old woman on her knees gazed with wonder at the sight.

When the pail was full the old woman rose, put her arm through the handle, and said to Finette, " Madam, all is yours, the house, the cow, and everything else. Hurrah! I am going to the town to live like a lady with nothing to do. Oh, dear, how I wish I were only sixty!" And, shaking her crutch, without looking backward, she set out on a run toward Kerver Castle.

THE FAIRY RING

Finette entered the house. It was a wretched hovel, dark, low, damp, bad-smelling, and full of dust and spiders' webs —a horrible refuge for a woman accustomed to living in the giant's grand castle. Without seeming troubled, Finette went to the hearth, on which a few green boughs were smoking, took another golden bullet from her purse, and threw it into the fire, saying:

"Golden bullet, precious treasure,
Save me, if it be thy pleasure"

The gold melted, bubbled up, and spread all over the house like running water, and behold! the whole cottage, the walls, the thatch, the wooden rocking chair, the stool, the chest, the bed, the cow's horns, everything, even to the spiders in their webs, was turned to gold. The house gleamed in the moonlight, among the trees, like a star in the night.

When Finette had milked the cow and drunk a little new milk, she threw herself on the bed without undressing, and, worn out by the fatigue of the day, fell asleep in the midst of her tears.

Old women do not know how to hold their tongues, at least in Brittany. Finette's hostess had scarcely reached the village when she hastened to the house of the steward. He was an important personage, who had more than once made her tremble when she had driven her cow into her neighbor's pasture by mistake. The steward listened to the old woman's story, shook his head, and said that it looked like witchcraft; then he mysteriously brought a pair of scales, weighed the guineas, which he found to be genuine and of full weight, kept as many of them as he could, and advised the owner to tell no one of this strange adventure. "If it should come to the ears of the bailiff or the seneschal," said he, "the least that would happen to you, mother, would be to lose every one of these beautiful bright guineas. Justice is impartial; it knows neither favor nor repugnance; it takes the whole."

The old woman thanked the steward for his advice, and promised to follow it. She kept her word so well that she

[126]

only told her story that evening to two neighbors, her dearest friends, both of whom swore on the heads of their little
children to keep it secret. The oath was a solemn one, and
so well kept that at noon the next day there was not a boy
of six in the village that did not point his finger at the old
woman, while the very dogs seemed to bark in their language,
" Here is the old woman with her guineas! "

A girl who amuses herself by filling milk-pails with gold is
not to be found every day. Even though she should be
something of a witch, such a girl would none the less be a
treasure in a family. The steward, who was a bachelor, made
this wise reflection that night on going to bed. Before dawn
he rose to make his rounds in the direction of the stranger's
cottage. By the first gleam of day he spied something shining in the distance like a light among the woods. On reaching the place he was greatly surprised to find a golden cottage
instead of the wretched hut that had stood there the day
before. But, on entering the house, he was much more surprised and delighted to find a beautiful young girl, with raven
hair, sitting by the window, and spinning on her distaff with
'he air of an empress.

Like all men the steward did himself justice, and knew,
at the bottom of his heart, that there was not a woman in the
world that would not be too happy to give him her hand.
Without hesitating therefore he declared to Finette that he
had come to marry her. The young girl burst out laughing,
upon which the steward flew into a passion.

" Take care! " said he, in a terrible voice; " I am the master here. No one knows who you are or whence you came.
The gold that you gave the old woman has raised suspicions.
There is magic in this house. If you do not accept me for a
husband this very instant I will arrest you, and before night
perhaps a witch will be burned before Kerver Castle."

" You are very amiable," said Finette, with a charming
grimace; " you have a peculiar way of paying court to ladies.
Even when they have decided not to refuse, a gallant man
spares their blushes."

"We Bretons are plain-spoken people," replied the stew‑
ard; "we go straight to the point. Marriage or prison, which
do you choose?"

"Oh!" cried Finette, laying down the distaff, "there are
the firebrands falling all over the room."

"Don't trouble yourself," said the steward, "I will pick
them up."

"Lay them carefully on the top of the ashes," returned
Finette. "Have you the tongs?"

"Yes," said the steward, picking up the crackling coals.

"*Abracadabra!*" cried Finette, rising. "Villain, may the
tongs hold you, and may you hold the tongs till sunset!"

No sooner said than done. The wicked steward stood
there all day with the tongs in his hand, picking up and
throwing back the burning coals that snapped in his face,
and the hot ashes that flew into his eyes. It was useless for
him to shout, pray, weep, and blaspheme; no one heard him.
If Finette had stayed at home she would doubtless have taken
pity on him; but, after putting the spell upon him she has‑
tened to the seashore, where, forgetting everything else, she
watched for Yvon in vain.

The moment that the sun set the tongs fell from the stew‑
ard's hands. He did not stop to finish his errand, but ran as
if the devil or justice were at his heels. He made such leaps,
he uttered such groans, he was so blackened, scorched, and
benumbed, that everyone in the village was afraid of him,
thinking that he was mad. The boldest tried to speak to him,
but he fled without answering, and hid himself in his house,
more ashamed than a wolf that has left his paw in the trap.

At evening, when Finette returned home in despair, in‑
stead of the steward she found another visitor little less for‑
midable. The bailiff had heard the story of the guineas, and
had also made up his mind to marry the stranger. He was
not rough like the steward, but a fat, good-natured man who
could not speak without bursting into a laugh, showing his
great yellow teeth, and puffing and blowing like an ox, though
at heart he was not less obstinate or less threatening than

his predecessor. Finette entreated the bailiff to leave her alone. He laughed and hinted to her in a good-natured way that, by right of his office, he had the power to imprison and hang people without process of law. She clasped her hands, and begged him with tears to go. For his only answer he took a roll of parchment from his pocket, wrote on it a contract of marriage, and declared to Finette that should he stay all night he would not leave the house till she had signed the promise.

"Nevertheless," said he, "if you do not like my person I have another parchment here on which I will write an agreement to live apart; and if my sight annoys you, you have only to shut your eyes."

"Why," said Finette, "I might decide to do as you wish if I were sure of finding a good husband in you; but I am afraid."

"Of what, my dear child?" asked the bailiff, smiling, and already as proud as a peacock.

"Do you think," said she, with a pettish air, "that a good husband would leave that door wide open, and not know that his wife was freezing with cold?"

"You are right, my dear," said the bailiff; "it was very stupid in me. I will go and shut it."

"Have you hold of the knob?" asked Finette.

"Yes, my charmer," answered the happy bailiff; "I am just shutting the door."

"*Abracadabra!*" cried Finette. "May you hold the door, villain, and may the door hold you till daybreak."

And behold, the door opened and shut, and slammed against the walls like an eagle flapping its wings. You may judge what a dance the poor captive kept up all night. Never had he tried such a waltz, and I imagine that he never wished to dance a second one of the same sort. Sometimes the door swung open with him in the street; sometimes it flew back and crushed him against the wall. He swung backward and forward, screaming, swearing, weeping, and praying, but all in vain; the door was deaf, and Finette asleep.

At daybreak his hands unclasped, and he fell in the road head foremost. Without waiting to finish his errand he ran as if the Moors were after him. He did not even turn around for fear that the door might be at his heels. Fortunately for him all were still asleep when he reached the village, and he could hide himself in bed without anyone seeing his deplorable plight. This was a great piece of good fortune for him for he was covered with whitewash from head to foot, and so pale, haggard, and trembling that he might have been taken for the ghost of a miller escaped from the infernal regions.

When Finette opened her eyes she saw by her bedside a tall man dressed in black, with a velvet cap and a sword. It was the seneschal of the barony of Kerver. He stood with his arms folded, gazing at Finette in a way that chilled the very marrow of her bones.

"What is your name, vassal?" said he in a voice of thunder.

"Finette, at your service, my lord," replied she, trembling.

"Is this house and furniture yours?"

"Yes, my lord, everything, at your service."

"I mean that it shall be at my service," returned the seneschal sternly. "Rise, vassal! I do you the honor to marry you, and to take yourself, your person, and your property under my guardianship."

"My lord," returned Finette, "this is much too great an honor for a poor girl like me, a stranger, without friends or kindred."

"Be silent, vassal!" replied the seneschal. "I am your lord and master; I have nothing to do with your advice. Sign this paper."

"My lord," said Finette, "I don't know how to write."

"Do you think that I do, either?" returned the seneschal, in a voice that shook the house. "Do you take me for a clerk? A cross—that is the signature of gentlemen."

He made a large cross on the paper, and handed the pen to Finette.

"Sign," said he. "If you are afraid to make a cross, infidel, you pass your own death sentence, and I shall take on myself to execute it." He drew his heavy sword from the scabbard as he spoke, and threw it on the table.

For her only answer, Finette leaped out of the window, and ran to the stable. The seneschal pursued her thither; but, on attempting to enter an unexpected obstacle stopped him. The frightened cow had backed at the sight of the young girl, and stood in the doorway with Finette clinging to her horns, and making of her a sort of buckler.

" You shall not escape me, sorceress! " cried the seneschal, and, with a grasp like that of Hercules, he seized the cow by the tail and dragged her out of the stable.

"*Abracadabra!*" cried Finette. " May the cow's tail hold you, villain, and may you hold the cow's tail till you have both been around the world together."

And behold! the cow darted off like lightning, dragging the unhappy seneschal after her. Nothing stopped the two inseparable comrades; they rushed over mountains and valleys, crossed marshes, rivers, quagmires, and brakes, glided over the seas without sinking, were frozen in Siberia and scorched in Africa, climbed the Himalayas, descended Mont Blanc, and at length after thirty-six hours of a journey, the like of which had never been seen, both stopped out of breath in the public square of the village.

A seneschal harnessed to a cow's tail is a sight not to be seen every day, and all the peasants in the neighborhood crowded together to wonder at the spectacle. But, torn as he was by the cactuses of Barbary and the thickets of Tartary, the seneschal had lost nothing of his haughty air. With a threatening gesture he dispersed the rabble, and limped to his house to taste the repose of which he began to feel the need.

VI

WHILE the steward, the bailiff, and the seneschal were experiencing these little unpleasantnesses, of which they did not think it proper to boast, preparations were being made

THE FAIRY RING

for a great event at Kerver Castle, namely, the marriage of Yvon and the fair-haired lady. Two days had passed in these preparations, and all the friends of the family had gathered together for twenty leagues round, when one fine morning Yvon and his bride, with the Baron and Baroness Kerver, took their seats in a great carriage adorned with flowers, and set out for the celebrated church of St. Maclou.

A hundred knights, in full armor, mounted on horses decked with ribbons, rode on each side of the betrothed couple, each with his visor raised and his lance at rest in token of honor. By the side of each baron, a squire, also on horseback, carried the seigniorial banner. At the head of the procession rode the seneschal with a gilded staff in his hand. Behind the carriage gravely walked the bailiff, followed by the vassals, while the steward railed at the serfs, a noisy and curious rabble.

As they were crossing a brook a league from the castle, one of the traces of the carriage broke, and they were forced to stop. The accident repaired, the coachman cracked his whip, and the horses started with such force that the new trace broke in three pieces. Six times this provoking piece of wood was replaced, and six times it broke anew without drawing the carriage from the hole where it was wedged.

Everyone had a word of advice to offer; even the peasants, as wheelwrights and carpenters, were not the last to make a show of their knowledge. This gave the steward courage; he approached the Baron, took off his cap, and, scratching his head:

"My lord," said he, "in the house that you see shining yonder among the trees there lives a woman who does things such as nobody else can do. Only persuade her to lend you her tongs, and, in my humble opinion, they will hold till morning."

The Baron made a sign, and ten peasants ran to the cottage of Finette, who very obligingly lent them her gold tongs. They were put in the place of the trace; the coachman cracked his whip, and off went the carriage like a feather.

[132]

Everyone rejoiced, but the joy did not last long. A hundred steps farther, lo! the bottom of the carriage gave way; little more and the noble Kerver family would have sunk quite out of sight. The wheelwrights and the carpenters set to work at once; they sawed planks, nailed them down fast, and in the twinkling of an eye repaired the accident. The coachman cracked his whip, and the horses started, when behold! half of the carriage was left behind; the Baroness Kerver sat motionless by the side of the bride, while Yvon and the Baron were carried off at full gallop. Here was a new difficulty. Three times was the carriage mended; three times it broke anew. There was every reason to believe that it was enchanted.

Everyone had a word of advice to offer. This gave the bailiff courage. He approached the Baron, and said in a low tone:

" My lord, in the house that you see shining yonder among the trees, there lives a woman who does things such as nobody else can do. Only persuade her to lend you her door for the bottom of the carriage, and, in my opinion, it will hold till morning."

The Baron made a sign, and twenty peasants ran to the cottage of Finette, who very obligingly lent them her gold door. They put it in the bottom of the carriage where it fitted as if it had been made expressly for it. The party took their seats in the carriage, the coachman cracked his whip, the church was in sight, and all the troubles of the journey seemed ended.

Not at all! Suddenly the horses stopped, and refused to draw. There were four of them. Six, eight, ten, twenty-four more were put to the carriage, but all in vain; it was impossible to stir them. The more they were whipped the deeper the wheels sunk into the ground like the colter of a plow.

What were they to do? To go on foot would have been a disgrace. To mount a horse and ride to the church like simple peasants, was not the custom of the Kervers. They tried to lift the carriage, they pushed the wheels, they shook it, they pulled it, but all in vain. Meanwhile the day was declining, and the hour for the marriage had passed.

Everyone had a word of advice to offer. This gave the seneschal courage. He approached the Baron, alighted from his horse, raised his velvet cap, and said:

"My lord, in the house that you see shining yonder among the trees, there lives a woman who does things such as nobody else can do. Only persuade her to lend you her cow to draw the carriage, and, in my opinion, she will draw it till morning."

The Baron made a sign, and thirty peasants ran to the cottage of Finette, who very obligingly lent them her golden-horned cow.

To go to church drawn by a cow was not, perhaps, what the ambitious bride had dreamed of, but it was better than to remain unmarried in the road. The heifer was harnessed therefore before the horses, and everybody looked on anxiously to see what this boasted animal was capable of doing.

But before the coachman had time to crack his whip, lo! the cow started off as if she were about to go around the world anew. Horses, carriage, Baron, betrothed, coachman, all were hurried away by the furious animal. In vain the knights spurred their horses to follow the pair; in vain the peasants ran at full speed, taking the crossroad and cutting across the meadows. The carriage flew as if it had wings; a pigeon could not have followed it.

On reaching the door of the church the party, a little disturbed by this rapid journey, would not have been sorry to alight. Everything was ready for the ceremony, and the bridal pair had long been expected; but, instead of stopping, the cow redoubled her speed. Thirteen times she ran round the church like lightning, then suddenly made her way in a straight line across the fields to the castle with such force that the whole party were almost shaken to pieces before their arrival.

THE FAIRY RING

VII

No more marriage was to be thought of for that day; but the tables were set and the dinner served, and the Baron Kerver was too noble a knight to take leave of his brave Bretons until they had eaten and drunk according to custom —that is, from sunset till sunrise, and even a little later.

Orders were given for the guests to take their seats. Ninety-six tables were ranged in eight rows. In front of them, on a large platform covered with velvet, with a canopy in the middle, was a table larger than the rest, and loaded with fruit and flowers, to say nothing of the roast hares and the peacocks smoking beneath their plumage. At this table the bridal pair were to have been seated in full sight in order that nothing might be lacking to the pleasures of the feast, and that the meanest peasant might have the honor of saluting them by emptying his cup of hydromel to the honor and prosperity of the high and mighty house of Kerver.

The Baron seated the hundred knights at his table, and placed their squires behind their chairs to serve them. At his right he put the bride and Yvon, but he left the seat at his left vacant, and, calling a page, " Child," said he, " run to the house of the stranger lady who obliged us only too much this morning. It was not her fault if her success exceeded her good will. Tell her that the Baron Kerver thanks her for her help, and invites her to the wedding feast of his son Lord Yvon."

On reaching the golden house, where Finette in tears was mourning for her beloved, the page bent one knee to the ground, and, in the Baron's name, invited the stranger lady to the castle to do honor to the wedding of Lord Yvon.

"Thank your master for me," answered the young girl proudly, " and tell him that if he is too noble to come to my house I am too noble to go to his."

When the page repeated this answer to his master the Baron Kerver struck the table such a blow that three plates flew into the air

THE FAIRY RING

"By my honor," said he, "this is spoken like a lady, and, for the first time, I own myself beaten. Quick, saddle my dun mare, and let my knights and squires prepare to attend me."

It was with this brilliant train that the Baron alighted at the door of the golden cottage. He begged Finette's pardon, held the stirrup for her, and seated her behind him on his own horse, neither more nor less than a duchess in person. Through respect he did not speak a single word to her on the way. On reaching the castle, he uncovered his head and led her to the seat of honor that he had chosen for her.

The Baron's departure had made a great excitement, and his return caused still greater surprise. Everyone asked who the lady could be that the Baron treated with such respect. Judging from her costume she was a foreigner; could she be the Duchess of Normandy or the Queen of France? The steward, the bailiff, and the seneschal were appealed to. The steward trembled, the bailiff turned pale, and the seneschal blushed, but all three were as mute as fishes. The silence of these important personages added to the general wonder.

All eyes were fixed on Finette, who felt a deadly chill at her heart, for Yvon saw but did not know her. He cast an indifferent glance at her, then began again to talk in a tender tone to the fair-haired lady, who smiled disdainfully.

Finette, in despair, took from the purse the golden bullet, her last hope. While talking with the Baron, who was charmed with her wit, she shook the little ball in her hand, and repeated in a whisper:

"Golden bullet, precious treasure,
Save me, if it be thy pleasure."

And behold, the bullet grew larger and larger until it became a goblet of chased gold, the most beautiful cup that ever graced the table of baron or king.

Finette filled the cup herself with spiced wine, and calling the seneschal, who was cowering behind her, she said in her gentlest tones, "My good seneschal, I entreat you to offer this goblet to Lord Yvon. I wish to drink his health, and I am sure that he will not refuse me this pleasure."

Yvon took the goblet, which the seneschal presented to him on a salver of enamel and gold, with a careless hand, bowed to the stranger, drank the wine, and, setting the cup on the table before him, turned to the fair-haired lady who occupied all his thoughts. The lady seemed anxious and vexed. He whispered a few words in her ear that seemed to please her, for her eyes sparkled, and she placed her hand again in his.

Finette cast down her head and began to weep. All was over.

"Children," cried the Baron, in a voice of thunder, "fill your glasses. Let us all drink to the noble stranger who honors us with her presence. 'To the lovely lady of the golden cottage!'"

All began to huzzah and drink. Yvon contented himself with raising his goblet to a level with his eyes. Suddenly he started and stood mute, his mouth open and his eyes fixed, like a man who has a vision.

It was a vision. In the gold of the goblet Yvon saw his past life as in a mirror: the giant pursuing him; Finette dragging him along; both embarking in the ship that saved them; both landing on the shore of Brittany; he quitting her for an instant; she weeping at his departure. Where was she? By his side, of course. What other woman than Finette could be by the side of Yvon?

He turned toward the fair-haired lady, and cried out like a man treading on a serpent. Then, staggering as if he were drunk, he rose and looked around him with haggard eyes. At the sight of Finette he clasped his trembling hands, and, dragging himself toward her, fell on his knees and exclaimed, "Finette, forgive me!"

To forgive is the height of happiness. Before evening Finette was seated by the side of Yvon, both weeping and smiling.

And what became of the fair-haired lady? No one knows. At the cry of Yvon she disappeared; but it was said that a wretched old hag was seen flying on a broomstick over the castle walls, chased by the dogs; and it was the common opinion among the Kervers that the fair-haired lady was none other than the witch, the godmother of the giant. I am not sure enough of the fact, however, to dare warrant it. It is always prudent to believe, without proof, that a woman may be a witch, but it is never wise to say so.

What I can say on the word of an historian is that the feast, interrupted for a moment, went on gayer than ever. Early the next morning they went to the church, where, to the joy of his heart, Yvon married Finette, who was no longer afraid of evil spirits; after which they ate, drank, and danced for thirty-six hours, without anyone thinking of resting. The steward's arms were a little heavy, the bailiff rubbed his back at times, and the seneschal felt a sort of weariness in his limbs, but all three had a weight on their consciences which they could not shake off, and which made them tremble and flutter, till finally they fell on the ground and were carried off. Finette took no other vengeance on them; her only desire was to render all happy around her, far and near, who belonged to the noble house of Kerver. Her memory still lives in Brittany; and, among the ruins of the old castle, anyone will show you the statue of the good lady, with five bullets in her hand.

The Fair One with Golden Locks

THERE was once a king's daughter so beautiful that they named her the Fair One with Golden Locks. These golden locks were the most remarkable in the world, soft and fine, and falling in long waves down to her very feet. She wore them always thus, loose and flowing, surmounted with a wreath of flowers; and though such long hair was sometimes rather inconvenient, it was so exceedingly beautiful, shining in the sun like ripples of molten gold, that everybody agreed she fully deserved her name.

"SHE WORE THEM ALWAYS . . . LOOSE AND FLOWING"

Now there was a young king of a neighboring country, very handsome, very rich, and wanting nothing but a wife to make him happy. He heard so much of the various perfections of the Fair One with Golden Locks that at last, without even seeing her, he fell in love with her so desperately that he could neither eat nor drink, and resolved to send an ambassador at once to demand her in marriage. So he ordered a magnificent equipage—more than a hundred horses and a hundred footmen—in order to bring back to him the Fair One with Golden Locks, who, he never doubted, would be only too happy to become his queen. Indeed, he felt so sure of her that he refurnished the whole palace, and had made, by all the dressmakers of the city, dresses enough to last a lady for a lifetime. But, alas! when the ambassador arrived and delivered his message, either the princess was in a bad humor or the offer did not appear to be to her taste, for she returned her best thanks to his majesty, but said she had not the slightest wish or intention to be married. She also, being a prudent damsel, declined receiving any of the presents which the King had sent her; except that, not quite to offend his majesty, she retained a box of English pins, which were in that country of considerable value.

When the ambassador returned, alone and unsuccessful, all the court was very much affected, and the King himself began to weep with all his might. Now, there was in the palace household a young gentleman named Avenant, beautiful as the sun, besides being at once so amiable and so wise that the King confided to him all his affairs; and everyone loved him, except those people—to be found in all courts—who were envious of his good fortune. These malicious folk hearing him say gayly, " If the King had sent me to fetch the Fair One with Golden Locks, I know she would have come back with me," repeated the saying in such a manner that it appeared as if Avenant thought overmuch of himself and his beauty, and felt sure the Princess would have followed him all over the world; which, when it came to the ears of the King, as it was meant to do, irritated him so much that he commanded Avenant to be imprisoned in a high tower, and left to die there of hunger. The guards accordingly carried off the young man, who had quite forgotten his idle speech, and had not the least idea what fault he had committed. They ill-treated him very much and then left him, with nothing to eat and only water to drink. This, however, kept him alive for a few days, during which he did not cease to complain aloud, and to call upon the King, saying, " O King, what harm have I done? You have no subject more faithful than I. Never have I had a thought which could offend you."

And it so befell that the King, coming by chance, or else from a sense of remorse, past the tower, was touched by the voice of the young Avenant, whom he had once so much regarded. In spite of all the courtiers could do to prevent him, he stopped to listen, and overheard these words. The tears rushed into his eyes; he opened the door of the tower and called, "Avenant!" Avenant came, creeping feebly along, fell at the King's knees, and kissed his feet:

" O sire, what have I done that you should treat me so cruelly?"

" You have mocked me and my ambassador; for you said if I had sent you to fetch the Fair One with Golden Locks, you would have been successful and brought her back."

" I did say it, and it was true," replied Avenant fearlessly; " for I should have told her so much about your majesty and your various high qualities, which no one knows so well as myself, that I am persuaded she would have returned with me."

" I believe it," said the King, with an angry look at those who had spoken ill of his favorite; he then gave Avenant a free pardon, and took him back with him to the court.

After having supplied the famished youth with as much supper as he could eat, the King admitted him to a private audience and said: " I am as much in love as ever with the Fair One with Golden Locks, so I will take thee at thy word, and send thee to try and win her for me."

" Very well, please your majesty," replied Avenant cheerfully; " I will depart to-morrow."

The King, overjoyed with his willingness and hopefulness, would have furnished him with a still more magnificent equipage and suite than the first ambassador, but Avenant refused to take anything except a good horse to ride and letters of introduction to the Princess's father. The King embraced him and eagerly saw him depart.

It was on a Monday morning when, without any pomp or show, Avenant thus started on his mission. He rode slowly and meditatively, pondering over every possible means of persuading the Fair One with Golden Locks to marry the King; but, even after several days' journey toward her country, no clear project had entered into his mind. One morning, when he had started at break of day, he came to a great meadow with a stream running through it, along which were planted willows and poplars. It was such a pleasant, rippling stream that he dismounted and sat down on its banks. There he perceived, gasping on the grass, a large golden carp, which, in leaping too far after gnats, had thrown itself quite out of the water, and now lay dying on the greensward. Avenant took pity on it, and though he was very hungry, and the fish was very fat, and he would well enough have liked it for his breakfast, still he lifted it gently and put it back into the stream. No sooner had the carp touched the fresh cool water than it revived and swam away; but shortly returning, it spoke to him from the water in this wise:

"Avenant, I thank you for your good deed. I was dying, and you have saved me. I will recompense you for this one day."

After this pretty little speech, the fish popped down to the bottom of the stream, according to the habit of carp, leaving Avenant very much astonished, as was natural.

Another day he met with a raven that was in great distress, being pursued by an eagle, which would have swallowed him up in no time. "See," thought Avenant, "how the stronger oppress the weaker! What right has an eagle to eat up a raven?" So taking his bow and arrow, which he always carried, he shot the eagle dead, and the raven, delighted, perched in safety on an opposite tree.

"Avenant," screeched he, though not in the sweetest voice in the world; "you have generously succored me, a poor miserable raven. I am not ungrateful, and I will recompense you one day."

"Thank you," said Avenant, and continued his road.

Entering in a thick wood, so dark with the shadows of early morning that he could scarcely find his way, he heard an owl hooting, as if in great tribulation. She had been caught by the nets spread by birdcatchers to entrap finches, larks, and other small birds. "What a pity," thought Avenant, "that men must always torment poor birds and beasts who have done them no harm!" So he took out his knife, cut the net, and let the owl go free. She went sailing up into the air, but immediately returned, hovering over his head on her brown wings.

"Avenant," said she, "at daylight the birdcatchers would have been here, and I should have been caught and killed. I have a grateful heart; I will recompense you one day."

These were the three principal adventures that befell Avenant on his way to the kingdom of the Fair One with Golden Locks. Arrived there, he dressed himself with the greatest care, in a habit of silver brocade, and a hat adorned with plumes of scarlet and white. He threw over all a rich mantle, and carried a little basket in which was a lovely little dog, an offering of respect to the Princess. With this he presented himself at the palace gates, where, even though he came alone, his mien was so dignified and graceful, so altogether charming, that everyone did him reverence, and was eager to run and tell the Fair One with Golden Locks that Avenant, another ambassador from the King her suitor, awaited an audience.

"Avenant!" repeated the Princess. "That is a pretty name; perhaps the youth is pretty too."

"So beautiful," said the ladies of honor, "that while he

stood under the palace window we could do nothing but look at him."

"How silly of you!" sharply said the Princess. But she desired them to bring her robe of blue satin, to comb out her long hair and adorn it with the freshest garland of flowers, to give her her high-heeled shoes, and her fan. "Also," added she, "take care that my audience chamber is well swept and my throne well dusted. I wish in everything to appear as becomes the Fair One with Golden Locks."

This done, she seated herself on her throne of ivory and ebony, and gave orders for her musicians to play, but softly, so as not to disturb conversation. Thus, shining in all her beauty, she admitted Avenant to her presence.

He was so dazzled that at first he could not speak; then he began and delivered his harangue to perfection.

"Gentle Avenant," returned the princess, after listening to all his reasons for her returning with him, "your arguments are very strong, and I am inclined to listen to them; but you must first find for me a ring which I dropped into the river about a month ago. Until I recover it I can listen to no propositions of marriage."

Avenant, surprised and disturbed, made her a profound reverence and retired, taking with him the basket and the little dog Cabriole, which she refused to accept. All night long he sat sighing to himself: "How can I ever find a ring which she dropped into the river a month ago? She has set me an impossibility."

"My dear master," said Cabriole, "nothing is an impossibility to one so young and charming as you are. Let us go at daybreak to the riverside."

Avenant patted him, but replied nothing; until, worn out with grief, he slept. Before dawn Cabriole wakened him, saying, "Master, dress yourself and let us go to the river."

There Avenant walked up and down, with his arms folded and his head bent, but saw nothing. At last he heard a voice calling from a distance, "Avenant, Avenant!"

The little dog ran to the waterside—"Never believe me

again, master, if it is not a golden carp with a ring in its mouth!"

"Yes, Avenant," said the carp, "this is the ring which the Princess has lost. You saved my life in the willow meadow, and I have recompensed you. Farewell!"

Avenant took the ring gratefully and returned to the palace with Cabriole, who scampered about in great glee. Craving an audience, he presented the Princess with her ring, and begged her to accompany him to his master's kingdom. She took the ring, looked at it, and thought she was surely dreaming.

"Some fairy must have assisted you, fortunate Avenant," said she.

"Madam, I am fortunate only in my desire to obey your wishes."

"Obey me still," she said graciously. "There is a prince named Galifron, whose suit I have refused. He is a giant as tall as a tower, who eats a man as a monkey eats a nut. He puts cannons into his pockets instead of pistols, and when he speaks his voice is so loud that everyone near him becomes deaf. Go and fight him, and bring me his head."

Avenant was thunderstruck; but after a time he recovered himself. "Very well, madam. I shall certainly perish, but I will perish like a brave man. I will depart at once to fight the Giant Galifron."

The Princess, now in her turn surprised and alarmed, tried every persuasion to induce him not to go, but in vain. Avenant armed himself and started, carrying his little dog in its basket. Cabriole was the only creature that gave him consolation: "Courage, master! While you attack the giant, I will bite his legs. He will stoop down to strike me, and then you can knock him on the head." Avenant smiled at the little dog's spirit, but he knew it was useless.

Arrived at the castle of Galifron, he found the road all strewn with bones and carcasses of men. Soon he saw the giant walking. His head was level with the highest trees, and he sang in a terrific voice:

THE FAIRY RING

> " Bring me babies to devour;
> More—more—more—more—
> Men and women, tender and tough;
> All the world holds not enough."

To which Avenant replied, imitating the tune:

> "Avenant you here may see,
> He is come to punish thee;
> Be he tender, be he tough,
> To kill thee, giant, he is enough."

Hearing these words, the giant took up his massive club, looked around for the singer, and, perceiving him, would have slain him on the spot, had not a raven, sitting on a tree close by, suddenly flown down upon him and picked out both his eyes. Then Avenant easily killed him and cut off his head, while the raven, watching him, said:

"You shot the eagle who was pursuing me. I promised to recompense you, and to-day I have done it. We are quits."

"No, it is I who am your debtor, Sir Raven," replied Avenant as, hanging the frightful head to his saddle bow, he mounted his horse and rode back to the city of the Fair One with Golden Locks.

There everybody followed him, shouting, " Here is brave Avenant, who has killed the giant," until the Princess, hearing the noise, and fearing it was Avenant himself who was killed, appeared, all trembling; and even when he appeared with Galifron's head, she trembled still, although she had nothing to fear.

"Madam," said Avenant, " your enemy is dead, so I trust you will accept the hand of the king, my master."

"I cannot," replied she, thoughtfully, " unless you first bring me a vial of the water in the Grotto of Darkness. It is six leagues in length, and guarded at the entrance by two fiery dragons. Within it is a pit, full of scorpions, lizards, and serpents, and at the bottom of this place flows the Fountain of Beauty and Health. All who wash in it become, if ugly, beautiful; and if beautiful, beautiful forever; if old, young; and if young, young forever. Judge then, Avenant, if I can quit my kingdom without carrying with me some of this miraculous water."

"Madam," replied Avenant, "you are already so beautiful that you require it not; but I am an unfortunate ambassador whose death you desire. I will obey you, though I know I shall never return."

So he departed with his only friends—his horse and his faithful dog Cabriole; while all who met him looked at him compassionately, pitying so pretty a youth bound on such a hopeless errand. But, however kindly they addressed him, Avenant rode on and answered nothing, for he was too sad at heart.

He reached a mountain-side, where he sat down to rest, leaving his horse to graze and Cabriole to run after the flies. He knew that the Grotto of Darkness was not far off, yet he looked about him like one who sees nothing. At last he perceived a rock as black as ink, whence came a thick smoke; and in a moment appeared one of the two dragons, breathing out flames. It had a yellow-and-green body, claws, and a long tail. When Cabriole saw the monster, the poor little dog hid himself in terrible fright. But Avenant resolved to die bravely; so taking a vial which the Princess had given him, he prepared to descend into the cave.

"Cabriole," said he, "I shall soon be dead. Then fill this vial with my blood and carry it to the Fair One with Golden Locks, and afterwards to the King my master, to show him I have been faithful to the last."

While he was thus speaking a voice called, "Avenant, Avenant!" and he saw an owl sitting on a hollow tree. Said the owl: "You cut the net in which I was caught, and I vowed to recompense you. Now is the time. Give me the vial. I know every corner of the Grotto of Darkness. I will fetch you the water of beauty."

Delighted beyond words, Avenant delivered up his vial; the owl flew with it into the grotto, and in less than half an hour reappeared, bringing it quite full and well corked. Avenant thanked her with all his heart, and joyfully took once more the road to the city.

THE FAIRY RING

The Fair One with Golden Locks had no more to say. She consented to accompany him back, with all her suite, to his master's court. On the way thither she saw so much of him, and found him so charming, that Avenant might have married her himself had he chosen; but he would not have been false to his master for all the beauties under the sun. At length they arrived at the King's city, and the Fair One with Golden Locks became his spouse and queen. But she still loved Avenant in her heart, and often said to the king her lord: "But for Avenant I should not be here; he has done all sorts of impossible deeds for my sake; he has fetched me the water of beauty, and I shall never grow old—in short, I owe him everything."

And she praised him in this sort so much that at length the King became jealous, and though Avenant gave him not the slightest cause of offense, he shut him up in the same high tower once more—but with irons on his hands and feet, and a cruel jailer besides, who fed him with bread and water only. His sole companion was his little dog Cabriole.

When the Fair One with Golden Locks heard of this, she reproached her husband for his ingratitude, and then, throwing herself at his knees, implored that Avenant might be set free. But the King only said, "She loves him!" and refused the prayer. The Queen entreated no more, but fell into a deep melancholy.

When the King saw it, he thought she did not care for him because he was not handsome enough; and that if he could wash his face with her water of beauty, it would make her love him more. He knew that she kept it in a cabinet in her chamber, where she could find it always.

Now it happened that a waiting maid, in cleaning out this cabinet, had, the very day before knocked down the vial, which was broken in a thousand pieces, and all the contents were lost. Very much alarmed, she then remembered seeing in a cabinet belonging to the King, a similar vial. This she fetched and put in the place of the other one, in which was the water of beauty. But the King's vial contained the water

of death. It was a poison, used to destroy great criminals—
that is, noblemen, gentlemen, and such like. Instead of hanging
them or cutting their heads off, like common people, they
were compelled to wash their faces with this water, upon
which they fell asleep and woke no more. So it happened that
the king, taking up this vial, believing it to be the water of
beauty, washed his face with it, fell asleep, and—died.

Cabriole heard the news, and, gliding in and out among the
crowd which clustered round the young and lovely widow,
whispered softly to her, " Madam, do not forget poor Avenant." If she had been disposed to do so, the sight of his
little dog would have been enough to remind her of him—
his many sufferings and his great fidelity. She rose up, without speaking to anybody, and went straight to the tower where
Avenant was confined. There, with her own hands, she struck
off his chains, and putting a crown of gold on his head and a
purple mantle on his shoulders, said to him, " Be King—and
my husband."

Avenant could not refuse, for in his heart he had loved her
all the time. He threw himself at her feet, and then took the
crown and scepter, and ruled her kingdom like a king. All
the people were delighted to have him as their sovereign. The
marriage was celebrated in all imaginable pomp, and Avenant
and the Fair One with Golden Locks lived and reigned happily
together all their days.

The Little Good Mouse

ONCE upon a time there lived a king and queen who
loved each other so much that they were never happy
unless they were together. Day after day they went
out hunting or fishing; night after night they went to balls
or to the opera; they sang and danced and ate sugarplums,
and were the gayest of the gay, and all their subjects followed
their example so that the kingdom was called the Joyous Land.

Now in the next kingdom everything was as different as it could possibly be. The King was sulky and savage, and never enjoyed himself at all. He looked so ugly and cross that all his subjects feared him, and he hated the very sight of a cheerful face; so if he ever caught anyone smiling he had his head cut off that very minute. This kingdom was very appropriately called the Land of Tears. Now when this wicked King heard of the happiness of the jolly King, he was so jealous that he collected a great army and set out to fight him, and the news of his approach was soon brought to the King and Queen. The Queen, when she heard of it, was frightened out of her wits, and began to cry bitterly. "Sire," she said, "let us collect all our riches and run away as far as ever we can, to the other side of the world."

But the King answered:

"Fie, madam! I am far too brave for that. It is better to die than to be a coward."

Then he assembled all his armed men, and after bidding the Queen a tender farewell, he mounted his splendid horse and rode away. When he was lost to sight the Queen could do nothing but weep and wring her hands and cry.

"Alas! If the King is killed, what will become of me and of my little daughter?" and she was so sorrowful that she could neither eat nor sleep.

The King sent her a letter every day, but at last, one morning, as she looked out of the palace window, she saw a messenger approaching in hot haste.

"What news, courier? What news?" cried the Queen, and he answered:

"The battle is lost and the King is dead, and in another moment the enemy will be here."

The poor Queen fell back insensible, and all her ladies carried her to bed, and stood round her weeping and wailing. Then began a tremendous noise and confusion, and they knew that the enemy had arrived, and very soon they heard the King himself stamping about the palace seeking the Queen. Then her ladies put the little Princess into her arms, and covered her up, head and all, in the bedclothes, and ran for their lives, and the poor Queen lay there shaking and hoping she would not be found. But very soon the wicked King clattered into the room, and in a fury because the Queen would not answer when he called to her, he tore back her silken coverings and tweaked off her lace cap, and when all her lovely hair came tumbling down over her shoulders, he wound it three times round his hand and threw her over his shoulder, where he carried her like a sack of flour.

The poor Queen held her little daughter safe in her arms and shrieked for mercy, but the wicked King only mocked her, and begged her to go on shrieking, as it amused him, and so mounted his great black horse, and rode back to his own country. When he got there he declared that he would have the Queen and the little Princess hanged on the nearest tree; but his courtiers said that seemed a pity, for when the baby grew up she would be a very nice wife for the King's only son.

The King was rather pleased with this idea, and shut the Queen up in the highest room of a tall tower, which was very tiny, and miserably furnished with a table and a very hard bed upon the floor. Then he sent for a fairy who lived near his kingdom, and after receiving her with more politeness than he generally showed, and entertaining her at a sumptuous feast, he took her up to see the Queen. The fairy was so touched by the sight of her misery that when she kissed her hand she whispered:

" Courage, madam! I think I see a way to help you."

The Queen, a little comforted by these words, received her graciously, and begged her to take pity upon the poor little Princess, who had met with such a sudden reverse of fortune. But the King got very cross when he saw them whispering together, and cried harshly:

" Make an end of these fine speeches, madam. I brought you here to tell me if the child will grow up pretty and fortunate."

Then the fairy answered that the Princess would be as pretty and clever and well brought-up as it was possible to be, and the old King growled to the Queen that it was lucky for her that it was so, as they would certainly have been hanged if it were otherwise. Then he stamped off, taking the fairy with him, and leaving the poor Queen in tears.

"How can I wish my little daughter to grow up pretty if she is to be married to that horrid little dwarf, the King's son," she said to herself, "and yet, if she is ugly we shall both be killed. If I could only hide her away somewhere, so that the cruel King could never find her."

As the days went on, the Queen and the little Princess grew thinner and thinner, for their hard-hearted jailer gave them every day only three boiled peas and a tiny morsel of black bread, so that they were always terribly hungry.

At last, one evening, as the Queen sat at her spinning wheel —for the King was so avaricious that she was made to work day and night—she saw a tiny, pretty little mouse creep out of a hole, and said to it:

"Alas, little creature! what are you coming to look for here? I have only three peas for my day's provision, so unless you wish to fast you must go elsewhere."

But the mouse ran hither and thither, and danced and capered so prettily, that at last the Queen gave it her last pea, which she was keeping for her supper, saying: "Here, little one, eat it up; I have nothing better to offer you, but I give this willingly in return for the amusement I have had from you."

She had hardly spoken when she saw upon the table a delicious little roast partridge, and two dishes of preserved fruit. "Truly," said she, "a kind action never goes unrewarded"; and she and the little Princess ate their supper with great satisfaction, and then the Queen gave what was left to the little mouse, who danced better than ever afterwards. The next morning came the jailer with the Queen's allowance of three peas, which he brought in upon a large dish to make them look smaller; but as soon as he set it down the little mouse came and ate up all three, so that when the Queen wanted her dinner there was nothing left for her. Then she was quite provoked, and said:

"What a bad little beast that mouse must be! If it goes on like this I shall be starved." But when she glanced at the dish again it was covered with all sorts of nice things to eat, and the Queen made a very good dinner and was gayer than usual over it. But afterwards as she sat at her spinning wheel she began to consider what would happen if the little Princess did not grow up pretty enough to please the King, and she said to herself:

"Oh, if I could only think of some way of escaping!"

As she spoke she saw the little mouse playing in a corner with some long straws. The Queen took them and began to plait them, saying:

"If only I had straws enough I would make a basket with them, and let my baby down in it from the window to any kind passer-by who would take care of her."

By the time the straws were all plaited the little mouse had dragged in more and more, until the Queen had plenty to make her basket, and she worked at it day and night, while the little mouse danced for her amusement; and at dinner and supper time the Queen gave it the three peas and the bit of black bread, and always found something good in the dish in their place. She really could not imagine where all the nice things came from. At last one day when the basket was finished, the Queen was looking out of the window to see how long a cord she must make to lower it to the bottom of the tower, when she noticed a little old woman who was leaning upon her stick and looking up at her. Presently she said:

"I know your trouble, madam. If you like, I will help you."

"Oh, my dear friend," said the Queen; "if you really wish to be of use to me you will come at the time that I will appoint, and I will let down my poor little baby in a basket. If you will take her and bring her up for me, when I am rich I will reward you splendidly."

"I don't care about the reward," said the old woman, "but there is one thing I should like. You must know that I am very particular about what I eat, and if there is one thing that I fancy above all others, it is a plump, tender little mouse. If there is such a thing in your garret just throw it down to me, and in return I will promise that your little daughter shall be well taken care of."

The Queen when she heard this began to cry, but made no answer, and the old woman after waiting a few minutes asked her what was the matter.

"Why," said the Queen, "there is only one mouse in this garret, and that is such a dear, pretty little thing that I cannot bear to think of its being killed."

"What!" cried the old woman in a rage. "Do you care more for a miserable mouse than for your own baby? Good-by, madam! I leave you to enjoy its company, and for my own part I thank my stars that I can get plenty of mice without troubling you to give them to me."

And she hobbled off grumbling and growling. As to the Queen, she was so disappointed that, in spite of finding a better dinner than usual, and seeing the little mouse dancing in its merriest mood, she could do nothing but cry. That night when her baby was fast asleep she packed it into the basket, and wrote on a slip of paper, "This unhappy little girl is called Delicia!" This she pinned to its robe, and then very sadly she was shutting the basket when in sprang the little mouse and sat on the baby's pillow.

"Ah! little one," said the Queen, "it cost me dear to save your life. How shall I know now whether my Delicia is being taken care of or not? Anyone else would have let the greedy old woman have you and eat you up, but I could not bear to do it." Whereupon the mouse answered:

"Believe me, madam, you will never repent of your kindness."

The Queen was immensely astonished when the mouse began to speak, and still more so when she saw its little sharp nose turn to a beautiful face, and its paws to hands and feet; then it suddenly grew tall, and the Queen recognized the fairy who had come with the wicked King to visit her.

The fairy smiled at her astonished look, and said:

"I wanted to see if you were faithful and capable of feeling a real friendship for me, for you see we fairies are rich in everything but friends, and those are hard to find."

"It is not possible that *you* should want for friends, you charming creature," said the Queen, kissing her.

"Indeed it is so," the fairy said. "For those who are only friendly with me for their own advantage, I do not count at all. But when you cared for the poor little mouse you could not have known there was anything to be gained by it, and to try you further I took the form of the old woman whom you talked to from the window, and then I was convinced that you really loved me." Then, turning to the little Princess, she kissed her rosy lips three times, saying:

"Dear little one, I promise that you shall be richer than your father, and shall live a hundred years, always pretty and happy, without fear of old age and wrinkles."

The Queen, quite delighted, thanked the fairy gratefully, and begged her to take charge of the little Delicia and bring her up as her own daughter. This she agreed to do, and then they shut the basket and lowered it carefully, baby and all, to the ground at the foot of the tower. The fairy then changed herself back into the form of a mouse, and this delayed her a few seconds, after which she ran nimbly down the straw rope, only to find when she got to the bottom that the baby had disappeared.

In the greatest terror she ran up again to the Queen, crying:

"All is lost! my enemy Cancaline has stolen the Princess away. You must know that she is a cruel fairy who hates me, and as she is older than I am and has more power, I can do nothing against her. I know no way of rescuing Delicia from her clutches."

When the Queen heard this terrible news she was heart-broken, and begged the fairy to do all she could to get the poor little Princess back again. At this moment in came the jailer, and when he missed the little Princess he at once told the King, who came in a great fury, asking what the Queen had done with her. She answered that a fairy, whose name she did not know, had come and carried her off by force. Upon this the King stamped upon the ground, and cried in a terrible voice:

"You shall be hung! I always told you you should." And without another word he dragged the unlucky Queen out into the nearest wood, and climbed up into a tree to look for a branch to which he could hang her. But when he was quite high up, the fairy, who had made herself invisible and followed them, gave him a sudden push, which made him lose his footing and fall to the ground with a crash and break four of his teeth, and while he was trying to mend them the fairy carried the Queen off in her flying chariot to a beautiful castle, where she was so kind to her that but for the loss of Delicia the Queen would have been perfectly happy. But though the good little mouse did her very utmost, they could not find out where Cancaline had hidden the little Princess.

Thus fifteen years went by, and the Queen had somewhat recovered from her grief, when the news reached her that the son of the wicked King wished to marry the little maiden who kept the turkeys, and that she had refused him; the wedding dresses had been made, nevertheless, and the festivities were to be so splendid that all the people for leagues round were flocking in to be present at them. The Queen felt quite curious about a little turkey maiden who did not wish to be a queen, so the little mouse conveyed herself to the poultry yard to find out what she was like.

She found the turkey maiden sitting upon a big stone, barefooted and miserably dressed in an old, coarse, linen gown and cap; the ground at her feet was all strewn with robes of gold and silver, ribbons and laces, diamonds and pearls, over which the turkeys were stalking to and fro, while the king's ugly, disagreeable son stood opposite her, declaring angrily that if she would not marry him she should be killed.

The turkey maiden answered proudly:

"I never will marry you! You are too ugly and too much

[155]

like your cruel father. Leave me in peace with my turkeys, which I like far better than all your fine gifts."

The little mouse watched her with the greatest admiration, for she was as beautiful as the spring; and as soon as the wicked Prince was gone, she took the form of an old peasant woman and said to her:

"Good day, my pretty one! you have a fine flock of turkeys there."

The young turkey maiden turned her gentle eyes upon the old woman and answered:

"Yet they wish me to leave them to become a miserable queen! What is your advice upon the matter?"

"My child," said the fairy, "a crown is a very pretty thing, but you know neither the price nor the weight of it."

"I know so well that I have refused to wear one," said the little maiden, "though I don't know who was my father or who was my mother, and I have not a friend in the world."

"You have goodness and beauty, which are of more value than ten kingdoms," said the wise fairy. "But tell me, child, how came you here, and how is it you have neither father nor mother nor friend?"

"A fairy called Cancaline is the cause of my being here," answered she, "for while I lived with her I got nothing but blows and harsh words, until at last I could bear it no longer, and ran away from her without knowing where I was going, and as I came through a wood the wicked Prince met me and offered to give me charge of the poultry yard. I accepted gladly, not knowing that I should have to see him day by day. And now he wants to marry me, but that I will never consent to."

Upon hearing this the fairy became convinced that the little turkey maiden was none other than the Princess Delicia.

"What is your name, my little one?" said she.

"I am called Delicia, if it please you," she answered.

Then the fairy threw her arms round the Princess's neck, and nearly smothered her with kisses, saying:

THE FAIRY RING

"Ah, Delicia! I am a very old friend of yours, and I am truly glad to find you at last; but you might look nicer than you do in that old gown, which is only fit for a kitchenmaid. Take this pretty dress and let us see the difference it will make."

So Delicia took off the ugly cap, and shook out all her fair shining hair, and bathed her hands and face in clear water from the nearest spring till her cheeks were like roses, and when she was adorned with the diamonds and the splendid robe the fairy had given her she looked the most beautiful princess in the world, and the fairy with great delight, cried:

"Now you look as you ought to look, Delicia. What do you think about it yourself?"

And Delicia answered:

"I feel as if I were the daughter of some great king."

"And would you be glad if you were?" asked the fairy.

"Indeed I should," answered she.

"Ah, well," said the fairy, "to-morrow I may have some pleasant news for you."

So she hurried back to her castle, where the Queen sat busy with her embroidery, and cried:

"Well, madam, will you wager your thimble and your golden needle that I am bringing you the best news you could possibly hear?"

"Alas!" sighed the Queen, "since the death of the jolly King and the loss of my Delicia, all the news in the world is not worth a pin to me."

"There, there, don't be melancholy," said the fairy. "I assure you the Princess is quite well, and I have never seen her equal for beauty. She might be a queen to-morrow if she chose"; and then she told all that had happened, and the Queen first rejoiced over the thought of Delicia's beauty, and then wept at the idea of her being a turkey maiden.

"I will not hear of her being made to marry the wicked King's son," she said. "Let us go at once and bring her here."

[157]

In the meantime the wicked Prince, who was very angry with Delicia, had sat himself down under a tree, and cried and howled with rage and spite until the King heard him, and cried out from the window:

"What is the matter with you, that you are making all this disturbance?"

The Prince replied:

"It is all because our turkey maiden will not love me!"

"Won't love you, eh!" said the King. "We'll very soon see about that!" So he called his guards and told them to go and fetch Delicia. "See if I don't make her change her mind pretty soon!" said the wicked King with a chuckle.

Then the guards began to search the poultry yard, and could find nobody there but Delicia, who, with her splendid dress and her crown of diamonds, looked such a lovely princess that they hardly dared to speak to her. But she said to them very politely:

"Pray tell me what you are looking for here?"

"Madam," they answered, "we are sent for an insignificant little person called Delicia."

"Alas!" said she, "that is my name. What can you want with me?"

So the guards tied her hands and feet with thick ropes, for fear she might run away, and brought her to the King, who was waiting with his son.

When he saw her he was very much astonished at her beauty, which would have made anyone less hard-hearted sorry for her. But the wicked King only laughed and mocked at her, and cried: "Well, little fright, little toad! why don't you love my son, who is far too handsome and too good for you? Make haste and begin to love him this instant, or you shall be tarred and feathered."

Then the poor little Princess, shaking with terror, went down on her knees, crying:

"Oh, don't tar and feather me, please! It would be so uncomfortable. Let me have two or three days to make up my mind, and then you shall do as you like with me."

"I FEEL AS IF I WERE THE DAUGHTER OF SOME GREAT KING"

"I FELL AS IF A WERE THE DAUGHTER OF SOME GREAT KING."

THE FAIRY RING

The wicked Prince would have liked very much to see her tarred and feathered, but the King ordered that she should be shut up in a dark dungeon. It was just at this moment that the Queen and the fairy arrived in the flying chariot, and the Queen was dreadfully distressed at the turn affairs had taken, and said miserably that she was destined to be unfortunate all her days. But the fairy bade her take courage.

"I'll pay them out yet," said she, nodding her head with an air of great determination.

That very same night, as soon as the wicked King had gone to bed, the fairy changed herself into the little mouse, and creeping up on to his pillow nibbled his ear so that he squealed out quite loudly and turned over on his other side; but that did no good, for the little mouse only set to work and gnawed away at the second ear until it hurt more than the first one.

Then the King cried "Murder!" and "Thieves!" and all his guards ran to see what was the matter, but they could find nothing and nobody, for the little mouse had run off to the Prince's room and was serving him in exactly the same way. All night long she ran from one to the other, until at last, driven quite frantic by terror and want of sleep, the King rushed out of the palace crying:

"Help! help! I am pursued by rats."

The Prince when he heard this got up also, and ran after the King, and they had not gone far when they both fell into the river and were never heard of again.

Then the good fairy ran to tell the Queen, and they went together to the black dungeon where Delicia was imprisoned. The fairy touched each door with her wand, and it sprang open instantly; but they had to go through forty before they came to the Princess, who was sitting on the floor looking very dejected. But when the Queen rushed in and kissed her twenty times in a minute, and laughed and cried and told her all her history, the Princess was wild with delight. Then the fairy showed her all the wonderful dresses and jewels she had brought for her, and said:

THE FAIRY RING

"Don't let us waste time; we must go and harangue the people."

So she walked first, looking very serious and dignified, and wearing a dress the train of which was at least ten ells long. Behind her came the Queen wearing a blue velvet robe embroidered with gold and a diamond crown that was brighter than the sun itself. Last of all walked Delicia, who was so beautiful that it was nothing short of marvelous.

They proceeded through the streets, returning the salutations of all they met, great or small, and all the people turned and followed them, wondering who these noble ladies could be.

When the audience hall was quite full, the fairy said to the subjects of the wicked King that if they would accept Delicia, who was the daughter of the jolly King, as their Queen, she would undertake to find a suitable husband for her, and would promise that during their reign there should be nothing but rejoicing and merrymaking, and all dismal things should be entirely banished. Upon this the people cried with one accord: "We will, we will! We have been gloomy and miserable too long already." And they all took hands and danced round the Queen and Delicia and the good fairy, singing: "Yes, yes; we will, we will!"

Then there were feasts and fireworks in every street in the town, and early the next morning the fairy, who had been all over the world in the night, brought back with her in her flying chariot the most handsome and good-tempered Prince she could find anywhere. He was so charming that Delicia loved him from the moment their eyes met, and as for him, of course he could not help thinking himself the luckiest prince in the world. The Queen felt that she had really come to the end of her misfortunes at last, and they all lived happily ever after.

THE FAIRY RING

The Story of Blanche and Vermilion

THERE was once upon a time a widow, a very good kind of woman, who had two daughters, both very amiable. The elder was called "Blanche" and the younger "Vermilion." They had received these names because one of them had the fairest complexion that was ever seen, and the other had cheeks and lips as red as coral.

One day, as the good woman was seated near the door of her cottage spinning, she perceived a poor old woman who could hardly hobble along with the assistance of her stick. "You appear to be very much tired, my good woman," said the widow; "sit down here and rest yourself awhile"; and she then desired one of her daughters to fetch her a chair. Both of them immediately rose, but Vermilion outran her sister and brought the chair.

"Will you please to drink?" said the good old dame to the old woman. "With all my heart," answered she; "and I feel even as if I could eat a little if you could give me a bit of something nice." "You shall be welcome to anything that I have," said the good widow; "but, as I am poor, it will be nothing out of the common way." At the same time she desired her daughters to lay the table for the good old dame, who straightway seated herself at it.

The widow then told the elder daughter to go and gather some plums from a tree that she had planted herself, and was very fond of. Blanche, instead of obeying her mother willingly, murmured, and said to herself, "So it is for this old gormandizer that I have been so very careful of my plum tree." She, however, dared not refuse to fetch a few plums, but she gave them with much reluctance and very ungraciously. "You, Vermilion," said the good woman to her younger daughter, "have no fruit to give to this good dame, for your grapes are not ripe." "That's true," said Vermilion; "but I hear my hen cackling, so she must have laid an egg, and if the gentlewoman would like a new-laid egg she is very welcome to it"; and without waiting for any answer from the old woman, she ran off to seek her egg. The moment she presented it, however, the old woman disappeared and was replaced by a beautiful lady who said to the mother: "I am about to recompense your two daughters according to their deserts. The elder shall become a great queen, and the younger a farmer's wife." With these words she struck the house with her wand; it disappeared, and in its place rose a nice, snug-looking farm. "That is your portion," said she to Vermilion. "I know that I have given each of you what you like best." Having thus said, the fairy departed; and the good woman and her two daughters remained in great surprise.

They went into the farmhouse, and were charmed with the neatness of the furniture. The chairs were only of wood, but they were so bright that one might see one's face in them as in a looking-glass. The bedding was of Irish linen, as white as snow. In the pens were sheep; four oxen and the like number of cows were in the cowhouses, and the yard was well stocked with all sorts of domestic animals, as poultry, ducks, pigeons, etc. There was also a pretty garden, planted with different kinds of fruit, vegetables, and flowers.

Blanche regarded without any feelings of jealousy the fairy's gift to her sister. Her only thoughts were concerning the pleasures she anticipated in being a queen. All at once she heard a huntsman's horn, and going to the door to see the party pass, she appeared so beautiful to the King that he resolved to marry her, and did so accordingly. Blanche, when she was become a queen, said to her sister Vermilion: "I do not wish that you should marry a farmer; come to court with me, sister; I will procure you a great lord for your husband." "I am very much obliged to you, sister," replied Vermilion, "but I am accustomed to a country life, and do not wish to change it."

Queen Blanche then set out, and she was so gratified that she passed several nights without sleeping, for joy. The first few months she was so taken up with fine clothes, balls, and plays that she thought of nothing else. But she soon grew used to these things, and nothing now amused her; on the contrary, she was very discontented. All the ladies of the court showed her great respect when they were in her presence; but she knew that they did not like her, and that they said to each other behind her back, " See how this peasant girl plays the fine lady! The King must have had very poor taste to take such a personage for his consort." The King heard of these remarks, and they made him reflect on what he had done. He began to think that he had acted wrongly in marrying Blanche, and as his passion for her had cooled, he soon neglected her.

When the courtiers perceived that the King no longer loved his wife, they paid her little or no attention. She was very unfortunate, for she had not a single friend to whom she could impart her grief. She observed that it was the fashion at court to sacrifice one's friend to one's interest, to smile on one's bitterest enemy, and to tell lies continually. She was obliged to be serious, because she was told that a queen ought always to look grave and majestic. She had several children, and during all this time she was constantly attended by a physician, who examined everything that she ate, and ordered everything that she liked to be removed from the table. She was allowed no salt in her soup, she was forbidden to quit the house when she felt inclined to take a walk—in a word, she was contradicted from morning till night. Governesses were engaged for her children, who brought them up in direct opposition to her wishes; yet she was not permitted to find fault. Poor Queen Blanche was dying with sorrow, and she grew so thin that it was pitiable to see her. She had not seen her sister once during the three years that she had been a queen, because she thought it would be demeaning her high rank to pay a visit to a farmer's wife; but when she was quite oppressed with melancholy, she came to the resolution of spending a few days in the country to restore herself. She asked leave of the King to go, who permitted her very willingly, for he thought that he should thus get rid of her for some time. She set out, and arrived in the dusk of the evening at Vermilion's farm. As she was drawing near, she observed about the door a company of shepherds and shepherdesses who were dancing and merrymaking in high glee. "Alas!" said the Queen sighing, "there was once a time when I could divert myself like these poor people, and no one found fault with me." Directly she came in sight, her sister ran to embrace her. She looked so happy, she had grown so plump, that the Queen could not forbear crying when she looked at her.

Vermilion had married a farmer's son, who had no fortune; but he never ceased to remember that his wife had brought him all that he possessed, and he strove by his obliging disposition to show his gratitude. Vermilion had not many servants; but those that she had were as fond of her as if she had been their mother, because she treated them well. All her neighbors also liked her, and they were all zealous in showing their love. She had not much money, nor had she any occasion for much, for her farm yielded her corn, wine, and oil. Her herds furnished her with milk, with which she made butter and cheese. She spun the wool supplied by her sheep into the materials of clothes for herself, her husband, and her two children. They all enjoyed excellent health, and in the evening, when the period of working had passed, they diverted themselves with all sorts of pastimes. "Alas!" cried the Queen, "the fairy made me a very evil present when she gave me a crown. Contentment is not to be found in magnificent palaces, but only in the innocent employments of a country life." These words had hardly passed her lips when the fairy appeared. "It was not my intention, when I made you Queen, to reward, but to punish you," said the fairy to her, "for giving me your plums with so much ill will. To be truly contented and happy, you must, like your sister, possess only what is necessary, and wish for nothing more." "Ah, madam!" faltered Blanche, "you are sufficiently revenged; I entreat you to put an end to my unhappiness."

"It is at an end," answered the fairy. "The King, who no longer loves you, has just married another wife, and his officers will arrive here to-morrow to desire you, in his name, never to return to his court." It came to pass exactly as the fairy had foretold. Blanche passed the remainder of her days with her sister Vermilion, in all happiness and reasonable pleasure, and she never thought of the court again except to thank the fairy for having brought her from it to her native village.

Prince Desire and Princess Mignonetta

THERE was once upon a time a king who was passionately fond of a princess; but she could not be married, because she was enchanted. He went to consult a fairy, to ascertain what he ought to do to make the Princess love him. The fairy said to him, " You know that the Princess has a large cat, of which she is very fond; well, she can marry that person only who can succeed in treading on her cat's tail." The King said to himself, " That will not be very difficult to accomplish "; and he quitted the fairy, determined rather to crush the cat's tail than to fail in treading on it. He hastened to his mistress's palace; Master Puss came to meet him, very consequentially, as was his wont; the King lifted up his foot, but when he thought to have put it on the cat's tail, Puss turned round so quickly that he trod on nothing but the floor. He was a week trying to tread on this fatal tail, which appeared to be full of quicksilver, for it was continually moving. But, at last, the King had the good fortune to surprise Master Puss while he was asleep, and trod upon his tail with all his weight. Puss awakened, mewing horribly, and immediately took the shape of a tall man, who, looking at the King with eyes full of anger, said to him: " You may now marry the Princess, since you have dissolved the enchantment which prevented you; but I will be revenged. You shall have a son who will always be unfortunate until the time when he shall become aware that his nose is too long; and, if you take any umbrage at what I threaten, you shall immediately be put to death."

Although the King was frightened at the sight of this tall man, who was an enchanter, he could not help laughing at his threat. "If my son's nose should be too long," said he to himself, "unless he should be either blind or silly, he will certainly be able to see or feel it." When the enchanter had disappeared, the King went to find the Princess, who consented to marry him. However, he did not live long with her, for he died eight months after the wedding. Shortly after his death, the Queen gave birth to a young Prince, who was called Desire. He had the finest large blue eyes in the world, and a pretty little mouth; but his nose was so large that it covered half his face. The Queen was inconsolable when she saw this large nose; but the ladies who were with her told her that the nose was not so large as it appeared to her to be; that it was a Roman nose, and that history averred that all heroes had large noses. The Queen, who loved her son to excess, was charmed with this discourse; and, by continually looking at Desire, his nose no longer appeared to be so very long. The Prince was brought up very carefully; and, as soon as he could speak, all kinds of shocking stories were told him of people who had short noses. No one was allowed to remain near him whose nose did not a little resemble his own; and the courtiers, to show their respect to the Queen and her son, pulled their children's noses several times a day, with a view of lengthening them. They had, however, a difficult task; for their sons appeared to have hardly any nose at all compared with Prince Desire's. When he became old enough to understand it, he was instructed in history; and, whenever any great prince or handsome princess was mentioned to him, he or she was always spoken of as having a long nose. The room was hung round with pictures in which all the figures had large noses; and Desire grew so accustomed to regard length of nose as an ornament, that he would not for an empire have parted with an atom of his. When he had reached the age of twenty, it was thought expedient for him to marry; and the portraits of various princesses were submitted to him. He was in raptures with

"HE WAS A WEEK TRYING TO TREAD ON THIS FATAL TAIL"

that of Mignonetta, the daughter of a great king, and heiress to several kingdoms; of the kingdoms, however, Desire thought not at all, he was so much struck with her beauty.

The Princess Mignonetta, although he was thus charmed with her, had a little turned-up nose which harmonized admirably with her other features, but which very much perplexed the courtiers. They had acquired such a habit of ridiculing small noses, that they sometimes could not forbear laughing at that of the Princess; but Desire would not suffer a jest on this subject; and he banished two courtiers from his presence, who dared to make insinuations against Mignonetta's nose. The others, warned by their fate, were more cautious; and there was one who said to the Prince, that, in truth, a man could not be amiable who had not a large nose, but that it was not the same in respect to woman; for a wise man, who spoke Greek, had informed him that he had read in an old manuscript that the fair Cleopatra had the end of her nose turned up. The Prince made a magnificent present to the courtier who told him this good news, and dispatched ambassadors to demand Mignonetta in marriage. His proposal was accepted, and he was so anxious to see her, that he went more than nine miles on the road to meet her; but as he was just stepping forward to kiss her hand, the enchanter appeared and carried off the Princess before his face, leaving him quite inconsolable.

Desire resolved never to reënter his kingdom, until he had discovered Mignonetta. He would not allow any of his courtiers to accompany him, and, mounting a good horse, he laid the bridle on his neck, and allowed him to choose his own road. The horse presently came to a large plain, which he traversed the whole day without seeing a single house. Both horse and rider were ready to die with hunger; at last, as night was about to set in, they discovered a cave in which a light was burning. Desire entered, and saw a little old woman, who appeared to be more than a hundred years old. She put on her spectacles to look at the Prince; bu, she was a long time adjusting them, for her nose was too short. The Prince and the fairy (for it was a fairy) burst out laughing as they looked at each other; exclaiming simultaneously, "Oh, what a comical nose!" "Not so comical as yours," said Desire; "but, madam, let us leave our noses as they are, and have the goodness to give me something to eat; for both I and my poor horse are dying with hunger."

"With all my heart," answered the fairy. "Although your nose is ridiculous, you are not the less the son of my best friend. I loved the King, your father, like my own brother; but he had a very handsome nose." "And what is there wanting in mine?" asked Desire. "Oh, it wants nothing," answered the fairy; "on the contrary, there is far too much of it; but no matter; a man may be very good, and yet have too large a nose. I was saying, then, that I was your father's friend; at that time he frequently came to see me; and you must know that in those days I was very pretty; your father told me so. I must repeat to you a conversation that we had together the last time he saw me." "Very well, madam," said Desire; "I will listen to you with a great deal of pleasure when I have had my supper; consider, if you please, that I have eaten nothing to-day." "The poor child is right," said the fairy; "I did not think of that. I will prepare your supper; and, while you are eating, I will tell you my history in a few words; for I do not like long tales. A long tongue is still more insufferable than a large nose; and I remember, when I was young, that I was admired for not being a great talker; the Queen, my mother, used frequently to have it mentioned to her; for, such as you see me, I am a great king's daughter. My father—" "Your father ate when he was hungry," said the Prince, interrupting her. "Yes, he did, doubtless," said the fairy, "and you also will have your supper in a moment: I was merely going to tell you that my father—" "But I will not listen to a word until I have something to eat," said the Prince, growing angry. He checked himself, however, for he wanted

something of the fairy, and said: " I know that the pleasure
I should take in listening to you would make me forget my
own hunger; but my horse, who will not understand you, is
in need of some food." This compliment made the fairy
blush prettily. " You shall wait no longer," said she to
Desire, calling her domestics; " you are very polite, and, in
spite of the size of your nose, you are very amiable." " Plague
take the old woman with my nose! " said the Prince to himself; " one would have sworn that my mother had stolen what
is wanting in hers, to make mine with; if I were not hun-
grv, I would leave this prate-a-pace, who fancies that she
is a little talker. One must be very stupid not to perceive
one's own defects; that comes of her being born a princess:
flatterers have spoiled her, and persuaded her that she is a
little talker."

While that was passing in the Prince's mind, the servants
laid the table; and the Prince wondered at the fairy, who
kept asking them a thousand questions, solely to have the
pleasure of talking: he was especially surprised at a waiting
woman, who, in everything that she saw, praised her mistress for her discretion. " Egad! " thought he, as he was
eating, " I am delighted to have found my way here. This
example demonstrates to me how wisely I have acted in not
listening to flatterers, who praise all princes very shame-
lessly, concealing our defects from us, or representing them
to us as perfections; but as for me, I shall never be their
dupe; I know my own defects, God be thanked." Poor
Desire quite thought he was right, and little imagined that
those who had praised his nose had ridiculed it in their
hearts, as the waiting woman was ridiculing the fairy; for
the Prince observed that she turned her head aside every
now and then to laugh. With regard to himself, he did not
say a word, but ate away as fast as he could. " Prince,"
said the fairy to him, when he began to be satisfied, " move
a little I entreat you; your nose makes so large a shadow
that it prevents me from seeing what is on my plate. By
the way, with regard to your father: I went to his court

when he was quite a child; but it is forty years since I first retired into this solitude. Tell me a little how things are going on at court now; are the ladies still as fond of running about? In my time they used to go on the same day to the promenade, to the assembly, to the theater, to the ball— But how long your nose is! I cannot grow used to it." " In truth, madam," answered Desire, " do not say any more about my nose; it is as it is, and in what does it concern you? I am contented with it, and do not wish that it was any shorter; everyone to his taste." " Oh, I perceive now I have hurt your feelings, my poor Desire," said the fairy, " but I did not intend to do so; on the contrary, I am your friend, and I wish to do you a service; but notwithstanding that, I cannot help being shocked at your nose; I will not, however, mention it to you again; I will even constrain myself to think that you are snub-nosed; though in truth there are materials enough in it to make three reasonable noses."

Desire, who had finished his supper, grew so tired of the fairy's tedious prattle about his nose that he sprang on his horse and rode away from the cavern. He continued his journey; and wherever he went, he thought that everybody was mad, for everybody talked about his nose; nevertheless, he had been so accustomed to hear it asserted that his nose was handsome, that he could not reconcile to himself the idea that it was too long.

The old fairy, who wished to do him a service in spite of himself, determined to shut up Mignonetta in a crystal palace, and place this palace in the Prince's road. Desire, transported with joy, strove to break it; but he could not succeed: in despair, he wished to approach near it, so as at least to speak to the Princess, who, on her part, stretched her hand close to the crystal wall of the palace. He was very anxious to kiss her hand; but turn his head which way he would, he could not place his mouth near it, his nose constantly preventing him. He then perceived for the first time its extraordinary length, and feeling all over it with his hand, "I must confess," said he, "that my nose is too large." At the moment he pronounced those words, the crystal palace vanished, and the fairy appeared leading Mignonetta by the hand, and saying: "Confess that you are greatly obliged to me. I vainly wished to speak to you about your nose; but you would never have acknowledged its defect unless it had become an obstacle to your wishes. In this way self-love conceals from us all the defects of our minds and bodies. In vain reason endeavors to unveil them to us; we can never perceive them until the same self-love that blinds us to them finds them to be opposed to its interests." Desire, whose nose had become an ordinary nose, profited by this lesson. He married Mignonetta, and lived very happily with her to a good old age.

The Yellow Dwarf

THERE once lived a widowed Queen, who had one daughter. There had been several other children, you must know, but one by one they had died, until the beautiful Princess All-fair was the only child left.

Time passed on, and every day the maiden grew more and more lovely, and, to tell the truth, she not only grew lovelier, but she also became very vain indeed.

Well, by the time she reached the age of eighteen, All-fair was so charming that she had won the hearts of twenty noble kings, and they were all courting her at the same time.

But never a smile did they get from the fair Princess. There was not a man living, be he king or peasant, who was good enough to become her husband, she said.

So when the twenty kings heard this, nineteen of them took their hats at once, and set off in a body to search for brides who were a little less charming and a little easier to please.

But the twentieth man, the King of the Golden Mines,

was so much in love with All-fair, that he stayed behind in the hope that she would change her mind.

"This will never do," said the Queen one day. "Here am I getting quite old, and I want to see All-fair safely married and settled down before I die. I must go and visit the Desert Fairy, and see if she will give me some advice as to how I can manage my stubborn daughter."

Now you must know that it was a very hard task indeed to reach the Desert Fairy, for she was guarded by two fierce and terrible lions. The only way to get past the animals was to throw them a huge cake made from crocodiles' eggs, millet, and sugar candy.

So the Queen set to work, and with her own royal hands she prepared one of these cakes; then she placed it in a basket and set out for the home of the Desert Fairy.

Well, the day was hot, and the cake was heavy, and before long the Queen was lying fast asleep under a big tree.

Suddenly a terrible roar awakened her, and she looked round for her cake to throw to the angry lions, but to her horror it was gone.

"What is to become of me?" cried the poor Queen in terror, and she burst into tears.

"Hem! hem!" cried a small voice, and the Queen looked all around her to see who could be speaking.

At last she looked upward, and there, in the branches of the big orange tree overhead, sat a little yellow man. He was just half a yard high, and he was eating oranges as quickly as ever he could; in fact, he didn't even stop eating while he spoke to the Queen, which, of course, was very rude.

"Ah, Queen!" he went on, "there is only one way by which you can escape the lions, and that is by letting me marry your daughter."

The Queen was so surprised that she even stopped crying. The idea of that hideous little creature marrying her beautiful daughter was quite absurd, and she was just about to tell him so when again she heard the dreadful roaring of the lions. "Be quick and make up your mind!" cried the

Yellow Dwarf. (He was called the Yellow Dwarf, you know, because he lived in the orange tree, and he had eaten so much of the fruit that his skin had become the same color.) "Just remember you have no cake to throw to the lions."

So, to save her life, the Queen was forced to give her consent to a marriage between the Yellow Dwarf and her beautiful daughter.

No sooner did she agree to the match than she began to feel very drowsy, and the next minute the Queen found herself safely back in her own palace.

She was so filled with sadness at the thought of her promise to the dwarf that a fit of deep gloom settled upon her, and for weeks she never smiled.

The Princess was quite at a loss to know what had come over her mother; so in the end she, too, made up her mind to visit the Desert Fairy in the hope that she would be able to tell her what ailed the Queen.

Then All-fair set to work and made a cake from the crocodiles' eggs, millet, and sugar candy, and when it was ready she started off for the Desert Fairy's grotto.

She soon reached the fatal orange tree, and the fruit looked so very tempting that All-fair laid her cake upon the ground and began to pick and eat the ripe oranges.

Just then one of the lions gave a terrible roar, and All-fair looked for her cake to throw to them. Alas, it was gone! and the maiden began to weep bitterly.

"Dry your eyes, lovely Princess!" cried a voice, and, looking up, All-fair spied the Yellow Dwarf.

"You need not trouble to go to the Desert Fairy," went on the dwarf, "for I can tell you what ails your mother."

"I shall be obliged if you will tell me at once, then," replied All-fair.

"Oh, it is all your fault," said the Yellow Dwarf.

"How dare you say such things!" cried the Princess. "It is nothing of the sort."

"Oh, yes, it is," answered the dwarf, with a grin. "Your

[173]

mother is sorry now that she promised you to me in marriage."

"I am sure my mother did not promise me to a fright like you," cried the angry Princess, "and I will not marry you!"

"Oh, please yourself," answered the Yellow Dwarf; "but if you don't marry me you will make a fine meal for the lions, that is all."

Just at that moment the lions began to roar louder than ever.

"Well, to save my life," cried poor All-fair, "I will agree to marry you."

"I wouldn't have you now," said the dwarf, with an air of disdain.

"Oh, please do," begged All-fair, "or I shall be torn to pieces by the lions!"

"I'll marry you out of charity then," said the Yellow Dwarf. "But don't suppose that I really want a vain creature like you."

At that instant the Princess found herself growing very drowsy, and the next minute she was back again at the palace, and on her finger was a ring made of a single red hair, which she could not take off.

After that All-fair grew sad, for she feared that the Yellow Dwarf might claim her.

Of course nobody knew the cause of her sadness, and they all wondered what it could be.

So the Queen's ministers held a cabinet meeting, and they agreed to ask the Princess once more if she would marry, for they thought the excitement of choosing her wedding gown would rouse her from her gloom.

To the great surprise of them all, All-fair said she was quite willing to do as they wished. So the King of the Golden Mines had his reward for waiting so long, for the Princess chose him as her husband. He was very rich and powerful, and so gallant, that All-fair thought when once she was his wife she need fear the Yellow Dwarf no more.

The wedding day arrived at last, and as the guests were

THE FAIRY RING

on their way to the church they saw a big box moving toward them, and on the top sat a very ugly old woman.

"Stop!" she cried, with a dreadful frown. "Do you remember the promise you made to my friend, the Yellow Dwarf? I am the Desert Fairy, and if All-fair does not marry the dwarf she will taste my wrath, you will find."

This speech made the brave King of the Golden Mines so angry that he drew his sword, and shouted loudly:

"Begone, or I will take your evil life!"

As soon as he uttered these words, off flew the top of the box, and out came the Yellow Dwarf seated upon a big, black Spanish cat.

"Not so fast!" cried the Yellow Dwarf. "I am your rival, so do not vent your wrath upon the Desert Fairy. I claim the Princess for my bride, and in token of her promise to me, on her finger you will find a ring made of a single red hair."

"It is false!" cried the King of the Golden Mines, and he made a dash, sword in hand, for the Yellow Dwarf.

But quick as thought the dwarf drew his sword also, and he rode forward on his Spanish cat.

Well, they fought long and fiercely, but the King was not able to overcome the dwarf because he was protected by two enormous giants, who stood one on each side of him.

Suddenly the Desert Fairy stepped forward, and on her head was a wreath of big, curling snakes. Raising her lance, she struck the Princess such a blow that All-fair sank fainting into her mother's arms.

"Revenge!" shouted the King of the Golden Mines, and he rushed to the aid of his love, as a brave man would, of course.

But, alas! he was too late, for the dwarf had torn her from her mother's arms, lifted her on to his Spanish cat, and the next minute they were flying through the air beyond his reach.

The poor King was so surprised that all he could do was to gaze up toward the clouds and wonder what would happen next. Suddenly a mist gathered before his eyes, and he felt himself being carried up into the air also.

Now you must know that the ugly old Desert Fairy had fallen madly in love with the King of the Golden Mines, and she had made up her mind that he should never marry All-fair; so she carried him off to secure him for herself.

Up into the air they went until they reached a gloomy cave. Then the fairy set him down, and restored his sight by means of her magic arts.

"He is sure to fall in love with me," she cried to herself, "now that All-fair is safely out of the way!"

But it was not a bit of use, for she was so ugly that the King only looked the other way the whole time, and this made her very angry indeed.

So the fairy tried another plan. She took the form of a beautiful maiden, and placed the King in a splendid chariot, drawn by two snow-white swans.

Then she, too, stepped in, and together they sailed away through the air.

"He'll never resist my charms this time," she said to herself. But she found out her mistake very soon, I can tell you. You see, although the fairy could change her form at will, her feet always remained the same, and the King caught sight of two ugly webbed feet, that looked as if they belonged to a griffin; so he was not deceived at all, and knew her to be the Desert Fairy, in spite of the disguise.

On and on they went, and once the King chanced to look downward. There he saw a castle built of bright polished steel, and on the balcony stood All-fair weeping very bitterly.

All-fair chanced to look upward, and she spied the chariot drawn by the snow-white swans. Although it passed along very quickly, she could see the King seated inside with a lovely maiden, and as she did not know it was the Desert Fairy, she felt very jealous indeed.

Soon the chariot alighted at a lonely palace, shut in by a wall of emeralds on one side and the sea on the other.

THE FAIRY RING

Well, the King just cast his eyes around the place, and made up his mind not to stay there long.

"I'll escape somehow," he said to himself; and he did, too, before very long.

He pretended to be in love with the Desert Fairy, and this pleased and flattered her so much that she began to treat him very kindly indeed. She even allowed him to walk alone on the seashore for half an hour each day.

One morning as the King stood upon the beach he was surprised to see a charming mermaid rise up from the water.

"King of the Golden Mines," she said, "I know your story, and have the power to set you free. I can also restore your Princess All-fair to you once more. Now, as I am an enemy of the Desert Fairy, I will do this for you."

The King thanked her, of course, and the mermaid bade him set himself upon her tail, and away they sailed at full speed across the blue ocean until they had gone many miles.

"The Princess, you must know," said the mermaid, "is being kept a prisoner by the Yellow Dwarf. She is in a bright steel castle, and in another hour we shall reach the place."

On they went still farther, and at length the mermaid set the King down upon the seashore.

"The rest of the journey," she said, "you must take alone, and you will have many enemies to fight before you reach the Princess. But," she added, "I will present you with this magic sword, which will overcome everything, so long as you never let it out of your hand."

The King took the sword, and thanked the mermaid again and again, and then he set out to seek the steel castle.

But before he had gone a hundred yards, four terrible griffins attacked him, and the King stood a good chance of being torn to pieces by their long claws. Just in time, however, he remembered his magic sword, and no sooner did the four griffins behold it than they sank to the ground, blinded by its brightness.

After that it was an easy matter to cut off their heads, and the King went on his way again.

THE FAIRY RING

Soon after he met six big dragons, and each one was covered with scales like cast iron. But by means of his magic sword the King was able to kill them also, and then he hoped his troubles were nearly over.

Alas! before he had gone many yards, twenty-four nymphs, all lovely as the sun, set themselves right in his path.

"Our business," they said, "is to keep you from reaching the steel castle. If we let you pass, all our lives will be sacrificed. We have done you no harm, so do go back again that our innocent lives may be spared."

Well, the King scarcely knew how to act; it seemed a pity to destroy such lovely creatures, and yet get to the steel castle he must.

"Strike! Strike!" cried a voice loudly, "or you will lose your Princess forever!"

So his Majesty destroyed the whole twenty-four of them, and at that moment the steel castle appeared in sight.

On the balcony stood All-fair, just as she had been when he passed through the air in the chariot drawn by swans.

"Princess," he cried, "your faithful lover has returned at last!"

"Faithful indeed!" replied All-fair angrily. "You were not faithful when I saw you being carried through the air in company with a beautiful maiden."

"Indeed I was," replied the King of the Golden Mines. "The maiden you saw was the wicked Desert Fairy. She carried me off to an island, and there I should be now, if a kind mermaid had not set me free."

Then the King cast himself at her feet; but, unfortunately, he managed to drop the magic sword over the balcony.

Out popped the ugly Yellow Dwarf from behind a big cabbage, where he was hiding, and he snapped up the sword in a trice.

The Princess gave a loud shriek when she set eyes on the dwarf, but the little man, who knew well what a treasure the sword was, just uttered two magic words, with the weapon

[178]

THE MERMAID TAKING THE KING OF THE GOLDEN MINES TO THE STEEL CASTLE

in his hand, and there appeared two terrible giants, who at once bound the King in chains in spite of his struggles.

" Now," chuckled the Yellow Dwarf, " your lover is in my power. If he will consent to your becoming my bride, I will set him free at once."

" Never ! " cried the King of the Golden Mines.

" Then take that," replied the Yellow Dwarf, and he buried the magic sword in the heart of the King.

The poor Princess was filled with sorrow at the loss of her lover, and she cried loudly :

" Hideous dwarf, you have gained nothing by slaying my lover, for I will never marry you. Since he is dead, I will die too."

Then she seized the sword and plunged it into her own heart.

The good mermaid was very unhappy when she heard what had taken place, but as her only power lay in the magic sword, she could help them no further.

So she changed them into two palm trees, growing side by side, and every time the soft breezes blew, their branches caressed and kissed each other, so they were happy together, after all, in spite of the ugly Yellow Dwarf.

Graciosa and Percinet

ONCE upon a time there lived a King and Queen who had one charming daughter. She was so graceful and pretty and clever that she was called Graciosa, and the Queen was so fond of her that she could think of nothing else.

Every day she gave the Princess a lovely new frock of gold brocade, or satin, or velvet, and when she was hungry she had bowls full of sugarplums, and at least twenty pots of jam. Everybody said she was the happiest princess in the world. Now there lived at this same court a very rich old Duchess whose name was Grumbly. She was more frightful than tongue can tell; her hair was red as fire, and she had but one eye, and that not a pretty one! Her face was as broad as a full moon, and her mouth was so large that everybody who met her would have been afraid they were going to be eaten up, only she had no teeth. As she was as cross as she was ugly, she could not bear to hear everyone saying how pretty and how charming Graciosa was; so she presently went away from the court to her own castle, which was not far off. But if anybody who went to see her happened to mention the charming Princess, she would cry angrily:

"It's not true that she is lovely. I have more beauty in my little finger than she has in her whole body."

Soon after this, to the great grief of the Princess, the Queen was taken ill and died, and the King became so melancholy that for a whole year he shut himself up in his palace. At last his physicians, fearing that he would fall ill, ordered that he should go out and amuse himself; so a hunting party was arranged, but as it was very hot weather the King soon grew tired, and said he would dismount and rest at a castle which they were passing.

This happened to be the Duchess Grumbly's castle, and when she heard that the King was coming she went out to meet him, and said that the cellar was the coolest place in the whole castle if he would condescend to come down into it. So down they went together, and the King seeing about two hundred great casks ranged side by side, asked if it was only for herself that she had this immense store of wine.

"Yes, sire," answered she, "it is for myself alone, but I shall be most happy to let you taste some of it. Which do you like, canary, St. Julien, champagne, hermitage sack, raisin, or cider?"

"Well," said the King, "since you are so kind as to ask me, I prefer champagne to anything else."

Then Duchess Grumbly took up a little hammer and

tapped upon the cask twice, and out came at least a thousand crowns.

"What's the meaning of this?" said she, smiling.

Then she tapped the next cask, and out came a bushel of gold pieces.

"I don't understand this at all," said the Duchess, smiling more than before.

Then she went on to the third cask, tap, tap, and out came such a stream of diamonds and pearls that the ground was covered with them.

"Ah!" she cried, "this is altogether beyond my comprehension, sire. Some one must have stolen my good wine and put all this rubbish in its place."

"Rubbish, do you call it, Madam Grumbly?" cried the King. "Rubbish! why there is enough there to buy ten kingdoms."

"Well," said she, "you must know that all those casks are full of gold and jewels, and if you like to marry me it shall all be yours."

Now the King loved money more than anything else in the world, so he cried joyfully:

"Marry you? why, with all my heart! to-morrow if you like."

"But I make one condition," said the Duchess; "I must have entire control of your daughter to do as I please with her."

"Oh, certainly, you shall have your own way; let us shake hands upon the bargain," said the King.

So they shook hands and went up out of the cellar of treasure together, and the Duchess locked the door and gave the key to the King.

When he returned to his own palace Graciosa ran out to meet him, and asked if he had had good sport.

"I have caught a dove," answered he.

"Oh! do give it to me," said the Princess, "and I will keep it and take care of it."

"I can hardly do that," said he, "for, to speak more

plainly, I mean that I met the Duchess Grumbly, and have promised to marry her."

"And you call her a dove?" cried the Princess. "I should have called her a screech owl."

"Hold your tongue," said the King very crossly. "I intend you to behave prettily to her. So now go and make yourself fit to be seen, as I am going to take you to visit her."

So the Princess went very sorrowfully to her own room, and her nurse, seeing her tears, asked what was vexing her.

"Alas! who would not be vexed?" answered she, "for the King intends to marry again, and has chosen for his new bride my enemy, the hideous Duchess Grumbly."

"Oh, well!" answered the nurse, "you must remember that you are a Princess, and are expected to set a good example in making the best of whatever happens. You must promise me not to let the Duchess see how much you dislike her."

At first the Princess would not promise, but the nurse showed her so many good reasons for it that in the end she agreed to be amiable to her stepmother.

Then the nurse dressed her in a robe of pale green and gold brocade, and combed out her long fair hair till it floated round her like a golden mantle, and put on her head a crown of roses and jasmine with emerald leaves.

When she was ready nobody could have been prettier, but she still could not help looking sad.

Meanwhile the Duchess Grumbly was also occupied in attiring herself. She had one of her shoe heels made an inch or so higher than the other, that she might not limp so much, and put a cunningly made glass eye in the place of the one she had lost. She dyed her red hair black, and painted her face. Then she put on a gorgeous robe of lilac satin lined with blue, and a yellow petticoat trimmed with violet ribbons, and because she had heard that queens always rode into their new dominions, she ordered a horse to be made ready for her to ride.

While Graciosa was waiting until the King should be ready to set out, she went down all alone through the garden into a little wood, where she sat down upon a mossy bank and began to think. And her thoughts were so doleful that very soon she began to cry, and she cried and cried, and forgot all about going back to the palace, until she suddenly saw a handsome page standing before her. He was dressed in green, and the cap which he held in his hand was adorned with white plumes. When Graciosa looked at him he went down on one knee, and said to her:

"Princess, the King awaits you."

The Princess was surprised, and, if the truth must be told, very much delighted at the appearance of this charming page, whom she could not remember to have seen before. Thinking he might belong to the household of the Duchess, she said:

"How long have you been one of the King's pages?"

"I am not in the service of the King, madam," answered he, "but in yours."

"In mine?" said the Princess with great surprise. "Then how is it that I have never seen you before?"

"Ah, Princess!" said he, "I have never before dared to present myself to you, but now the King's marriage threatens you with so many dangers that I have resolved to tell you at once how much I love you already, and I trust that in time I may win your regard. I am Prince Percinet, of whose riches you may have heard, and whose fairy gift will, I hope, be of use to you in all your difficulties, if you will permit me to accompany you under this disguise."

"Ah, Percinet!" cried the Princess, "is it really you? I have so often heard of you and wished to see you. If you will indeed be my friend, I shall not be afraid of that wicked old Duchess any more."

So they went back to the palace together, and there Graciosa found a beautiful horse which Percinet had brought for her to ride. As it was very spirited he led it by the bridle, and this arrangement enabled him to turn and look

[183]

at the Princess often, which he did not fail to do. Indeed, she was so pretty that it was a real pleasure to look at her. When the horse which the Duchess was to ride appeared beside Graciosa's, it looked no better than an old cart horse, and as to their trappings, there was simply no comparison between them, as the Princess's saddle and bridle were one glittering mass of diamonds. The King had so many other things to think of that he did not notice this, but all his courtiers were entirely taken up with admiring the Princess and her charming page in green, who was more handsome and distinguished looking than all the rest of the court put together.

When they met the Duchess Grumbly she was seated in an open carriage trying in vain to look dignified. The King and the Princess saluted her, and her horse was brought forward for her to mount. But when she saw Graciosa's she cried angrily:

"If that child is to have a better horse than mine, I will go back to my own castle this very minute. What is the good of being a Queen, if one is to be slighted like this?"

Upon this the King commanded Graciosa to dismount and to beg the Duchess to honor her by mounting her horse. The Princess obeyed in silence, and the Duchess, without looking at her or thanking her, scrambled up upon the beautiful horse, where she sat looking like a bundle of clothes, and eight officers had to hold her up for fear she should fall off.

Even then she was not satisfied, and was still grumbling and muttering, so they asked her what was the matter.

"I wish that page in green to come and lead the horse, as he did when Graciosa rode it," said she very sharply.

And the King ordered the page to come and lead the Queen's horse. Percinet and the Princess looked at one another, but said never a word, and then he did as the King commanded, and the procession started in great pomp. The Duchess was greatly elated, and as she sat there in state would not have wished to change places even with Graciosa. But at the moment when it was least expected the beautiful

THE FAIRY RING

horse began to plunge and rear and kick, and finally to run away at such a pace that it was impossible to stop him.

At first the Duchess clung to the saddle, but she was very soon thrown off and fell in a heap among the stones and thorns, and there they found her, shaken to a jelly, and collected what was left of her as if she had been a broken glass. Her bonnet was here and her shoes there, her face was scratched, and her fine clothes were covered with mud. Never was a bride seen in such a dismal plight. They carried her back to the palace and put her to bed, but as soon as she recovered enough to be able to speak, she began to scold and rage, and declared that the whole affair was Graciosa's fault, that she had contrived it on purpose to try and get rid of her, and that if the King would not have her punished, she would go back to her castle and enjoy her riches by herself.

At this the King was terribly frightened, for he did not at all want to lose all those barrels of gold and jewels. So he hastened to appease the Duchess, and told her she might punish Graciosa in any way she pleased.

Thereupon she sent for Graciosa, who turned pale and trembled at the summons, for she guessed that it promised nothing agreeable for her. She looked all about for Percinet, but he was nowhere to be seen; so she had no choice but to go to the Duchess Grumbly's room. She had hardly got inside the door when she was seized by four waiting women, who looked so tall and strong and cruel that the Princess shuddered at the sight of them, and still more when she saw them arming themselves with great bundles of rods, and heard the Duchess call out to them from her bed to beat the Princess without mercy. Poor Graciosa wished miserably that Percinet could only know what was happening and come to rescue her. But no sooner did they begin to beat her than she found, to her great relief, that the rods had changed to bundles of peacocks' feathers, and though the Duchess's women went on till they were so tired that they could no longer raise their arms from their sides, yet she was

[185]

not hurt in the least. However, the Duchess thought she must be black and blue after such a beating; so Graciosa, when she was released, pretended to feel very ill, and went away into her own room, where she told her nurse all that had happened, and then the nurse left her, and when the Princess turned round there stood Percinet beside her. She thanked him gratefully for helping her so cleverly, and they laughed and were very merry over the way they had taken in the Duchess and her waiting maids; but Percinet advised her still to pretend to be ill for a few days and after promising to come to her aid whenever she needed him, he disappeared as suddenly as he had come.

The Duchess was so delighted at the idea that Graciosa was really ill that she herself recovered twice as fast as she would have done otherwise, and the wedding was held with great magnificence. Now as the King knew that, above all other things, the Queen loved to be told that she was beautiful, he ordered that her portrait should be painted, and that a tournament should be held, at which all the bravest knights of his court should maintain against all comers that Grumbly was the most beautiful princess in the world.

Numbers of knights came from far and wide to accept the challenge, and the hideous Queen sat in great state in a balcony hung with cloth of gold to watch the contests, and Graciosa had to stand up behind her, where her loveliness was so conspicuous that the combatants could not keep their eyes off her. But the Queen was so vain that she thought all their admiring glances were for herself, especially as, in spite of the badness of their cause, the King's knights were so brave that they were the victors in every combat.

However, when nearly all the strangers had been defeated, a young unknown knight presented himself. He carried a portrait, inclosed in a box incrusted with diamonds, and he declared himself willing to maintain against them all, that the Queen was the ugliest creature in the world, and that the Princess whose portrait he carried was the most beautiful.

So one by one the knights came out against him, and one by one he vanquished them all, and then he opened the box, and said that, to console them, he would show them the portrait of his queen of beauty, and when he did so, everyone recognized the Princess Graciosa. The unknown knight then saluted her gracefully and retired, without telling his name to anybody. But Graciosa had no difficulty in guessing that it was Percinet.

As to the Queen, she was so furiously angry that she could hardly speak; but she soon recovered her voice, and overwhelmed Graciosa with a torrent of reproaches.

"What!" she said, "do you dare to dispute with me for the prize of beauty, and expect me to endure this insult to my knights? But I will not bear it, proud Princess. I will have my revenge."

"I assure you, madam," said the Princess, "that I had nothing to do with it and am quite willing that you shall be declared queen of beauty."

"Ah! you are pleased to jest, popinjay!" said the Queen, "but it will be my turn soon!"

The King was speedily told what had happened, and how the Princess was in terror of the angry Queen, but he only said:

"The Queen must do as she pleases. Graciosa belongs to her!"

The wicked Queen waited impatiently until night fell, and then she ordered her carriage to be brought. Graciosa, much against her will, was forced into it, and away they drove, and never stopped until they reached a great forest, a hundred leagues from the palace. This forest was so gloomy and so full of lions, tigers, bears, and wolves that nobody dared pass through it even by daylight, and here they set down the unhappy Princess in the middle of the black night, and left her in spite of all her tears and entreaties. The Princess stood quite still at first from sheer bewilderment, but when the last sound of the retreating carriage died away in the distance she began to run aimlessly hither and thither, sometimes knocking herself against a tree, sometimes tripping over a stone, fearing every minute that she would be eaten up by the lions. Presently she was too tired to advance another step, so she threw herself down upon the ground and cried miserably:

"O Percinet! where are you? Have you forgotten me altogether?"

She had hardly spoken when all the forest was lighted up with a sudden glow. Every tree seemed to be sending out a soft radiance, which was clearer than moonlight and softer than daylight, and at the end of a long avenue of trees opposite to her the Princess saw a palace of clear crystal which blazed like the sun. At that moment a slight sound behind her made her turn around, and there stood Percinet himself.

"Did I frighten you, my Princess?" said he. "I come to bid you welcome to our fairy palace, in the name of the Queen, my mother, who is prepared to love you as much as I do." The Princess joyfully mounted with him into a little sledge, drawn by two stags, which bounded off and drew them swiftly to the wonderful palace, where the Queen received her with the greatest kindness, and a splendid banquet was served at once. Graciosa was so happy to have found Percinet, and to have escaped from the gloomy forest and all its terrors, that she was very hungry and very merry, and they were a gay party. After supper they went into another lovely room, where the crystal walls were covered with pictures, and the Princess saw with great surprise that her own history was represented, even down to the moment when Percinet found her in the forest.

"Your painters must indeed be diligent," she said, pointing out the last picture to the Prince.

"They are obliged to be, for I will not have anything forgotten that happens to you," he answered.

When the Princess grew sleepy, twenty-four charming maidens put her to bed in the prettiest room she had ever seen, and then sang to her so sweetly that Graciosa's dreams were all of mermaids, and cool sea waves, and caverns, in which she wandered with Percinet; but when she woke up again her first thought was that, delightful as this fairy palace seemed to her, yet she could not stay in it, but must go back to her father. When she had been dressed by the twenty-four maidens in a charming robe which the Queen had sent for her, and in which she looked prettier than ever, Prince Percinet came to see her, and was bitterly disappointed when she told him what she had been thinking. He begged her to consider again how unhappy the wicked Queen would make her, and how, if she would but marry him, all the fairy palace would be hers, and his one thought would be to please her. But, in spite of everything he could say, the Princess was quite determined to go back, though he at last persuaded her to stay eight days, which were so full of pleasure and amusement that they passed like a few hours. On the last day, Graciosa, who had often felt anxious to know what was going on in her father's palace, said to Percinet that she was sure that he could find out for her, if he would, what reason the Queen had given her father for her sudden disappearance. Percinet at first offered to send his courier to find out, but the Princess said:

"Oh! isn't there a quicker way of knowing than that?"

"Very well," said Percinet, "you shall see for yourself."

So up they went together to the top of a very high tower, which, like the rest of the castle, was built entirely of rock crystal.

There the Prince held Graciosa's hand in his, and made her put the tip of her little finger into her mouth, and look toward the town, and immediately she saw the wicked Queen go to the King, and heard her say to him: "That miserable Princess is dead, and no great loss either. I have ordered that she shall be buried at once."

And then the Princess saw how she dressed up a log of wood and had it buried, and how the old King cried, and all the people murmured that the Queen had killed Graciosa with her cruelties, and that she ought to have her head cut

off. When the Princess saw that the King was so sorry for
her pretended death that he could neither eat nor drink, she
cried:

"Ah, Percinet! take me back quickly, if you love me."

And so, though he did not want to at all, he was obliged to
promise that he would let her go.

"You may not regret me, Princess," he said sadly, "for
I fear that you do not love me well enough; but I foresee
that you will more than once regret that you left this fairy
palace where we have been so happy."

But, in spite of all he could say, she bade farewell to the
Queen, his mother, and prepared to set out; so Percinet,
very unwillingly, brought the little sledge with the stags and
she mounted beside him. But they had hardly gone twenty
yards when a tremendous noise behind her made Graciosa
look back, and she saw the palace of crystal fly into a million
splinters, like the spray of a fountain, and vanish.

"O Percinet!" she cried, "what has happened? The
palace is gone!"

"Yes," he answered, "my palace is a thing of the past;
you will see it again, but not until after you have been
buried."

"Now you are angry with me," said Graciosa in her most
coaxing voice, "though after all I am more to be pitied than
you are."

When they drew near the palace the Prince made the sledge
and themselves invisible, so the Princess got in unobserved,
and ran up to the great hall where the King was sitting all by
himself. At first he was very much startled by Graciosa's
sudden appearance, but she told him how the Queen had left
her out in the forest, and how she had caused a log of wood
to be buried. The King, who did not know what to think,
sent quickly and had it dug up, and sure enough it was as
the Princess had said. Then he caressed Graciosa, and made
her sit down to supper with him, and they were as happy
as possible. But some one had by this time told the wicked
Queen that Graciosa had come back, and was at supper with

the King, and in she flew in a terrible fury. The poor old King quite trembled before her, and when she declared that Graciosa was not the Princess at all, but a wicked impostor, and that if the King did not give her up at once she would go back to her own castle and never see him again, he had not a word to say, and really seemed to believe that it was not Graciosa after all. So the Queen in great triumph sent for her waiting women, who dragged the unhappy Princess away and shut her up in a garret; they took away all her jewels and her pretty dress, and gave her a rough cotton frock, wooden shoes, and a little cloth cap. There was some straw in a corner, which was all she had for a bed, and they gave her a very little bit of black bread to eat. In this miserable plight Graciosa did indeed regret the fairy palace, and she would have called Percinet to her aid, only she felt sure he was still vexed with her for leaving him, and thought that she could not expect him to come.

Meanwhile the Queen had sent for an old fairy, as malicious as herself, and said to her:

"You must find me some task for this fine Princess which she cannot possibly do, for I mean to punish her, and if she does not do what I order, she will not be able to say that I am unjust." So the old fairy said she would think it over, and come again the next day. When she returned she brought with her a skein of thread, three times as big as herself; it was so fine that a breath of air would break it, and so tangled that it was impossible to see the beginning or the end of it.

The Queen sent for Graciosa, and said to her:

"Do you see this skein? Set your clumsy fingers to work upon it, for I must have it disentangled by sunset, and if you break a single thread it will be the worse for you." So saying she left her, locking the door behind her with three keys.

The Princess stood dismayed at the sight of the terrible skein. If she did but turn it over to see where to begin, she broke a thousand threads, and not one could she disentangle. At last she threw it into the middle of the floor, crying:

"O Percinet! this fatal skein will be the death of me if you will not forgive me and help me once more."

And immediately in came Percinet as easily as if he had all the keys in his own possession.

"Here I am, Princess, as much as ever at your service," said he, "though really you are not very kind to me."

Then he just stroked the skein with his wand, and all the broken threads joined themselves together, and the whole skein wound itself smoothly off in the most surprising manner, and the Prince, turning to Graciosa, asked if there was nothing else that she wished him to do for her, and if the time would never come when she would wish for him for his own sake.

"Don't be vexed with me, Percinet," she said. "I am unhappy enough without that."

"But why should you be unhappy, my Princess?" cried he. "Only come with me and we shall be as happy together as the day is long."

"But suppose you get tired of me?" said Graciosa.

The Prince was so grieved at this want of confidence that he left her without another word.

The wicked Queen was in such a hurry to punish Graciosa that she thought the sun would never set; and indeed it was before the appointed time that she came with her four fairies, and as she fitted the three keys into the locks she said:

"I'll venture to say that the idle minx has not done anything at all—she prefers to sit with her hands before her to keep them white."

But as soon as she entered, Graciosa presented her with the ball of thread in perfect order, so that she had no fault to find, and could only pretend to discover that it was soiled, for which imaginary fault she gave Graciosa a blow on each cheek, that made her white-and-pink skin turn green and yellow. And then she sent her back to be locked into the garret once more.

THE FAIRY RING

Then the Queen sent for the fairy again and scolded her furiously. "Don't make such a mistake again; find me something that it will be quite impossible for her to do," she said.

So the next day the fairy appeared with a huge barrel full of the feathers of all sorts of birds. There were feathers from nightingales, canaries, goldfinches, linnets, tomtits, parrots, owls, sparrows, doves, ostriches, bustards, peacocks, larks, partridges, and every sort that you can think of. These feathers were all mixed up in such confusion that the birds themselves could not have chosen out their own. "Here," said the fairy, "is a little task which it will take all your prisoner's skill and patience to accomplish. Tell her to pick out and lay in a separate heap the feathers of each bird. She would need to be an enchanter to do it."

The Queen was more than delighted at the thought of the despair this task would cause the Princess. She sent fo. her, and with the same threats as before locked her up with the three keys, ordering that all the feathers should be sorted by sunset. Graciosa set to work at once, but before she had taken out a dozen feathers she found that it was perfectly impossible to know one from another.

"Ah, well," she sighed, "the Queen wishes to kill me, and if I must die I must. I cannot ask Percinet to help me again, for if he really loved me he would not wait till I called him, he would come without that."

"I am here, my Graciosa," cried Percinet, springing out of the barrel, where he had been hiding. "How can you still doubt that I love you with all my heart?"

Then he gave three strokes of his wand upon the barrel, and all the feathers flew out in a cloud and settled down in neat little separate heaps all round the room.

"What should I do without you, Percinet?" said Graciosa gratefully. But still she could not quite make up her mind to go with him and leave her father's kingdom forever; so she begged him to give her more time to think of it, and he had to go away disappointed once more.

When the wicked Queen came at sunset she was amazed

and infuriated to find the task done. However, she complained that the heaps of feathers were badly arranged, and for that the Princess was beaten and sent back to her garret. Then the Queen sent for the fairy once more, and scolded her until she was fairly terrified, and promised to go home and think of another task for Graciosa, worse than either of the others.

At the end of three days she came again, bringing with her a box.

"Tell your slave," said she, "to carry this wherever you please, but on no account to open it. She will not be able to help doing so, and then you will be quite satisfied with the result." So the Queen came to Graciosa and said:

"Carry this box to my castle, and place it upon the table in my own room. But I forbid you on pain of death to look at what it contains."

Graciosa set out, wearing her little cap and wooden shoes and the old cotton frock, but even in this disguise she was so beautiful that all the passers-by wondered who she could be. She had not gone far before the heat of the sun and the weight of the box tired her so much that she sat down to rest in the shade of a little wood which lay on one side of a green meadow. She was carefully holding the box upon her lap when she suddenly felt the greatest desire to open it.

"What could possibly happen if I did?" she said to herself. "I should not take anything out. I should only just see what was there."

And without further hesitation she lifted the cover.

Instantly out came swarms of little men and women, no taller than her finger, and scattered themselves all over the meadow, singing and dancing, and playing the merriest games, so that at first Graciosa was delighted and watched them with much amusement. But presently, when she was rested and wished to go on her way, she found that, do what she would, she could not get them back into their box. If she chased them in the meadow they fled into the wood, and if she pursued them into the wood they dodged around trees and behind sprigs of moss, and with peals of elfin laughter scampered back again into the meadow.

At last, weary and terrified, she sat down and cried.

"It is my own fault," she said sadly. "Percinet, if you can still care for such an imprudent Princess, do come and help me once more."

Immediately Percinet stood before her.

"Ah, Princess!" he said, "but for the wicked Queen I fear you would never think of me at all."

"Indeed I should," said Graciosa; "I am not so ungrateful as you think. Only wait a little and I believe I shall love you quite dearly."

Percinet was pleased at this, and with one stroke of his wand compelled all the willful little people to come back to their places in the box, and then rendering the Princess invisible he took her with him in his chariot to the castle.

When the Princess presented herself at the door, and said that the Queen had ordered her to place the box in her own room, the governor laughed heartily at the idea.

"No, no, my little shepherdess," said he, "that is not the place for you. No wooden shoes have ever been over that floor yet."

Then Graciosa begged him to give her a written message telling the Queen that he had refused to admit her. This he did, and she went back to Percinet, who was waiting for her, and they set out together for the palace. You may imagine that they did not go the shortest way, but the Princess did not find it too long, and before they parted she had promised that if the Queen was still cruel to her, and tried again to play her any spiteful trick, she would leave her and come to Percinet forever.

When the Queen saw her returning she fell upon the fairy, whom she had kept with her, and pulled her hair, and scratched her face, and would really have killed her if a fairy could be killed. And when the Princess presented the letter and the box she threw them both upon the fire without opening them, and looked very much as if she would like to throw the Princess after them. However, what she really did do was to have a great hole as deep as a well dug in her garden, and the top of it covered with a flat stone. Then she went and walked near it, and said to Graciosa and all her ladies who were with her:

"I am told that a great treasure lies under that stone: let us see if we can lift it."

So they all began to push and pull at it, and Graciosa among the others, which was just what the Queen wanted; for as soon as the stone was lifted high enough, she gave the Princess a push which sent her down to the bottom of the well, and then the stone was let fall again, and there she was a prisoner. Graciosa felt that now indeed she was hopelessly lost; surely not even Percinet could find her in the heart of the earth.

"This is like being buried alive," she said with a shudder. "O Percinet! if you only knew how I am suffering for my want of trust in you! But how could I be sure that you would not be like other men and tire of me from the moment you were sure I loved you?"

As she spoke she suddenly saw a little door open, and the sunshine blazed into the dismal well. Graciosa did not hesitate an instant, but passed through into a charming garden. Flowers and fruit grew on every side, fountains plashed, and birds sang in the branches overhead, and when she reached a great avenue of trees and looked up to see where it would lead her, she found herself close to the palace of crystal. Yes! there was no mistaking it, and the Queen and Percinet were coming to meet her.

"Ah, Princess!" said the Queen, "don't keep this poor Percinet in suspense any longer. You little guess the anxiety he has suffered while you were in the power of that miserable Grumbly."

The Princess kissed her gratefully, and promised to do as she wished in everything, and holding out her hand to Percinet, with a smile, she said:

" Do you remember telling me that I should not see your palace again until I had been buried? I wonder if you guessed that when that happened, I should tell you that I love you with all my heart, and will marry you whenever you like?"

Prince Percinet joyfully took the hand that was given him, and, for fear the Princess should change her mind, the wedding was held at once with the greatest splendor, and Graciosa and Percinet lived happily ever after.

Drak, the Fairy

IN the last century there lived in the little town of Gaillac, in Languedoc, a young merchant, who, having arrived at an age when he wished to settle down in life, sought a wife. Providing she was sweet-tempered, witty, rich, pretty, and of good family, he was not particular about the rest; for Michael knew that he must be moderate in his desires. Unhappily, he could not see in Gaillac one who appeared worthy of his choice. All the young girls had some known fault, not to mention those which were not known. At length he was told of a young lady of Lavaur, endowed with innumerable good qualities and a dowry of twenty thousand crowns. This sum was exactly that required by Michael to establish himself in business; so he instantly fell in love with the young lady of Lavaur. He obtained an introduction to the family, who liked his appearance, and gave him a good reception. But the young heiress had many suitors, from whom she hesitated to make a definite choice. After several discussions it was decided by her parents that the contending lovers should be brought together at a ball, and after having compared them a choice should be made.

On the appointed day Michael set out for Lavaur. His portmanteau was packed with his finest clothes: an apple-green coat, a lavender vest, breeches of black velvet, silk stockings

with silver trees, buckled shoes, powder box, and a satin ribbon for his queue. His horse was harnessed with gay trappings. Furthermore, the prudent traveler, not having a pistol
to put in his holsters, had slipped in a little bottle of wine and
several slices of almond cake, in order to have something at
hand to keep his courage up. For in reality now that the
day had come he was in a very anxious state, and when he
saw in the distance the church of Lavaur he felt quite taken
aback. He slackened the pace of his horse, then dismounted,
and in order to reflect upon what he should do at the ball
he entered a little wood and sat down on the turf. He drew
from his holsters, to keep him company, the almond cake and
the bottle; the latter he placed between his knees, so that without thinking of it he varied his reflections by sips of wine
and mouthfuls of cake. These distractions somewhat enliv-
ened him and gave him confidence, so much so that he began
to discover in himself a number of virtues and excellences,
which could not fail to insure him the victory.

The sun having disappeared from the horizon he was about
to pursue his journey, when he heard a sound behind him
among the leaves, as of a multitude of little footsteps tramp-
ling the grass in tune to the music of a flute and cymbals.
Astonished, he turned around, and by the light of the first
stars, he perceived a troop of fairies, who were running headed
by the King, Tambourinet. In their rear, turning over and
over like a wheel, was the buffoon of the little people—Drak,
the fairy.

The fairies surrounded the traveler, and gave him a thousand welcomes and good wishes. Michael, who had drunk
too freely not to be brave, welcomed them as old acquaintances, and seeing their little eyes fixed upon the cake he
began to crumble and throw it to them as one would to the
birds. In spite of their numbers, each one had his crumb
with the exception of Drak, who arrived when everyone had
finished. Tambourinet next asked what was in the bottle,
and passed it from hand to hand till it reached the buffoon,
who, finding it empty, threw it away.

Michael burst out laughing.

"That is justice, my little man," said he to the fairy. "For those who arrive late, there remains nothing but regret."

"I will make you remember what you have just said," cried Drak in anger.

"And how?" asked the traveler ironically. "Do you think, now, you are big enough to revenge yourself?"

Drak disappeared without answering; and Michael, after taking leave of Tambourinet, mounted his horse again.

He had not gone a hundred paces, when the saddle turned and threw him roughly to the ground. He arose a little stunned, rebuckled the straps, and mounted his horse again. A little farther on, as he was going over a bridge, the right stirrup bent slightly, and he found himself thrown in the middle of the rivulet. He got out again in a very bad humor, and fell the third time over the pebbles in the road, hurting himself so much that he could hardly proceed. He began to think if he persisted in riding in the saddle he would be unable to present himself at all to the family of the young lady, so he decided to ride his horse barebacked, and take the saddle upon his shoulder. In this manner he made his entry into Lavaur amid the loud laughter of the people who were sitting at their doors.

"Laugh! laugh! you great stupids," murmured Michael; "is it very marvelous that a man should carry his saddle when it will not carry him?"

At length he reached the inn, where he alighted, and asked for a room in which to change his traveling clothes. Having obtained a chamber, he proceeded with much care to open his portmanteau and lay out carefully on the bed the articles for his toilet.

His first consideration was whether he should powder his hair white or yellow. Having decided it should be white, he seized the swans-down powder puff, and commenced the operation on the right side. But at the moment when he had finished that side he saw that an invisible hand had powdered the other side yellow, so that his head had the appearance of a half-peeled lemon. Michael, stupefied, hastened to mix the powder with the comb, and finding himself too pressed for time to seek to think out the reason of the mischance (he was always a slow thinker) stretched out his hand toward the reel on which the satin for his queue was wound. The reel escaped from his fingers and fell to the ground.

Michael went to pick it up, but it seemed to roll before him. Twenty times he was about to seize it, and twenty times his impatient hands missed it. One would have said he looked like a kitten playing with a reel. At length, seeing that time was going, he lost patience and resigned himself to wear his old ribbon.

He now hastened to put on his morocco shoes. He buckled the right, then having finished the left, he stooped to admire them, but as he did so the right buckle fell to the ground. He replaced it, but no sooner had he done so than the left followed suit. He had hardly put that right before the other one claimed his attention again in the same manner as before. He proceeded thus for some time, without being able to get both buckles fastened together.

Furious, he finished by putting on his traveling boots, and was about to take his velvet breeches, when, immediately he approached the bed, lo! the breeches began of their own accord to walk about the room.

Michael, petrified, stood mute, with his arm extended, contemplating with a frightened air this incongruous dance. But you may guess how he looked when he saw the vest, coat, and hat join the breeches at their respective places, and form a sort of counterfeit of himself, which commenced to walk about and parody his attitudes.

Pale with fear he drew back to the window; but at this moment the Michaelesque figure turned toward him, and he saw under the cocked hat the grimacing face of Drak, the fairy.

Michael uttered a cry.

" It is you, you villain, is it? I'll make you repent of your insolence if you don't instantly give me back my clothes."

So saying, he rushed to take them; but the fairy, turning

"MICHEAL, PETRIFIED, STOOD MUTE, . . . CONTEMPLATING WITH A
FRIGHTENED AIR THIS INCONGRUOUS DANCE"

sharply around, ran to the other side of the room. Michael was beside himself with anger and impatience, and rushed again toward the fairy, who this time passed between his legs and rushed out on to the staircase. Michael pursued him angrily up four flights of stairs till they arrived at the garret, where the fairy dodged him round and round, and then skipped out of the window. Michael, exasperated, took the same route. The malicious fairy led him from roof to roof, dragging the velvet breeches, the vest, and coat in all the gutters, to Michael's despair. At length, after a peregrination of an hour or two across this Pyrenees of the cats and swallows, Drak gained a high chimney at the foot of which his pursuer was forced to stop.

Drak, leaning over toward Michael, who was out of breath and discouraged, said:

"You see, my good friend, you have forced me to spoil your ball dress; but, happily, I see underneath me the copper of a laundress, where everything can be put right for you."

With these words Drak shook the velvet breeches over the chimney pot.

"What are you doing, rascal?" cried Michael.

"I am sending your dress to the wash!" said the fairy.

And so saying, the vest, coat, and hat followed the breeches into the smoking gulf.

The young gallant sat down upon the roof with a cry of despair; but rising immediately, said with resolution:

"Well, I'll go to the ball in my traveling dress."

"Hark!" interrupted the fairy.

The sound of a bell rang out from a neighboring steeple. Midnight struck! Michael counted the twelve strokes, and could not restrain a cry. It was the hour designated by the parents when they would proclaim to the suitors who had presented themselves at the ball their daughter's choice for a husband. He wrung his hands in despair.

"Unhappy man that I am!" he cried. "When I arrive all will be over; she and her parents will laugh at me."

"And that would be justice, my big man," replied Drak,

with a pointed sneer. "For you have said yourself, '*For
those who arrive late, there remains nothing but regret.*' This
will serve you, I hope, as a lesson, and prevent you another
time from laughing at the feeble; for from henceforth you
will know that the smallest are big enough to avenge themselves."

Drakesbill and His Friends

DRAKESBILL was very little, and that is why some
people called him Bill Drake; but, tiny as he was,
he knew a thing or two. He was a great worker
and laid up every cent that he earned; and, long before he
was half as tall as a gray goose he had saved a hundred dol-
lars in gold. The King of the country, who never did anything but spend money, heard that Drakesbill had some gold
pieces, and he made haste to borrow them. How very kind
and gracious he was until he heard the little yellow coins
jingle in his pocket! And how proud it made Drakesbill feel
to have it said that he had lent money to the King!

A year went by—two years, three years—and the King
seemed to have forgotten him. He did not even offer to pay
Drakesbill the interest, and the little fellow was very uneasy
lest he should lose all his money. At last he made up his
mind that he would go and see the King and tell him that
he needed the gold pieces very much.

So, early one morning, Drakesbill, as spruce and fresh as
a young robin, went down the highroad toward the King's
palace, singing, "Quack, quack, quack, when shall I get my
money back?"

He had not gone far when he met friend Fox coming home
from his rounds among the farmyards.

"Good morning, my good neighbor," said friend Fox;
"where are you going so early in the day?"

"I am going to the King to ask him to pay me what he
owes me."

"Oh, take me with you!"

"One can't have too many friends," thought Drakesbill. Then he said: "Certainly I will take you; but you walk on four legs, and you will soon get tired. So make yourself very small, get into my mouth, creep under my tongue—and I will carry you."

Friend Fox thanked him very kindly, made himself very small, and was out of sight like a letter in a letterbox.

Then Drakesbill was off again, all spruce and fresh as a spring morning, and still singing, "Quack, quack, quack, when shall I get my money back?"

He had not gone far when he met his lady friend Ladder leaning against her wall. "Good morning, ducky darling," said the lady friend, "whither away, so bold and gay, this fine, new day?"

"I am going to the King to ask him to pay me what he owes me."

"Oh, take me with you!"

"One can't have too many friends," thought Drakesbill. Then he said, "Certainly I will take you; but you have such long wooden legs that you will soon get tired. So make yourself very small, get into my mouth, creep under my tongue—and I will carry you."

The Ladder thanked him, made herself very small, and went to keep company with friend Fox.

Then Drakesbill was off again, spruce and fresh as any dapper little dandy, and singing, "Quack, quack, quack, when shall I get my money back?"

He had not gone far when he met his sweetheart, laughing River, wandering quietly in the sunshine.

"Good morning, my spoonbill," she said, "whither do you go, so happy and slow, while the soft breezes blow?"

"I am going to the King, you know, for he owes me money, and I want him to pay me back."

"Oh, take me with you!"

"One can't have too many friends," thought Drakesbill. Then he said: "Certainly I will take you; but you always sleep while you run, and you will soon get tired. So make yourself very small, get into my mouth, creep under my tongue— and I will carry you."

The River thanked him very kindly, and then, glou! glou! glou! she went to take her place between friend Fox and friend Ladder.

And Drakesbill was off again, spruce and fresh as a busy bee, and singing, " Quack, quack, quack, when shall I get my money back? "

A little farther on he met neighbor Wasp-nest, taking his wasps out for some fresh air.

" Good morning, neighbor Bill," said Wasp-nest; " whither do we run, so full of fun, in the bright warm sun? "

" Oh, don't you know that the King owes me money? And I am going down to see him and make him pay me," answered Drakesbill.

" Oh, take us with you! "

" One can't have too many friends," thought Drakesbill. Then he said: " Certainly I will take you; but there are so many of you that you will soon get tired. So make yourself quite small, get into my mouth, creep under my tongue— and I will carry you."

Neighbor Wasp-nest thanked him very kindly, and then buzz, buzz, buzz, file right! march! There wasn't much more room, but by getting close together everybody was made quite comfortable.

And then Drakesbill went on singing.

In the afternoon he came to the great city where the King lived; and as he marched straight up High Street, he sang as loud as he could, " Quack, quack, quack! Oh, when shall I get my money back? "

When he came to the King's palace he climbed up the step; and then he stood on tiptoe, and knocked at the door, toc! toc! toc!

" Who's there? " asked the doorkeeper, looking out through the keyhole.

" 'Tis I, Drakesbill. I want to speak with the King."

THE FAIRY RING

"Speak with the King? Nonsense! That is easier said than done. The King is in the parlor counting out his money."

"That is just what I want to see him do," said Drakesbill. "Tell him I am here, and then he will know my business."

The doorkeeper went into the parlor to speak with the King. But he was not there; he was in the kitchen, just sitting down to dinner with a white napkin round his neck.

"Good! good!" said the King. "I know the rascal. Fetch him in and put him with the turkeys and chickens."

The doorkeeper went back to the door.

"Walk in, sir!"

"Good!" said Drakesbill to himself. "Now I can see how the folks eat at the King's table."

"This way, this way!" said the doorkeeper. "Now step through that gate. There you are!"

"What! In the poultry yard? How? What?"

How vexed the little fellow was! And no wonder.

"Just wait," he said at last. "I think I'll show them a thing or two. Quack, quack, quack, when shall I get my money back?"

But turkeys and chickens are queer things, as you know, and think themselves a good deal better than other folks. When they saw what a funny little fellow had come among them, and when they heard him singing his queer song, they began to ask one another:

"Who is he? What is he doing here?"

Then they all rushed upon him, and if he had not had his wits about him they would have pecked him to death in no time. But, as good luck would have it, he remembered his friend Fox, and he cried out:

> "Fox, friend Fox, from your hiding place
> Come quick, or sad will be my case!"

Then friend Fox, who was only waiting for these words, leaped out from his hiding place, as big as life and as happy as a sunflower; and he threw himself on the wicked fowls, and snip, snap! crish, crash! he tore them in pieces; and at the end of five minutes not one of them was left alive. And Drakesbill, spruce and fresh as ever, began to sing again, "Quack, quack, quack, when shall I get my money back?"

But the King was very angry when the poultry woman and the cook and the doorkeeper all rushed into the kitchen where he was eating and told him what had happened. He ordered them to seize this naughty little Drakesbill and throw him into the well, and thus make an end of him.

"I am lost! I am lost!" cried Drakesbill as he fell fluttering down into the deep, dark hole. "I can never climb out of this place."

Then he happened to think of his lady friend Ladder, and he sang:

> "Ladder, Ladder, from beneath my tongue
> Come quick, or soon my song will be sung!"

Friend Ladder, who had only been waiting for these words, leaped quickly out, as tall as a flag pole and as charming as a walking stick; and she stood with her feet at the bottom of the well and her two arms resting upon the top; and Drakesbill climbed nimbly on her back, and hip! hop! hup! how soon he was up and singing louder than ever, "Quack, quack, quack, when shall I get my money back?"

The King, who was still at the table, heard him singing, and the song made him so angry that he almost choked.

"Can't anybody make that fellow hush?" he cried.

Then he ordered his men to build a great fire, and, when it was hot, to throw Drakesbill into it and burn him up for a wicked wizard.

But Drakesbill was not much afraid this time; he remembered his sweetheart River. Just when the flames were the highest, and the captain of the King's men was going to toss him into them, he sang out:

> "River, River, outward flow,
> Or into the fire I must go!"

THE FAIRY RING

Then friend River, who had only been waiting for these
words, flowed quickly out, as strong as a storm and as swift
as the wind; and she put out the fire, and drowned all the
people that had kindled it; and, glou! glou! glou! she flowed
into the King's palace and stood four feet deep in the great
hall. And Drakesbill, spruce and fresh as ever, swam hither
and thither, singing, " Quack, quack, quack, when shall I get
my money back?"

Of course, after all this had happened, the King was more
angry than he had ever been before; and when he saw Drakesbill swimming about so coolly, while he had to stand on the
table to keep his feet dry, he could hardly hold himself.

"Bring the fellow here, and I'll finish him with the carving knife! bring him here quick!" he cried.

Two servants rushed out and seized Drakesbill very rudely.
They dragged him toward the King, who was standing with
drawn carving knife. The King's brave men with swords in
their hands were all around him. "It is all over with me
now," said Drakesbill. "I don't see how I can live through
this!"

But just then he thought of his neighbor Wasp-nest, and he
cried out:

"Wasp-nest, Wasp-nest, hither fly,
Or Drakesbill soon will have to die!"

Then Wasp-nest, who had been waiting for these words,
began to wake up his wasps, and things changed very
quickly.

"Buzz, buzz, buzz! Charge!" cried Wasp-nest. And the
wasps rushed out and threw themselves upon the King and
his brave men, and stung them so badly that they ran and
jumped right out from the windows, and nobody in the palace
ever saw them again.

As for Drakesbill, he could only sit still and wonder what
was going to happen next. But after a while he remembered
his money, and began to sing as before. Then, as the house
was very still, he thought that he might as well look around a

little while; perhaps he would find his hundred yellow pieces of gold.

It was of no use, however. He peeped into all the corners and opened all the drawers. There was not a dollar in the house. The King had spent everything.

By and by Drakesbill found his way into the room where the King's throne stood, and as he was very tired he sat down to rest among the cushions of velvet and gold.

When the people saw the King and his brave men running away from the wasps they felt sure that they would never come back. So they crowded into the palace to see what was the matter. And the only person they found there was little Drakesbill sitting by himself on the throne. Then they all shouted:

"The King is dead! long live the King!
How glad we'll be to be ruled by this thing!"

And one of them ran and fetched the golden crown; and they put it on Drakesbill's head and hailed him as King. And Drakesbill, who had made up his mind not to be surprised at anything, sat very still and took it all as a matter of course.

"He doesn't look much like a king," whispered a few idle fellows; but they were soon driven out of the hall and made to understand that it was wrong even to think such words.

"He will be the best king we have ever had," said others. And some who had known him before said: "A Drakesbill is better any day than a king who does nothing but spend our money."

And that is the way in which little Drakesbill became King. When he had been crowned, and the people had finished shouting, he made a speech from the throne. "Ladies and gentlemen," he said, "I am very hungry. Let us all go to supper."

THE FAIRY RING

Riquet with the Tuft

*O*NCE upon a time there was a Queen who had a son, so ugly and misshapen that it was doubted for a long time whether his form was really human. A fairy, who was present at his birth, affirmed, nevertheless, that he would be worthy to be loved, as he would have an excellent wit; she added, moreover, that by virtue of the gift she had bestowed upon him, he would be able to impart equal intelligence to the one whom he loved best. All this was some consolation to the poor Queen, who was much distressed at having brought so ugly a little monkey into the world. It is true that the child was no sooner able to speak than he said a thousand pretty things, and that in all his ways there was a certain air of intelligence, with which everyone was charmed. I had forgotten to say that he was born with a little tuft of hair on his head, and so he came to be called Riquet with the Tuft; for Riquet was the family name.

About seven or eight years later, the Queen of a neighboring kingdom had two daughters. The elder was fairer than the day, and the Queen was so delighted that it was feared some harm might come to her from her great joy. The same fairy who had assisted at the birth of little Riquet was present upon this occasion, and in order to moderate the joy of the Queen she told her that this little Princess would have no gifts of mind at all, and that she would be as stupid as she was beautiful. The Queen was greatly mortified on hearing this, but shortly after, she was even more annoyed when her second little daughter was born and proved to be extremely ugly. "Do not distress yourself, madam," said the fairy to her, "your daughter will find compensation, for she will have so much intelligence that her lack of beauty will scarcely be perceived."

"Heaven send it may be so!" replied the Queen; "but are there no means whereby a little more understanding might be given to the elder, who is so lovely?" "I can do nothing for her in the way of intelligence, madam," said the fairy, "but everything in the way of beauty; as, however, there is nothing in my power I would not do to give you comfort, I will bestow on her the power of conferring beauty on any man or woman who shall please her." As these two Princesses grew up their endowments also became more perfect, and nothing was talked of anywhere but the beauty of the elder and the intelligence of the younger. It is true that their defects also greatly increased with their years. The younger became uglier every moment, and the elder more stupid every day. She either made no answer when she was spoken to, or else said something foolish. With this she was so clumsy that she could not even place four pieces of china on a mantel shelf without breaking one of them, or drink a glass of water without spilling half of it on her dress. Notwithstanding the attraction of beauty, the younger, in whatever society they might be, nearly always bore away the palm from her sister. At first everyone went up to the more beautiful to gaze at and admire her; but they soon left her for the cleverer one, to listen to her many pleasant and amusing sayings; and people were astonished to find that in less than a quarter of an hour the elder had not a soul near her, while all the company had gathered around the younger. The elder, though very stupid, noticed this, and would have given, without regret, all her beauty for half the sense of her sister. Discreet as she was, the Queen could not help often reproaching her with her stupidity, which made the poor Princess ready to die of grief.

One day, when she had gone by herself into a wood to weep over her misfortune, she saw approaching her a little man of very ugly and unpleasant appearance, but magnificently dressed. It was the young Prince Riquet with the Tuft, who, having fallen in love with her from seeing her portraits, which were sent all over the world, had left his father's kingdom that he might have the pleasure of beholding her and speaking to her. Enchanted at meeting her thus alone, he addressed her with all the respect and politeness imaginable.

Having remarked, after paying her the usual compliments
that she was very melancholy, he said to her: "I cannot understand, madam, how a person as beautiful as you are can be
so unhappy as you appear; for, although I can boast of having seen an infinite number of beautiful people, I can say
with truth that I have never seen one whose beauty could be
compared with yours."

"You are pleased to say so, sir," replied the Princess, and
there she stopped.

"Beauty," continued Riquet, "is so great an advantage that
it ought to take the place of every other, and, possessed of
it, I see nothing that can have power to afflict one."

"I would rather," said the Princess, "be as ugly as you
are and have intelligence, than possess the beauty I do and
be as stupid as I am."

"There is no greater proof of intelligence, madam, than the
belief that we have it not; it is the nature of that gift, that the
more we have, the more we believe ourselves to be without it."

"I do not know how that may be," said the Princess, "but
I know well enough that I am very stupid, and this is the
cause of the grief that is killing me."

"If that is all that troubles you, madam, I can easily put
an end to your sorrow."

"And how would you do so?" said the Princess.

"I have the power, madam," said Riquet with the Tuft, "to
give as much intelligence as it is possible to possess to the person whom I love best; as you, madam, are that person, it will
depend entirely upon yourself whether or not you become
gifted with this amount of intelligence—provided that you are
willing to marry me."

The Princess was stricken dumb with astonishment, and replied not a word.

"I see," said Riquet with the Tuft, "that this proposal
troubles you, and I am not surprised, but I will give you a
full year to consider it."

The Princess had so little sense, and at the same time was
so anxious to have a great deal, that she thought the end

of that year would never come; so she at once accepted the offer that was made her. She had no sooner promised Riquet with the Tuft that she would marry him that day twelve months than she felt herself quite another person from what she had previously been. She found she was able to say whatever she pleased, with a readiness past belief, and to say it in a clever, but easy and natural manner. She immediately began a sprightly and well-sustained conversation with Riquet with the Tuft, and was so brilliant in her talk that the Prince began to think he had given her more wit than he had reserved for himself. On her return to the palace, the whole court was puzzled to account for a change so sudden and extraordinary; for instead of the number of foolish things which they had been accustomed to hear from her, she now made as many sensible and exceedingly witty remarks. All the court was in a state of joy not to be described. The younger sister alone was not altogether pleased, for, having lost her superiority over her sister in the way of intelligence, she now appeared by her side merely as a very unpleasing-looking person.

The King now began to be guided by his elder daughter's advice, and at times even held his council in her apartments. The news of the change of affairs was spread abroad, and all the young princes of the neighboring kingdoms exerted themselves to gain her affection, and nearly all of them asked her hand in marriage. She found none of them, however, intelligent enough to please her, and she listened to all of them without engaging herself to one.

At length arrived a prince so rich and powerful, so clever and so handsome, that she could not help listening willingly to his addresses. Her father, having perceived this, told her that he left her at perfect liberty to choose a husband for herself, and that she had only to make known her decision. As the more intelligence we possess, the more difficulty we find in making up our mind on such a matter as this, she begged her father, after having thanked him, to allow her time to think about it.

She went by chance to walk in the same wood in which
she had met Riquet with the Tuft, in order to meditate more
uninterruptedly over what she had to do. While she was
walking, deep in thought, she heard a dull sound beneath her
feet, as of many persons running to and fro and busily occupied. Having listened more attentively she heard one say,
"Bring me that saucepan"; another, "Give me that kettle";
another, "Put some wood on the fire." At the same moment the ground opened, and she saw beneath her what
appeared to be a large kitchen, full of cooks, scullions, and
all sorts of servants necessary for the preparation of a magnificent banquet. There came forth a band of about twenty
to thirty cooks, who went and established themselves in an
avenue of the wood, at a very long table, and who, each
with the larding pin in his hand and the tail of his fur
cap over his ear, set to work, keeping time to a harmonious
song.

The Princess, astonished at this sight, asked the men for
whom they were working.

"Madam," replied the chief among them, "for Prince
Riquet with the Tuft, whose marriage will take place to-
morrow." The Princess, still more surprised than she was
before, and suddenly recollecting that it was just a twelvemonth from the day on which she had promised to marry
Prince Riquet with the Tuft, was overcome with trouble and
amazement. The reason of her not having remembered her
promise was, that when she made it she had been a very
foolish person, and since she became gifted with the new
mind that the Prince had given her, she had forgotten all
her follies.

She had not taken another thirty steps when Riquet with
the Tuft presented himself before her, gaily and splendidly
attired, like a prince about to be married. "You see,
madam," said he, "I keep my word punctually, and I doubt
not that you have come hither to keep yours, and to make
me, by the giving of your hand, the happiest of men."

"I confess to you frankly," answered the Princess, "that

I have not yet made up my mind on that matter, and that I doubt if I shall ever be able to do so in the way you wish."

"You astonish me, madam," said Riquet with the Tuft.

"I have no doubt I do," said the Princess; "and assuredly, had I to deal with a stupid person, with a man without intelligence, I should feel greatly perplexed. 'A Princess is bound by her word,' he would say to me, 'and you must marry me, as you have promised to do so.' But as the person to whom I speak is, of all men in the world, the one of greatest sense and understanding, I am certain he will listen to reason. You know that, when I was no better than a fool, I nevertheless could not decide to marry you—how can you expect, now that I have the mind which you have given me, and which renders me much more difficult to please than before, that I should take to-day a resolution which I could not then? If you seriously thought of marrying me you did very wrong to take away my stupidity, and so enable me to see more clearly than I saw then."

"If a man without intelligence," replied Riquet with the Tuft, "who reproached you with your breach of promise, might have a right, as you have just intimated, to be treated with indulgence, why would you, madam, that I should receive less consideration in a matter which affects the entire happiness of my life? Is it reasonable that persons of intellect should be in a worse position than those that have none? Can you assert this—you who have so much, and who so earnestly desired to possess it? But let us come to the point, if you please. Setting aside my ugliness, is there anything in me that displeases you? Are you dissatisfied with my birth, my understanding, my temper, or my manners?"

"Not in the least," replied the Princess; "I admire in you everything you have mentioned."

"If that is so," rejoined Riquet with the Tuft, "I shall soon be happy, as you have it in your power to make me the most pleasing-looking of men."

"How can that be done?" asked the Princess.

"It can be done," said Riquet with the Tuft, "if you love

me sufficiently to wish that it should be. And in order, madam, that you should have no doubt about it, know that the same fairy who, on the day I was born, endowed me with the power to give intelligence to the person I chose, gave you also the power to render handsome the man you should love, and on whom you should wish to bestow this favor."

" If such be the fact," said the Princess, " I wish, with all my heart, that you should become the handsomest and most lovable Prince in the world, and I bestow the gift on you to the fullest extent in my power."

The Princess had no sooner pronounced these words than Riquet with the Tuft appeared to her eyes, of all men in the world, the handsomest, the best-made, and most attractive she had ever seen. There are some who assert that it was not the spell of the fairy, but love alone that caused this metamorphosis. They say that the Princess, having reflected on the preserverance of her lover, on his prudence, and on all the good qualities of his heart and mind, no longer saw the deformity of his body, or the ugliness of his features; that his hump appeared to her nothing more than a good-natured shrug of his shoulders, and that instead of noticing, as she had done, how badly he limped, she saw in him only a certain lounging air, which charmed her. They say also that his eyes, which squinted, only seemed to her the more brilliant for this; and that the crookedness of his glance was to her merely expressive of his great love; and, finally, that his great red nose had in it, to her mind, something martial and heroic. However this may be, the Princess promised on the spot to marry him, provided he obtained the consent of the King, her father. The King, having learned that his daughter entertained a great regard for Riquet with the Tuft, whom he knew also to be a very clever and wise Prince, received him with pleasure as his son-in-law. The wedding took place the next morning, as Riquet with the Tuft had foreseen, and according to the orders which he had given a long time before.

No beauty, no talent, has power above
Some indefinite charm discern'd only by love.

The White Cat

T HERE was once a king who had three sons, all handsome, brave, and noble of heart. Nevertheless, some wicked courtiers made their father believe they were eager to wear his crown, which, though he was old, he had no mind to resign. He therefore invented a plan to get them out of the kingdom and prevent their carrying out any undutiful projects. Sending for them to a private audience, he conversed with them kindly, and said: " You must be sensible, my dear children, that my great age prevents me from attending as closely as I have hitherto done to state affairs. I fear this may be injurious to my subjects; I therefore desire to place my crown on the head of one of you; but it is no more than just that, in return for such a present, you should procure me some amusement in my retirement, before I leave the capital forever. I cannot help thinking that a little dog, handsome, faithful, and engaging, would be the very thing to make me happy; so that, without bestowing a preference on either of you, I declare that he who brings me the most perfect little dog shall be my successor."

The Princes were much surprised at the fancy of their father to have a little dog, yet they accepted the proposition with pleasure; and accordingly, after taking leave of the King, who presented them with abundance of money and jewels, and appointed that day twelvemonth for their return, they set off on their travels.

Before separating, however, they took some refreshment together in an old palace about three miles out of town, where they mutually agreed to meet in the same place on that day twelvemonth, and go all together with their presents to court. They also agreed to change their names and travel incognito.

Each took a different road; but it is intended to relate the adventures of only the youngest, who was the most beautiful, amiable, and accomplished prince in the world. As he traveled from town to town, he bought all the handsome dogs that fell in his way; and as soon as he saw one that was handsomer than those he had, he made a present of the rest, for twenty servants would scarcely have been sufficient to take care of all the dogs he was continually purchasing. At length, wandering he knew not whither, he found himself in a forest; night suddenly came on, and with it a violent storm of thunder, lightning, and rain. To add to his perplexity, he lost his way. After he had groped about for a long time, he perceived a light, which made him suppose that he was not far from some house. He accordingly pursued his way toward it, and in a short time found himself at the gates of the most magnificent palace he had ever beheld. The entrance door was of gold, covered with sapphires, which shone so that scarcely could the strongest eyesight bear to look at it. This was the light the Prince had seen from the forest. The walls were of transparent porcelain, variously colored, and represented the history of all the fairies that had existed from the beginning of the world. The Prince, coming back to the golden door, observed a deer's foot fastened to a chain of diamonds; he could not help wondering at the magnificence he beheld, and the security in which the inhabitants seemed to live. "For," said he to himself, "nothing could be easier than for thieves to steal this chain, and as many of the sapphire stones as would make their fortunes." He pulled the chain and heard a bell, the sound of which was exquisite. In a few moments the door was opened; yet he perceived nothing but twelve hands in the air, each holding a torch. The Prince was so astonished that he durst not move a step—when he felt himself gently pushed on by some other hands from behind him. He walked on in great perplexity till he entered a vestibule inlaid with porphyry and lapis stone, where the most melodious voice he had ever heard chanted the following words:

> "Welcome, Prince, no danger fear,
> Mirth and love attend you here;
> You shall break the magic spell,
> That on a beauteous lady fell.

> "Welcome, Prince, no danger fear,
> Mirth and love attend you here."

The Prince now advanced with confidence, wondering what these words could mean; the hands moved him forward toward a large door of coral, which opened of itself to give him admittance into a splendid apartment built of mother-of-pearl, through which he passed into others, so richly adorned with paintings and jewels, and so resplendently lighted with thousands of lamps, girandoles, and lusters, that he imagined he must be in an enchanted palace. When he had passed through sixty apartments, all equally splendid, he was stopped by the hands, and a large easy chair advanced of itself toward the fireplace; then the hands, which he observed were extremely white and delicate, took off his wet clothes, and supplied their place with the finest linen imaginable, adding a comfortable wrapping gown embroidered with gold and pearls.

The hands next brought him an elegant dressing table, and combed his hair so very gently that he scarcely felt their touch. They held before him a beautiful basin, filled with perfumes, for him to wash his face and hands, and afterwards took off the wrapping gown and dressed him in a suit of clothes of still greater splendor. When his toilet was complete, they conducted him to an apartment he had not yet seen, and which also was magnificently furnished. There was a table spread for supper, and everything upon it was of the purest gold adorned with jewels. The Prince observed there were two covers set, and was wondering who was to be his companion, when his attention was suddenly caught by a small figure not a foot high which just then entered the room and advanced toward him. It had on a long black veil, and was supported by two cats dressed in mourning and with swords by their sides. They were followed by a numerous retinue of cats, some carrying cages full of rats, and others mouse traps full of mice.

The Prince was at a loss what to think. The little figure now approached, and throwing aside her veil, he beheld a most beautiful white cat. She seemed young and melancholy, and addressing herself to him, she said: "My Prince, you are welcome; your presence affords me the greatest pleasure."

"Madam," replied he, "I would fain thank you for your generosity, nor can I help observing that you must be an extraordinary creature to possess, with your present form, the gift of speech and the most magnificent palace I have ever seen."

"All this is very true," answered the beautiful cat; "but, Prince, I am not fond of talking, and least of all do I like compliments; let us therefore sit down to supper."

The trunkless hands then placed the dishes on the table, and the Prince and White Cat seated themselves at it. The first dish was a pie made of young pigeons, and the next was a fricassee of the fattest mice. The view of the one made the Prince almost afraid to taste the other, till the White Cat, who guessed his thoughts, assured him that there were certain dishes at table which had been dressed on purpose for him, in which there was not a morsel of either rat or mouse. Accordingly, he ate heartily of such as she recommended. When supper was over, he perceived that the White Cat had a portrait set in gold hanging to one of her feet. He begged her permission to look at it, when, to his astonishment, he saw the portrait of a handsome young man who exactly resembled himself! He thought there was something most extraordinary in all this; yet, as the White Cat sighed and looked very sorrowful, he did not venture to ask any questions. He conversed with her on different subjects, and found her extremely well versed in everything that was passing in the world. When night was far advanced, his hostess wished him a good night, and he was conducted by the hands to his bedchamber, which was different still from anything he had seen in the palace, being hung with the wings of butterflies mixed with the most curious feathers. His bed was of gauze, festooned with bunches of the gayest ribbons, and the looking-glasses reached from the floor to the ceiling. The Prince was undressed and put into bed by the hands without speaking a word. He, however, slept little, and in the morning was awakened by a confused noise. The hands took him out of bed and put on him a handsome hunting jacket. He looked into the courtyard and perceived more than five hundred cats busily employed in preparing for the field—for this was a day of festival. Presently the White Cat came to his apartment, and having politely inquired after his health, she invited him to partake of their amusement. The Prince willingly acceded, and mounted a wooden horse, richly caparisoned, which had been prepared for him, and which he was assured would gallop to admiration. The beautiful White Cat mounted a monkey; she wore a dragoon's cap, which made her look so fierce that all the rats and mice ran away in the utmost terror.

Everything being ready, the horns sounded and away they went. No hunting was ever more agreeable. The cats ran faster than the hares and rabbits, and when they caught any they turned them out to be hunted in the presence of the White Cat, and a thousand cunning tricks were played. Nor were the birds in safety, for the monkey made nothing of climbing up the trees with the White Cat on his back, to the nests of the young eagles. When the chase was over, the whole retinue returned to the palace. The White Cat immediately exchanged her dragoon's cap for the veil, and sat down to supper with the Prince, who, being very hungry, ate heartily, and afterwards partook with her of the most delicious wines. He then was conducted to his chamber as before, and wakened in the morning to renew the same sort of life, which day after day became so charming to him that he no longer thought of anything but of pleasing the sweet little creature who received him so courteously. Accordingly, every day was spent in new amusements. The Prince had almost forgotten his country and relations, and sometimes even regretted that he was not a cat, so great was his affection for his mewing companions.

"Alas!" said he to the White Cat, "how will it afflict me to leave you, whom I love so much! Either make yourself a lady or make me a cat." She smiled at the Prince's wish, but offered no reply.

At length the twelvemonth was nearly expired. The White Cat, who knew the very day when the Prince was to reach his father's palace, reminded him that he had but three days longer to look for a perfect little dog. The Prince, astonished at his own forgetfulness, began to afflict himself, when the cat told him not to be so sorrowful, since she would not only provide him with a little dog, but also with a wooden horse which should convey him safely home in less than twelve hours.

" Look here," said she, showing him an acorn, " this contains what you desire."

The Prince put the acorn to his ear, and heard the barking of a little dog. Transported with joy, he thanked the cat a thousand times, and the next day, bidding her tenderly adieu, he set out on his return.

The Prince arrived first at the place of rendezvous, and was soon joined by his brothers. They mutually embraced, and began to give an account of their success, when the youngest showed them only a little mongrel cur, telling them that he thought it could not fail to please the King, from its extraordinary beauty. The brothers trod on each other's toes under the table, as much as to say, "We have little to fear from this sorry-looking animal." The next day they went together to the palace. The dogs of the two elder brothers were lying on cushions, and so curiously wrapped around with embroidered quilts that one would scarcely venture to touch them. The youngest produced his cur, and all wondered how the Prince could hope to receive a crown for such a shabby present. The King examined the two little dogs of the elder Princes, and declared he thought them so equally beautiful that he knew not to which, with justice, he could give the preference. They accordingly began to dispute, when the youngest Prince, taking his acorn from his pocket, soon ended their contention; for a little dog appeared which could with ease go through the smallest ring, and was besides a miracle of beauty. The King could not possibly hesitate in declaring his satisfaction; yet, as he was not more inclined than the year before to part with his crown, he told his sons that he was extremely obliged to them for the pains they had taken, and since they had succeeded so well, he wished they would make a second attempt;

THE FAIRY RING

he therefore begged they would take another year in order to procure a piece of cambric fine enough to be drawn through the eye of a small needle.

The three Princes thought this very hard; yet they set out, in obedience to the King's command. The two eldest took different roads, and the youngest remounted his wooden horse, and in a short time arrived at the palace of his beloved White Cat, who received him with the greatest joy, while the trunkless hands helped him to dismount and provided him with immediate refreshment. Afterwards the Prince gave the White Cat an account of the admiration which had been bestowed on the beautiful little dog, and informed her of the further injunction of his father.

"Make yourself perfectly easy, dear Prince," said she; "I have in my palace some cats who are perfect adepts in making such cambric as the King requires; so you have nothing to do but to give me the pleasure of your company while it is making and I will procure you all the amusement possible."

She accordingly ordered the most curious fireworks to be played off in sight of the window of the apartment in which they were sitting, and nothing but festivity and rejoicing was heard throughout the palace for the Prince's return. As the White Cat frequently gave proofs of an excellent understanding, the Prince was by no means tired of her company; she talked with him of state affairs, of theaters, of fashions—in short, she was at a loss on no subject whatever; so that when the Prince was alone he had plenty of amusement in thinking how it could possibly be that a small white cat should be endowed with all the attractions of the very best and most charming of women.

The twelvemonth in this manner again passed insensibly away, but the cat took care to remind the Prince of his duty in proper time. "For once, my Prince," said she, "I will have the pleasure of equipping you as suits your high rank." And, looking into the courtyard, he saw a superb car, ornamented all over with gold, silver, pearls, and diamonds, drawn by twelve horses as white as snow, and harnessed in the most sumptuous trappings; and behind the car a thousand guards, richly appareled, were waiting to attend on the Prince's person. She then presented him with a nut: " You will find in it," said she, " the piece of cambric I promised you; do not break the shell till you are in the presence of the King your father." Then, to prevent the acknowledgments which the Prince was about to offer, she hastily bade him adieu.

Nothing could exceed the speed with which the snow-white horses conveyed this fortunate Prince to his father's palace, where his brothers had just arrived before him. They embraced each other, and demanded an immediate audience of the King, who received them with the greatest of kindness. The Princes hastened to place at the feet of his majesty the curious present he had required them to procure. The eldest produced a piece of cambric so extremely fine that his friends had no doubt of its passing through the eye of a needle, which was now delivered to the King, having been kept locked up in the custody of his majesty's treasurer all the time. But when the King tried to draw the cambric through the eye of the needle it would not pass, though it failed but very little. Then came the second Prince, who made as sure of obtaining the crown as his brother had done, but, alas! with no better success; for though his piece of cambric was exquisitely fine, yet it could not be drawn through the eye of the needle. It was now the turn of the youngest Prince, who accordingly advanced, and opening an elegant little box inlaid with jewels, took out a walnut and cracked the shell, imagining he should immediately perceive his piece of cambric; but what was his astonishment to see nothing but a filbert! He did not, however, lose his hopes; he cracked the filbert, and it presented him with a cherry stone. The lords of the court, who had assembled to witness this extraordinary trial, could not, any more than the Princes his brothers, refrain from laughing, to think he should be so silly as to claim the crown on no better pretensions. The Prince, however, cracked the cherry stone, which was filled with a kernel; he divided it, and found in the middle a grain of wheat, and in that a grain of millet seed. He was now absolutely confounded, and could not help muttering between his teeth, " O White Cat, White Cat, thou hast deceived me! " At this instant he felt his hand scratched by the claw of a cat, upon which he again took courage, and opening the grain of millet seed, to the astonishment of all present he drew forth a piece of cambric four hundred yards long, and fine enough to be threaded with perfect ease through the eye of the needle.

When the King found he had no pretext left for refusing the crown to his youngest son, he sighed deeply, and it was easy to be seen that he was sorry for the Prince's success.

" My sons," said he, " it is so gratifying to the heart of a father to receive proofs of his children's love and obedience, that I cannot refuse myself the satisfaction of requiring of you one thing more. You must undertake another expedition. That one of you who, by the end of the year, brings me the most beautiful lady shall marry her and obtain my crown."

So they again took leave of the King and of each other, and set out without delay; and in less than twelve hours our young Prince arrived, in his splendid car, at the palace of his dear White Cat. Everything went on as before till the end of another year. At length only one day remained of the year, when the White Cat thus addressed him: " To-morrow, my Prince, you must present yourself at the palace of your father and give him a proof of your obedience. It depends only on yourself to conduct thither the most beautiful princess ever yet beheld, for the time is come when the enchantment by which I am bound may be ended. You must cut off my head and tail," continued she, " and throw them into the fire."

" I! " said the Prince hastily—" I cut off your head and tail! You surely mean to try my affection, which, believe me, beautiful cat, is truly yours."

" You mistake me, generous Prince," said she; " I do not doubt your regard, but if you wish to see me in any other form than that of a cat you must consent to do as I desire, when you will have done me a service I shall never be able sufficiently to repay."

THE FAIRY RING

The Prince's eyes filled with tears as she spoke, yet he considered himself obliged to undertake the dreadful task; and the cat continuing to press him with the greatest eagerness, with a trembling hand he drew his sword, cut off her head and tail, and threw them into the fire. No sooner was this done than the most beautiful lady his eyes had ever seen stood before him, and ere he had sufficiently recovered from his surprise to speak to her, a long train of attendants, who at the same moment as their mistress were changed to their natural shapes, came to offer their congratulations to the Queen and inquire her commands. She received them with the greatest kindness, and ordering them to withdraw, thus addressed the astonished Prince:

"Do not imagine, dear Prince, that I have always been a cat, or that I am of obscure birth. My father was the monarch of six kingdoms; he tenderly loved my mother, and left her always at liberty to follow her own inclinations. Her prevailing passion was to travel, and a short time before my birth, having heard of some fairies who were in possession of the largest gardens filled with the most delicious fruits, she had so strong a desire to eat some of them that she set out for the country where they lived. She arrived at their abode, which she found to be a magnificent palace, glittering on all sides with gold and precious stones. She knocked a long time at the gates, but no one came, nor could she perceive the least sign that it had any inhabitant. The difficulty, however, did but increase the violence of my mother's longing, for she saw the tops of the trees above the garden walls loaded with the most luscious fruits. The Queen, in despair, ordered her attendants to place tents close to the door of the palace; but, having waited six weeks without seeing anyone pass the gates, she fell sick of vexation and her life was despaired of.

"One night, as she lay half asleep, she turned herself about, and opening her eyes, perceived a little old woman, very ugly and deformed, seated in the easy chair by her bedside. 'I and my sister fairies,' said she, 'take it very ill that your majesty should so obstinately persist in getting some of our fruit:

[225]

but since so precious a life is at stake, we consent to give you as much as you can carry away provided you will give us in return what we shall ask.' ' Ah, kind fairy!' cried the Queen, 'I will give you anything that I possess, even my very kingdoms, on condition that I eat of your fruit.' The old fairy then informed the Queen that what they required was that she should give them the child she was going to have as soon as it should be born, adding that every possible care should be taken of it, and that it should become the most accomplished princess. The Queen replied that however cruel the conditions she must accept them, since nothing but the fruit could save her life. In short, dear Prince," continued the lady, " my mother instantly got out of bed, was dressed by her attendants, entered the palace, and satisfied her longing. Having eaten her fill, she ordered four thousand mules to be procured and loaded with the fruit, which had the virtue of continuing all the year round in a state of perfection. Thus provided, she returned to the King my father, who, with the whole court, received her with rejoicings, as it was before imagined she would die of disappointment. All this time the Queen said nothing to my father of the promise she had made to give her daughter to the fairies, so that when the time was come that she expected my birth she grew very melancholy; till at length, being pressed by the King, she declared to him the truth. Nothing could exceed his affliction when he heard that his only child, when born, was to be given to the fairies. He bore it, however, as well as he could for fear of adding to my mother's grief, and also believing he should find some means of keeping me in a place of safety, which the fairies would not be able to approach. As soon, therefore, as I was born, he had me conveyed to a tower in the palace, to which there were twenty flights of stairs and a door to each, of which my father kept the key, so that none came near me without his consent. When the fairies heard of what had been done, they sent first to demand me, and on my father's refusal, they let loose a monstrous dragon, which devoured men, women, and children, and which, by the breath of its nostrils, destroyed everything it came near, so that even the trees and plants began to die. The grief of the King was excessive, and, finding that his whole kingdom would in a short time be reduced to famine, he consented to give me into their hands. I was accordingly laid in a cradle of mother-of-pearl, ornamented with gold and jewels, and carried to their palace, when the dragon immediately disappeared. The fairies placed me in a tower, elegantly furnished, but to which there was no door, so that whoever approached was obliged to come by the windows, which were a great height from the ground. From these I had the liberty of getting out into a delightful garden, in which were baths, and every sort of cooling fruit. In this place was I educated by the fairies, who behaved to me with the greatest kindness; my clothes were splendid, and I was instructed in every kind of accomplishment; in short, Prince, if I had never seen anyone but themselves I should have remained very happy. One day, however, as I was talking at the window with my parrot, I perceived a young gentleman who was listening to our conversation. As I had never seen a man but in pictures, I was not sorry for the opportunity of gratifying my curiosity. I thought him a very pleasing object, and he at length bowed in the most respectful manner, without daring to speak, for he knew that I was in the palace of the fairies. When it began to grow dark he went away, and I vainly endeavored to see which road he took. The next morning, as soon as it was light, I again placed myself at the window, and had the pleasure of seeing that the gentleman had returned to the same place. He now spoke to me through a speaking trumpet, and informed me he thought me a most charming lady, and that he should be very unhappy if he did not pass his life in my company.

"I resolved to find some means of escaping from my tower, and was not long in devising the means for the execution of my project. I begged the fairies to bring me a netting needle, a mesh, and some cord, saying I wished to make some nets to amuse myself with catching birds at my window. This they readily complied with, and in a short time I completed a ladder long enough to reach to the ground. I now sent my parrot to the Prince to beg he would come to the usual place, as I wished to speak with him. He did not fail; and finding the ladder, mounted it, and quickly entered my tower. This at first alarmed me, but the charms of his conversation had restored me to tranquillity, when all at once the window opened, and the Fairy Violent, mounted on the dragon's back, rushed into the tower. My beloved Prince thought of nothing but how to defend me from their fury, for I had had time to relate to him my story previous to this cruel interruption, but their numbers overpowered him, and the Fairy Violent had the barbarity to command the dragon to devour my lover before my eyes. In my despair I would have thrown myself also into the mouth of the horrible monster, but this they took care to prevent, saying my life should be preserved for greater punishment. The fairy then touched me with her wand and I instantly became a white cat. She next conducted me to this palace, which belonged to my father, and gave me a train of cats for my attendants, together with the twelve hands that waited on your highness. She then informed me of my birth and the death of my parents, and pronounced upon me what she imagined the greatest of maledictions; that I should not be restored to my natural figure until a young prince, the perfect resemblance of him I had lost, should cut off my head and tail. You are that perfect resemblance, and accordingly you ended the enchantment. I need not add that I already love you more than my life; let us therefore hasten to the palace of the King your father, and obtain his approbation to our marriage."

The Prince and Princess accordingly set out side by side, in a car of still greater splendor than before, and reached the palace just as the two brothers had arrived with two beautiful princesses. The King, hearing that each of his sons had succeeded in finding what he had required, again began to think of some new expedient to delay the time of his resigning the crown; but when the whole court with the King was assembled to pass judgment, the Princess who accompanied the youngest, perceiving his thoughts by his countenance, stepped majestically forward and thus addressed him:

"It is a pity that your majesty, who is so capable of governing, should think of resigning the crown! I am fortunate enough to have six kingdoms in my possession; permit me to bestow one on each of the eldest princes, and to enjoy the remaining four in the society of the youngest. And may it please your majesty to keep your own kingdom, and make no decision concerning the beauty of three princesses, who, without such a proof of your majesty's preference, will no doubt live happily together!"

The air resounded with the applauses of the assembly. The young Prince and Princess embraced the King, and next their brothers and sisters. The three weddings immediately took place, and the kingdoms were divided as the Princess had proposed.

Prince Cherry

LONG ago there lived a monarch who was such a very honest man that his subjects entitled him the Good King. One day, when he was out hunting, a little white rabbit, which had been half killed by his hounds, leaped right into his majesty's arms. Said he, caressing it: "This poor creature has put itself under my protection, and I will allow no one to injure it." So he carried it to his palace, had prepared for it a neat little rabbit hutch, with abundance of the daintiest food such as rabbits love, and there he left it.

The same night, when he was alone in his chamber, there appeared to him a beautiful lady. She was dressed neither in gold, nor silver, nor brocade, but her flowing robes were white as snow, and she wore a garland of white roses on her head. The Good King was greatly astonished at the sight, for his door was locked, and he wondered how so dazzling a lady could possibly enter; but she soon removed his doubts.

"I am the Fairy Candide," said she, with a smiling and

gracious air. "Passing through the wood where you were hunting, I took a desire to know if you were as good as men say you are. I therefore changed myself into a white rabbit, and took refuge in your arms. You saved me and now I know that those who are merciful to dumb beasts will be ten times more so to human beings. You merit the name your subjects give you: you are the Good King. I thank you for your protection, and shall be always one of your best friends. You have but to say what you most desire, and I promise you your wish shall be granted."

"Madam," replied the King, "if you are a fairy, you must know without my telling you the wish of my heart. I have one well-beloved son, Prince Cherry. Whatever kindly feeling you have toward me, extend it to him."

"Willingly," said Candide. "I will make him the hand-somest, richest, or most powerful prince in the world. Choose whichever you desire for him."

"None of the three," returned the father. "I only wish him to be good—the best prince in the whole world. Of what use would riches, power, or beauty be to him if he were an evil man?"

"You are right," said the fairy; "but I cannot make him good. He must do that himself. I can only change his external fortunes; for his personal character the utmost I can promise is to give him good counsel, reprove him for his faults, and even punish him if he will not punish himself. You mortals can do the same with your children."

"Ah, yes!" said the King, sighing. Still he felt that the kindness of a fairy was something gained for his son, and died not long after, content and at peace.

Prince Cherry mourned deeply, for he dearly loved his father, and would have gladly given all his kingdoms and treasures to keep him in life a little longer. Two days after the Good King was no more, Prince Cherry was sleeping in his chamber when he saw the same dazzling vision of the Fairy Candide.

"I promised your father," said she, "to be your best friend, and in pledge of this take what I now give you"; and she placed a small gold ring upon his finger. "Poor as it looks, it is more precious than diamonds, for whenever you do ill it will prick your finger. If, after that warning, you still continue in evil, you will lose my friendship and I shall become your direst enemy."

So saying she disappeared, leaving Cherry in such amazement that he would have believed it all a dream save for the ring on his finger.

He was for a long time so good that the ring never pricked him at all, and this made him so cheerful and pleasant in his humor that everybody called him "Happy Prince Cherry." But one unlucky day he was out hunting and found no sport, which vexed him so much that he showed his ill temper by his looks and ways. He fancied his ring felt very tight and uncomfortable, but as it did not prick him he took no heed of this, until, reëntering his palace, his little pet dog, Bibi, jumped up upon him, and was sharply told to get away. The creature, accustomed to nothing but caresses, tried to attract his attention by pulling at his garments, when Prince Cherry turned and gave it a severe kick. At this moment he felt in his finger a prick like a pin.

"What nonsense!" said he to himself. "The fairy must be making game of me. Why, what great evil have I done! I, the master of a great empire, cannot I kick my own dog?"

A voice replied, or else Prince Cherry imagined it: "No, sire; the master of a great empire has a right to do good, but not evil. I—a fairy—am as much above you as you are above your dog. I might punish you, kill you, if I chose; but I prefer leaving you to amend your ways. You have been guilty of three faults to-day—bad temper, passion, cruelty. Do better to-morrow."

The Prince promised, and kept his word awhile; but he had been brought up by a foolish nurse who indulged him in every way, and was always telling him that he would be a king one day, when he might do as he liked in all things. He found out now that even a king cannot always do that; it vexed him and made him angry. His ring began to prick him so often that his little finger was continually bleeding. He disliked this, as was natural, and soon began to consider whether it would not be easier to throw the ring away altogether than to be constantly annoyed by it. It was such a queer thing for a king to have always a spot of blood on his finger! At last, unable to put up with it any more, he took his ring off and hid it where he would never see it, and believed himself the happiest of men, for he could now do exactly what he liked. He did it, and became every day more and more miserable.

One day he saw a young girl so beautiful that, being always accustomed to have his own way, he immediately determined to espouse her. He never doubted that she would be only too glad to be made a queen, for she was very poor. But Zelia— that was her name—answered, to his great astonishment, that she would rather not marry him.

"Do I displease you?" asked the Prince, into whose mind it had never entered that he could displease anybody.

"Not at all, my Prince," said the honest peasant maiden. "You are very handsome, very charming; but you are not like your father the Good King. I will not be your queen, for you would make me miserable."

At these words the Prince's love seemed all to turn to hatred. He gave orders to his guards to convey Zelia to a prison near the palace, and then took counsel with his foster brother, the one of all his evil companions who most incited him to do wrong.

"Sire," said this man, "if I were in your majesty's place, I would never vex myself about a poor silly girl. Feed her on bread and water till she comes to her senses, and if she still refuses you, let her die in torment, as a warning to your other subjects should they venture to dispute your will. You will be disgraced should you suffer yourself to be conquered by a simple girl."

"But," said Prince Cherry, "shall I not be disgraced if I harm a creature so perfectly innocent?"

"No one is innocent who disputes your majesty's authority,"

said the courtier bowing; "and it is better to commit an in-
justice than allow it to be supposed you can ever be contradicted with impunity."

This touched Cherry on his weak point—his good impulses
faded; he resolved once more to ask Zelia if she would marry
him, and if she again refused, to sell her as a slave. Arrived at
the cell in which she was confined, what was his astonishment
to find her gone! He knew not whom to accuse, for he had
kept the key in his pocket the whole time. At last the foster
brother suggested that the escape of Zelia might have been
contrived by an old man, Suliman by name, the Prince's former tutor, who was the only one who now ventured to blame
him for anything that he did. Cherry sent immediately and
ordered his old friend to be brought to him loaded heavily
with irons. Then, full of fury, he went and shut himself up
in his own chamber, where he went raging to and fro, till
startled by a noise like a clap of thunder. The Fairy Candide
stood before him.

"Prince," said she in a severe voice, "I promised your
father to give you good counsels, and to punish you if you
refused to follow them. My counsels were forgotten, my pun-
ishments despised. Under the figure of a man you have been
no better than the beasts you chase. Like a lion in fury, a
wolf in gluttony, a serpent in revenge, and a bull in brutality.
Take, therefore, in your new form the likeness of all these
animals."

Scarcely had Prince Cherry heard these words than to his
horror he found himself transformed into what the fairy
had named. He was a creature with the head of a lion, the
horns of a bull, the feet of a wolf, and the tail of a serpent.
At the same time he felt himself transported to a distant forest where, standing on the bank of a stream, he saw reflected
in the water his own frightful shape, and heard a voice
saying:

"Look at thyself, and know that thy soul has become a
thousand times uglier even than thy body."

Cherry recognized the voice of Candide, and in his rage

would have sprung upon her and devoured her; but he saw nothing, and the same voice said behind him:

"Cease thy feeble fury, and learn to conquer thy pride by being in submission to thine own subjects."

Hearing no more, he soon quitted the stream, hoping at least to get rid of the sight of himself; but he had scarcely gone twenty paces when he tumbled into a pitfall that was laid to catch bears; the bear hunters, descending from some trees hard by, caught him, chained him, and, only too delighted to get hold of such a curious-looking animal, led him along with them to the capital of his own kingdom.

There great rejoicings were taking place, and the bear hunters, asking what it was all about, were told that it was because Prince Cherry, the torment of his subjects, had just been struck dead by a thunderbolt—just punishment of all his crimes. Four courtiers, his wicked companions, had wished to divide his throne between them, but the people had risen up against them and offered the crown to Suliman, the old tutor whom Cherry had ordered to be arrested.

All this the poor monster heard. He even saw Suliman sitting upon his own throne, and trying to calm the populace by representing to them that it was not certain Prince Cherry was dead; that he might return one day to reassume with honor the crown which Suliman only consented to wear as a sort of viceroy.

"I know his heart," said the honest and faithful old man; "it is tainted, but not corrupt. If alive, he may yet reform, and be all his father over again to you, his people, whom he has caused to suffer so much."

These words touched the poor beast so deeply that he ceased to beat himself against the iron bars of the cage in which the hunters carried him about, became gentle as a lamb, and suffered himself to be taken quietly to a menagerie, where were kept all sorts of strange and ferocious animals—a place which he had often visited as a boy, but in which he never thought he should be shut up himself.

However, he owned he had deserved it all, and began to

make amends by showing himself very obedient to his keeper.
This man was almost as great a brute as the animals he had
charge of, and when he was in ill humor he used to beat them
without rhyme or reason. One day, while he was sleeping,
a tiger broke loose and leaped upon him, eager to devour him.
Cherry at first felt a thrill of pleasure at the thought of being
revenged; then, seeing how helpless the man was, he wished
himself free, that he might defend him. Immediately the doors
of his cage opened. The keeper, waking up, saw the strange
beast leap out, and imagined, of course, that he was going
to be slain at once. Instead, he saw the tiger lying dead, and
the strange beast creeping up and laying itself at his feet to be
caressed. But as he lifted up his hand to stroke it, a voice was
heard saying, " Good actions never go unrewarded "; and, instead of the frightful monster, there crouched on the ground
nothing but a pretty little dog.

Cherry, delighted to find himself thus metamorphosed, caressed the keeper in every possible way, till at last the man
took him up in his arms and carried him to the King, to
whom he related this wonderful story from beginning to end.
The Queen wished to have the charming little dog, and Cherry
would have been exceedingly happy could he have forgotten
that he was originally a man and a King. He was lodged most
elegantly, had the richest of collars to adorn his neck, and
heard himself praised continually. But his beauty rather
brought him into trouble, for the Queen, afraid lest he might
grow too large for a pet, took advice of dog doctors, who
ordered that he should be fed entirely upon bread, and that
very sparingly, so poor Cherry was sometimes nearly starved.

One day when they gave him his crust for breakfast, a fancy
seized him to go and eat it in the palace garden; so he took the
bread in his mouth and trotted away toward a stream which
he knew, and where he sometimes stopped to drink. But instead of the stream he saw a splendid palace glittering with
gold and precious stones. Entering the doors was a crowd of
men and women magnificently dressed, and within there was
singing and dancing and good cheer of all sorts. Yet, how-

ever grandly and gayly the people went in, Cherry noticed that those who came out were pale, thin, ragged, half-naked, covered with wounds and sores. Some of them dropped dead at once; others dragged themselves on a little way and then lay down, dying of hunger, and vainly begged a morsel of bread from others who were entering in—who never took the least notice of them.

Cherry perceived one woman who was trying feebly to gather and eat some green herbs. "Poor thing!" said he to himself; "I know what it is to be hungry, and I want my breakfast badly enough; but still it will not kill me to wait till dinner time, and my crust may save the life of this poor woman."

So the little dog ran up to her and dropped his bread at her feet; she picked it up and ate it with avidity. Soon she looked quite recovered, and Cherry, delighted, was trotting back again to his kennel when he heard loud cries, and saw a young girl dragged by four men to the door of the palace, which they were trying to compel her to enter. Oh, how he wished himself a monster again, as when he slew the tiger!—for the young girl was no other than his beloved Zelia. Alas! what could a poor little dog do to defend her? But he ran forward and barked at the men, and bit their heels, until at last they chased him away with heavy blows. And then he lay down outside the palace door, determined to watch and see what had become of Zelia.

Conscience pricked him now. "What!" thought he, "I am furious against these wicked men, who are carrying her away, and did I not do the same myself? Did I not cast her into prison and intend to sell her as a slave? Who knows how much more wickedness I might not have done to her and others if Heaven's justice had not stopped me in time?"

While he lay thinking and repenting, he heard a window open, and saw Zelia throw out of it a bit of dainty meat. Cherry, who felt hungry enough by this time, was just about to eat it when the woman to whom he had given his crust snatched him up in her arms.

"Poor little beast!" cried she, patting him, "every bit of food in that palace is poisoned. You shall not touch a morsel."

At the same time the voice in the air repeated again, "Good actions never go unrewarded"; and Cherry found himself changed into a beautiful little white pigeon. He remembered with joy that white was the color of the Fairy Candide, and began to hope that she was taking him into favor again.

So he stretched his wings, delighted that he might now have a chance of approaching his fair Zelia. He flew up to the palace windows, and, finding one of them open, entered and sought everywhere, but he could not find Zelia. Then, in despair, he flew out again, resolved to go over the world until he beheld her once more.

He took flight at once, and traversed many countries, swiftly as a bird can, but found no trace of his beloved. At length in a desert, sitting beside an old hermit in his cave and partaking with him his frugal repast, Cherry saw a poor peasant girl, and recognized Zelia. Transported with joy he flew in, perched on her shoulder, and expressed his delight and affection by a thousand caresses.

She, charmed with the pretty little pigeon, caressed it in her turn, and promised it that, if it would stay with her, she would love it always.

"What have you done, Zelia?" said the hermit, smiling; and while he spoke the white pigeon vanished, and there stood Prince Cherry in his own natural form. "Your enchantment ended, Prince, when Zelia promised to love you. Indeed, she has loved you always, but your many faults constrained her to hide her love. These are now amended, and you may both live happy if you will, because your union is founded upon mutual esteem."

Cherry and Zelia threw themselves at the feet of the hermit, whose form also began to change. His soiled garments became of dazzling whiteness, and his long beard and withered face grew into the flowing hair and lovely countenance of the Fairy Candide.

"Rise up, my children," said she; "I must now transport

you to your palace, and restore to Prince Cherry his father's crown, of which he is now worthy."

She had scarcely ceased speaking when they found themselves in the chamber of Suliman, who, delighted to find again his beloved pupil and master, willingly resigned the throne, and became the most faithful of his subjects.

King Cherry and Queen Zelia reigned together for many years, and it is said that the former was so blameless and strict in all his duties that though he constantly wore the ring which Candide had restored him, it never once pricked his finger enough to make it bleed.

The Wild Swans

FAR away in the land to which the swallows fly when it is winter, dwelt a king who had eleven sons, and one daughter named Eliza. The eleven brothers were princes, and each went to school with a star on his breast and a sword by his side. They wrote with diamond pencils on gold slates, and learned their lessons so quickly and read so easily that everyone might know they were princes. Their sister Eliza sat on a little stool of plate glass, and had a book full of pictures which had cost as much as half a kingdom. Oh, these children were indeed happy, but they were not to remain so always. Their father, who was King of the country, married a very wicked Queen who did not love the poor children at all. They knew this from the very first day after the wedding. In the palace there were great festivities, and the children played at receiving company; but instead of having, as usual, all the cakes and apples that were left, she gave them some sand in a teacup and told them to pretend it was cake. The week after she sent little Eliza into the country to a peasant and his wife, and then she told the King so many untrue things about the young princes that he gave himself no more trouble respecting them.

THE FAIRY RING

"Go out into the world and get your own living," said the
Queen. "Fly like great birds who have no voice." But she
could not make them ugly as she wished, for they were turned
into eleven beautiful wild swans. Then, with a strange cry,
they flew through the windows of the palace, over the park, to
the forest beyond. It was yet early morning when they passed
the peasant's cottage, where their sister Eliza lay asleep in her
room. They hovered over the roof, twisted their long necks,
and flapped their wings; but no one heard them or saw them,
so they were at last obliged to fly away, high up in the clouds;
and over the wide world they flew till they came to a thick,
dark wood, which stretched far away to the seashore. Poor
little Eliza was alone in her room playing with a green leaf,
for she had no other playthings, and she pierced a hole through
the leaf and looked through it at the sun, and it was as if she
saw her brothers' clear eyes, and when the warm sun shone
on her cheeks she thought of all the kisses they had given her.
One day passed just like another; sometimes the winds rustled
through the leaves of the rosebush, and would whisper to the
roses, "Who can be more beautiful than you?" But the roses
would shake their heads and say, "Eliza is." And when the old
woman sat at the cottage door on Sunday and read her hymn
book, the wind would flutter the leaves and say to the book,
"Who can be more pious than you?" and then the hymn book
would answer, "Eliza." And the roses and the hymn book
told the real truth. At fifteen she returned home, but when the
Queen saw how beautiful she was, she became full of spite and
hatred toward her. Willingly would she have turned her into
a swan, like her brothers, but she did not dare to do so yet,
because the King wished to see his daughter. Early one morning the Queen went into the bathroom; it was built of marble,
and had soft cushions trimmed with the most beautiful tapestry.
She took three toads with her and kissed them, and said to
one: "When Eliza comes to the bath, seat yourself upon her
head, that she may become as stupid as you are." Then she
said to another: "Place yourself on her forehead, that she may
become as ugly as you are, and that her father may not know

[239]

her." "Rest on her heart," she whispered to the third, "then she will have evil inclinations, and suffer in consequence." So she put the toads into clear water, and they turned green immediately. She next called Eliza and helped her to undress and get into the bath. As Eliza dipped her head under the water one of the toads sat on her hair, a second on her forehead, and a third on her breast, but she did not seem to notice them, and when she rose out of the water there were three red poppies floating upon it. Had not the creatures been venomous or been kissed by the witch they would have been changed into red roses. At all events they became flowers, because they had rested on Eliza's head, and on her heart. She was too good and too innocent for witchcraft to have any power over her. When the wicked Queen saw this, she rubbed her face with walnut juice, so that she was quite brown; then she tangled her beautiful hair and smeared it with disgusting ointment, till it was quite impossible to recognize the beautiful Eliza.

When her father saw her, he was much shocked and declared she was not his daughter. No one but the watchdog and the swallows knew her, and they were only dumb animals and could say nothing. Then poor Eliza wept, and thought of her eleven brothers who were all away. Sorrowfully she stole away from the palace, and walked the whole day over fields and moors till she came to the great forest. She knew not in what direction to go; but she was so unhappy and longed so for her brothers who had been, like herself, driven out into the world, that she was determined to seek them. She had been but a short time in the wood when night came on, and she quite lost the path; so she laid herself down on the soft moss, offered up her evening prayer, and leaned her head against the stump of a tree. All nature was still, and the soft, mild air fanned her forehead. The light of hundreds of glow-worms shone amidst the grass and the moss, like green fire; and if she touched a twig with her hand ever so lightly, the brilliant fireflies fell down around her like shooting stars.

All night long she dreamed of her brothers. She and they

were children again playing together. She saw them writing with their diamond pencils on golden slates, while she looked at the beautiful picture book which had cost half a kingdom. They were not writing lines and letters, as they used to do, but descriptions of the noble deeds they had performed, and of all they had discovered and seen. In the picture book, too, everything was living. The birds sang, and the people came out of the book and spoke to Eliza and her brothers; but, as the leaves turned over they darted back again to their places, that all might be in order.

When she awoke the sun was high in the heavens, yet she could scarcely see him, for the lofty trees spread their branches thickly over her head, and his beams were glancing through the leaves here and there like a golden mist. There was a sweet fragrance from the fresh verdure, and the birds almost perched upon her shoulders. She heard water rippling from a number of springs, all flowing into a lake with golden sands. Bushes grew thickly around the lake, and at one spot an opening had been made by a deer, through which Eliza went down to the water. The lake was so clear that, had not the wind rustled the branches of the trees and the bushes so that they moved, they would have appeared as if painted in the depths of the lake, for every leaf was reflected in the water, whether it stood in the shade or the sunshine. As soon as Eliza saw her own face, she was quite terrified at finding it so brown and ugly; but when she wetted her little hand and rubbed her eyes and forehead the white skin gleamed forth once more; and, after she had undressed and dipped herself in the fresh water, a more beautiful king's daughter could not be found in the wide world. As soon as she had dressed herself again, and braided her long hair, she went to the bubbling spring and drank some water out of the hollow of her hand. Then she wandered far into the forest, not knowing whither she went. She thought of her brothers, and felt sure that God would not forsake her. It is God who makes the wild apples grow in the wood to satisfy the hungry, and He now led her to one of these trees, which was so loaded with fruit that the boughs bent beneath its weight. Here she held her noonday repast, placed props under the boughs, and then went into the gloomiest depths of the forest. It was so still that she could hear the sound of her own footsteps, as well as the rustling of every withered leaf which she crushed under her feet. Not a bird was to be seen, not a sunbeam could penetrate through the large dark boughs of the trees. The lofty trunks stood so close together that when she looked before her it seemed as if she were inclosed within trelliswork. Such solitude she had never known before. The night was very dark. Not a single glow-worm glittered in the moss.

Sorrowfully she laid herself down to sleep, and after a while it seemed to her as if the branches of the trees parted over her head, and that the mild eyes of angels looked down upon her from heaven. When she awoke in the morning, she knew not whether she had dreamed this or if it had really been so. Then she continued her wandering, but she had not gone many steps forward when she met an old woman with berries in her basket, and begged a few to eat. Then Eliza asked her if she had seen eleven princes riding through the forest.

"No," replied the old woman, "but I saw yesterday eleven swans, with gold crowns on their heads, swimming on the river close by." Then she led Eliza a little distance farther to a sloping bank, at the foot of which wound a little stream. The trees on its banks stretched their long leafy branches across the water toward each other, and where the growth prevented them from meeting naturally, the roots had torn themselves away from the ground, so that the branches might mingle their foliage as they hung over the stream. Eliza bade the old woman farewell and walked by the flowing river till she reached the shore of the open sea. And there before the young maiden's eyes lay the glorious ocean, but not a sail appeared on its surface; not even a boat could be seen. How was she to go farther? She noticed how the countless pebbles on the seashore had been smoothed and rounded by the action of the water. Glass, iron, stones, everything that lay there mingled together, had taken its shape from the same power, and felt as smooth, or even smoother, than her own delicate hand. "The water rolls on without weariness," she said, "till all that is hard becomes smooth; so will I be unwearied in my task. Thanks for your lessons, bright rolling waves; my heart tells me you will lead me to my dear brothers." On the foam-covered seaweeds lay eleven white swan feathers, which she gathered up and placed together. Drops of water lay upon them; whether they were dewdrops or tears no one could say. Lonely as it was on the seashore she did not observe it, for the ever-moving sea showed more changes in a few hours than the most varying lake could produce during a whole year. If a black heavy cloud arose, it was as if the sea said, "I can look dark and angry too"; and then the wind blew, and the waves turned to white foam as they rolled. When the wind slept and the clouds glowed with the red sunlight, then the sea looked like a rose leaf. But however quietly its white glassy surface rested, there was still a motion on the shore, as its waves rose and fell like the breast of a sleeping child. When the sun was about to set, Eliza saw eleven white swans with golden crowns on their heads flying toward the land, one behind the other, like a long white ribbon. Then Eliza went down the slope from the shore and hid herself behind the bushes. The swans alighted quite close to her, and flapped their great white wings. As soon as the sun had disappeared under the water, the feathers of the swans fell off, and eleven beautiful princes, Eliza's brothers, stood near her. She uttered a loud cry, for, although they were very much changed, she knew them immediately. She sprang into their arms and called them each by name. Then, how happy the princes were at meeting their little sister again! for they recognized her, although she had grown so tall and beautiful. They laughed and they wept, and very soon understood how wickedly their mother had acted to them all. "We brothers," said the eldest, "fly about as wild swans so long as the sun is in the sky, but as soon as it sinks behind the hills, we recover our human shape. Therefore must we always be near a resting place for our feet before sunset; for if we should be flying toward the clouds at the time we recovered our natural form as men, we should fall deep into the sea. We do not dwell here but in a land just as fair, that lies beyond the ocean, which we have to cross for a long distance; there is no island in our passage upon which we could pass the night; nothing but a little rock rising out of the sea, upon which we can scarcely stand with safety, even closely crowded together. If the sea is rough, the foam dashes over us, yet we thank God even for this rock; we have passed whole nights upon it, or we should never have reached our beloved fatherland, for our flight across the sea occupies two of the longest days in the year. We have permission to visit our home once in every year and to remain eleven days, during which we fly across the forest to look once more at the palace where our father dwells and where we were born, and at the church where our mother lies buried. Here it seems as if the very trees and bushes were related to us. The wild horses leap over the plains as we have seen them in our childhood. The charcoal burners sing the old songs to which we have danced as children. This is our fatherland to which we are drawn by loving ties; and here we have found you, our dear little sister. Two days longer we can remain here, and then must we fly away to a beautiful land which is not our home; and how can we take you with us? We have neither ship nor boat."

"How can I break this spell?" said their sister. And then she talked about it nearly the whole night, only slumbering for a few hours. Eliza was awakened by the rustling of the swans' wings as they soared above. Her brothers were again changed to swans, and they flew in circles wider and wider till they were far away; but one of them, the youngest swan, remained behind and laid his head in his sister's lap, while she stroked his wings, and they remained together the whole day. Toward evening the rest came back, and as the sun went down they resumed their natural forms. "To-morrow," said one, "we shall fly away, not to return again till a whole year has passed. But we cannot leave you here. Have you courage to go with us? My arm is strong enough to carry you through

the wood; and will not all our wings be strong enough to fly
with you over the sea?"

"Yes, take me with you," said Eliza. Then they spent the
whole night in weaving a net with the pliant willow and rushes.
It was very large and strong. Eliza laid herself down on the
net, and when the sun rose and her brothers again became wild
swans, they took up the net with their beaks and flew up to the
clouds with their dear sister, who still slept. The sunbeams
fell on her face, therefore one of the swans soared over her
head, so that his broad wing might shade her. They were
far from the land when Eliza woke. She thought she must still
be dreaming, it seemed so strange to her to feel herself being
carried so high in the air over the sea. By her side lay a
branch full of beautiful ripe berries and a bundle of sweet roots;
the youngest of her brothers had gathered them for her, and
placed them by her side. She smiled her thanks to him; she
knew it was the same who had hovered over her to shade her
with his wings. They were now so high that a large ship
beneath them looked like a white sea gull skimming the waves.
A great cloud floating behind them appeared like a vast mountain, and upon it Eliza saw her own shadow and those of the
eleven swans, looking gigantic in size. Altogether it formed a
more beautiful picture than she had ever seen; but as the sun
rose higher, and the clouds were left behind, the shadowy picture vanished away. Onward the whole day they flew through
the air like a winged arrow, yet more slowly than usual, for
they had their sister to carry. The weather seemed inclined to
be stormy, and Eliza watched the sinking sun with great anxiety, for the little rock in the ocean was not yet in sight. It
appeared to her as if the swans were making great efforts with
their wings. Alas! she was the cause of their not advancing
more quickly. When the sun set they would change to men,
fall into the sea, and be drowned. Then she offered a prayer
from her inmost heart, but still no appearance of the rock.
Dark clouds came nearer, the gusts of wind told of a coming
storm, while from a thick, heavy mass of clouds the lightning
burst forth flash after flash. The sun had reached the edge of

the sea, when the swans darted down so swiftly that Eliza's
head trembled; she believed they were falling, but they again
soared onward. Presently she caught sight of the rock just
below them, and by this time the sun was half hidden by the
waves. The rock did not appear larger than a seal's head
thrust out of the water. They sank so rapidly that at the
moment their feet touched the rock the sun shone only like a
star, and at last disappeared like the last spark in a piece of
burned paper. Then she saw her brothers standing closely
around her with their arms linked together. There was but
just room enough for them, and not the smallest space to spare.
The sea dashed against the rock and covered them with spray.
The heavens were lighted up with continual flashes, and peal
after peal of thunder rolled. But the sister and brothers sat
holding each other's hands and singing hymns, from which
they gained hope and courage. In the early dawn the air
became calm and still, and at sunrise the swans flew away
from the rock with Eliza. The sea was still rough, and from
their high position in the air the white foam on the dark green
waves looked like millions of swans swimming on the water
As the sun rose higher Eliza saw before her, floating in the air,
a range of mountains with shining masses of ice on their sum-
mits. In the center rose a castle apparently a mile long, with
rows of columns rising one above another, while around it
palm trees waved and flowers bloomed as large as mill wheels.
She asked if this was the land to which they were hastening.
The swans shook their heads, for what she beheld were the
beautiful ever-changing cloud palaces of the " Fata Morgana," into which no mortal can enter. Eliza was still gazing
at the scene when mountains, forests, and castles melted away,
and twenty stately churches rose in their stead, with high
towers and pointed Gothic windows. Eliza even fancied she
could hear the tones of the organ, but it was the music of the
murmuring sea which she heard. As they drew nearer to the
churches, these also changed into a fleet of ships, which seemed
to be sailing beneath her; but as she looked again, she found it
was only a sea mist gliding over the ocean. So there continued

to pass before her eyes a constant change of scene, till at last she saw the real land to which they were bound, with its blue mountains, its cedar forests, and its cities and palaces. Long before the sun went down she sat on a rock in front of a large cave, on the floor of which the overgrown yet delicate green creeping plants looked like an embroidered carpet. "Now we shall expect to hear what you dream of to-night," said the youngest brother, as he showed his sister her bedroom.

"Heaven grant that I may dream how to save you!" she replied. And this thought took such hold upon her mind that she prayed earnestly to God for help, and even in her sleep she continued to pray. Then it appeared to her as if she were flying high in the air, toward the cloudy palace of the "Fata Morgana," and a fairy came out to meet her, radiant and beautiful in appearance, and yet very much like the old woman who had given her berries in the wood, and who had told her of the swans with golden crowns on their heads. "Your brothers can be released," said she, "if you have only courage and perseverance. True, water is softer than your own delicate hands, and yet it polishes stones into shapes; it feels no pain as your fingers would feel, it has no soul, and cannot suffer such agony and torment as you will have to endure. Do you see the stinging nettle which I hold in my hand? Quantities of the same sort grow around the cave in which you sleep, but none will be of any use to you unless they grow upon the graves in a churchyard. These you must gather even while they burn blisters on your hands. Break them to pieces with your hands and feet, and they will become flax, from which you must spin and weave eleven coats with long sleeves; if these are then thrown over the eleven swans the spell will be broken. But remember, that from the moment you commence your task until it is finished, even should it occupy years of your life, you must not speak. The first word you utter will pierce through the hearts of your brothers like a deadly dagger. Their lives hang upon your tongue. Remember all I have told you." And as she finished speaking, she touched her hand lightly with the nettle, and a pain as of burning fire awoke Eliza.

It was broad daylight, and close by where she had been sleeping lay a nettle like the one she had seen in her dream. She fell on her knees and offered her thanks to God. Then she went forth from the cave to begin her work with her delicate hands. She groped in among the ugly nettles, which burned great blisters on her hands and arms, but she determined to bear it gladly if she could only release her dear brothers. So she bruised the nettles with her bare feet and spun the flax. At sunset her brothers returned and were very much frightened when they found her dumb. They believed it to be some new sorcery of their wicked stepmother. But when they saw her hands they understood what she was doing on their behalf, and the youngest brother wept, and where his tears fell the pain ceased and the burning blisters vanished. She kept at her work all night, for she could not rest till she had released her dear brothers. During the whole of the following day, while her brothers were absent, she sat in solitude, but never before had the time flown so quickly. One coat was already finished and she had begun the second when she heard a huntsman's horn and was struck with fear. The sound came nearer and nearer; she heard the dogs barking, and fled with terror into the cave. She hastily bound together the nettles she had gathered into a bundle and sat upon them. Immediately a great dog came bounding toward her out of the ravine, and then another and another; they barked loudly, ran back, and then came again. In a very few minutes all the huntsmen stood before the cave, and the handsomest of them was the King of the country. He advanced toward her, for he had never seen a more beautiful maiden.

"How did you come here, my sweet child?" he asked. But Eliza shook her head. She dared not speak, at the cost of her brothers' lives. And she hid her hands under her apron, so that the King might not see how she must be suffering.

"Come with me," he said; "here you cannot remain. If you are as good as you are beautiful, I will dress you in silk

248]

and velvet, I will place a golden crown on your head, and you shall dwell and rule and make your home in my richest castle." And then he lifted her on his horse. She wept and wrung her hands, but the King said: "I wish only your happiness. A time will come when you will thank me for this." And then he galloped away over the mountains, holding her before him on his horse, and the hunters followed behind them. As the sun went down they approached a fair, royal city, with churches and cupolas. On arriving at the castle the King led her into marble halls where large fountains played, and where the walls and the ceilings were covered with rich paintings. But she had no eyes for all these glorious sights; she could only mourn and weep. Patiently she allowed the women to array her in royal robes, to weave pearls in her hair, and draw soft gloves over her blistered fingers. As she stood before them in all her rich dress, she looked so dazzlingly beautiful that the court bowed low in her presence. Then the King declared his intention of making her his bride, but the archbishop shook his head, and whispered that the fair young maiden was only a witch who had blinded the King's eyes and enchanted his heart. But the King would not listen to this; he ordered the music to sound, the daintiest dishes to be served, and the loveliest maidens to dance. Afterwards he led her through fragrant gardens and lofty halls, but not a smile appeared on her lips or sparkled in her eyes. She looked the very picture of grief. Then the King opened the door of a little chamber in which she was to sleep; it was adorned with rich green tapestry, and resembled the cave in which he had found her. On the floor lay the bundle of flax which she had spun from the nettles, and under the ceiling hung the coat she had made. These things had been brought away from the cave as curiosities by one of the huntsmen.

"Here you can dream yourself back again in the old home in the cave," said the King; "here is the work with which you employed yourself. It will amuse you now in the midst of all this splendor to think of that time."

When Eliza saw all these things which lay so near her heart, a smile played around her mouth and the crimson blood rushed to her cheeks. She thought of her brothers, and their release made her so joyful that she kissed the King's hand. Then he pressed her to his heart. Very soon the joyous church bells announced the marriage feast, and that the beautifui dumb girl out of the wood was to be made Queen of the country. Then the archbishop whispered wicked words in the King's ear, but they did not sink into his heart. The marriage was still to take place, and the archbishop himself had to place the crown on the bride's head; in his wicked spite he pressed the narrow circlet so tightly on her forehead that it caused her pain. But a heavier weight encircled her heart—sorrow for her brothers. She felt not bodily pain. Her mouth was closed; a single word would cost her brothers their lives. But she loved the kind, handsome King, who did everything to make her happy, more and more each day; she loved him with her whole heart, and her eyes beamed with the love she dared not speak. Oh, if she had only been able to confide in him and tell him of her grief! But dumb she must remain till her task was finished. Therefore at night she crept away into her little chamber, which had been decked out to look like the cave, and quickly wove one coat after another. But when she began the seventh she found she had no more flax. She knew that the nettles she wanted to use grew in the churchyard, and that she must pluck them herself. How should she get out there? "Oh, what is the pain in my fingers to the torment which my heart endures?" said she. "I must venture; I shall not be denied help from heaven." Then with a trembling heart, as if she were about to perform a wicked deed, she crept into the garden in the broad moonlight, and passed through the narrow walks and the deserted streets till she reached the churchyard. Then she saw on one of the broad tombstones a group of ghouls. These hideous creatures took off their rags, as if they intended to bathe, and then, clawing open the grassy graves with their long skinny fingers, pulled out the bones and threw them about! Eliza had to pass close by them, and they fixed their wicked glances upon her, but she prayed silently, gathered the burning nettles, and carried them home with her to the castle. One person only had seen her, and that was the archbishop—he was awake while everybody was asleep. Now he thought his opinion was evidently correct. All was not right with the Queen. She was a witch, and had enchanted the King and all the people. Secretly he told the King what he had seen and what he feared, and as the hard words came from his tongue, the carved images of the saints shook their heads as if they would say, " It is not so. Eliza is innocent."

But the archbishop interpreted it in another way; he believed that they witnessed against her, and were shaking their heads at her wickedness. Two large tears rolled down the King's cheeks, and he went home with doubt in his heart, and at night pretended to sleep, but there came no real sleep to his eyes, for he saw Eliza get up every night and disappear in her own chamber. From day to day his brow became darker, and Eliza saw it and did not understand the reason, but it alarmed her and made her heart tremble for her brothers. Her hot tears glittered like pearls on the regal velvet and diamonds, while all who saw her were wishing they could be queens. In the meantime she had almost finished her task; only one coat of mail was wanting, but she had no flax left, and not a single nettle. Once more only, and for the last time, must she venture to the churchyard and pluck a few handfuls. She thought with terror of the solitary walk, and of the horrible ghouls, but her will was firm, as well as her trust in Providence. Eliza went, and the King and the archbishop followed her. They saw her vanish through the wicket gate into the churchyard, and when they came nearer they saw the ghouls sitting on the tombstone as Eliza had seen them, and the King turned away his head, for he thought she was with them—she whose head had rested on his breast that very evening. " The people must condemn her," said he, and she was very quickly condemned by everyone to suffer death by fire. Away from the gorgeous regal halls was she led to a dark, dreary cell, where the wind whistled through the iron bars. Instead of the velvet and silk dresses, they gave her the coats of mail which she had woven to cover her, and the bundle of nettles for a pillow; but nothing they could give her would have pleased her more. She continued her task with joy, and prayed for help, while the street boys sang jeering songs about her, and not a soul comforted her with a kind word. Toward evening she heard at the grating the flutter of a swan's wing; it was her youngest brother—he had found his sister, and she sobbed for joy, although she knew that very likely this would be the last night she would have to live. But still she could hope, for her task was almost finished and her brothers were come. Then the archbishop arrived, to be with her during her last hours, as he had promised the King. But she shook her head, and begged him, by looks and gestures, not to stay, for in this night she knew she must finish her task, otherwise all her pain and tears and sleepless nights would have been suffered in vain. The archbishop withdrew, uttering bitter words against her; but poor Eliza knew that she was innocent, and diligently continued her work.

The little mice ran about the floor; they dragged the nettles to her feet, to help as well as they could, and the thrush sat outside the grating of the window and sang to her the whole night long, as sweetly as possible, to keep up her spirits.

It was still twilight and at least an hour before sunrise when the eleven brothers stood at the castle gate and demanded to be brought before the King. They were told it could not be, it was yet almost night, and as the King slept they dared not disturb him. They threatened, they entreated. Then the guard appeared, and even the King himself, inquiring what all the noise meant. At this moment the sun rose. The eleven brothers were seen no more, but eleven wild swans flew away over the castle.

And now all the people came streaming forth from the gates of the city to see the witch burned. An old horse drew the cart on which she sat. They had dressed her in a garment of coarse sackcloth. Her lovely hair hung loose on her shoulders, her cheeks were deadly pale, her lips moved silently, while her fingers still worked at the green flax. Even on the way to

"ELIZA WENT, AND THE KING AND THE ARCHBISHOP FOLLOWED HER"

death she would not give up her task. The ten coats of mail lay at her feet, she was working hard at the eleventh, while the mob jeered her and said, " See the witch, how she mutters! She has no hymn book in her hand. She sits there with her ugly sorcery. Let us tear it in a thousand pieces."

And then they pressed toward her, and would have destroyed the coats of mail, but at the same moment eleven wild swans flew over her and alighted on the cart. Then they flapped their large wings and the crowd drew on one side in alarm.

" It is a sign from heaven that she is innocent," whispered many of them, but they ventured not to say it aloud.

As the executioner seized her by the hand to lift her out of the cart, she hastily threw the eleven coats of mail over the swans, and they immediately became eleven handsome princes; but the youngest had a swan's wing instead of an arm, for she had not been able to finish the last sleeve of the coat.

" Now I may speak! " she exclaimed. " I am innocent."

Then the people, who saw what happened, bowed to her as before a saint, but she sank lifeless in her brother's arms, overcome with suspense, anguish, and pain.

" Yes, she is innocent," said the eldest brother; and then he related all that had taken place, and while he spoke there rose in the air a fragrance as from millions of flowers. Every piece of fagot in the pile had taken root, and thrown out branches, and appeared a thick hedge, large and high, covered with roses, while above all bloomed a white and shining blossom that glittered like a star. This flower the King plucked and placed in Eliza's bosom, when she awoke from her swoon with peace and happiness in her heart. And all the church bells rang of themselves and the birds came in great troops. And a marriage procession returned to the castle such as no king had ever before seen.

THE FAIRY RING

The Story of Coquerico

ONCE upon a time there was a handsome hen who lived like a great lady in the poultry yard of a rich farmer, surrounded by a numerous family that clucked about her, and none of which clamored more loudly or picked up the corn faster with his beak than a poor little deformed and crippled chicken. This was precisely the one that the mother loved best. It is the way with all mothers; the weakest and most unsightly are always their favorites. This misshapen creature had but one eye, one wing, and one leg in good condition; it might have been thought that Solomon had executed his memorable sentence on Coquerico, for that was the name of the wretched chicken, and cut him in two with his famous sword. When a person is one-eyed, lame, and one-armed, he may reasonably be expected to be modest; but our Castilian ragamuffin was prouder than his father, the best spurred, most elegant, bravest, and most gallant cock to be seen from Burgos to Madrid. He thought himself a phœnix of grace and beauty, and passed the best part of the day in admiring himself in the brook. If one of his brothers ran against him by accident, he abused him, called him envious and jealous, and risked his only remaining eye in battle; if the hens clucked on seeing him, he said it was to hide their spite because he did not condescend to look at them.

One day, when he was more puffed up with vanity than usual, he resolved no longer to remain in such a narrow sphere, but to go out into the world, where he would be better appreciated.

"My lady mother," said he, "I am tired of Spain; I am going to Rome to see the Pope and cardinals."

"What are you thinking of, my poor child!" cried his mother. "Who has put such a folly into your head? Never has one of our family been known to quit his country, and, for this reason, we are the honor of our race, and are proud

[254]

of our genealogy. Where will you find a poultry yard like this—mulberry trees to shade you, a whitewashed hen roost, a magnificent dunghill, worms and corn everywhere, brothers that love you, and three great dogs to guard you from the foxes? Do you not think that at Rome itself you will regret the ease and plenty of such a life?"

Coquerico shrugged his crippled wing in token of disdain. "You are a simple woman, my good mother," said he; "everything is accounted worthy of admiration by him who has never quitted his dunghill. But I have wit enough to see that my brothers have no ideas, and that my cousins are nothing but rustics. My genius is stifling in this hole; I wish to roam the world and seek my fortune."

"But, my son, have you never looked in the brook?" resumed the poor hen. "Don't you know that you lack an eye, a leg, and a wing? To make your fortune, you need the eyes of a fox, the legs of a spider, and the wings of a vulture. Once outside of these walls, you are lost."

"My good mother," replied Coquerico, "when a hen hatches a duck, she is always frightened on seeing it run to the water. You know me no better. It is my nature to succeed by my wit and talent. I must have a public capable of appreciating the charms of my person; my place is not among inferior people."

"My son," said the hen, seeing all her counsels useless, "my son, listen at least to your mother's last words. If you go to Rome, take care to avoid St. Peter's Church; the saint, it is said, dislikes cocks, especially when they crow. Shun, moreover, certain personages called cooks and scullions; you will know them by their paper caps, their tucked-up sleeves, and the great knives which they wear at their sides. They are licensed assassins, who track our steps without pity, and cut our throats without giving us time to cry mercy. And now, my child," she added, raising her claw, "receive my blessing. May St. James, the patron saint of pilgrims, protect thee!"

Coquerico pretended not to see the tear that trembled in

his mother's eye, nor did he trouble himself any more about his father, who bristled his plumage and seemed about to call him back. Without caring for those whom he left behind, he glided through the half-open door, and, once outside, flapped his only wing and crowed three times, to celebrate his freedom—"Cock-a-doodle-doo!"

As he half-flew, half-hopped over the fields, he came to the bed of a brook which had been dried up by the sun. In the middle of the sands, however, still trickled a tiny thread of water, so small that it was choked by a couple of dead leaves that had fallen into it.

"My friend," exclaimed the Streamlet at the sight of our traveler, "my friend, you see my weakness; I have not even the strength to carry away these leaves which obstruct my passage, much less to make a circuit, so completely am I exhausted. With a stroke of your beak you can restore me to life. I am not an ingrate; if you oblige me, you may count on my gratitude the first rainy day, when the water from heaven shall have restored my strength."

"You are jesting?" said Coquerico. "Do I look like one whose business it is to sweep the brooks? Apply to those of your own sort." And, with his sound leg, he leaped across the Streamlet.

"You will remember me when you least expect it," murmured the Brook, but with so feeble a voice that it was lost on the proud cock.

A little farther on, Coquerico saw the Wind lying breathless on the ground.

"Dear Coquerico, come to my aid," it cried; "here on earth we should help each other. You see to what I am reduced by the heat of the day; I, who in former times uprooted the olive trees and lashed the waves to frenzy, lie here well nigh slain by the dog star. I suffered myself to be lulled to sleep by the perfume of the roses with which I was playing; and lo! here I am, stretched almost lifeless upon the ground. If you will raise me a couple of inches with your beak and fan me a little with your wing, I shall have the strength to mount to yonder white clouds which I see in the distance, where I shall receive aid enough from my family to keep me alive till I gain fresh strength from the next whirlwind.

"My lord," answered the spiteful Coquerico, "your excellency has more than once amused himself by playing tricks at my expense. It is not a week since your lordship glided like a traitor behind me, and diverted himself by opening my tail like a fan and covering me with confusion in the face of nations. Have patience, therefore, my worthy friend; mockers always have their turn; it does them good to repent, and to learn to respect those whose birth, wit, and beauty should screen them from the jests of a fool." And Coquerico, bristling his plumage, crowed three times in his shrillest voice and proudly strutted onward.

A little farther on he came to a newly mown field, where the farmers had piled up the weeds in order to burn them. Coquerico approached a smoking heap, hoping to find some stray kernels of corn, and saw a little flame which was charring the green stalks without being able to set them on fire.

"My good friend," cried the Flame to the newcomer, "you are just in time to save my life; I am dying for want of air. I cannot imagine what has become of my cousin, the Wind, who cares for nothing but his own amusement. Bring me a few dry straws to rekindle my strength, and you will not have obliged an ingrate."

"Wait a moment," said Coquerico, "and I will serve you as you deserve, insolent fellow that dares ask my help!" And behold! he leaped on the heap of dried weeds, and trampled it down till he smothered both Flame and smoke; after which he exultingly shouted three times "Cock-a-doodle-doo!" and flapped his wings, as if he had done a great deed.

Proudly strutting onward and crowing, Coquerico at last arrived at Rome, the place to which all roads lead. Scarcely had he reached the city when he hastened to the great church of St. Peter. Grand and beautiful as it was, he did not stop to admire it, but, planting himself in front of the main entrance, where he looked like a fly among the great columns, he raised himself on tiptoe and began to shout "Cocka-doodle-doo!" only to enrage the saint and disobey his mother.

He had not yet ended his song when one of the Pope's guards, who chanced to hear him, laid hands on the insolent wretch who dared thus to insult the saint, and carried him home in order to roast him for supper.

"Quick!" said he to his wife on entering the house, "give me some boiling water; here is a sinner to be punished."

"Pardon, pardon, Madam Water!" cried Coquerico. "O good and gentle Water, the best and purest thing in the world, do not scald me, I pray you!"

"Did you have pity on me when I implored your aid, ungrateful wretch?" answered the Water, boiling with indignation. And with a single gush it inundated him from head to foot, and left not a bit of down on his body.

The unhappy Coquerico stripped of all his feathers, the soldier took him and laid him on the gridiron.

"O Fire, do not burn me!" cried he, in an agony of terror. "O beautiful and brilliant Fire, the brother of the Sun and the cousin of the Diamond, spare an unhappy creature; restrain thy ardor and soften thy flame; do not roast me!"

"Did you have pity on me when I implored your aid, ungrateful wretch?" answered the Fire, and, fiercely blazing with anger, in an instant it burned Coquerico to a coal.

The soldier, seeing his roast chicken in this deplorable condition, took him by the leg and threw him out of the window. The Wind bore the unhappy fowl to a dunghill, where it left him for a moment.

"O Wind," murmured Coquerico, who still breathed, "oh, kindly zephyr, protecting breeze, behold me cured of my vain follies; let me rest on the paternal dunghill."

"Let you rest!" roared the Wind. "Wait and I will teach

you how I treat ingrates." And with one blast it sent him so high in the air that, as he fell back, he was transfixed by a steeple.

There St. Peter was awaiting him. With his own hand he nailed him to the highest steeple in Rome, where he is still shown to travelers. However high placed he may be, all despise him because he turns with the slightest wind; black, dried up, stripped of his feathers, and beaten by the rain, he is no longer called Coquerico, but Weathercock; and thus expiates, and must expiate eternally, his disobedience, vanity, and wickedness.

The Bird-Cage Maker

IN a town of the ancient kingdom of Castile there lived, in former ages, a youth called Bartolo, who tried to eke out a living by making cages for birds, and taking them round to sell at the neighboring villages. But his trade was a poor one, and he judged himself in luck if he sold one cage in the day, and as may be supposed, he knew what sorrow and privation were.

One day as he was proceeding to a village he heard sounds of revelry, the buzz of many people, and the strains of a band of music. This merrymaking was a procession of children dressed in white, carrying in their midst a beautiful child crowned with roses, in a chariot covered with white satin, and ornamented with acacia and myrtle. This procession was in honor of *Maya*, the personification of Spring, and took place to announce the entry of Spring. In front of the little chariot some children danced, and held in their hands tin platters for contributions; and, as may be imagined, all, or nearly all, the spectators dropped their coins into them.

Bartolo moved away in a desponding mood, saying to himself as he walked on: "Is this the justice of the world? There they are, flinging their money into these platters just because these children come in procession to announce to them that it is the month of May, as though they could not know it by looking in an almanac. They barter and grind me down to the lowest price for my cages, even when I chance to sell one."

Full of these bitter thoughts he walked on sadly, for the voices of two importunate enemies were making themselves heard within him—these were hunger and thirst: the one clamored for food and the other for drink. Bartolo had nothing in his wallet but his clasp knife, and had had nought for his breakfast but hopes, and these made him sharp and active.

He had reached a plantation when he perceived a well-dressed individual coming toward him. Pressed by hunger Bartolo, taking his cap off respectfully, approached and said: "Excuse me, sir, but could you kindly give me a trifle? I promise I will return it as soon as I earn some money."

"Don't you think that it is a shameful thing for a man like you, young and with a good, healthy appearance, to be demanding charity of people? Does it not strike you that you have a duty to earn your living by working at your trade?"

"Yes, sir, certainly, but my trade does not fulfill its own duty. Most people like to see the birds flying about free rather than in cages, and, therefore, day by day I find myself poorer than before."

At first the stranger doubted what he heard, but the bird-cage maker gave him so detailed an account of his work and the small profits he derived, that he became interested and sympathized with his ill fortune. Bartolo was a man who always knew how to excite great interest in himself.

"Come, come," the stranger said, smiling, "I will do something for you. As I cannot find customers for your cages, I will afford you a powerful means by which you shall never more be in want."

He then blew a whistle, and Bartolo saw flying before him

a bird blue as the sky, which came and perched on one of his cages.

"See here," added the stranger, "what will compensate for all your past misery. From this day forward you have only to formulate a wish and say slowly and distinctly, ' *Bluest of blue birds, do your duty!* ' and your wish will be granted to you."

"By my faith!" cried the bird-cage maker, "but I will try it at once. For the last twenty years I have wished to kill hunger: ' Bluest of blue birds, do your duty! ' "

Scarcely were the words out of his mouth than he saw suddenly spread before him on the grass a breakfast fit for a prince, laid on a service of exquisite silver and glass and the whitest of cloths. Bartolo, astonished, flung himself on his knees before his benefactor to thank him, but he raised him up saying:

"I am the good genius of the honest workingmen of Castile. Sit down and eat without fear. Take advantage of your lucky star," and then suddenly disappeared.

Bartolo reverently bent down and kissed the spot upon which he had stood, unable to find adequate expression of his gratitude. He then sat down and ate his breakfast. After his meal, Bartolo judged that a man who had feasted in such an elegant manner ought to have other, better clothing than his well-worn working suit; and, lifting his staff, he cried to the bird: "Bluest of blue birds, do your duty!" In an instant his old suit became transformed into one of richest velvet, embroidered in gold and silver, and his rough staff into a splendid horse fully caparisoned, and having round its neck a collar of silver bells.

More astonished than ever, Bartolo suspended to the saddle the cage with the blue bird, leaped on the horse, and went his way, as proud of his dress as a donkey of its ears.

Setting spurs to his horse, he soon reached the gates of a splendid castle. Some feast was taking place within. The guests were all seated under a shady bower, deploring that they had been disappointed of the minstrels who were to have played.

Bartolo, on learning this, advanced to the bower, and, after elegantly saluting the lord and lady of the castle, in a most refined voice said:

"If it be right for a simple knight to offer his services to such a distinguished company of rank and beauty, I think I could promise to provide what you are requiring."

"Oh, do! at once, please!" cried all the ladies, who were longing to dance.

"Bluest of blue birds, do your duty!" said Bartolo.

Suddenly, in the distance, was heard the noise of many feet, and a troop of musicians with their instruments appeared, to the great delight of the company.

The lord of the castle thanked the stranger, and desired him to open the ball with his eldest daughter, a maiden fair and lovely, like a snowbird.

When the ball was at its height, the bird-cage maker ordered an elegant banquet to be served, during which the bluest of blue birds was commanded to sing some songs, which were very much admired. Games of chance followed, and Bartolo, taking advantage of his good fortune, distributed among the ladies pearls, bracelets, and rings of precious stones. All those present were surprised beyond measure, because the lord of the castle was known to be extremely niggardly and mean.

The lord of the castle, who knew how all this had been done through the agency of the bird, and being himself of an inordinately avaricious nature, thought he might do a fine stroke of business were he to buy the creature. Hence, calling his unknown guest away to his study, he proposed to him to purchase the bird for what price he should quote.

"You would never give me my price," replied Bartolo.

"For it I would give my castle with its nine forests," said the lord of the castle.

"It is not enough!"

"Very well, I will add my olive plantations and vineyards."

"That is still insufficient!" cried Bartolo.

"I will add the orchards, gardens, and houses."

"I want something else!"

"What, still more? Why, man, you must want paradise itself!"

"Not so; I want what you can give me this very moment. I want your daughter with whom I danced just now! Let her be my bride."

"What, my daughter!" cried the old miser, in an ecstasy of joy; "by my faith, we shall soon conclude the bargain. Why did you not say so before?"

He went to seek the girl, and told her of the engagement he had entered into. But his daughter, in utter amazement, cried out:

"But what if he be a wicked elf, and all he does be witchcraft?"

"You have an amulet of coral hanging from your neck; it is an antidote against all witchery."

"And what if he be Satan himself?"

"I will give you a piece of blessed candle, and he will have no power over you," replied the unrelenting father.

Taking her hand, he led her to the stranger, who was already on his horse, and assisted her to mount behind her future husband. Taking the cage with the bluest of birds, he watched the retreating forms of the pair as the horse carried them away swifter than the wind, and when out of sight, he proceeded to join his guests. The company were all gathered in knots discussing the extraordinary powers of the bird and all the events which had taken place.

"Peace! peace!" cried the lord of the castle, as he entered; "I will perform more marvelous things than ever he did. I have given him my daughter to wed in exchange for the bird, and this blue bird will render me more wealthy than the King of Aragon. Approach, and see the wonders I will work with it."

He took the cage, and lifting it up to look at the bird, was astonished to find that it was not blue at all, but a large gray bird, which turned to stare at him in an insolent manner, gave a fierce peck at the door of the cage with its beak, flung it open, and flew out of the window uttering a terrible screech.

The lord of the castle stood with open mouth, not knowing what to do or say. His guests broke out in peals of laughter at his discomfiture and the well-deserved punishment for his unseemly avarice in exchanging his beautiful daughter for a worthless bird.

Meanwhile, Bartolo was galloping on with his bride to the nearest town to be married, and when he arrived at the first hostelry, he wished to dismount and engage the most splendid suite of apartments for his intended wife, but he found himself utterly penniless. He had not calculated that in parting with the bird he had parted with his luck, and therefore as soon as he dismounted the horse disappeared and his elegant dress became changed for the shabby one he had worn before he met the kind individual who had wished to befriend him. When the beautiful daughter of the lord of the castle beheld the transformation which had taken place she ran back to her father as fast as she could, fright lending wings to her feet.

Bartolo had to return to his old life of making cages and to his miserable existence.

The Twelve Months

THERE was once a woman who was left a widow with two children. The elder, who was only her stepdaughter, was named Dobrunka; the younger, who was as wicked as her mother, was called Katinka. The mother worshiped her daughter, but she hated Dobrunka, simply because she was as beautiful as her sister was ugly. Dobrunka did not even know that she was pretty, and she could not understand why her stepmother flew into a rage at the mere

sight of her. The poor child was obliged to do all the work
of the house; she had to sweep, cook, wash, sew, spin, weave,
cut the grass, and take care of the cow, while Katinka lived
like a princess, that is to say, did nothing.

Dobrunka worked with a good will, and took reproaches
and blows with the gentleness of a lamb; but nothing soothed
her stepmother, for every day added to the beauty of the elder
sister and the ugliness of the younger. "They are growing
up," thought the mother, "and suitors will soon appear who
will refuse my daughter when they see this hateful Dobrunka,
who grows beautiful on purpose to spite me. I must get
rid of her, cost what it may."

One day in the middle of January, Katinka took a fancy
for some violets. She called Dobrunka and said: "Go to
the forest and bring me a bunch of violets, that I may put
them in my bosom and enjoy their fragrance."

"Oh, sister, what an idea!" answered Dobrunka; "as if
there were any violets under the snow!"

"Hold your tongue, stupid lass," returned her sister, "and
do as I bid you. If you do not go to the forest and bring
me back a bunch of violets, I will beat you to a jelly." Upon
this the mother took Dobrunka by the arm, put her out of
the door, and drew the bolt on her.

The poor girl went to the forest weeping bitterly. Every
thing was covered with snow; there was not even a footpath. She lost her way, and wandered about till, famishing
with hunger and perishing with cold, she entreated God to
take her from this wretched life.

All at once she saw a light in the distance. She went on,
climbing higher and higher, until at last she reached the top
of a huge rock, upon which a great fire was built. Around
the fire were twelve stones, and on each stone sat a motionless figure, wrapped in a large mantle, his head covered
with a hood which fell over his eyes. Three of these
mantles were white like the snow, three were green like the
grass of the meadows, three were golden like the sheaves
of ripe wheat, and three were purple like the grapes of the

vine. These twelve figures, gazing at the fire in silence, were the Twelve Months of the year.

Dobrunka knew January by his long white beard. He was the only one that had a staff in his hand. The poor girl was terribly frightened. She drew near, saying, in a timid voice: "My good sirs, please let me warm myself by your fire; I am freezing with cold."

January nodded his head. "Why have you come here, my child?" he asked. "What are you looking for?"

"I am looking for violets," replied Dobrunka.

"This is not the season for them; there are no violets in the time of snow," said January, in his gruff voice.

"I know it," replied Dobrunka sadly; "but my sister and mother will beat me to a jelly if I do not bring them some. My good sirs, please tell me where I can find them."

Old January rose, and, turning to a young man in a green mantle, put his staff in his hand, and said to him, "Brother March, this is your business."

March rose in turn, and stirred the fire with the staff, when behold! the flames rose, the snow melted, the buds put forth on the trees, the grass turned green under the bushes, the flowers peeped through the verdure, and the violets opened— it was spring.

"Make haste, my child, and gather your violets," said March.

Dobrunka gathered a large bouquet, thanked the Twelve Months, and joyfully ran home. You can imagine the astonishment of Katinka and the stepmother. The fragrance of the violets filled the whole house.

"Where did you find these fine things?" asked Katinka, in a disdainful voice.

"Up yonder on the mountain," answered her sister. "It looked like a great blue carpet under the bushes."

Katinka put the bouquet in her bosom, and did not even thank the poor child.

The next morning the wicked sister, as she sat idling by the stove, took a fancy for some strawberries.

"MARCH ROSE IN TURN, AND STIRRED THE FIRE WITH THE STAFF, WHEN, BEHOLD! . . . IT WAS SPRING"

"MARCH ROSE IN TURN, AND STIRRED THE FIRE WITH THE STAFF, WHEN BEHOLD! . . . IT WAS SPRING."

THE FAIRY RING

"Go to the forest and bring me some strawberries," said she to Dobrunka.

"Oh, sister, what an idea! as if there were any strawberries under the snow!"

"Hold your tongue, stupid lass, and do as I bid you. If you don't go to the forest and bring me back a basket of strawberries, I will beat you to a jelly."

The mother took Dobrunka by the arm, put her out of the door, and drew the bolt on her.

The poor girl returned to the forest, looking with all her eyes for the light that she had seen the day before. She was fortunate enough to spy it, and she reached the fire trembling and almost frozen.

The Twelve Months were in their places, motionless and silent.

"My good sirs," said Dobrunka, "please let me warm myself by your fire; I am almost frozen with cold."

"Why have you returned?" asked January. "What are you looking for?"

"I am looking for strawberries," answered she.

"This is not the season for them," returned January, in his gruff voice; "there are no strawberries under the snow."

"I know it," replied Dobrunka sadly; "but my mother and sister will beat me to a jelly if I do not bring them some. My good sirs, please tell me where I can find them."

Old January rose, and, turning to a man in a golden mantle, he put his staff in his hand, saying, "Brother June, this is your business."

June rose in turn and stirred the fire with the staff, when behold! the flames rose, the snow melted, the earth grew green, the trees were covered with leaves, the birds sang, and the flowers opened—it was summer. Thousands of little white stars enameled the turf, then turned to red strawberries, looking, in their green cups, like rubies set in emeralds.

"Make haste, my child, and gather your strawberries," said June.

Dobrunka filled her apron, thanked the Twelve Months,

[267]

and joyfully ran home. You may imagine the astonishment of Katinka and the stepmother. The fragrance of the strawberries filled the whole house.

"Where did you find these fine things?" asked Katinka, in a disdainful voice.

"Up yonder on the mountain," answered her sister; "there were so many of them that they looked like blood poured on the ground."

Katinka and her mother devoured the strawberries without even thanking the poor child.

The third day the wicked sister took a fancy for some red apples. The same threats, the same insults, and the same violence followed. Dobrunka ran to the mountain, and was fortunate enough to find the Twelve Months warming themselves, motionless and silent.

"You here again, my child?" said old January, making room for her by the fire. Dobrunka told him, with tears, how, if she did not bring home some red apples, her mother and sister would beat her to death.

Old January repeated the ceremonies of the day before. "Brother September," said he to a gray-bearded man in a purple mantle, "this is your business."

September rose and stirred the fire with the staff, when behold! the flames ascended, the snow melted, and the trees put forth a few yellow leaves, which fell one by one before the wind—it was autumn. The only flowers were a few late pinks, daisies, and immortelles. Dobrunka saw but one thing, an apple tree with its rosy fruit.

"Make haste, my child; shake the tree," said September.

She shook it, and an apple fell; she shook it again, and a second apple followed.

"Make haste, Dobrunka, make haste home!" cried September, in an imperious voice.

The good child thanked the Twelve Months, and joyfully ran home. You may imagine the astonishment of Katinka and the stepmother.

"Fresh-plucked apples in January! Where did you get these apples?" asked Katinka.

"Up yonder on the mountain; there is a tree there that is as red with them as a cherry tree in July."

"Why did you bring only two? You ate the rest on the way."

"Oh, sister, I did not touch them; I was only permitted to shake the tree twice, and but two apples fell."

"Begone, you wretch!" cried Katinka, striking her sister, who ran away crying.

The wicked girl tasted one of the apples; she had never eaten anything so delicious in her life, neither had her mother. How they regretted not having any more!

"Mother," said Katinka, "give me my fur cloak. I will go to the forest and find the tree, and, whether I am permitted or not, I will shake it so hard that all the apples will be ours."

The mother tried to stop her. A spoiled child listens to nothing. Katinka wrapped herself in her fur cloak, drew the hood over her head, and hastened to the forest.

Everything was covered with snow; there was not even a footpath. Katinka lost her way, but she pushed on, spurred by pride and covetousness. She spied a light in the distance. She climbed and climbed till she reached the place, and found the Twelve Months each seated on his stone, motionless and silent. Without asking their permission, she approached the fire.

"Why have you come here? What do you want? Where are you going?" asked old January gruffly.

"What matters it to you, old fool?" answered Katinka. "It is none of your business where I came from or whither I am going." She plunged into the forest. January frowned, and raised his staff above his head. In the twinkling of an eye the sky was overcast, the fire went out, the snow fell, and the wind blew. Katinka could not see the way before her. She lost herself, and vainly tried to retrace her steps. The snow fell and the wind blew. She called her mother, she called her sister, she prayed to God. The snow fell and the wind blew. Katinka froze, her limbs stiffened, and she fell motionless. The snow still fell and the wind still blew.

The mother went without ceasing from the window to the door, and from the door to the window. The hours passed, and Katinka did not return.

"I must go and look for my daughter," said she. "The child has forgotten herself with those hateful apples." She took her fur cloak and hood, and hastened to the mountain. Everything was covered with snow; there was not even a footpath. She plunged into the forest, calling her daughter. The snow fell and the wind blew. She walked on with feverish anxiety, shouting at the top of her voice. The snow still fell and the wind still blew.

Dobrunka waited through the evening and the night, but no one returned. In the morning she took her wheel and spun a whole distaff full; there was still no news. "What can have happened?" said the good girl, weeping. The sun was shining through an icy mist, and the ground was covered with snow. Dobrunka prayed for her mother and sister. They did not return; and it was not till spring that a shepherd found the two bodies in the forest.

Dobrunka remained the sole mistress of the house, the cow, and the garden, to say nothing of a piece of meadow adjoining the house. But when a good and pretty girl has a field under her window, the next thing that follows is a young farmer, who offers her his heart and hand. Dobrunka was soon married. The Twelve Months did not abandon their child. More than once, when the north wind blew fearfully and the windows shook in their frames, old January stopped up all the crevices of the house with snow, so that the cold might not enter this peaceful abode.

Dobrunka lived to a good old age, always virtuous and happy, having, according to the proverb, winter at the door, summer in the barn, autumn in the cellar, and spring in the heart.

The Bee, the Harp, the Mouse, and the Bum-Clock

ONCE there was a widow, and she had one son, called Jack. Jack and his mother owned just three cows. They lived well and happy for a long time; but at last hard times came down on them, and the crops failed, and poverty looked in at the door, and things got so sore against the poor widow that for want of money and for want of necessities she had to make up her mind to sell one of the cows. "Jack," she said one night, "go over in the morning to the fair to sell the branny cow."

Well and good: in the morning my brave Jack was up early, and took a stick in his fist and turned out the cow, and off to the fair he went with her; and when Jack came into the fair, he saw a great crowd gathered in a ring in the street. He went into the crowd to see what they were looking at, and there in the middle of them he saw a man with a wee, wee harp, a mouse, and a bum-clock,* and a bee to play the harp. And when the man put them down on the ground and whistled, the bee began to play the harp, and the mouse and the bum-clock stood up on their hind legs and took hold of each other and began to waltz. And as soon as the harp began to play and the mouse and the bum-clock to dance, there wasn't a man or woman, or a thing in the fair that didn't begin to dance also; and the pots and pans, and the wheels and reels jumped and jigged all over the town, and Jack himself and the branny cow were as bad as the next.

There was never a town in such a state before or since, and after a while the man picked up the bee, the harp, and the mouse, and the bum-clock and put them into his pocket, and the men and women, Jack and the cow, the pots and pans, wheels and reels that had hopped and jigged now

*Cockroach.

[271]

stopped, and everyone began to laugh as if to break its heart. Then the man turned to Jack. "Jack," says he, "how would you like to be master of all these animals?"

"Why," says Jack, "I should like it fine."

"Well, then," says the man, "how will you and me make a bargain about them?"

"I have no money," says Jack.

"But you have a fine cow," says the man. "I will give you the bee and the harp for it."

"Oh, but," Jack says, says he, "my poor mother at home is very sad and sorrowful entirely, and I have this cow to sell and lift her heart again."

"And better than this she cannot get," says the man. "For when she sees the bee play the harp, she will laugh if she never laughed in her life before."

"Well," says Jack, says he, "that will be grand."

He made the bargain. The man took the cow; and Jack started home with the bee and the harp in his pocket, and when he came home his mother welcomed him back.

"And Jack," says she, "I see you have sold the cow."

"I have done that," says Jack.

"Did you do well?" says the mother.

"I did well, and very well," says Jack.

"How much did you get for her?" says the mother.

"Oh," says he, "it was not for money at all I sold her, but for something far better."

"O, Jack! Jack!" says she, "what have you done?"

"Just wait until you see, mother," says he, "and you will soon say I have done well."

Out of his pocket he takes the bee and the harp and sets them in the middle of the floor, and whistles to them, and as soon as he did this the bee began to play the harp, and the mother she looked at them and let a big, great laugh out of her, and she and Jack began to dance, the pots and pans, the wheels and reels began to jig and dance over the floor, and the house itself hopped about also.

When Jack picked up the bee and the harp again the dancing all stopped, and the mother laughed for a long time. But when she came to herself she got very angry entirely with Jack, and she told him he was a silly, foolish fellow, that there was neither food nor money in the house, and now he had lost one of her good cows also. " We must do some thing to live," says she. " Over to the fair you must go to-morrow morning, and take the black cow with you and sell her."

And off in the morning at an early hour brave Jack started, and never halted until he was in the fair. When he came into the fair he saw a big crowd gathered in a ring in the street. Said Jack to himself, " I wonder what they are look-ing at."

Into the crowd he pushed, and saw the wee man this day again with a mouse and a bum-clock, and he put them down in the street and whistled. The mouse and the bum-clock stood up on their hind legs and got hold of each other and began to dance there and jig, and as they did there was not a man or woman in the street who didn't begin to jig also, and Jack and the black cow, and the wheels and the reels, and the pots and pans, all of them were jigging and dancing all over the town, and the houses themselves were jumping and hopping about, and such a place Jack or anyone else never saw before.

When the man lifted the mouse and the bum-clock into his pocket they all stopped dancing and settled down, and everybody laughed right hearty. The man turned to Jack. " Jack," says he, " I am glad to see you; how would you like to have these animals?"

" I should like well to have them," says Jack, says he, " only I cannot."

" Why cannot you?" says the man.

" Oh!" says Jack, says he, " I have no money, and my poor mother is very downhearted. She sent me to the fair to sell this cow and bring some money to lift her heart."

" Oh!" says the man, says he, " if you want to lift your mother's heart I will sell you the mouse, and when you set the bee to play the harp and the mouse to dance to it, your mother will laugh if she never laughed in her life before."

"But I have no money," says Jack, says he, "to buy your mouse."

"I don't mind," says the man, says he, "I will take your cow for it."

Poor Jack was so taken with the mouse, and had his mind so set on it, that he thought it was a grand bargain entirely, and he gave the man his cow and took the mouse and started off for home; and when he got home his mother welcomed him.

"Jack," says she, "I see you have sold the cow."

"I did that," says Jack.

"Did you sell her well?" says she.

"Very well indeed," says Jack, says he.

"How much did you get for her?"

"I didn't get money," says he, "but I got value."

"O Jack! Jack!" says she, "what do you mean?"

"I will soon show you that, mother," says he, taking the mouse out of his pocket and the harp and the bee, and setting all on the floor; and when he began to whistle, the bee began to play, and the mouse got up on its hind legs and began to dance and jig, and the mother gave such a hearty laugh as she never laughed in her life before. To dancing and jigging herself and Jack fell, and the pots and pans and the wheels and reels began to dance and jig over the floor, and the house jigged also. And when they were tired of this, Jack lifted the harp and the mouse and the bee and put them in his pocket, and his mother she laughed for a long time.

But when she got over that she got very downhearted and very angry entirely with Jack. "And oh, Jack!" she says, "you are a stupid, good-for-nothing fellow. We have neither money nor meat in the house, and here you have lost two of my good cows, and I have only one left now. To-morrow morning," she says, "you must be up early and take this cow to the fair and sell her. See you get something to lift my heart up."

" I will do that," says Jack, says he. So he went to his bed, and early in the morning he was up and turned out the spotty cow and went to the fair.

When Jack got to the fair he saw a crowd gathered in a ring in the street. " I wonder what they are looking at, anyhow," says he. He pushed through the crowd, and there he saw the same wee man he had seen before, with a bum-clock; and when he put the bum-clock on the ground he whistled, and the bum-clock began to dance; and the men, women, and children in the street, and Jack and the spotty cow began to dance and jig also, and everything on the street and about it—the wheels and reels, the pots and pans began to jig, and the houses themselves began to dance likewise. And when the man lifted the bum-clock and put it in his pocket everybody stopped jigging and dancing and everyone laughed aloud. The wee man turned and saw Jack.

" Jack, my brave boy," says he, " you will never be right fixed until you have this bum-clock, for it is a very fancy thing to have."

" Oh! but," says Jack, says he, " I have no money."

" No matter for that," says the man; " you have a cow, and that is as good as money to me."

" Well," says Jack, " I have a poor mother who is very downhearted at home, and she sent me to the fair to sell this cow and raise some money and lift her heart."

" Oh! but Jack," says the wee man, " this bum-clock is the very thing to lift her heart, for when you put down your harp and bee and mouse on the floor, and put the bum-clock along with them she will laugh if she never laughed in her life before."

" Well, that is surely true," says Jack, says he, " and I think I will make a swap with you."

So Jack gave the cow to the man and took the bum-clock himself, and started for home. His mother was glad to see Jack back, and says she, " Jack, I see that you have sold the cow."

" I did that, mother," says Jack.

"Did you sell her well, Jack?" says the mother.

"Very well indeed, mother," says Jack.

"How much did you get for her?" says the mother.

"I didn't take any money for her, mother, but value," says Jack, and he takes out of his pocket the bum-clock and the mouse, and set them on the floor and began to whistle, and the bee began to play the harp and the mouse and the bum-clock stood up on their hind legs and began to dance, and Jack's mother laughed very hearty, and everything in the house— the wheels and the reels and the pots and pans went jigging and hopping over the floor, and the house itself went jigging and hopping about likewise.

When Jack lifted up the animals and put them in his pocket everything stopped, and the mother laughed for a good while. But after a while, when she came to herself and saw what Jack had done and how they were now without either money, or food, or a cow, she got very, very angry at Jack and scolded him hard, and then sat down and began to cry.

Poor Jack, when he looked at himself, confessed that he was a stupid fool entirely. "And what," says he, "shall I now do for my poor mother?" He went out along the road, thinking and thinking, and he met a wee woman who said: "Good morrow to you, Jack," says she, "how is it you are not trying for the King's daughter of Ireland?"

"What do you mean?" says Jack.

Says she: "Didn't you hear what the whole world has heard, that the King of Ireland has a daughter who hasn't laughed for seven years, and he has promised to give her in marriage and to give the kingdom along with her to any man who will take three laughs out of her."

"If that is so," says Jack, says he, "it is not here I should be."

Back to the house he went and gathers together the bee, the harp, the mouse, and the bum-clock, and putting them into his pocket he bade his mother good-by, and told her it wouldn't be long till she got good news from him, and off he hurries.

When he reached the castle there was a ring of spikes all

around the castle and men's heads on nearly every spike there.

"What heads are these?" Jack asked one of the King's soldiers.

"Any man that comes here trying to win the King's daughter and fails to make her laugh three times loses his head and has it stuck on a spike. These are the heads of the men that failed," says he.

"A mighty big crowd," says Jack, says he. Then Jack sent word to tell the King's daughter and the King that there was a new man who had come to win her.

In a very little time the King and the King's daughter and the King's court all came out and sat themselves down on gold-and-silver chairs in front of the castle, and ordered Jack to be brought in until he should have his trial. Jack, before he went, took out of his pocket the bee, the harp, the mouse, and the bum-clock, and he gave the harp to the bee, and he tied a string to one and the other, and took the end of the string himself, and marched into the castle yard before all the court, with his animals coming on a string behind him.

When the Queen and the King and the court and the princes saw poor ragged Jack with his bee and mouse and bum-clock hopping behind him on a string they set up one roar of laughter that was long and loud enough, and when the King's daughter herself lifted her head and looked to see what they were laughing at, and saw Jack and his paraphernalia, she opened her mouth and she gave such a laugh as was never heard before.

Then Jack dropped a low courtesy and said: "Thank you, my lady; I have one of the three parts of you won."

Then he drew up his animals in a circle and began to whistle, and the minute he did the bee began to play the harp, and the mouse and the bum-clock stood up on their hind legs, got hold of each other, and began to dance, and the King and the King's court and Jack himself began to dance and jig, and everything about the King's castle — pots and pans, wheels and reels, and the castle itself began to dance also. And the

King's daughter, when she saw this, opened her mouth again and gave a laugh twice louder than she did before, and Jack, in the middle of his jigging, drops another courtesy, and says: "Thank you, my lady; that is two of the three parts of you won."

Jack and his menagerie went on playing and dancing, but Jack could not get the third laugh out of the King's daughter, and the poor fellow saw his big head in danger of going on the spike. Then the brave mouse came to Jack's help and wheeled round upon its heel, and as it did so its tail swept into the bum-clock's mouth, and the bum-clock began to cough and cough and cough. And when the King's daughter saw this she opened her mouth again, and she laughed the loudest and hardest and merriest laugh that was ever heard before or since; and, "Thank you, my lady," says Jack, dropping another courtesy; "I have all of you won."

Then when Jack stopped his menagerie the King took himself and the menagerie within the castle. He was washed and combed and dressed in a suit of silk and satin, with all kinds of gold and silver ornaments, and then was led before the King's daughter. And true enough she confessed that a handsomer and finer fellow than Jack she had never seen, and she was very willing to be his wife.

Jack sent for his poor old mother and brought her to the wedding, which lasted nine days and nine nights, every night better than the other. All the lords and ladies and gentry of Ireland were at the wedding. I was at it, too, and got brogues, broth and slippers of bread, and came jigging home on my head.

THE FAIRY RING

The Long Leather Bag

ONCE on a time, long, long ago, there was a widow woman who had three daughters. When their father died, their mother thought they never would want, for he had left her a long leather bag filled with gold and silver. But he was not long dead, when an old Hag came begging to the house one day and stole the long leather bag filled with gold and silver, and went away out of the country with it, no one knew where.

So from that day, the widow woman and her three daughters were poor, and she had a hard struggle to live and to bring up her three daughters.

But when they were grown up, the eldest said one day: "Mother, I'm a young woman now, and it's a shame for me to be here doing nothing to help you or myself. Bake me a bannock and cut me a callop, till I go away to push my fortune."

The mother baked her a whole bannock, and asked her if she would have half of it with her blessing, or the whole of it without. She said to give her the whole bannock without.

So she took it and went away. She told them if she was not back in a year and a day from that, then they would know she was doing well, and making her fortune.

She traveled away and away before her, far farther than I could tell you, and twice as far as you could tell me, until she came into a strange country, and going up to a little house, she found an old Hag living in it. The Hag asked her where she was going. She said she was going to push her fortune.

Said the Hag: "How would you like to stay here with me, for I want a maid?"

"What will I have to do?" said she.

"You will have to wash me and dress me, and sweep the hearth clean; but on the peril of your life, never look up the chimney," said the Hag.

"All right," she agreed to this.

[279]

THE FAIRY RING

The next day, when the Hag arose, she washed her and dressed her, and when the Hag went out, she swept the hearth clean, and she thought it would do no harm to have one wee look up the chimney. And there, what did she see but her own mother's long leather bag of gold and silver! So she took it down at once, and getting it on her back, started away for home as fast as she could run.

But she had not gone far when she met a horse grazing in a field, and when he saw her he said: " Rub me! Rub me! for I haven't been rubbed these seven years."

But she only struck him with a stick she had in her hand, and drove him out of her way.

She had not gone much farther when she met a sheep, who said: " Oh, shear me! Shear me! for I haven't been shorn these seven years."

But she struck the sheep, and sent it scurrying out of her way.

She had not gone much farther when she met a goat tethered, and he said: " Oh, change my tether! Change my tether! for it hasn't been changed these seven years."

But she flung a stone at him, and went on.

Next she came to a limekiln, and it said: " Oh, clean me! Clean me! for I haven't been cleaned these seven years."

But she only scowled at it, and hurried on.

After another bit she met a cow, and it said:

" Oh, milk me! Milk me! for I haven't been milked these seven years."

She struck the cow out of her way, and went on.

Then she came to a mill. The mill said: " Oh, turn me! Turn me! for I haven't been turned these seven years."

But she did not heed what it said, only went in and lay down behind the mill door, with the bag under her head, for it was then night.

When the Hag came into her hut again and found the girl gone, she ran to the chimney and looked up to see if she had carried off the bag. She flew into a great rage, and she started to run as fast she could after her.

[280]

THE FAIRY RING

She had not gone far when she met the horse, and she said: "Oh, horse, horse of mine, did you see this maid of mine, with my tig, with my tag, with my long leather bag, and all the gold and silver I have earned since I was a maid?"

"Aye," said the horse, "it is not long since she passed here."

So on she ran, and it was not long till she met the sheep, and said she: "Sheep, sheep of mine, did you see this maid of mine, with my tig, with my tag, with my long leather bag, and all the gold and silver I have earned since I was a maid?"

"Aye," said the sheep, "it is not long since she passed here."

So she goes on, and it was not long before she met the goat, and said she: "Goat, goat of mine, did you see this maid of mine, with my tig, with my tag, with my long leather bag, and all the gold and silver I have earned since I was a maid?"

"Aye," said the goat, "it is not long since she passed here."

So she goes on, and it was not long before she met the limekiln, and said she: "Limekiln, limekiln of mine, did you see this maid of mine, with my tig, with my tag, with my long leather bag, and with all the gold and silver I have earned since I was a maid?"

"Aye," said the limekiln, "it is not long since she passed here."

So she goes on, and it was not long before she met the cow, and said she: "Cow, cow of mine, did you see this maid of mine, with my tig, with my tag, with my long leather bag, and all the gold and silver I have earned since I was a maid?"

"Aye," said the cow, "it is not long since she passed here."

So she goes on, and it was not long before she met the mill, and said she: "Mill, mill of mine, did you see this maid of mine, with my tig, with my tag, with my long leather bag, and all the gold and silver I have earned since I was a maid?"

And the mill said: "Yes, she is sleeping behind the door."
She went in and struck her with a white rod, and turned

[281]

her into a stone. She then took the bag of gold and silver on her back and went away back home.

A year and a day had gone by after the eldest daughter left home, and when they found she had not returned, the second daughter got up, and she said: " My sister must be doing well and making her fortune, and isn't it a shame for me to be sitting here doing nothing, either to help you, mother, or myself? Bake me a bannock," said she, " and cut me a callop, till I go away to push my fortune."

The mother did this, and asked her would she have half the bannock with her blessing, or the whole bannock without.

She said the whole bannock without, and she set off. Then she said: " If I am not back here in a year and a day, you may be sure that I am doing well and making my fortune," and then she went away.

She traveled away and away on before her, far farther than I could tell you, and twice as far as you could tell me, until she came into a strange country, and going up to a little house, she found an old Hag living in it. The old Hag asked her where she was going. She said she was going to push her fortune.

Said the Hag: " How would you like to stay here with me, for I want a maid?"

" What will I have to do?" says she.

" You'll have to wash me and dress me, and sweep the hearth clean; and on the peril of your life never look up the chimney," said the Hag.

" All right," she agreed to this.

The next day, when the Hag arose, she washed her and dressed her, and when the Hag went out she swept the hearth, and she thought it would do no harm to have one wee look up the chimney. And there, what did she see but her own mother's long leather bag of gold and silver! So she took it down at once, and getting it on her back, started away for home as fast as she could run.

But she had not gone far when she met a horse grazing

THE FAIRY RING

in a field, and when he saw her he said: "Rub me! Rub me! for I haven't been rubbed these seven years."

But she only struck him with a stick she had in her hand and drove him out of her way.

She had not gone much farther when she met the sheep, who said: "Oh, shear me! Shear me! for I haven't been shorn in seven years."

But she struck the sheep and sent it scurrying out of her way.

She had not gone much farther when she met the goat tethered, and he said: "Oh, change my tether! Change my tether! for it hasn't been changed in seven years."

But she flung a stone at him and went on.

Next she came to the limekiln, and that said: "Oh, clean me! Clean me! for I haven't been cleaned these seven years."

But she only scowled at it and hurried on.

Then she came to the cow, and it said: "Oh, milk me, Milk me! for I haven't been milked these seven years."

She struck the cow out of her way and went on.

Then she came to the mill. The mill said: "Oh, turn me! Turn me! for I haven't been turned these seven years."

But she did not heed what it said, only went in and lay down behind the mill door, with the bag under her head, for it was then night.

When the Hag came into her hut again and found the girl gone, she ran to the chimney and looked up to see if she had carried off the bag. She flew into a great rage, and she started to run as fast as she could after her.

She had not gone far when she met the horse, and she said: "Oh, horse, horse of mine, did you see this maid of mine, with my tig, with my tag, with my long leather bag, and all the gold and silver I have earned since I was a maid?"

"Aye," said the horse, "it is not long since she passed here."

So on she ran, and it was not long until she met the sheep, and said she: "Oh, sheep, sheep of mine, did you see this maid of mine, with my tig, with my tag, with my long leather

[283]

bag, and all the gold and silver I have earned since I was a maid?"

"Aye," said the sheep, "it is not long since she passed here."

So she goes on, and it was not long before she met the goat, and said: "Goat, goat of mine, did you see this maid of mine, with my tig, with my tag, with my long leather bag, and all the gold and silver I have earned since I was a maid?"

"Aye," said the goat, "it is not long since she passed here."

So she goes on, and it was not long before she met the limekiln, and said she: "Limekiln, limekiln of mine, did you see this maid of mine, with my tig, with my tag, with my long leather bag, and all the gold and silver I have earned since I was a maid?"

"Aye," said the limekiln, "it is not long since she passed here."

So she goes on, and it was not long before she met the cow, and says she: "Cow, cow of mine, did you see this maid of mine, with my tig, with my tag, with my long leather bag, and all the gold and silver I have earned since I was a maid?"

"Aye," said the cow, "it is not long since she passed here."

So she goes on, and it was not long before she met the mill, and said she: "Mill, mill of mine, did you see this maid of mine, with my tig, with my tag, with my long leather bag, and all the gold and silver I have earned since I was a maid?"

And the mill said: "Yes, she is sleeping behind the door."

She went in and struck her with a white rod, and turned her into a stone. She then took the bag of gold and silver on her back and went home.

When the second daughter had been gone a year and a day and she hadn't come back, the youngest daughter said: "My two sisters must be doing very well indeed, and making great fortunes when they are not coming back, and it's a shame for me to be sitting here doing nothing, either to help you, mother, or myself. Make me a bannock and cut me a callop, till I go away and push my fortune."

The mother did this, and asked her would she have half of the bannock with her blessing, or the whole bannock without.

She said: " I will have half of the bannock with your blessing, mother."

The mother gave her a blessing and half a bannock, and she set out.

She traveled away and away on before her, far farther than I could tell you, and twice as far as you could tell me, until she came into a strange country, and going up to a little house, she found an old Hag living in it. The Hag asked her where she was going. She said she was going to push her fortune.

Said the Hag: " How would you like to stay here with me, for I want a maid?"

" What will I have to do?" said she.

" You'll have to wash me and dress me, and sweep the hearth clean; and on the peril of your life never look up the chimney," said the Hag.

" All right," she agreed to this.

The next day when the Hag arose, she washed her and dressed her, and when the Hag went out she swept the hearth, and she thought it would do no harm to have one wee look up the chimney, and there, what did she see but her own mother's long leather bag of gold and silver! So she took it down at once, and getting it on her back, started away for home as fast as she could run.

When she got to the horse, the horse said: " Rub me! Rub me! for I haven't been rubbed these seven years."

" Oh, poor horse, poor horse," she said, " I'll surely do that." And she laid down her bag and rubbed the horse.

Then she went on, and it wasn't long before she met the sheep, who said: " Oh, shear me! Shear me! for I haven't been shorn these seven years."

"Oh, poor sheep, poor sheep," she said, "I'll surely do that," and she laid down the bag and sheared the sheep.

On she went till she met the goat who said: "Oh, change my tether! Change my tether! for it hasn't been changed these seven years."

"Oh, poor goat, poor goat," she said, "I'll surely do that," and she laid down the bag and changed the goat's tether.

Then she went on till she met the limekiln. The limekiln said: "Oh, clean me! Clean me! for I haven't been cleaned these seven years."

"Oh, poor limekiln, poor limekiln," she said, "I'll surely do that," and she laid down the bag and cleaned the limekiln.

Then she went on and met the cow. The cow said: "Oh, milk me! Milk me! for I haven't been milked these seven years."

"Oh, poor cow, poor cow," she said, "I'll surely do that," and she laid down the bag and milked the cow.

At last she reached the mill. The mill said: "Oh, turn me! Turn me! for I haven't been turned these seven years."

"Oh, poor mill, poor mill," she said, "I'll surely do that," and she turned the mill too.

As night was on her she went in and lay down behind the mill door to sleep.

When the Hag came into her hut again and found the girl gone, she ran to the chimney to see if she had carried off the bag. She flew into a great rage, and started to run as fast as she could after her.

She had not gone far until she came up to the horse and said: "Oh, horse, horse of mine, did you see this maid of mine, with my tig, with my tag, with my long leather bag, and all the gold and silver I have earned since I was a maid?"

The horse said: "Do you think I have nothing to do but watch your maids for you? You may go somewhere else and look for information."

Then she came upon the sheep. "Oh, sheep, sheep of mine, have you seen this maid of mine, with my tig, with my tag with my long leather bag, and all the gold and silver I have earned since I was a maid?"

The sheep said: "Do you think I have nothing to do but watch your maids for you? You may go somewhere else and look for information."

Then she went on till she met the goat. "Oh, goat, goat of mine, have you seen this maid of mine, with my tig, with my tag, with my long leather bag, and all the gold and silver I have earned since I was a maid?"

The goat said: "Do you think I have nothing to do but watch your maids for you? You can go somewhere else and look for information."

Then she went on till she came to the limekiln. "Oh, lime-kiln, limekiln of mine, did you see this maid of mine, with my tig, with my tag, with my long leather bag, and all the gold and silver I have earned since I was a maid?"

Said the limekiln: "Do you think I have nothing to do but watch your maids for you? You may go somewhere else and look for information."

Next she met the cow. "Oh, cow, cow of mine, have you seen this maid of mine, with my tig, with my tag, with my long leather bag, and all the gold and silver I have earned since I was a maid?"

The cow said: "Do you think I have nothing to do but watch your maids for you? You may go somewhere else and look for information."

Then she got to the mill. "Oh, mill, mill of mine, have you seen this maid of mine, with my tig, with my tag, with my long leather bag, and all the gold and silver I have earned since I was a maid?"

The mill said: "Come nearer and whisper to me."

She went nearer to whisper to the mill, and the mill dragged her under the wheels and ground her up.

The old Hag had dropped the white rod out of her hand, and the mill told the young girl to take this white rod and strike two stones behind the mill door. She did that, and her two sisters stood up. She hoisted the leather bag on her back, and the three of them set out and traveled away and away till they reached home.

The mother had been crying all the time while they were away, and was now ever so glad to see them, and rich and happy they all lived ever after.

The Widow's Daughter

THERE was once a poor widow woman, living in the North of Ireland, who had one daughter named Nabla. And Nabla grew up both idle and lazy, till at length, when she had grown to be a young woman, she was both thriftless and useless, fit only to sit with her heels in the ashes and croon to the cat the day long. Her mother was annoyed with her, so that one day, when Nabla refused to do some little trifle about the house, her mother got out a good stout sally rod and came in and thrashed her soundly with it.

As her mother was giving Nabla the whacking she had so richly earned, who should happen to be riding past but the King's son himself. He heard the mother beating and scolding, and Nabla crying and pleading within. So he drew rein, and at the top of his voice shouted to know what was the matter. The widow came to the door, courtesying when she saw who he was. Not wishing to give out a bad name on her daughter, she told the King's son that she had a daughter who killed herself working the leelong day and refused to rest when her mother asked her, so that she had always to be beaten before she would stop.

"What work can your daughter do?" the Prince asked.

"She can spin, weave, and sew, and do every work that ever a woman did," the mother replied.

Now, it so happened that a twelvemonth before the Prince had taken a notion of marrying, and his mother, anxious he should have none but the best wife, had, with his approval, sent messengers over all Ireland to find him a woman who could perform all a woman's duties, including the three accomplishments the widow named—spinning, that is, weaving and sewing. But all the candidates whom the messengers had secured were found unsatisfactory on being put to trial, and the Prince had remained unwedded. When, now, the King's son heard this account of Nabla from her own mother he said:

"You are not fit to have the charge of such a good girl. For twelve months, through all parts of my mother's kingdom, search was being made for just such a young woman that she might become my wife. I'll take Nabla with me."

Poor Nabla was rejoiced and her mother astonished. The King's son helped Nabla to a seat behind him on the horse's back and bidding adieu to the widow, rode off.

When he had got Nabla home, he introduced her to his mother, telling the Queen that by good fortune he had secured the very woman they had so long sought in vain. The Queen asked what Nabla could do, and he replied that she could spin, weave, and sew, and do everything else a woman should; and, moreover, she was so eager for work that her mother was beating her within an inch of her life to make her rest herself when he arrived on the scene at Nabla's own cottage. The Queen said that was well.

She took Nabla to a large room and gave her a heap of silk and a golden wheel, and told her she must have all the silk spun into thread in twenty-four hours. Then she bolted her in.

Poor Nabla, in amazement, sat looking at the big heap of silk and the golden wheel. And at length she began to cry, for she had not spun a yard of thread in all her life. As she cried an ugly woman, having one of her feet as big as a bolster, appeared before her.

"What are you crying for?" she asked.

Nabla told her, and the woman said, "I'll spin the silk for you if you ask me to the wedding."

"I'll do that," Nabla said. And then the woman sat down

to the wheel, and working it with her big foot, very soon had
the whole heap spun.

When the Queen came and found all spun she said: "That
is good." Then she brought in a golden loom and told Nabla
she must have all that thread woven in twenty-four hours.

When the Queen had gone, Nabla sat down and looked
from the thread to the loom and from the loom to the thread,
wondering, for she had not in all her life even thrown a
shuttle. At length she put her face in her hands and began
to cry. There now appeared to her an ugly woman with one
hand as big as a pot hanging by her side. She asked Nabla
why she cried. Nabla told her, and then the woman said:

"I'll weave all that for you if you'll give me the promise
of your wedding."

Nabla said she would surely. So the woman sat down to
the golden loom, and very soon had all the thread woven
into webs.

When again the Queen came and found all woven she said:
"That is good." And then she gave Nabla a golden needle
and thimble and said that in twenty-four hours more she
must have all the webs made into shirts for the Prince.

Again when the Queen had gone, Nabla, who had never
even threaded a needle in all her life, sat for a while looking
at the needle and thimble and looking at the webs of silk,
and again she broke down, and began to cry heartily.

As she cried an ugly woman with a monstrously big nose
came into the room and asked:

"Why do you cry?"

When Nabla had told her, the ugly woman said:

"I'll make up all those webs into shirts for the Prince if
you promise me the wedding."

"I'll do that," Nabla said, "and a thousand welcomes."

So the woman with the big nose, taking the needle and
thimble, sat down, and in a short time had made all the silk
into shirts and disappeared again.

When the Queen came a third time and found all the silk
made up in shirts she was mightily pleased and said:

[290]

THE FAIRY RING

" You are the very woman for my son, for he'll never want a housekeeper while he has you."

Then Nabla and the Prince were betrothed, and on the wedding night there was a gay and a gorgeous company in the hall of the castle. All was mirth and festivity. But as they were about to sit down to a splendid repast there was a loud knock at the door. A servant opened it and there came in an ugly old woman with one foot as big as a bolster who, amid the loud laughter of the company, hobbled along the floor and took a seat at the table. She was asked of which party was she, the bride or the groom's, and she replied that she was of the bride's party. When the Prince heard this he believed that she was one of Nabla's poor friends. He went up to her and asked her what had made her foot so big.

"Spinning," she said, " I have been all my life at the wheel, and that's what it has done for me."

"Then, by my word," said the Prince, striking the table a great blow, " my wife shall not turn a wheel while I'm here to prevent it!"

As the guests were again settling themselves another knock came to the door. A servant opening it, let in a woman with one hand as big as a pot. The weight of this hand hanging by her side gave her body a great lean over, so that as she hobbled along the floor the company at the table lay back, laughing and clapping their hands at the funny sight. This woman, taking a seat at the table, was asked by whose invitation she was there, to which she replied that she was of the bride's party. Then the Prince went up to her and inquired what caused her hand to be so big.

"Weaving," she said. " I have slaved at the shuttle all my life; that's what has come on me."

"Then," the Prince said, striking the table a thundering blow, " by my word, my wife shall never throw a shuttle again while I live to prevent it."

A third time the guests were ready to begin their repast, when again there came a knock to the door. Everyone looked up; and they saw the servant now admit an ugly old woman

[291]

with the most monstrous nose ever beheld. This woman likewise took a chair at the table. She was then asked who had invited her—the bride or the groom. She said she was one of the bride's party. Then the Prince, going up to her, asked her why her nose had come to be so very big.

"It's with sewing," she said. "All my life I have been bending my head over sewing, so that every drop of blood ran down into my nose, swelling it out like that."

Then the Prince struck the table a blow that made the dishes leap and rattle.

"By my word," he said, "my wife shall never either put a needle in cloth again, or do any other sort of household work while I live to prevent it."

And the Prince faithfully kept his word. He was always on the lookout to try and catch Nabla spinning, weaving, or sewing, or doing any other sort of work, for he thought she might at any time try to work on the sly.

Poor Nabla, however, never did anything to confirm his uneasiness, but, taking her old mother to stay in the castle with her, lived happy and contented, and as lazy as the day was long, ever after.

Munachar and Manachar

THERE once lived a Munachar and a Manachar, a long time ago, and it is a long time since it was, and if they were alive now they would not be alive then. They went out together to pick raspberries, and as many as Munachar used to pick Manachar used to eat. Munachar said he must go look for a rod to make a gad to hang Manachar, who ate his raspberries every one; and he came to the rod. "What news to-day?" said the rod. "It is my own news that I'm seeking. Going looking for a rod, a rod to make a gad, a gad to hang Manachar, who ate my raspberries every one.

"AN UGLY OLD WOMAN WITH THE MOST MONSTROUS NOSE EVER BEHELD"

"You will not get me," said the rod, "until you get an ax to cut me." He came to the ax. "What news to-day?" said the ax. "It's my own news I'm seeking. Going looking for an ax, an ax to cut a rod, a rod to make a gad, a gad to hang Manachar, who ate my raspberries every one."

"You will not get me," said the ax, "until you get a flag to edge me." He came to the flag. "What news to-day?" says the flag. "It's my own news I'm seeking. Going looking for a flag, flag to edge ax, ax to cut a rod, a rod to to make a gad, a gad to hang Manachar, who ate my raspberries every one."

"You will not get me," says the flag, "till you get water to wet me." He came to the water. "What news to-day?" says the water. "It's my own news I'm seeking. Going looking for water, water to wet flag, flag to edge ax, ax to cut a rod, a rod to make a gad, a gad to hang Manachar, who ate my raspberries every one."

"You will not get me," said the water, "until you get a deer who will swim me." He came to the deer. "What news to-day?" says the deer. "It's my own news I'm seeking. Going looking for a deer, deer to swim water, water to wet flag, flag to edge ax, ax to cut a rod, a rod to make a gad, a gad to hang Manachar, who ate my raspberries every one.

"You will not get me," said the deer, "until you get a hound who will hunt me." He came to the hound. "What news to-day?" says the hound. "It's my own news I'm seeking. Going looking for a hound, hound to hunt deer, deer to swim water, water to wet flag, flag to edge ax, ax to cut a rod, a rod to make a gad, a gad to hang Manachar, who ate my raspberries every one."

"You will not get me," said the hound, "until you get a bit of butter to put in my claw." He came to the butter. "What news to-day?" says the butter. "It's my own news I'm seeking. Going looking for butter, butter to go in claw of hound, hound to hunt deer, deer to swim water, water to wet flag, flag to edge ax, ax to cut a rod, a rod to make a gad, a gad to hang Manachar, who ate my raspberries every one."

"You will not get me," said the butter, "until you get a cat who shall scrape me." He came to the cat. "What news to-day?" said the cat. "It's my own news I'm seeking. Going looking for a cat, cat to scrape butter, butter to go in claw of hound, hound to hunt deer, deer to swim water, water to wet flag, flag to edge ax, ax to cut a rod, a rod to make a gad, a gad to hang Manachar, who ate my raspberries every one."

"You will not get me," said the cat, "until you get milk which you will give me." He came to the cow. "What news to-day?" said the cow. "It's my own news I'm seeking. Going looking for a cow, cow to give me milk, milk I will give to the cat, cat to scrape butter, butter to go in claw of hound, hound to hunt deer, deer to swim water, water to wet flag, flag to edge ax, ax to cut a rod, a rod to make a gad, a gad to hang Manachar, who ate my raspberries every one."

"You will not get any milk from me," said the cow, "until you bring me a whisp of straw from those threshers yonder." He came to the threshers. "What news to-day?" said the threshers. "It's my own news I'm seeking. Going looking for a whisp of straw to give to the cow, the cow to give me milk, milk I will give to the cat, cat to scrape butter, butter to go in claw of hound, hound to hunt deer, deer to swim water, water to wet flag, flag to edge ax, ax to cut a rod, a rod to make a gad, a gad to hang Manachar, who ate my raspberries every one."

"You will not get any whisp of straw from us," said the threshers, "until you bring us the makings of a cake from the miller over yonder." He came to the miller. "What news to-day?" said the miller. "It's my own news I'm seeking. Going looking for the makings of a cake which I will give the threshers, the threshers to give me a whisp of straw, the whisp of straw I will give to the cow, the cow to give me milk, milk I will give to the cat, cat to scrape butter, butter to go in claw of hound, hound to hunt deer, deer to swim water, water to wet flag, flag to edge ax, ax to cut a rod, a rod to make a gad, a gad to hang Manachar, who ate my raspberries every one."

"You will not get any makings of a cake from me," said the miller, "till you bring me the full of that sieve of water from the river over there."

He took the sieve in his hand and went over to the river, but as often as ever he would stoop and fill it with water, the moment he raised it the water would run out of it again, and sure, if he had been there, from that day till this, he never could have filled it. A crow went flying by him, over his head, "Daub! daub!" said the crow. "My blessings on ye, then," said Munachar, "but it's the good advice you have"; and he took the red clay and the daub that was by the brink, and he rubbed it to the bottom of the sieve, until all the holes were filled, and then the sieve held the water, and he brought the water to the miller, and the miller gave him the makings of a cake, and he gave the makings of the cake to the threshers, and the threshers gave him a whisp of straw, and he gave the whisp of straw to the cow, and the cow gave him milk, the milk he gave to the cat, the cat scraped the butter, the butter went into the claw of the hound, the hound hunted the deer, the deer swam the water, the water wet the flag, the flag sharpened the ax, the ax cut the rod, and the rod made a gad, and when he had it ready to hang Manachar he found that Manachar had BURST.

The Road to Fortune

ONE fine morning two young men were strolling together through the fields, when they perceived, at a great distance, a very high hill, on the top of which stood a beautiful castle, which sparkled so brightly in the sunshine that the youths were quite delighted, and could not help gazing at it.

THE FAIRY RING

"Let us go to it," said one of the lads.

"It is easy to say, 'Let us go,' but how can we walk so far?" retorted the other, who was a lazy fellow.

"You may do it easily," replied a clear voice behind them.

On looking around to see whence these words came, they perceived a beautiful fairy standing on a large ball, which rolled along with her upon it in the direction of the castle.

"It is no very difficult task for her, at all events. Look, she can get forward without moving a limb," said the lazy one, throwing himself down on the grass.

The other, however, was not so easily satisfied; for, without stopping to reflect, he started off after the fairy as fast as he could run, and catching hold of the skirts of her robe cried, "Who art thou?"

"I am Fortune," answered the fairy, "and yonder is my castle—follow me there! If thou reachest it before midnight, I will receive thee as a friend; but remember, shouldst thou arrive one moment later, my door will be closed against thee."

With these words the fairy drew her robe from the hand of the young man, and went off so quickly upon her ball that she was soon out of sight.

The youth immediately ran back to his companion and told him all that had happened, adding: "I intend taking the fairy's advice. Will you accompany me?"

"Are you mad?" inquired the other; "for my part, if I had a good horse I should not mind the journey, but as for walking all that way, I certainly shall not attempt it."

"Farewell then," answered his comrade, who started off at a brisk pace in the direction of the castle.

The lazy one, however, reasoned thus to himself: "Exert yourself as much as you please, my worthy friend. Good fortune often comes while we are dozing; perhaps it may be my case to-day." And without more ado he stretched himself on the grass and fell fast asleep; not, however, before he had cast a longing glance at the beautiful castle on the hill. After sleeping some time he felt as though there were a warm wind blowing on his ear, and when he had stretched his slothful limbs and rubbed his sleepy eyes, he perceived a beautiful milk-white horse, ready saddled, standing beside him, shaking his mane and neighing lustily in the clear morning air.

"Ah, did I not say as much?" cried the youth. "Oh, if people would but trust to Fate! Come here, you fine creature! We must be good friends." So saying, he threw himself into the saddle, and the steed galloped off with him as swift as the wind. Thus mounted, our lazy friend very soon overtook his industrious companion, and hailing him as he passed cried: "Show respect to my horse's heels!" The other, however, continued on at a steady pace, without paying much heed to his satire.

About midday, on arriving at the summit of a beautiful hill, the horse suddenly stopped. "Quite right," cried his rider; "I find you are a very sagacious creature—'soft and fairly' is a good proverb; the castle is now not very far off, but my appetite is a great deal nearer." So dismounting, he sought out a shady slope, and having laid down in the moss with his feet against the stump of a tree, he began to take some refreshment—for happily he had a good supply of bread and sausage in his pocket, and a pleasant drink in his flask. As soon as the youth had satisfied his appetite, he began to feel rather drowsy, and, as is usual with indolent people, he gave full vent to the inclination, stretched himself on the moss, and fell into a sound sleep. Never had man a more pleasant sleep, nor accompanied with more delightful dreams. He imagined that he was already in the castle, reposing on silken cushions; and that all that he desired came to him immediately upon his beckoning with his little finger. After thus enjoying himself for some time, it seemed as though a firework went off with a great explosion; this was followed by strains of soft music, which went to the tune of a song he had often heard, every verse of which terminated with these words:

THE FAIRY RING

"Healthful limbs and spirits gay,
Bear the traveler on his way."

This continued some time, when he awoke with the song still ringing in his ears; then rubbing his eyes, he perceived that the setting sun was fast sinking behind the castle, and heard the voice of his companion singing from the valley before him the very words he had heard in his dream.

"What a time I have slept!" cried the lazy fellow. "It is high time that I was getting on my way. Come here, my steed! where are you?" But no steed was to be found; the only creature that he could see, after looking all around, was an old gray donkey, grazing on the top of a hill at some distance. He shouted and whistled with all his might, but the horse was gone quite out of hearing, and the old donkey did not seem to pay the least attention. So, after exerting his lungs to no purpose, the lazy fellow was obliged to go and try to make friends with the gray old beast, which allowed itself to be quietly mounted, and then trudged slowly on with him.

But our youth found this kind of traveling very different from the previous stage, for then he not only proceeded at a much quicker pace, but had a more comfortable seat, which was by no means an unimportant consideration with him. In the course of a short time it began to grow dark, and heavy clouds overspread the sky; already he could perceive that the castle was being lighted up, and now he began to be very frightened and anxious to get forward. The donkey, however, did not seem in any way to partake of his feelings, but continued on at even a slower pace than before. At length it became quite dark, and the donkey, after going slower and slower, came to a dead stand in the midst of a thick wood. All his entreaties were of no use, nor were threats and kicks of more avail—the donkey would not move. At last the rider became so exasperated that he struck it with his fist; but this did not much improve our lazy friend's condition, for the obstinate brute instantly flung up its hind legs, and by that process released itself of its burden, which fell heavily on the ground. It required much less violence than our youth experienced in his fall to prove to him that he was not lying on a satin couch, for his legs and arms were dreadfully bruised. He remained some time in this miserable plight, but the bright and inviting appearance of the lights in the castle at length attracted his attention. "Ah!" thought he, "what beautiful beds must there be in that fine building!"

This thought alone aroused for a moment his sluggish energies, and he managed to get on his feet. "Perhaps," thought he, "the gray old donkey may by this time have got into a better temper." So he searched about for him in every direction; but after knocking his head against the trees here, tearing his face with the thorns there, and stumbling over roots and stones for a full quarter of an hour without finding it, he gave up the search as hopeless. It was high time, however, that he made some effort to get out of this dismal wood, which every now and then resounded with dreary howls, sounding very much as though they proceeded from the throats of hungry wolves. At last, when quite bewildered with fear, he suddenly stumbled against something soft and slimy; he knew by the touch that it was not the donkey, but fancying it to be in the form of a saddle, he was about to bestride it at once; yet he found it so cold and damp to the touch that he quite shuddered at the thought. He was still hesitating when the castle clock struck, and he counted eleven. Recollecting that it was drawing near to the eventful time and that he had no other hope, he threw himself on what appeared to be the saddle. He found his seat tolerably easy, as it was very soft, and at his back was something to lean against; another great advantage was that the creature on which he was mounted seemed to be very surefooted; there was, however, one great objection to it, and that was the creeping pace at which it moved, for it went along much slower than even the obstinate donkey.

Proceeding thus for some time, he got so near to the

castle that he could count the windows, and in this occupation he was engaged when suddenly the moon shone out from between the clouds, and, oh, horror! what did he behold. The creature on which he sat was neither a horse nor a donkey, but an enormous snail, quite as large as a calf, and its house which it carried upon its back had served him to lean against! Now he could well understand why he had come at such a creeping pace. He turned as cold as death, and his hair stood on end with fright! But there was now no time for fear, for the castle clock had already made the woods resound with the first stroke of the midnight hour, just as his steed crawled out from the wood. Then how great was the young man's astonishment when he beheld the castle of Fortune in all its grandeur! Hitherto he had sat quietly on the snail, without hastening it, or in any way interfering with its pace; at the sight of the castle, however, he dashed both his heels into its sides, and attempted to urge it on. To this treatment the snail was quite unaccustomed, and instantly it drew its head into its shell and left the youth sprawling on the ground. The castle clock rang out the second stroke. Had the lazy fellow but mustered up resolution and trusted to his feet even then, he might have reached the castle in time. But no, there he stood crying bitterly and screaming out: "A beast! a beast! of whatever kind it may be, to carry me to yon castle."

The inmates of the building had already begun to extinguish the lights, and the moon being hidden by the clouds, he was again in total darkness. As the clock struck the third time he heard something moving near him, and, as well as he could make out in the dark, it seemed like a saddled horse: "Ah, that is my long-lost steed," cried he, "that Heaven has kindly sent to me at the needful moment!" As quickly as his lazy limbs would enable him, he leaped on the back of the creature. There was now only a little elevation to be surmounted, and he could easily see his companion standing at the open door of the castle waving his cap and beckoning him on. The clock chimed out the fourth stroke when the creature whereon he sat began to move slowly; then went the fifth and sixth strokes, and it began to advance a little at a very awkward pace; at the seventh, the creature began to move, first sideways and then went backward! To his great horror and surprise the rider found that he could not throw himself off, though he struggled with all his might. By a passing ray of the moon, he discovered that the new steed on which he was riding was a horrid monster with ten legs, and from either side there extended a large claw with which it held him fast by the arms. The youth screamed loudly for help, but all to no purpose; the animal still kept receding farther and farther from the castle, while the eventful moment approached nearer and nearer, until the twelfth stroke proclaimed the midnight hour. A flitting ray of the moon displayed the castle once more to his view in all its splendor. But in the same moment the youth heard the door shut, and the rattling noise of chains and bolts. The entrance to the castle of Fortune was closed against him forever! The moon now shone again in full luster and discovered the horrid monster, that still kept carrying him away, to be nothing more nor less than an enormous crab. Where he went to on this uncommon steed I cannot tell; for the fact is, nobody ever troubled themselves further about the lazy fellow.

The Golden Crab

ONCE upon a time there was a fisherman who had a wife and three children. Every morning he used to go out fishing, and whatever fish he caught he sold to the King. One day, among the other fishes, he caught a golden crab. When he came home he put all the fishes together into a great dish, but he kept the crab separate because it shone so beautifully, and placed it upon a high shelf in the cupboard Now, while the old woman, his wife, was cleaning the fish, and had tucked up her gown so that her feet were visible, she suddenly heard a voice, which said:

> "Let down, let down thy petticoat
> That lets thy feet be seen."

She turned around in surprise, and then she saw the little creature, the golden crab.

"What! You can speak, can you, you ridiculous crab?" she said, for she was not quite pleased at the crab's remark. Then she took him up and placed him on a dish.

When her husband came home and they sat down to dinner, they presently heard the crab's little voice saying: " Give me some, too." They were all very much surprised, but they gave him something to eat. When the old man came to take away the plate which had contained the crab's dinner, he found it full of gold, and as the same thing happened every day he soon became very fond of the crab.

One day the crab said to the fisherman's wife: " Go to the King and tell him I wish to marry his younger daughter."

The old woman went accordingly and laid the matter before the King, who laughed a little at the notion of his daughter marrying a crab, but did not decline the proposal altogether, because he was a prudent monarch and knew that the crab was likely to be a prince in disguise. He said, therefore, to the fisherman's wife: " Go, old woman, and tell the crab I will give him my daughter if by to-morrow morning he can build a wall in front of my castle much higher than my tower, upon which all the flowers of the world must grow and bloom."

The fisherman's wife went home and gave this message.

Then the crab gave her a golden rod and said: " Go and strike with this rod three times upon the ground on the place which the King showed you, and to-morrow morning the wall will be there."

The old woman did so and went away again.

The next morning, when the King awoke, what do you

think he saw? The wall stood there before his eyes, exactly as he had bespoken it!

Then the old woman went back to the King and said to him: "Your majesty's orders have been fulfilled."

"That is all very well," said the King, "but I cannot give away my daughter until there stands in front of my palace a garden in which there are three fountains, of which the first must play gold, the second diamonds, and the third brilliants."

So the old woman had to strike again three times upon the ground with the rod, and the next morning the garden was there. The King now gave his consent, and the wedding was fixed for the very next day.

Then the crab said to the old fisherman:

"Now take this rod; go and knock with it on a certain mountain; then a black man will come out and ask you what you wish for. Answer him thus: 'Your master, the King, has sent me to tell you that you must send him his golden garment that is like the sun.' Make him give you, besides, the queenly robes of gold and precious stones which are like the flowery meadows, and bring them both to me, and bring me also the golden cushion."

The old man went and did his errand. When he had brought the precious robes the crab put on the golden garment and then crept upon the golden cushion, and in this way the fisherman carried him to the castle, where the crab presented the other garment to his bride. Now the ceremony took place, and when the married pair were alone together the crab made himself known to his young wife, and told her how he was the son of the greatest king in the world, and how he was enchanted, so that he became a crab by day and was a man only at night and he could also change himself into an eagle as often as he wished. No sooner had he said this than he shook himself and immediately became a handsome youth; but the next morning he was forced to creep back again into his crabshell. And the same thing happened every day. But the Princess's affection for the crab and the polite attention with which she behaved to him surprised the royal family very much. They suspected some secret, but though they spied and spied, they could not discover it. Thus a year pased away and the Princess had a son, whom she called Benjamin. But her mother still thought the whole matter very strange. At last she said to the King that he ought to ask his daughter whether she would not like to have another husband instead of the crab. But when the daughter was questioned she only answered:

" I am married to the crab, and him only will I have."

Then the King said to her: " I will appoint a tournament in your honor and I will invite all the princes in the world to it, and if any one of them pleases you you shall marry him."

In the evening the Princess told this to the crab, who said to her: " Take this rod; go to the garden gate and knock with it; then a black man will come out and say to you, ' Why have you called me and what do you require of me?' Answer him thus: ' Your master the King has sent me hither to tell you to send him his golden armor and his steed and the silver apple.' And bring them to me."

The Princess did so and brought him what he desired.

The following evening the Prince dressed himself for the tournament. Before he went he said to his wife: " Now mind you do not say when you see me that I am the crab. For if you do this evil will come of it. Place yourself at the window with your sisters; I will ride by and throw you the silver apple. Take it in your hand, but if they ask who I am, say that you do not know." So saying, he kissed her, repeated his warning once more, and went away.

The Princess went with her sisters to the window and looked on at the tournament. Presently her husband rode by and threw the apple up to her. She caught it in her hand and went with it to her room, and by and by her husband came back to her. But her father was much surprised that she did not seem to care about any of the princes; he therefore appointed a second tournament.

"IN THIS WAY THE FISHERMAN CARRIED HIM TO THE CASTLE"

The crab then gave his wife the same directions as before, only this time the apple which she received from the black man was of gold. But before the Prince went to the tournament he said to his wife: " Now I know you will betray me to-day."

But she swore to him that she would not tell who he was. He then repeated his warning and went away.

In the evening, while the Princess, with her mother and sisters, was standing at the window, the Prince suddenly galloped past on his steed and threw her the golden apple.

Then her mother flew into a passion, gave her a box on the ear, and cried out: " Does not even that prince please you, you fool?"

The Princess in her fright exclaimed: " That is the crab himself!"

Her mother was still more angry because she had not been told sooner, ran into her daughter's room where the crab shell was still lying, took it up and threw it into the fire. Then the poor Princess cried bitterly, but it was of no use; her husband did not come back.

Now we must leave the Princess and turn to the other persons in the story. One day an old man went to a stream to dip in a crust of bread which he was going to eat, when a dog came out of the water, snatched the bread from his hand, and ran away. The old man ran after him, but the dog reached a door, pushed it open, and ran in, the old man following him. He did not overtake the dog, but found himself above a staircase, which he descended. Then he saw before him a stately palace, and entering, he found in a large hall a table set for twelve persons. He hid himself in the hall behind a great picture, that he might see what would happen. At noon he heard a great noise, so that he trembled with fear. When he took courage to look out from behind the picture he saw twelve eagles flying in. At this sight his fear became still greater. The eagles flew to the basin of a fountain that was there and bathed themselves, when suddenly they were changed into twelve handsome youths. Now they seated themselves at the table and one of them took up a goblet filled with wine and said, "A health to my father!" And another said, "A health to my mother!" and so the healths went round. Then one of them said:

> "A health to my dearest lady,
> Long may she live and well!
> But a curse on the cruel mother
> Who burned my golden shell!"

And so saying, he wept bitterly. Then the youths rose from the table, went back to the great stone fountain, turned themselves into eagles again and flew away.

Then the old man went away too, returned to the light of day and went home. Soon after he heard that the Princess was ill, and that the only thing that did her good was having stories told to her. He therefore went to the royal castle, obtained an audience of the Princess, and told her about the strange things he had seen in the underground palace. No sooner had he finished than the Princess asked him whether he could find the way to that palace.

"Yes, certainly," he answered.

And now she desired him to guide her thither at once. The old man did so, and when they came to the palace he hid her behind the great picture and advised her to keep quite still, and he placed himself behind the picture also. Presently the eagles came flying in and changed themselves into young men, and in a moment the Princess recognized her husband among them all and tried to come out of her hiding place; but the old man held her back. The youths seated themselves at the table; and now the Prince said again, while he took up the cup of wine:

> "A health to my dearest lady,
> Long may she live and well!
> But a curse on the cruel mother
> Who burned my golden shell!"

THE FAIRY RING

Then the Princess could restrain herself no longer, but ran forward and threw her arms around her husband. And immediately he knew her again and said:

"Do you remember how I told you that day that you would betray me? Now you see that I spoke the truth. But all that evil time is past. Now listen to me: I must still remain enchanted for three months. Will you stay here with me till that time is over?"

So the Princess stayed with him and said to the old man: "Go back to the castle and tell my parents that I am staying here."

Her parents were very much vexed when the old man came back and told them this, but as soon as the three months of the Prince's enchantment were over he ceased to be an eagle and became once more a man, and they returned home together. And then they lived happily, and we who hear the story are happier still.

The Table, the Ass, and the Stick

ONCE upon a time, a long time ago, there lived a Tailor and his three sons; but they only had one Goat, which, as it had to give milk enough for all, had to feed well every day. The sons had to lead it to pasture in turns, and one morning, when it was the turn of the eldest, he took it into the churchyard, where grew the richest grass, and let it eat its fill. In the evening, when it was time to return, he said:

"Goat, have you eaten well?"

And the Goat answered:

> "'Tis said that enough is as good as a feast,
> And I've had enough for a wise little beast."

"Then we will go home," said the youth; and he led the Goat home by its halter, and tied it up in the stable for the night.

"Well," said the Tailor, "has the Goat eaten well?"

"It has eaten as much as it can," answered the boy.

But the father wanted to make sure; so he went into the stable and stroked the Goat, saying:

"Goat, have you eaten well?"

The wicked Goat replied:

> "How can I have eaten well?
> I wandered where the dead lie,
> But nothing found to feed upon."

"What do you say?" cried the Tailor, and running in to his son he cried, "Oh, you wicked boy! you told me the Goat had eaten well, and I find him shivering in the stable almost famished!" and, seizing his yard measure, he chased the boy out of the house in great wrath.

The next day it was the second son's turn, and he chose a place under the hedge in the garden where there grew some fine rich grass, which the Goat was not long in eating up completely. When the evening came, and it was time to go home, this lad, too, asked the Goat if it had had enough, and it answered as before:

> "'Tis said that enough is as good as a feast,
> And I've had enough for a wise little beast."

"Then we will go home," said the boy, and he took it to the stable and tied it up. When he went into the house, the Tailor met him, and asked him:

"Has the Goat eaten well?"

"It has eaten as much as it can," answered his son.

But the Tailor would make sure for all that, and nothing would satisfy him but that he should go to the stable and ask the Goat for himself.

> "How can I have eaten well?
> I roamed all day along the hedge,
> And nothing found to feed upon,"

answered the Goat.

"You bad rascal, to starve such a splendid animal!" cried

the Tailor, running back to the house and catching up his yard measure. Then with cuffs and blows he chased his second son out of the house.

The next day it was the third boy's turn, and he found a spot where there was some lovely young grass; and when it was time to go home, he asked the Goat the same question, and obtained the same answer:

> " 'Tis said that enough is as good as a feast,
> And I've had enough for a wise little beast."

So the lad led the Goat home, and he put it in the stable; and soon the Tailor came and asked if the Goat had had enough.

"Yes," replied the boy.

But the old man would go and make sure for all that.

> "How can I have eaten well?
> I sought all day among the leaves,
> And nothing found to feed upon,"

was the wicked Goat's answer.

"The scamp!" cried the Tailor in a fury; "he is as bad as the others, and out he shall go!" and he drove the poor boy out with the yard measure, dealing him fearful blows.

Now the Tailor was left alone to look after the Goat, and next day he went to it and said:

"Come, pretty creature, I will take you myself to pasture," and he took it to the lettuce bed, and there it fed all day. When night came he asked it, as the boys had done, if it had eaten well, and it said:

> " 'Tis said that enough is as good as a feast,
> And I've had enough for a wise little beast."

So they went home, and he put it in the stable; but as he was going, he said once more:

"Goat, have you eaten well?"

The wicked animal, not thinking for the moment to whom he was replying, answered with the usual complaint:

THE FAIRY RING

"How can I have eaten well?
I only frisked about the bed,
And nothing found to feed upon."

When the old man heard this he was horrified, for he saw at once how things had stood all the time, and that he had driven his boys away for no reason whatever.

"Oh, you brute!" he said. "You, too, shall be driven out; and I will take care that you never dare to appear among honest tailors again."

So he rushed into the house for his razor, and shaved the Goat's head as smooth as your face; and because the yard measure was too good to use upon him, he fetched his whip and gave the Goat such a sound thrashing that it was only too glad to scamper out of the stable and make off as fast as its legs could carry it.

When the Tailor returned into his house he was overcome with sorrow for the three sons whom he had driven from home, and who were wandering no one knew where.

However, the eldest boy had apprenticed himself to a carpenter, and he worked with him well and merrily till his time was out. Then his master gave him a table, which, though it looked only like an ordinary common wooden one, yet if its owner stood before it and said, "Table, Table, spread yourself," it at once became covered with all sorts of good things, meat and wine and everything necessary for a splendid meal.

"Now I shall never want again," the young man said to himself, and he went on journeying merrily, never troubling himself whether his lodging was good or bad, or whether there was anything to eat or not.

Sometimes he did not go to an inn at all, but just stopped where he was, under a hedge or in a wood, and there he would put down his table and cry, "Table, Table, spread yourself," and then in the twinkle of an eye he had before him as much as he liked to eat and drink.

One day he made up his mind to turn his steps homeward, as his father's anger, he knew, was sure to have died down by then, and they could live very comfortably together **with** his lucky table. It happened that one evening he came to an inn that was full of people, who invited him to eat in their company.

"No, not a mouthful, unless you consent to be my guests," answered the boy.

The people of course laughed, and thought he was joking; but their mirth soon changed to wonder when he set down his table in their midst, and saw that at his command, "Table, Table, spread yourself," it at once covered itself with all sorts of delicious things, quite as good as the host could have given them, and smelling very tempting to the hungry guests.

"Pray be seated, friends," said the Carpenter cheerily; and the people, seeing he really meant it, sat down at once and began to ply their knives and forks very merrily.

The thing that surprised them the most was, that whenever they emptied one dish, another full one always appeared immediately in its place; and the innkeeper, who was looking on, said to himself, "My friend, you could do very well with such a table as that in your own kitchen"; but he kept his own counsel. The guests sat up very late that night, but at last they went to bed. The Carpenter lay down, too, with his magic table beside him.

Now the landlord couldn't get to sleep that night at all for thinking and wishing, till suddenly he remembered that in the lumber room there was a table that he didn't use, and which was as like the one he coveted as two pins. Breathlessly and very cautiously he made his way to the garret and fetched it, and put it beside the lad's bed in place of the lucky table, which he carried away and hid in a safe place. The next day the Carpenter paid for his lodging and went on his way, not noticing any difference in the table, which he hoisted on his back. At midday he reached his home, and his father was overjoyed to see him.

"Well, my dear boy," said the old man, "what have you been doing all these months?"

"I have been apprenticed to a carpenter," answered the lad.

THE FAIRY RING

"And a very good trade, too; and what have you brought home with you?"

"The most wonderful thing I ever set eyes on," said his son, setting down the table.

"Uhm! I don't think much of that; it looks a very common piece of furniture," said the father, looking at it all around.

"But," cried the boy, "it is a magic table, and when I say, 'Table, Table, spread yourself,' it is at once covered with good things, which will make your mouth water. Invite all our friends in, and you will see what a feast there will be."

When the guests had all arrived, he fetched his table, and placing it in the middle of the room, he commanded it to spread itself. But the table remained just like any other table, which takes no notice when you speak to it; and the poor lad saw at once that somebody had robbed him. Of course the guests thought he was an impostor and laughed at him, and went home without any feast, to the poor Carpenter's shame. So the Tailor had to take up his needle again and stitch away as fast as ever, and the boy had to leave home again and work for another carpenter.

Meantime, the second son had taken service with a miller, and when he had learned everything, his master said:

"Because you have worked for me faithfully I will give you this ass, which, though it can neither draw nor carry, is a clever beast, nevertheless."

"What can it do, then?" said the boy.

"Why, if you only pat it and cry 'Bricklebit,' gold will drop out of its mouth like potatoes into a sack," replied the Miller.

"That is grand," said the boy; so, thanking his master, he started on his journey. Now he was rich, for he only had to say "Bricklebit" and a torrent of gold pieces came out of the ass's mouth, and were there for the picking up. Wherever he went he ordered the best of everything, and the more he had to pay for it the better he was pleased.

Soon he got tired of wandering about the world and thought he would like to go home and see his father, whose

[312]

anger had, no doubt, died down by this time; or, if not, it certainly would when he saw what a rich ass he had brought home with him.

Now it chanced that he came to the very same inn where his brother had lost his table, and when the landlord came out and offered to take the animal to the stable he said: "No, I will take him myself, for I want to see where he goes."

The landlord was surprised, but thought that one who would look after his own beast must be a poor man. But the boy, putting his hand in his pocket, drew out two gold pieces, and ordered the best the house contained. The landlord was very much astonished indeed, and ran and fetched him the best of everything. When he had eaten his fill the boy asked what more he owed, and the landlord, being a greedy man, said that two more gold pieces would pay the bill. The youth put his hand in his pocket and found it empty.

"Wait a moment, my friend, and I will fetch some gold," he said carelessly, and picking up the tablecloth, he went out.

The landlord didn't at all understand what was going on, but being inquisitive he crept out after the youth, and as the stable door was bolted carefully, the landlord had to glue his eye to a hole in the wall. Then he saw the boy spread out the cloth and say "Bricklebit," and immediately gold began to drop out of the ass's mouth in showers, as if it were hailing.

"Thunder and lightning!" gasped the landlord, running back to the house, "did one ever see the like of this! Why, that is the finest and fattest purse I ever set eyes on, and I must see what I can do to obtain it."

Later in the evening the lad paid his bill and went to bed; but when he was well asleep, the wicked landlord crept into the stable and took away the ass, and tied up an ordinary one in its stead.

The next day the youth went on his way with the ass, which he never noticed had been changed, and arrived at midday at his father's house. His father was delighted to see him again, and asked what trade he had learned. The boy told him that he was a miller.

"And what have you brought home with you?" said the old man.

"Only an ass," replied the boy.

"Ah, my lad, you had better have brought a goat. We have asses enough about already."

"Perhaps so," retorted the boy; "but wait till you see what this ass can do. I have only to say 'Bricklebit' and gold drops out of his mouth in heaps. Just send for all your friends, and we will make them rich in a trice."

"Indeed," said the Tailor, "that is not a bad idea. If what you say is true, I shall never need to do any more tailoring," and he hurried out and gathered all his friends in.

They arrived in high excitement, as you may be sure, and the youth bade them stand in a circle while he spread out a cloth under the ass's head.

"Now," he said proudly, "listen to me," and he called, "Bricklebit!"

But nothing happened, and it seemed that the ass could not coin gold after all; for it is not an easy thing to do, as you will agree.

The poor youth was very rueful, for he saw that some one had robbed him, and he was obliged to apologize to the guests, who only sneered and jeered at him and departed as poor as they came.

So the Tailor had to take up his needle once more and stitch away as fast as ever, and the boy had to go and work for another miller.

Meantime, the third son had apprenticed himself to a turner. But it takes a long time to learn to be a turner, and he was still with his master when his brothers sent a message to tell him how they had fared, and all about the wicked landlord who had robbed them of their precious belongings.

Time went on, and soon he had learned everything, and he took leave of his master, who gave him a sack, saying:

THE FAIRY RING

" In the sack lies a stick."

" I will take the sack gladly," said the youth, " for it will be handy. But of what use is the stick, except to make the sack heavier?"

" This is the use of the stick: if you want to punish anyone at any time, you have only to say, ' Come forth, Stick!' and the stick will slip out of the sack and lay about your enemy's shoulders in such a lively fashion that he will be as quiet as a tortoise for days afterwards, and it will not cease beating till you say, ' Stop, Stick, and into the sack!' "

The youth thanked him and went on his way, and when any rogue interfered with him, he only had to cry, " Come forth, Stick!" and out it came and gave them a sound thrashing, until he told it to stop, and then it slipped back so quickly that nobody saw where it went.

One night he arrived at the very inn where his brothers had been deceived, and putting his sack on the table, he began to boast of all the curious things he had seen.

" Yes," he said, " I have even known of a table which covers itself with food and wine in a twinkling. But that is not all, for I have seen an ass which coins gold, and scores of other wonderful things besides. But, when all is said and done, none have compared with what I carry in my sack."

The landlord opened his round eyes, saying:

" I wonder what it is?" and he thought to himself: " The sack must be full of precious stones. I must get hold of it, for all good luck runs in threes, and there is no reason why I should not succeed this time as I have done before."

As soon as it was time to go to bed the youth lay down on a bench and pillowed his head on his sack, and when the landlord thought he was fast asleep he came creeping softly to his side and pulled ever so gently at the sack to see if he could exchange it for another which he had all ready in his hand.

However, the boy was only waiting for this, and suddenly

[315]

he called out, "Come forth, Stick!" Immediately it sprang out and beat the landlord right merrily.

The landlord howled for mercy, but the Stick only hit the faster, till at last the rogue fell down exhausted.

"Now," said the Turner, ordering the stick to return to its bag, "if you do not deliver up to me the magic table and the lucky ass, the Stick shall begin again."

"No, no!" gasped the wretched man. "I will give them up if you will only spare me!"

"I will pardon you if you keep your word," said the youth; "but beware if you try to deceive me!"

Early next morning the Turner went on his way with the ass and the table to his father's house. When he arrived his father was overjoyed to see him, and asked him what trade he had learned.

"Dear father," he said, "I have become a turner."

"That is a difficult trade. And what have you brought home with you?"

"A sack and a stick, and a very valuable stick, too," said the son.

"What!" cried the old man. "A stick! Why, you can cut a stick off any tree!"

"Not a stick like this, for I have only to say, 'Come forth, Stick!' and it immediately slips out and lays about the shoulders of anyone who would injure me, so that he has to cry for mercy. By the aid of my stick I have got back the magic table and lucky ass which the thief of a landlord stole from my brothers. Now send for them, and call in all your friends, and I will give them a feast and fill their pockets with money as well."

The old Tailor could scarcely believe him, but he did as he was told. Then the youth spread a cloth on the floor and brought in the ass, telling his brother to speak to it.

The Miller called out, "Bricklebit!" and immediately the gold pieces began dropping out on to the floor in showers, till they all had as much as they could carry.

Then the table was brought in and the Carpenter said,

" Table, be spread! " and at once it was covered with all sorts of dainties. Then they had such a feast as the Tailor had never seen, and they all remained till late at night making merry.

The next day the happy Tailor gathered together all his needles and thread and measures and goose and put them away, and he lived happily with his sons forever after.

Now we must see what became of the Goat, whose fault it was that the brothers had been driven away. It was so ashamed of its shaven head that it crept into a fox's hole to hide itself. When the Fox came home he saw two great eyes glittering out of the blackness, and he was so terrified that he ran away. Soon he met a bear, who, noticing how frightened he looked, said:

" What has happened, Brother Fox, to make you look like that? "

" Oh! " he said, " in my lair is a fearful monster that rolled flaming eyes at me."

" We will soon turn him out," said the brave Bear. But when he looked in, he also was terrified at the glittering eyes and took to flight. He soon met a bee, and seeing that it was no good to sting him through his thick coat she said, in friendly fashion:

" You look very solemn, Mr. Bear. What has come over you? "

" Oh! " said the Bear, " in Brother Fox's lair is a fearful monster which rolls flaming eyes at us, and we daren't drive him out."

" Well, Mr. Bear," said the Bee, " I am sorry for you, and I believe I can help, though I am such a little creature that nobody thinks I can do any good in the world."

So she flew off to the Fox's lair, and dropping on to his bald head, stung him so terribly that the poor Goat rushed out madly, and he has never been heard of since.

The Little Brother and Sister

THERE was once a little Brother who took his Sister by the hand and said: "Since our own dear mother's death we have not had one happy hour; our stepmother beats us every day, and, if we come near her, kicks us away with her foot. Our food is the hard crusts of bread which are left, and even the dog under the table fares better than we, for he often gets a nice morsel. Come, let us wander forth into the wide world." So the whole day long they traveled over meadows, fields, and stony roads, and when it rained the Sister said, "It is Heaven crying in sympathy." By evening they came into a large forest, and were so wearied with grief, hunger, and their long walk that they laid themselves down in a hollow tree and went to sleep. When they awoke the next morning the sun had already risen high in the heavens, and its beams made the tree so hot that the little boy said to his Sister, "I am so thirsty; if I knew where there was a brook I would go and drink. Ah, I think I hear one running"; and so saying he got up, and taking his Sister's hand they went in search of the brook.

The wicked stepmother, however, was a witch, and had witnessed the departure of the two children; so sneaking after them secretly, as is the habit of witches, she had enchanted all the springs in the forest.

Presently they found a brook which ran trippingly over the pebbles, and the Brother would have drunk out of it, but the Sister heard how it said as it ran along, "Who drinks of me will become a tiger!" So the Sister exclaimed: "I pray you, Brother, drink not, or you will become a tiger and tear me to pieces!" So the Brother did not drink, although his thirst was so great, and he said, "I will wait till the next brook." As they came to the second the Sister heard it say, "Who drinks of me becomes a wolf!" The Sister ran up crying: "Brother, do not, pray do not, drink, or you will become a wolf and eat me up!" Then the Brother did not drink, say-

[318]

ing: "I will wait until we come to the next spring, but then I must drink, you may say what you will; my thirst is much too great." Just as they reached the third brook the Sister heard the voice saying: "Who drinks of me will become a fawn—who drinks of me will become a fawn!" So the Sister said: "Oh, my Brother! do not drink, or you will be changed to a fawn and run away from me!" But he had already kneeled down and drank of the water, and, as the first drops passed his lips, his shape became that of a fawn.

At first the Sister cried over her little changed Brother, and he wept too, and knelt by her very sorrowful; but at last the maiden said, "Be still, dear little Fawn, and I will never forsake you"; and, undoing her golden garter, she put it around his neck, and weaving rushes made a white girdle to lead him with. This she tied to him, and, taking the other end in her hand she led him away, and they traveled deeper and deeper into the forest. After they had walked a long distance they came to a little hut, and the maiden, peeping in, found it empty, and thought, "Here we can stay and dwell." Then she looked for leaves and moss to make a soft couch for the Fawn, and every morning she went out and collected roots and berries and nuts for herself and tender grass for the Fawn, which he ate out of her hand, and played happily around her. In the evening, when the Sister was tired and had said her prayers, she laid her head upon the back of the Fawn, which served for a pillow, on which she slept soundly. Had but the Brother regained his own proper form, their life would have been happy indeed.

Thus they dwelt in this wilderness, and some time had elapsed, when it happened that the King of the country held a great hunt in the forest; and now resounded through the trees the blowing of horns, the barking of dogs, and the lusty cries of the hunters, so that the little Fawn heard them and wanted very much to join. "Ah!" said he to his Sister, "let me go to the hunt, I cannot restrain myself any longer"; and he begged so hard that at last she consented. "But," said she to him, "return again in the evening, for I shall shut my door against the wild huntsmen, and, that I may know you, do you knock and say, 'Sister, let me in,' and if you do not speak I shall not open the door." As soon as she had said this, the little Fawn sprang off, quite glad and merry in the fresh breeze. The King and his huntsmen perceived the beautiful animal, and pursued him; but they could not catch him, and when they thought they had him for certain he sprang away over the bushes and got out of sight. Just as it was getting dark he ran up to the hut, and, knocking, said, "Sister mine, let me in." Then she undid the little door, and he went in and rested all night long upon his soft couch. The next morning the hunt was commenced again, and as soon as the little Fawn heard the horns and the tallyho of the sportsmen he could not rest, and said, "Sister, dear, open the door, I must be off." The Sister opened it, saying, "Return at evening, mind, and say the words as before." When the King and his huntsmen saw again the Fawn with the golden necklace, they followed him closely, but he was too nimble and quick for them. The whole day long they kept up with him, but toward evening the huntsmen made a circle around him, and one wounded him slightly in the hind foot, so that he could only run slowly. Then one of them slipped after him to the little hut, and heard him say, "Sister, dear, open the door," and saw that the door was opened and immediately shut behind. The huntsman, having observed all this, went and told the King what he had seen and heard, and he said, "On the morrow I will once more pursue him."

The Sister, however, was terribly frightened when she saw that her Fawn was wounded, and washing off the blood she put herbs upon the foot and said: "Go and rest upon your bed, dear Fawn, that the wound may heal." It was so slight that the next morning he felt nothing of it, and when he heard the hunting cries outside he exclaimed: "I cannot stop away —I must be there, and none shall catch me so easily again!" The Sister wept very much and told him: "Soon they will kill you, and I shall be here all alone in this forest, forsaken by all the world. I cannot let you go."

THE FAIRY RING

"I shall die here in vexation," answered the Fawn, "if you do not, for when I hear the horn I think I shall jump out of my skin." The Sister, finding she could not prevent him, opened the door with a heavy heart, and the Fawn jumped out, quite delighted, into the forest. As soon as the King perceived him he said to his huntsmen: "Follow him all day long till the evening, but let no one do him an injury." When the sun had set, the King asked his huntsmen to show him the hut; and as they came to it, he knocked at the door and said, "Let me in, dear Sister." Then the door was opened, and stepping in the King saw a maiden more beautiful than he had ever before seen. She was frightened when she saw not her Fawn, but a man step in who had a golden crown upon his head. But the King, looking at her with a friendly glance, reached her his hand, saying, "Will you go with me to my castle and be my dear wife?" "Oh, yes," replied the maiden; "but the Fawn must go too; him I will never forsake." The King replied: "He shall remain with you as long as you live, and shall want for nothing." In the meantime the Fawn had come in, and the Sister, binding the girdle to him, again took it in her hand, and led him away with her out of the hut.

The King took the beautiful maiden upon his horse, and rode to his castle, where the wedding was celebrated with great splendor, and she became Queen, and they lived together a long time; while the Fawn was taken care of and lived well, playing about the castle garden. The wicked stepmother, however, on whose account the children had wandered forth into the world, supposed that long ago the Sister had been torn in pieces by the wild beasts, and the little Brother hunted to death in his Fawn's shape by the hunters. As soon, therefore, as she heard how happy they had become, and how everything prospered with them, envy and jealousy were roused in her heart and left her no peace, and she was always thinking in what way she could work misfortune to them. Her own daughter, who was as ugly as night and had but one eye, for which she was continually reproached, said, "The luck of being a queen has never yet happened to me."

[321]

THE FAIRY RING

"Be quiet now," said the old woman, "and make yourself contented. When the time comes, I shall be at hand." As soon, then, as the time came when the Queen brought into the world a beautiful little boy, which happened when the King was out hunting, the old witch took the form of a chamber-maid, and got into the room where the Queen was lying, and said to her: "The bath is ready which will restore you and give you fresh strength; be quick, before it gets cold." Her daughter being at hand, they carried the weak Queen between them into the room, and laid her in the bath, and then, shutting the door, they ran off; but first they had made an immense fire in the stove, which must soon suffocate the young Queen.

When this was done the old woman took her daughter, and putting a cap on her, laid her in the bed in the Queen's place. She gave her, too, the form and appearance of the real Queen as far as she could; but she could not restore the lost eye, and so that the King might not notice it, she turned upon that side where there was no eye. When he came home at evening and heard that a son was born to him, he was much delighted, and prepared to go to his wife's bedside to see how she did. So the old woman called out in a great hurry: "For your life, do not undraw the curtains; the Queen must not yet see the light, and must be kept quiet." So the King went away, and did not discover that a false Queen was laid in the bed.

When midnight came and everyone was asleep, the nurse, who sat by herself, wide awake, near the cradle in the nursery, saw the door open and the true Queen come in. She took the child in her arms and rocked it awhile, and then, shaking up its pillow, laid it down in its cradle and covered it over again. She did not forget the Fawn either, but going to the corner where he was, stroked his back, and then went silently out at the door. The nurse asked in the morning of the guards if anyone had passed into the castle during the night, but they answered, "No, we have seen nobody." For many nights afterwards she came constantly, and never spoke a word; and the nurse saw her always, but she would not trust herself to speak about it to anyone.

[322]

THE FAIRY RING

When some time had passed away, the Queen one night began to speak, and said:

> "How fares my child, how fares my Fawn?
> Twice more will I come, but never again."

The nurse made no reply; but, when she had disappeared, went to the King and told him all. The King exclaimed: "Oh, heavens! what does this mean? The next night I will watch myself by the child." In the evening he went into the nursery, and about midnight the Queen appeared and said:

> "How fares my child, how fares my Fawn?
> Once more will I come, but never again."

And she nursed the child as she was used to do, and then disappeared. The King dared not speak, but he watched the following night, and this time she said:

> "How fares my child, how fares my Fawn?
> This time have I come, but never again."

At these words the King could hold back no longer, but sprang up and said, "You can be no other than my dear wife!" Then she answered, "Yes, I am your dear wife"; and at that moment her life was restored by God's mercy, and she was again as beautiful and charming as ever. She told the King the fraud which the witch and her daughter had practiced upon him, and he had them both tried and sentence pronounced against them. The daughter was taken into the forest, where the wild beasts tore her in pieces, but the old witch was led to the fire and miserably burned. And as soon as she was reduced to ashes the little Fawn was unbewitched, and received again his human form; and the Brother and Sister lived happily together to the end of their days.

THE FAIRY RING

The Old Griffin

THERE was once a king, but where he reigned and how he was called I know nothing about. He had no son, only a daughter, who was always ill, and no doctor could cure her; but it was prophesied to the King that his daughter would eat herself well with an apple. So he made it known all over the kingdom that whoever brought his daughter some apples with which she could eat herself well should marry her and be King. Now a peasant who had three sons heard of it; and he said to the eldest: " Go to the garden, take a basketful of those beautiful apples with the red cheeks, and carry them to the court. Perhaps the King's daughter will be able to eat herself well with them, and then you can marry her and be King." The chap did as he was bid and took to the road. When he had walked a little while he met quite a little iron man, who asked him what he had in his basket. So Hele, for that was his name, said, " Frogs' legs! " The Little Man then said, " Well, so it shall be and remain "; and then went on. At last Hele came to the castle, and had it announced that he had some apples which would cure the Princess if she ate them. At that the King was mightily pleased, and received Hele in court. Oh, dear! when he opened it, instead of apples he had frogs' legs in the basket, and they were kicking about still. The King flew into a great rage, and had him kicked out of the castle. When he got home he told his father how he had fared. Then the father sent his next son, whose name was Saeme, but it went just the same with him as with Hele. The little Iron Man met him very soon, and asked him what he had in the basket, and Saeme said, " Sow-thistles "; and the Little Man said, " Well, so it shall be and remain." When he arrived at the King's castle, and said he had apples with which the King's daughter could eat herself well, they would not let him in, and told him there had already been one who had made fools of them. But Saeme insisted he had really such apples; they should only let him in.

[324]

At last they believed him and took him before the King; but when he opened the basket he had nothing but sow-thistles. That annoyed the King most dreadfully, so that he had Saeme whipped out of the castle. When he got home he told them what had happened to him, and then came the youngest boy, whom they had always called Stupid Jack, and asked the father whether he, too, might go with apples. "Yes," said the father, "you are just the right sort of fellow; if the clever ones can't succeed, what will you be able to do?" The boy did not believe it. "Well, father, I will go too." "Get away, you stupid chap!" said the father; "you must wait till you grow wiser"; and then he turned his back upon him; but the boy tugged at his smock frock behind and said, "Now, father, I will go too." "Well, just as you like; go—you will be sure to come back," he answered in a spiteful way. The boy was beyond measure delighted, and jumped for joy. "Aye, there! act like a fool! You get stupider from one day to the next," said the father. That did not affect Jack a bit, who would not be disturbed in his joy. As night soon came on, he thought he would wait till the next morning; anyhow, he would not be able to get to court that day. He could not sleep that night in bed, and when he only slumbered a little he dreamed of beautiful maidens, of castles, gold, silver, and all that sort of thing. Early next morning he went his way, and soon the Little Man in his iron dress met him and asked him what he had in the basket. "Apples," he answered, "with which the King's daughter can eat herself well." "Well," said the Little Man, "such it shall be and remain." But at court they would not let Jack in at all; for that there had been two who had said they brought apples, and one had frogs' legs and the other sow-thistles. But Jack insisted tremendously he had no frogs' legs, but the most beautiful apples that grew in the kingdom. As he spoke so nicely the doorkeeper thought he could not be telling a lie, and let him in; and they did quite right, too, for when Jack uncovered the basket before the King, apples as yellow as gold came tumbling out. The King was delighted, and had some of them taken to his daughter at once, and waited in anxious expectation until they should bring him word what effect they had. Not long after news was brought him; but what think you it was? It was the daughter herself! As soon as she had eaten of those apples she had jumped out of bed quite well. What the King's delight was cannot be described.

But now the King would not give Jack his daughter to marry, and said that he must first make him a boat that would swim better on land than in the water. Jack agreed to the condition and went home and told his adventures. So the father sent Hele into the wood to make such a boat; he worked away diligently, and whistled the while. At midday, when the sun was at the highest, came the little Iron Man and asked what he was making. "Wooden bowls," answered he. The Little Man answered, "Well, so it shall be and remain." In the evening Hele thought he had made the boat, but when he was going to get into it, it turned to wooden bowls. The next day Saeme went into the wood, but he met with exactly the same fate as his brother. On the third day Stupid Jack went. He worked very hard, so that the wood resounded all through with his heavy blows, and he sang and whistled besides right merrily. The Little Man came to him at midday when it was very warm, and asked him what he was making. "A boat that will swim better on dry land than in the water," he answered, "and that when he had done it he should marry the King's daughter." "Well," said the Little Man, "such an one it shall be and remain." In the evening when the sun was setting like a ball of gold, Jack made ready his boat and all things belonging to it, and rowed toward the castle; but the boat went as fast as the wind. The King saw it a long way off, but would not give Jack his daughter yet, and said he must first take a hundred hares out grazing from early morning to late in the evening, and if one were missing he should not have his daughter. Jack was quite contented, and the next day went out with his herd to the meadow, and kept a sharp lookout that none should stray away. Not many hours had passed when a maid came from the castle, and

said Jack was to give her a hare directly, as some visitors had
arrived. But Jack saw through that well enough, and said he
would not give her one; the King might treat his visitors to
hare pepper. But the maid would not heed him, and at last
set to scolding. So Jack said that if the King's daughter came
herself he would give her a hare. The maid told them in the
castle, and the King's daughter did go herself. But in the
meantime the Little Man had come again to Jack and asked
him what he was doing there. Oh, he had to watch a
hundred hares so that none ran away, and then he might
marry the King's daughter and be King. "Good!" said the
Little Man, "there's a whistle for you, and when one runs
away, only just whistle and he will come back again." When
the King's daughter came, Jack put a hare into her apron,
but when she had gone about a hundred steps off, Jack whistled, and the hare jumped out of the cloth, and jump, jump!
was back to the herd directly. In the evening the hareherd
whistled again, and looked to see they were all right, and
drove them to the castle. The King wondered how Jack had
been able to take care of a hundred hares, so that none should
run off, but he would not yet give him his daughter so easily,
but said he must first get him a feather from the Old Griffin's
tail.

Jack started at once, and marched right briskly on. In the
evening he arrived at a castle, where he asked for a night's
lodging, for at that time there were no such things as hotels;
and the master of the castle greeted him very civilly, and
asked him where he was going to. Jack answered, "To the
Old Griffin." "Oh, indeed! to the Old Griffin; they say he
knows everything, and I have lost the key to an iron money
chest; perhaps you would be good enough to ask him where
it is!" "Certainly," said Jack, "that I will." Early the next
morning he started off again on his road, and arrived at another castle, where he again passed the night. When the
people learned that he was going to the Old Griffin, they said
a daughter was ill in the house; they had already tried every
possible remedy, but without effect; would he be kind enough

to ask Old Griffin what would cure her? Jack said he would
do it with pleasure, and went on again. He arrived at a lake,
and instead of a ferryboat there was a big man who had to
carry everybody over. The man asked him where he was
bound for? "To the Old Griffin," said Jack. "When you get
to him," said the man, "just ask him why I am obliged to
carry everybody over the water." "Yes, to be sure," said
Jack; "goodness gracious! yes, willingly!" The man then
took him up on his shoulder and carried him over. At last
Jack arrived at the Old Griffin's house, and only found the
wife at home, not Old Griffin. The woman asked him what
he wanted, so he told her he must have a feather from Old
Griffin's tail; and that in a castle they had lost the key to the
money chest, and he was to ask the Griffin where it was; and
then, in another castle, the daughter was ill, and he was to
know what would make her well again; then not far from
there were the water and the man who was obliged to carry
everybody over, and he should very much like to know why
the man was obliged to carry everybody over. "But," said
the woman, "look you, my good friend, no Christian can
speak with a Griffin; he eats them all up; but, if you like,
you can lie there under his bed, and at night when he is fast
asleep you can reach up and pull a feather out of his tail;
and as to those things that you want to know, I will ask him
myself." Jack was quite satisfied with the arrangement, and
got under the bed. In the evening Old Griffin came home,
and when he stepped into the room he said, "Wife, I smell a
Christian!" "Yes," said the wife, "there has been one here
to-day, but he went away again." So Old Griffin said no more.

In the middle of the night, when Griffin was snoring away
lustily, Jack reached up and pulled a feather out of his tail.
The Griffin jumped up suddenly and cried: "Wife, I smell
a Christian! and it was just as if some one had been plucking
at my tail." The wife said: "You have no doubt been dreaming. I have told you already that one has been here to-day,
but that he went away again. He told me all sorts of things;
that in one castle they had lost the key of the money chest

"IN THE MIDDLE OF THE NIGHT, WHEN GRIFFIN WAS SNORING AWAY LUSTILY,
JACK REACHED UP AND PULLED A FEATHER OUT OF HIS TAIL"

and could not find it." "Oh, the fools!" exclaimed the Griffin; "the key lies in the wood-shed, behind the door under a log of wood." "And further, he said that in another castle the daughter was ill, and they knew no means to cure her." "Oh, the fools!" said the Griffin, "under the cellar stairs a toad has made its nest of her hair, and if she got the hair back again she would be well." "And then, again, he said at a certain place there was a lake, and a man who was obliged to carry everybody over." "Oh, the fool!" said the Old Griffin, "if he were only to put somebody into the middle he need not carry any more over."

Early next morning the Old Griffin got up and went out, and Jack crept from under the bed with a beautiful feather, having heard what the Griffin had said about the key, the daughter, and the man. The wife repeated it all to him so that he should not forget, and then he started off toward home. He came to the man at the water first, and he asked him directly what the Griffin had said; but Jack said he must carry him over first, and then he would tell him. So he carried him over, and when they got there Jack told him he had only to put somebody into the middle and then he need carry no more. The man was delighted beyond measure, and told Jack that out of gratitude he should like to carry him over and back once more. But Jack said nay, he would save him the trouble; he was quite contented with him already, and then went on. Next he arrived at the castle where the daughter was ill; he took her on his shoulder, for she was not able to walk, and carried her down the cellar stairs, and then took the toad's nest from under the bottom step and put it into the daughter's hand, and all at once she jumped off his shoulder, up the stairs before him, strong and well. Now the father and mother were delighted indeed, and made Jack presents of gold and silver, and whatever he wanted they gave him.

When Jack arrived at the other castle he went straight to the wood-shed, and found the key right behind the door under the log of wood, and took it to the master. He was not a little pleased, and gave Jack in return a great deal of gold that was in the box and all sorts of things besides, such as cows and sheep and goats.

When Jack returned to the King with all these things, with the money and gold and silver, and the cows sheep, and goats, the King asked him how he had come by it all. So Jack said the Old Griffin would give one as much as one liked. The King thought he could find a use for that kind of gifts himself, and so started off to the Griffin; but when he got to the water he happened to be the first who had crossed over since Jack, and the man put him in the middle of the stream and walked off, and the King was drowned.

So Jack married the King's daughter and became King.

The Three Feathers

ONCE upon a time there lived a king who had three sons, two of whom were bright youths, but the youngest never had anything to say for himself, so he was set down by everyone as a simpleton.

Years went on, and the King felt himself growing old, and he thought it was time to decide which of his sons was to succeed him.

This was not so easy, so he told the youths that whoever should bring him the most beautiful carpet should be his heir, and, lest they should all want to go in the same direction and quarrel, he went up to the roof of the palace and blew three feathers up into the air, saying:

"As they fly, thither shall you follow."

One feather flew east, another west, and the third went in a straight line between the two for a little way, and then fell suddenly to the ground. So one brother went east, and another west, and poor Dummling was left to follow the third feather, which had gone no distance at all, whereat his brothers were much amused.

Dummling sat down beside his feather, feeling very sad and

doleful, and he was just thinking that all chance of the kingdom was at an end for him, when he discovered that all the time he was staring at a trapdoor in the ground. He lifted it, and found steps leading down into the earth, so he went down the stairs till he came to a door, and then he knocked.

Immediately he heard a voice singing:

> "Little frog, so green and cold,
> I prithee open and behold
> Who it is that knocks so bold,"

and the door opened, and he saw a large frog squatting in the middle of a circle of little ones. The big one bowed to him as he entered, and asked him what he sought.

"Please," said Dummling, taking off his cap and returning the bow, "I want to know if you can help me to get the most beautiful carpet in the world."

The Frog rolled her eyes for a minute, and then, turning to one of the little ones at her side, said:

"Go bring me hither the big casket," and the little frog hopped away, and came back dragging a large box.

Then the mother Frog took a key that hung around her neck on a chain, and opened the box and drew forth the most beautiful carpet that was ever seen.

Dummling was delighted with it, and thanking her very heartily, he hurried up the steps, eager to take it to the palace.

Meanwhile, the two brothers, never thinking that Dummling was clever enough to find any sort of carpet at all, said to each other:

"Let us buy the shawl of the first peasant woman we meet. That should be good enough to win us the kingdom."

So they bought a common old shawl at the first opportunity, and took it home to the palace, arriving just at the same moment as Dummling.

The King was astonished when the carpets were spread out before him and he saw the lovely thing Dummling had brought.

"The prize," said he, "should by rights belong to my youngest son."

But the others were so angry at this, and worried their father so much, that for very peace he had to consent to a new test.

So the King gave out that whoever should bring him the most beautiful ring should be King when he died, and he blew up the feathers as before, and bade the youths follow them.

The two eldest went east and west, but Dummling's feather did as it did the first time, and fell to earth just by the trap-door. So he pulled it up once again and went down the steps. When the door was opened, he told the big Frog that he wanted the most beautiful ring in the world. So she sent one of her little attendants hopping for her jewel casket, and, when it was come, she took out of it a ring that fairly blazed with diamonds and other jewels, and finer than the finest workmanship that could be obtained. You may imagine Dummling thanked her very warmly for the ring, and hurried off back to the palace as fast as his legs could carry him. He found his brothers had just arrived with rings they had taken no more pains to make than to beat two rusty nails into circlets. As soon as the King saw Dummling's lovely jewel, he cried out:

"The kingdom belongs to him."

But the brothers again flew into a passion at this, and said that a youth who had as little wit as Dummling could not possibly reign over the land. So they worried the father at last to make just one more condition; and this time he said that whoever should bring home the most beautiful woman in the world should succeed to the throne. A third time he blew the feathers into the air, and the youths set out after them.

Dummling's feather floated and fell just as before, and again he pulled up his trapdoor and went down into the presence of the old Frog, and told her that this time he wanted the most beautiful maiden in all the world.

"Hum!" said the Frog, "it is not everyone who gets that; still I will do my best for you, nevertheless. But first take

[332]

"THEN DUMMLING'S LOVELY MAIDEN SPRANG LIGHTLY AND GRACEFULLY
THROUGH THE RING"

THE FAIRY RING

this," and she gave Dummling a little toy cart made of a hollow carrot, to which were harnessed six beautiful white mice.

The youth looked at this rather doubtfully, and asked the mother Frog what he was to do with it.

" I will tell you," she said. " Take one of my little frog attendants and set her on the carrot."

So Dummling picked up the one that happened to be nearest him and put her on the carrot, and lo and behold! no sooner was she seated than she changed into a beautiful maiden, and the carrot and the mice into a grand chariot drawn by six prancing horses. As soon as he could stop rubbing his eyes from wonder, Dummling kissed the maiden, and drove off in triumph to the palace.

Meanwhile, the brothers, as usual, had taken no trouble whatever, and at the moment Dummling drove up in his glory they appeared with two peasant girls, who were not even pretty.

Of course the King had nothing for it but to award the kingdom to his youngest son, and, of course, the elder brothers still grumbled, and made such a fuss that at last the poor King had to consent to yet another trial.

To prove which was the best wife of the three, he decided that they should all jump through a hoop in the hall, and the one who did it most prettily was to be the winner.

And now all the court was gathered together in the hall to see the contest. The country girls jumped, but were so plump that they fell heavily and broke their arms and legs. Then Dummling's lovely maiden sprang lightly and gracefully through the ring, and landed safely on the other side.

So at last the brothers had to be content, and in time Dummling came to the throne and ruled wisely and well for many, many years.

THE FAIRY RING

The House in the Wood

THERE was once a poor Woodcutter who lived with his Wife and three Daughters in a little hut on the edge of a large forest. One morning, when he went out to his usual work, he said to his Wife: " Let my dinner be brought by our eldest Daughter, I shall not be ready to come home; and that she may not lose her way, I will take with me a bag of seeds and strew them on my path."

So when the sun was risen to the center of the heavens, the Maiden set out on her way, carrying a jug of soup. But the field and wood sparrows, the larks, blackbirds, goldfinches, and greenfinches, had many hours ago picked up the seeds, so that the Maiden could find no trace of the way. So she walked on, trusting to fortune, till the sun set and night came on. The trees soon began to rustle in the darkness, the owls to hoot, and the girl began to feel frightened. All at once she perceived a light shining at a distance among the trees. " People must dwell there," she thought, " who will keep me during the night "; and she walked toward the light. In a short time she came to a cottage where the windows were all lighted up, and when she knocked at the door a hoarse voice called from within, " Come in." The girl opened the door and perceived a hoary Old Man sitting at a table with his face buried in his hands, and his white beard flowing down over the table on to the ground. On the hearth lay three animals—a hen, a cock, and a brindled cow. The girl told the Old Man her adventures, and begged for a night's lodging. The Man said:

> " Pretty Hen, pretty Cock,
> And pretty brindled Cow,
> What have you to say to that? "

" Cluck! " said the animals, and as that meant they were satisfied, the Old Man said to the Maiden: " Here is abundance.

and to spare; go now into the kitchen and cook some supper for us."

The girl found plenty of everything in the kitchen, and cooked a good meal, but thought nothing about the animals. When she had finished she carried a full dish into the room, and, sitting down opposite the Old Man, ate till she had satisfied her hunger. When she had done she said: "I am very tired; where is my bed, where I shall lie down and sleep?" The animals replied:

> "You have eaten with him,
> You have drunk, too, with him;
> And yet you have not thought of us;
> Still you may pass the night here."

Thereupon the Old Man said: "Step down yon stair, and you will come to a room containing two beds, shake them up and cover them with white sheets, and then I will come and lie down to sleep myself." The Maiden stepped down the stair, and as soon as she had shaken up the beds and covered them afresh, she laid herself down in one bed, without waiting for the Old Man. But after some time the Old Man came, and, after looking at the girl with the light, shook his head when he saw she was fast asleep; and then, opening a trapdoor, dropped her down into the cellar below.

Late in the evening the Woodcutter arrived at home, and scolded his Wife because she had let him hunger all day long. "It is not my fault," she replied; "the girl was sent out with your dinner; she must have lost her way; but to-morrow she will return, no doubt." At daybreak the Woodcutter got up to go into the forest, and desired that the second Daughter should bring him his meal this time. "I will take a bag of peas," he said; "they are larger than corn seed, and the girl will therefore see them better and not lose my track." At noonday, accordingly, the girl set out with her father's dinner; but the peas had all disappeared, for the wood birds had picked them all up as they had on the day before, and not one was left So the poor girl wandered about in the forest till it was quite dark, and then she also arrived at the Old Man's hut, was invited in, and begged food and a night's lodging. The Man of the white beard asked his animals again:

> "Pretty Hen, and pretty Cock,
> And pretty brindled Cow,
> What have you to say to that?"

They answered again, "Cluck!" and everything thereupon occurred the same as on the previous day. The girl cooked a good meal, ate and drank with the Old Man, but never once thought of the animals; and when she asked for her bed, they made answer:

> "You have eaten with him,
> You have drunk, too, with him;
> And yet you have not thought of us;
> Still you may pass the night here!"

As soon as she was gone to sleep the Old Man came, and, after looking at her and shaking his head as before, dropped her into the cellar below.

Meanwhile the third morning arrived, and the Woodcutter told his Wife to send their youngest child with his dinner: "For," said he, "she is always obedient and good; she will keep in the right path and not run about like those idle hussies, her sisters!"

But the Mother refused, and said: "Shall I lose my youngest child too?"

"Be not afraid of that," said her husband; "the girl will not miss her way, she is too steady and prudent; but for more precaution I will take beans to strew, they are larger still than peas, and will show her the way better."

But by and by, when the girl went out with her basket on her arm, the wood pigeons had eaten up all the beans, and she knew not which way to turn. She was full of trouble, and thought with grief how her Father would want his dinner and how her dear Mother would grieve when she did not return. At length, when it became quite dark. she also perceïved the lighted cottage, and entering it, begged very politely to be allowed to pass the night there. The Old Man asked the animals a third time in the same words:

> "Pretty Hen, pretty Cock,
> And pretty brindled Cow,
> What have you to say to that?"

"Cluck, cluck!" said they. Thereupon the Maiden stepped up to the fire, near which they lay, and fondled the pretty Hen and Cock, smoothing their plumage down with her hands, while she stroked the Cow between her horns. Afterwards, when she had got ready a good supper at the Old Man's request, and had placed the dishes on the table, she thought to herself: "I must not appease my hunger till I have fed these good creatures. There is an abundance in the kitchen, I will serve them first." Thus thinking she went and fetched some corn and strewed it before the fowls, and then she brought an armful of hay and gave it to the Cow. "Now, eat away, you good creatures," said she to them, "and when you are thirsty you shall have a nice fresh draught." So saying she brought in a pailful of water; and the Hen and Cock perched themselves on its edge, put their beaks in, and then drew their heads up as birds do when drinking; the Cow also took a hearty draught. When the animals were thus fed, the Maiden sat down at table with the Old Man and ate what was left for her. In a short while the Hen and Cock began to fold their wings over their heads, and the brindled Cow blinked with both eyes. Then the Maiden asked: "Shall we not also take our rest?" The Old Man replied as before:

> "Pretty Hen, pretty Cock,
> And pretty brindled Cow,
> What have you to say to that?"

"Cluck, cluck!" replied the animals, meaning:

> "You have eaten with us,
> You have drunk, too, with us,
> You have thought of us kindly, too;
> And we wish you a good night's rest."

THE FAIRY RING

So the Maiden went down the stairs, and shook up the feather beds and laid on clean sheets, and when they were ready the Old Man came and lay down in one, with his white beard stretching down to his feet. The girl then lay down in the other bed, first saying her prayers before she went to sleep.

She slept quietly till midnight, and at that hour there began such a tumult in the house that it awakened her. Presently it began to crack and rumble in every corner of the room, and the doors were slammed back against the wall, and then the beams groaned as if they were being riven away from their fastenings, and the stairs fell down, and at last it seemed as if the whole roof fell in. Soon after that all was quiet, but the Maiden took no harm, and went quietly off again to sleep. When, however the bright light of the morning sun awoke her, what a sight met her eyes! She found herself lying in a large chamber, with everything around belonging to regal pomp. On the walls were represented gold flowers growing on a green silk ground; the bed was of ivory, and the curtains of red velvet, and on a stool close by was placed a pair of slippers ornamented with pearls. The Maiden thought it was all a dream; but presently in came three servants dressed in rich liveries, who asked her what were her commands. "Leave me," replied the Maiden; "I will get up at once and cook some breakfast for the Old Man, and also feed the pretty Hen, the pretty Cock, and the brindled Cow." She spoke thus because she thought the Old Man was already up; but when she looked round at his bed, she saw a stranger to her lying asleep in it. While she was looking at him, and saw that he was both young and handsome, he awoke, and starting up, said to the Maiden: "I am a king's son, who was long ago changed by a wicked old witch into the form of an old man, and condemned to live alone in the wood, with nobody to bear me company but my three servants in the form of a hen, a cock, and a brindled cow. And the enchantment was not to end until a maiden should come so kind-hearted that she should behave as well to my animals as she did to me; and such a one you have been;

and, therefore, this last midnight we were saved through you, and the old wooden hut has again become my royal palace."

When he had thus spoken the girl and he arose, and the Prince told his three servants to fetch to the palace the Father and Mother of the Maiden, that they might witness her marriage.

"But where are my two Sisters?" she asked. "I have put them in the cellar," replied the Prince, "and there they must remain till to-morrow morning, when they shall be led into the forest, and bound as servants to a collier, until they have reformed their tempers, and learned not to let poor animals suffer hunger."

Rapunzel

THERE was once a man and his wife who had long wished in vain for a child, when at last they had reason to hope that Heaven would grant their wish. There was a little window at the back of their house, which overlooked a beautiful garden, full of lovely flowers and shrubs. It was, however, surrounded by a high wall, and nobody dared to enter it, because it belonged to a powerful witch, who was feared by everyone.

One day the woman, standing at this window and looking into the garden, saw a bed planted with beautiful corn salad. It looked so fresh and green that it made her long to eat some of it. This longing increased every day, and as she knew it could never be satisfied, she began to look pale and miserable, and to pine away. Then her husband became alarmed, and said: "What ails you, my dear wife?"

"Alas!" she answered, "if I cannot get any of the corn salad from the garden behind our house to eat, I shall die."

Her husband, who loved her, thought: "Before you let your wife die, you must fetch her some of that corn salad, cost what it may." So in the twilight he climbed over the wall into the Witch's garden, hastily picked a handful of corn salad, and took it back to his wife. She immediately dressed it, and ate it up very eagerly. It was so very, very nice that the next day her longing for it increased threefold. She could have no peace unless her husband fetched her some more. So in the twilight he set out again; but when he got over the wall he was terrified to see the Witch before him.

"How dare you come into my garden like a thief, and steal my corn salad?" she said, with angry looks. "It shall disagree with you."

"Alas!" he answered, "be merciful to me; I am only here from necessity. My wife sees your corn salad from the window, and she has such a longing for it that she would die if she could not get some of it."

The anger of the Witch abated, and she said to him: "If it is as you say, I will allow you to take away with you as much corn salad as you like, but on one condition. You must give me the child which your wife is about to bring into the world. I will care for it like a mother, and all will be well with it." In his fear the man consented to everything, and when the baby was born the Witch appeared, gave it the name of Rapunzel (corn salad), and took it away with her.

Rapunzel was the most beautiful child under the sun. When she was twelve years old, the Witch shut her up in a tower which stood in a wood. It had neither staircase nor doors, and only a little window quite high up in the wall. When the Witch wanted to enter the tower, she stood at the foot of it and cried:

"Rapunzel, Rapunzel, let down your hair!"

Rapunzel had splendid long hair, as fine as spun gold. As soon as she heard the voice of the Witch she unfastened her plaits and twisted them around a hook by the window. They fell twenty ells downward, and the Witch climbed up by them.

It happened a couple of years later that the King's son rode through the forest and came close to the tower. From thence he heard a song so lovely that he stopped to listen. It was Rapunzel, who in her loneliness made her sweet voice resound to pass away the time. The King's son wanted to join her, and he sought for the door of the tower, but there was none to find.

He rode home, but the song had touched his heart so deeply that he went into the forest every day to listen to it. Once, when he was hidden behind a tree, he saw a witch come to the tower and call out:

"Rapunzel, Rapunzel, let down your hair!"

Then Rapunzel lowered her plaits of hair and the Witch climbed up to her.

"If that is the ladder by which one ascends, I will try my luck myself." And the next day, when it began to grow dark, he went to the tower and cried:

"Rapunzel, Rapunzel, let down your hair!"

The hair fell down at once, and the King's son climbed up by it.

At first Rapunzel was terrified, for she had never set eyes on a man before, but the King's son talked to her in a friendly way, and told her that his heart had been so deeply touched by her song that he had no peace, and he was obliged to see her. Then Rapunzel lost her fear, and when he asked if she would have him for her husband, and she saw that he was young and handsome, she thought, "He will love me better than old Mother Gothel." So she said, "Yes," and laid her hand in his. She said: "I will gladly go with you, but I do not know how I am to get down from this tower. When you come, will you bring a skein of silk with you every time? I will twist it into a ladder, and when it is long enough I will descend by it, and you can take me away with you on your horse."

She arranged with him that he should come and see her every evening, for the old Witch came in the daytime.

The Witch discovered nothing, till suddenly Rapunzel said to her: "Tell me, Mother Gothel, how can it be that you are so much heavier to draw up than the young Prince who will be here in a moment?"

"Oh, you wicked child, what do you say? I thought I

had separated you from all the world, and yet you have deceived me." In her rage she seized Rapunzel's beautiful hair, twisted it twice around her left hand, snatched up a pair of shears and cut off the plaits, which fell to the ground. She was so merciless that she took poor Rapunzel away into a wilderness, where she forced her to live in the greatest grief and misery.

In the evening of the day on which she had banished Rapunzel, the Witch fastened the plaits, which she had cut off, to the hook by the window, and when the Prince came and called, "Rapunzel, Rapunzel, let down your hair!" she lowered the hair. The Prince climbed up, but there he found, not his beloved Rapunzel, but the Witch, who looked at him with angry and wicked eyes.

"Ah!" she cried mockingly, "you have come to fetch your ladylove, but the pretty bird is no longer in her nest; and she can sing no more, for the cat has seized her, and it will scratch your own eyes out too. Rapunzel is lost to you; you will never see her again."

The Prince was beside himself with grief, and in his despair he sprang out of the window. He was not killed, but his eyes were scratched out by the thorns among which he fell. He wandered about blind in the wood, and had nothing but roots and berries to eat. He did nothing but weep and lament over the loss of his beloved wife Rapunzel. In this way he wandered about for some years, till at last he reached the wilderness where Rapunzel had been living in great poverty with the twins (a boy and a girl) who had been born to her.

He heard a voice which seemed very familiar to him, and he went toward it. The voice was Rapunzel's, and she knew him at once, and fell weeping upon his neck. Two of her tears fell upon his eyes, and they immediately grew quite clear, and he could see as well as ever.

He took her to his kingdom, where he was received with joy, and they lived long and happily together.

The Queen Bee

ONCE upon a time two princes started off in search of adventure, and, falling into a wild, free mode of life, did not come home again.

The third brother, who was called the Blockhead, set out to look for the other two. But when at last he found them, they mocked him for thinking of making his way in the world with his simplicity, while they, who were so much cleverer, could not get on.

They all three went on together till they came to an ant heap. The two elder princes wanted to disturb it, to see how the little ants crept away, carrying their eggs.

But the Blockhead said: "Leave the little creatures alone; I will not allow you to disturb them."

Then they went on farther till they came to a lake in which a great many ducks were swimming about. The two wanted to catch and roast a pair.

But the Blockhead would not allow it, and said: "Leave the creatures alone. You shall not kill them."

At last they came to a bee's nest, containing such a quantity of honey that it flowed around the trunk of the tree.

The two princes wanted to set fire to the tree and suffocate the bees, so as to remove the honey.

But the Blockhead stopped them again, and said: "Leave the creatures alone. I will not let you burn them."

At last the three brothers came to a castle, where the stables were full of stone horses, but not a soul was to be seen. They went through all the rooms till they came to a door quite at the end, fastened with three bolts. In the middle of the door was a lattice, through which one could see into the room.

There they saw a little gray man sitting at a table. They called to him once, twice; but he did not hear them. Finally, when they had called him the third time, he stood up and

[343]

opened the door and came out. He said not a word, but led them to a richly spread table, and when they had eaten and drunk, he took them each to a bedroom.

The next morning the little Gray Man came to the eldest Prince, beckoned, and led him to a stone tablet whereon were inscribed three tasks by means of which the castle should be freed from enchantment.

This was the first task: in the wood, under the moss, lay the Princess's pearls, a thousand in number. These had all to be found, and if at sunset a single one were missing, the seeker would be turned to stone.

The eldest went away, and searched all day, but when evening came, he had only found the first hundred, and it happened as the inscription foretold—he was turned to stone.

The next day the second brother undertook the quest; but he fared no better than the first, for he found only two hundred pearls, and he too was turned to stone.

At last came the Blockhead's turn; he searched in the moss, but the pearls were hard to find, and he got on but slowly.

Then he sat down on a rock and cried, and as he was sitting there, the Ant King, whose life he had saved, came up with five thousand ants, and it was not long before the little creatures had found all the pearls and laid them in a heap.

Now the second task was to get the key of the Princess's room out of the lake.

When the Blockhead came to the lake, the ducks, which he had once saved, swam up, dived, and brought up the key from the depths.

But the third task was the hardest. The Prince had to find out which was the youngest and prettiest of the princesses while they were asleep.

They were exactly alike, and could not be distinguished in any way, except that before going to sleep each had eaten a different kind of sweet. The eldest a piece of sugar, the second a little syrup, and the third a spoonful of honey.

Then the Queen of the Bees, whom the Blockhead had saved from burning, came and tried the lips of all three. Finally, she settled on the mouth of the one who had eaten the honey, and so the Prince recognized the right one.

Then the charm was broken and everything in the castle was set free, and those who had been turned to stone took human form again.

And the Blockhead married the youngest and sweetest Princess, and became King after her father's death, while his two brothers married the other sisters.

The Many-Furred Creature

THERE was once upon a time a king who had a wife with golden hair, and she was so beautiful that you couldn't find anyone like her in the world. It happened that she fell ill, and when she felt that she must soon die she sent for the King and said: "If you want to marry after my death, make no one queen unless she is just as beautiful as I am and has just such golden hair as I have. Promise me this." After the King had promised her this she closed her eyes and died.

For a long time the King was not to be comforted, and he did not even think of taking a second wife. At last his councilors said: "The King must marry again, so that we may have a Queen." So messengers were sent far and wide to seek for a bride equal to the late Queen in beauty. But there was no one in the wide world, and if there had been she could not have had such golden hair. Then the messengers came home again, not having been able to find a queen.

Now, the King had a daughter who was just as beautiful as her dead mother and had just such golden hair. One day, when she had grown up, her father looked at her and saw that she was exactly like her mother, so he said to his councilors: "I will marry my daughter to one of you and she shall be Queen, for she is exactly like her dead mother, and when I die her husband shall be King." But when the Princess heard of her father's decision she was not at all pleased and said to him: "Before I do your bidding I must have three dresses; one as golden as the sun, one as silver as the moon, and one as shining as the stars. Besides these, I want a cloak made of a thousand different kinds of skin. Every animal in your kingdom must give a bit of his skin to it." But she thought to herself: "This will be quite impossible, and I shall not have to marry some one I do not care for."

The King, however, was not to be turned from his purpose, and he commanded the most skilled maidens in his kingdom to weave the three dresses, one as golden as the sun, and one as silver as the moon, and one as shining as the stars; and he gave orders to all his huntsmen to catch one of every kind of beast in the kingdom and to get a bit of its skin to make the cloak of a thousand pieces of fur. At last, when all was ready, the King commanded the cloak to be brought to him, and he spread it out before the Princess and said: "To-morrow shall be your wedding day." When the Princess saw that there was no more hope of changing her father's resolution, she determined to flee away.

In the night, when everyone else was sleeping, she got up and took three things from her treasures, a gold ring, a little gold spinning wheel, and a gold reel. She put the sun, moon, and star dresses in a nut shell, drew on the cloak of many skins, and made her face and hands black with soot. Then she commended herself to God and went out and traveled the whole night till she came to a large forest. And as she was very much tired she sat down inside a hollow tree and fell asleep.

The sun rose and she still slept on and on, although it was nearly noon. Now, it happened that the King to whom this wood belonged was hunting in it. When his dogs came to the tree they sniffed and ran round and round it, barking.

THE FAIRY RING

The King said to the huntsmen: "See what sort of a wild beast is in there." The huntsmen went in and then came back and said: "In the hollow tree there lies a wonderful animal that we don't know, and we have never seen one like it. Its skin is made of a thousand pieces of fur; but it is lying down asleep." The King said: "See if you can catch it alive, and then fasten it to the cart and we will take it with us."

When the huntsmen seized the maiden, she awoke and was frightened and cried out to them: "I am a poor child, forsaken by father and mother. Take pity on me and let me go with you." Then they said to her: "Many-furred Creature, you can work in the kitchen. Come with us and sweep the ashes together." So they put her in the cart and went back to the palace. There they showed her a tiny room under the stairs, where no daylight came, and said to her: "Many-furred Creature, you can live and sleep here." Then she was sent into the kitchen, where she carried wood and water, poked the fire, washed vegetables, plucked fowls, swept up the ashes, and did all the dirty work.

So the Many-furred Creature lived for a long time in great poverty. Ah, beautiful king's daughter, what is going to befall you now?

It happened once when a great feast was being held in the palace that she said to the cook: "Can I go upstairs for a little bit and look on? I will stand outside the doors." The cook replied: "Yes, you can go up, but in half an hour you must be back here to sweep up the ashes." Then she took her little oil lamp and went into her little room, drew off her fur cloak, and washed off the soot from her face and hands, so that her beauty shone forth, and it was as if one sunbeam after another were coming out of a black cloud. Then she opened the nut and took out the dress as golden as the sun. And when she had done this she went up to the feast, and everyone stepped out of her way, for nobody knew her, and they thought she must be a king's daughter. But the King came toward her and gave her his hand, and danced

THE FAIRY RING

with her, thinking to himself, " My eyes have never beheld
anyone so fair!" When the dance was ended she courtesied
to him, and when the King looked around she had disappeared, no one knew whither. The guards who were standing
before the palace were called and questioned, but no one had
seen her.

She had run to her little room and had quickly taken off
her dress, made her face and hands black, put on the fur
cloak, and was once more the Many-furred Creature. When
she came into the kitchen and was setting about her work
of sweeping the ashes together the cook said to her: " Let
that wait till to-morrow, and just cook the King's soup for
me. I want to have a little peep at the company upstairs.
But be sure that you do not let a hair fall into it, otherwise
you will get nothing to eat in future!" So the cook went
away, and the Many-furred Creature cooked the soup for the
King. She made a bread soup as well as she possibly could,
and when it was done she fetched her gold ring from her
little room and laid it in the tureen in which the soup was
to be served up.

When the dance was ended the King had his soup brought
to him and ate it, and it was so good that he thought he
had never tasted such soup in his life. But when he came
to the bottom of the dish he saw a gold ring lying there,
and he could not imagine how it got in. Then he commanded
the cook to be brought before him. The cook was terrified
when he heard the command and said to the Many-furred
Creature: " You must have let a hair fall into the soup, and
if you have you deserve a good beating!"

When he came before the King, the King asked who had
cooked the soup. The cook answered: " I cooked it." But
the King said: " That's not true, for it was quite different and
much better soup than you have ever cooked." Then the cook
said: " I must confess. I did not cook the soup; the Many-
furred Creature did." " Let her be brought before me." said
the King.

When the Many-furred Creature came the King asked her

[348]

who she was. "I am a poor child without father or mother."
Then he asked her: "What do you do in my palace?" "I am
of no use except to have boots thrown at my head." "How
did you get the ring which was in the soup?" he asked. "I
know nothing at all about the ring," she answered. So the
King could find out nothing and was obliged to send her away.

After a time there was another feast, and the Many-furred
Creature begged the cook again to let her go and look on.
He answered: "Yes, but come back again in half an hour
and cook the King the bread soup that he likes so much."
So she ran away to her little room, washed herself quickly,
took out of the nut the dress as silver as the moon and put
it on. Then she went upstairs looking just like a king's
daughter, and the King came toward her, delighted to see her
again, and as the dance had just begun, they danced together.
But when the dance was ended she disappeared again so
quickly that the King could not see which way she went.

She ran to her little room and changed herself once more
into the Many-furred Creature, and went into the kitchen to
cook the bread soup. When the cook was upstairs she
fetched the golden spinning wheel and put it in the dish, so
that the soup was poured over it. It was brought to the
King, who ate it and liked it as much as the last time. He
had the cook sent to him, and again he had to confess that
the Many-furred Creature had cooked the soup. Then the
Many-furred Creature came before the King, but she said
again that she was of no use except to have boots thrown
at her head, and that she knew nothing at all of the golden
spinning wheel.

When the King had a feast for the third time things did
not turn out quite the same as they had before. The cook
said: "You must be a witch, Many-furred Creature, for you
always put something in the soup, so that it is much better
and tastes nicer to the King than any that I cook." But
because she begged hard he let her go up for the third time.
Now she put on the dress as shining as the stars and stepped
into the hall in it.

The King danced again with the beautiful maiden, and thought she had never looked so beautiful. And while he was dancing he put a gold ring on her finger without her seeing it, and he commanded that the dance should last longer than usual. When it was finished he wanted to keep her hands in his, but she broke from him and sprang so quickly away among the people that she vanished from his sight. She ran as fast as she could to her little room under the stairs, but because she had stayed too long beyond the half hour she could not stop to take off the beautiful dress, but only threw the fur cloak over it, and in her haste did not make herself quite black with the soot, one finger remaining white.

The Many-furred Creature now ran into the kitchen, cooked the King's bread soup, and when the cook had gone she laid the golden reel in the dish. When the King found the reel at the bottom, he had the Many-furred Creature brought to him, and then he saw the white finger and the ring which he had put on her hand in the dance. Then he took her hand and held her tightly, and as she was trying to get away she undid the fur cloak a little bit and the star dress shone out. The King seized the cloak and tore it off her. Her golden hair came down, and she stood there in her full splendor and could not hide herself away any more. And when the soot and ashes had been washed from her face she looked more beautiful than anyone in the world. But the King said: "You are my dear bride and we will never be separated from each other." So the wedding was celebrated and they lived happily ever after.

Snow-white and Rose-red

A POOR widow once lived in a little cottage with a garden in front of it, in which grew two rose trees, one bearing white roses and the other red. She had two children, who were just like the two rose trees; one was called Snow-white and the other Rose-red, and they were the sweetest and best children in the world, always diligent and always cheerful; but Snow-white was quieter and more gentle than Rose-red. Rose-red loved to run about the fields and meadows and to pick flowers and catch butterflies; but Snow-white sat at home with her mother and helped her in the household, or read aloud to her when there was no work to do. The two children loved each other so dearly that they always walked about, hand in hand, whenever they went out together, and when Snow-white said, "We will never desert each other," Rose-red answered, "No, not as long as we live"; and the mother added: "Whatever one gets she shall share with the other." They often roamed about in the woods gathering berries, and no beast offered to hurt them; on the contrary, they came up to them in the most confiding manner; the little hare would eat a cabbage leaf from their hands, the deer grazed beside them, the stag would bound past them merrily, and the birds remained on the branches and sang to them with all their might. No evil ever befell them; if they tarried late in the wood and night overtook them, they lay down together on the moss and slept till morning, and their mother knew they were quite safe and never felt anxious about them. Once, when they had slept the night in the wood and had been wakened by the morning sun, they perceived a beautiful child in a shining white robe sitting close to their resting place. The figure rose up, looked at them kindly, but said nothing and vanished into the wood. And when they looked round about them they became aware that they had slept quite close to a precipice, over which they would certainly have fallen had they gone on a few steps farther in the darkness. And when they told their mother of their adventure, she said what they had seen must have been the angel that guards good children.

Snow-white and Rose-red kept their mother's cottage so beautifully clean and neat that it was a pleasure to go into it. In summer Rose-red looked after the house, and every morning before her mother awoke she placed a bunch of flowers before the bed, and a rose from each tree. In winter Snow-white lit the fire and put on the kettle, which was made of brass, but so beautifully polished that it shone like gold. In the evening when the snowflakes fell, their mother said, "Snow-white, go and close the shutters"; and they drew round the fire, while the mother put on her spectacles and read aloud from a big book, and the two girls listened and sat and spun. Beside them on the ground lay a little lamb, and behind them perched a little white dove with its head tucked under its wings.

One evening as they sat thus cozily together some one knocked at the door as though he desired admittance. The mother said: "Rose-red, open the door quickly! it must be some traveler seeking shelter." Rose-red hastened to unbar the door, and thought she saw a poor man standing in the darkness outside; but it was no such thing, only a bear, who poked his thick black head through the door. Rose-red screamed aloud and sprang back in terror, the lamb began to bleat, the dove flapped its wings, and Snow-white ran and hid behind her mother's bed. But the bear began to speak, and said: "Don't be afraid; I won't hurt you. I am half frozen, and only wish to warm myself a little." "My poor bear," said the mother, "lie down by the fire, only take care you don't burn your fur." Then she called out: "Snow-white and Rose-red, come out; the bear will do you no harm; he is a good, honest creature." So they both came out of their hiding places, and gradually the lamb and dove drew near too, and they all forgot their fear. The bear asked the children to beat the snow a little out of his fur, and they fetched a brush and scrubbed him till he was dry. Then the beast stretched himself in front of the fire and growled quite happily and comfortably. The children soon grew quite at their ease with him and led their hapless guest a fearful life. They tugged his fur with their hands, put their small feet on his back, and rolled him about here and there, or took a hazel wand and beat him with it; and if he growled they only laughed. The bear submitted to everything with the best possible good nature, only when they went too far he cried: "O children, spare my life!

> "'Snow-white and Rose-red,
> Don't beat your lover dead.'"

When it was time to retire for the night and the others went to bed, the mother said to the bear: "You can lie there on the hearth, in Heaven's name; it will be shelter for you from the cold and wet." As soon as day dawned the children let him out, and he trotted over the snow into the wood. From this time on the bear came every evening at the same hour, and lay down by the hearth and let the children play what pranks they liked with him; and they grew so accustomed to him that the door was never shut till their black friend had made his appearance.

When spring came and all outside was green, the bear said one morning to Snow-white: "Now I must go away and not return again the whole summer." "Where are you going to, dear bear?" asked Snow-white. "I must go to the wood and protect my treasure from the wicked dwarfs. In winter, when the earth is frozen hard, they are obliged to remain underground, for they can't work their way through; but now, when the sun has thawed and warmed the ground, they break through and come up above to spy the land and steal what they can. What once falls into their hands and into their caves is not easily brought back to light." Snow-white was quite sad over their friend's departure, and when she unbarred the door for him the bear, stepping out, caught a piece of his fur in the door knocker, and Snow-white thought she caught sight of glittering gold beneath it, but she couldn't be certain of it; and the bear ran hastily away and soon disappeared behind the trees.

A short time after this the mother sent the children into the wood to collect fagots. They came in their wanderings upon a big tree which lay felled on the ground, and on the trunk among the long grass they noticed something jumping up and down, but what it was they couldn't distinguish

THE FAIRY RING

When they approached nearer they perceived a dwarf with a wizened face and a beard a yard long. The end of the beard was jammed into a cleft of the tree, and the little man sprang about like a dog on a chain, and didn't seem to know what he was to do. He glared at the girls with his fiery red eyes and screamed out: "What are you standing there for? Can't you come and help me?" "What were you doing, little man?" asked Rose-red. "You stupid, inquisitive goose!" replied the dwarf; "I wanted to split the tree in order to get little chips of wood for our kitchen fire; those thick logs that serve to make fires for coarse, greedy people like yourselves quite burn up all the little food we need. I had successfully driven in the wedge and all was going well, but the horrid wood was so slippery that it suddenly sprang out, and the tree closed up so rapidly that I had no time to take my beautiful white beard out, so here I am stuck fast and I can't get away; and you silly, smooth-faced, milk-and-water girls just stand and laugh. Ugh, what wretches you are!"

The children did all in their power, but they couldn't get the beard out; it was wedged in far too firmly. "I will run and fetch somebody," said Rose-red. "Crazy blockheads!" snapped the dwarf; "what's the good of calling anyone else? You're already two too many for me. Does nothing better occur to you than that?" "Don't be so impatient," said Snow-white. "I'll see you get help." And taking her scissors out of her pocket she cut the end off his beard. As soon as the dwarf felt himself free he seized a bagful of gold which was hidden among the roots of the tree, lifted it up, and muttered aloud: "Curse these rude wretches, cutting off a piece of my splendid beard!" With these words he swung the bag over his back and disappeared without as much as looking at the children again.

Shortly after this Snow-white and Rose-red went out to get a dish of fish. As they approached the stream they saw something which looked like an enormous grasshopper springing toward the water as if it were going to jump in. They ran forward and recognized their old friend, the dwarf.

THE FAIRY RING

" Where are you going to? " asked Rose-red. " You're surely not going to jump into the water? " " I'm not such a fool," screamed the dwarf. " Don't you see that horrid fish is trying to drag me in? " The little man had been sitting on the bank fishing, when unfortunately the wind had entangled his beard in the line; and when immediately afterwards a big fish bit, the feeble little creature had no strength to pull it out. The fish had the upper fin and dragged the dwarf toward him. He clung on with all his might to every rush and blade of grass, but it didn't help him much. He had to follow every movement of the fish and was in great danger of being drawn into the water. The girls came up just at the right moment, held him firm, and did all they could to disentangle his beard from the line; but in vain—beard and line were in a hopeless muddle. Nothing remained but to produce the scissors and cut the beard, by which a small part of it was sacrificed.

When the dwarf perceived what they were about, he yelled to them: " Do you call that manners, you toadstools! to disfigure a fellow's face? It wasn't enough that you shortened my beard before, but you must now needs cut off the best of it. I can't appear like this before my own people. I wish you'd been at Jericho first." Then he fetched a sack of pearls that lay among the rushes, and without saying another word he dragged it away and disappeared behind a stone.

It happened that soon after this the mother sent the two girls to the town to buy needles, thread, laces, and ribbons. Their road led over a heath where huge bowlders of rock lay scattered here and there. While trudging along they saw a big bird hovering in the air, circling slowly above them, but always descending lower, till at last it settled on a rock not far from them. Immediately afterwards they heard a sharp, piercing cry. They ran forward and saw with horror that the eagle had pounced on their old friend the dwarf and was about to carry him off. The tender-hearted children seized hold of the little man, and struggled so long with the bird that at last he let go his prey. When the dwarf had recovered from the first shock he screamed in his squeaking

[355]

THE FAIRY RING

voice: "Couldn't you have treated me more carefully? You have torn my thin little coat all to shreds, useless, awkward hussies that you are!" Then he took a bag of precious stones and vanished under the rocks into his cave. The girls were accustomed to his ingratitude, and went on their way and did their business in town. On their way home, as they were again passing the heath, they surprised the dwarf pouring out his precious stones on an open space, for he had thought no one would pass by at so late an hour. The evening sun shone on the glittering stones, and they glanced and gleamed so beautifully that the children stood still and gazed on them. "What are you standing there gaping for?" screamed the dwarf, and his ashen-gray face became scarlet with rage. He was about to go off with these angry words, when a sudden growl was heard and a black bear trotted out of the wood. The dwarf jumped up in a great fright, but he hadn't time to reach his place of retreat, for the bear was already close to him. Then he cried in terror: "Dear Mr. Bear, spare me! I'll give you all my treasure. Look at these beautiful precious stones lying there. Spare my life! What pleasure would you get from a poor, feeble little fellow like me? You won't feel me between your teeth. There, lay hold of these two wicked girls—they will be a tender morsel for you, as fat as young quails; eat them up, for Heaven's sake." But the bear, paying no attention to his words, gave the evil little creature one blow with his paw and he never moved again.

The girls had run away, but the bear called after them: "Snow-white and Rose-red, don't be afraid. Wait, and I'll come with you." Then they recognized his voice and stood still, and when the bear was quite close to them his skin suddenly fell off, and a beautiful man stood beside them, all dressed in gold. "I am a king's son," he said, "and have been doomed by that unholy little dwarf, who had stolen my treasure, to roam about the woods as a wild bear till his death should set me free. Now he has received his well-merited punishment."

Snow-white married him and Rose-red his brother, and they

[356]

"'WHAT ARE YOU STANDING THERE GAPING FOR?' SCREAMED THE DWARF"

divided the great treasure the dwarf had collected in his cave between them. The old mother lived for many years peacefully with her children; and she carried the two rose trees with her, and they stood in front of her window, and every year they bore the finest red and white roses.

The Frog Prince

*I*N times of yore, when wishes were both heard and granted, lived a king whose daughters were all beautiful, but the youngest was so lovely that the sun himself, who has seen so much, wondered at her beauty every time he looked in her face. Now, near the King's castle was a large dark forest; and in the forest, under an old linden tree, was a deep well. When the day was very hot, the King's daughter used to go to the wood and seat herself at the edge of the cool well; and when she became wearied she would take a golden ball, throw it up in the air, and catch it again. This was her favorite amusement. Once it happened that her golden ball, instead of falling back into the little hand that she stretched out for it, dropped on the ground and immediately rolled away into the water. The King's daughter followed it with her eyes, but the ball had vanished and the well was so deep that no one could see down to the bottom. Then she began to weep, wept louder and louder every minute, and could not console herself at all.

While she was thus lamenting, some one called to her: "What is the matter with you, King's daughter? You weep so bitterly that you would touch the heart of a stone."

She looked around to see whence the voice came, and saw a frog stretching his thick, ugly head out of the water.

"Ah, it is you, old water paddler!" said she. "I am crying for my golden ball, which has fallen into the well."

"Be content," answered the Frog, "I dare say I can give you some good advice; but what will you give me if I bring back your plaything to you?"

THE FAIRY RING

"Whatever you like, dear Frog," said she, "my clothes, my pearls, and jewels, even the golden crown I wear."

The Frog answered: "Your clothes, your pearls, and jewels, even your golden crown I do not care for; but if you will love me, and let me be your companion and playfellow; sit near you at your little table, eat from your little golden plate, drink from your little cup, and sleep in your little bed—if you will promise me this, then I will bring you back your golden ball from the bottom of the well."

"Oh, yes!" said she; "I promise you everything, if you will only bring me back my golden ball."

She thought to herself meanwhile: "What nonsense the silly Frog talks! He sits in the water with the other frogs and croaks, and cannot be anybody's playfellow."

But the Frog, as soon as he had received the promise, dipped his head under the water and sank down. In a little while up he came again with the ball in his mouth, and threw it on the grass. The King's daughter was overjoyed when she beheld her pretty plaything and picked it up and ran away with it.

"Wait! wait!" cried the Frog; "take me with you. I cannot run as fast as you."

Alas! of what use was it that he croaked after her as loud as he could. She would not listen to him, but hastened home, and soon forgot the poor Frog, who was obliged to plunge again to the bottom of his well.

The next day, when she was sitting at dinner with the King and all the courtiers, eating from her little golden plate, there came a sound of something creeping up the marble staircase—splish, splash; and when it had reached the top, it knocked at the door and cried: "Youngest King's daughter, open to me."

She ran, wishing to see who was outside; but when she opened the door, and there sat the Frog, she flung it hastily to again, and sat down at table, feeling very, very uncomfortable. The King saw that her heart was beating violently, and said: "Well, my child, why are you afraid? Is a giant standing outside the door to carry you off?"

"Oh, no!" answered she, "it is no giant, but a nasty frog. who yesterday, when I was playing in the wood near the well, fetched my golden ball out of the water. For this I promised him he should be my companion, but I never thought he could come out of his well. Now he is at the door, and wants to come in."

Again, the second time there was a knock, and a voice cried:

> "Youngest King's daughter,
> Open to me;
> Know you what yesterday
> You promised me
> By the cool water?
> Youngest King's daughter,
> Open to me."

Then said the King: "What you promised you must perform. Go and open the door."

She went and opened the door; the Frog hopped in, always following and following her till he came up to her chair. There he sat and cried out: "Lift me up to you on the table." She refused, till the King, her father commanded her to do it. When the Frog was on the table he said: "Now push your little golden plate nearer to me that we may eat together." She did as he desired, but one could easily see that she did it unwillingly. The Frog seemed to enjoy his dinner very much, but every morsel she ate stuck in the throat of the poor little Princess.

Then said the Frog: "I have eaten enough, and am tired; carry me to your little room, and make your little silken bed smooth, and we will lay ourselves down to sleep together."

At this the daughter of the King began to weep, for she was afraid of the cold frog, who wanted to sleep in her pretty clean bed.

But the King looked angrily at her, and said again: "What you have promised you must perform. The Frog is your companion."

It was no use to complain; whether she liked it or not, she was obliged to take the Frog with her up to her little bed.

So she picked him up with two fingers, hating him bitterly the while, and carried him upstairs. But when she got into bed, instead of lifting him up to her, she threw him with all her strength against the wall, saying: " Now, you nasty Frog, there will be an end of you ! "

But what fell down from the wall was not a dead frog, but a living young prince, with beautiful and loving eyes, who at once became, by her own promise and her father's will, her dear companion and husband. He told her how he had been cursed by a wicked sorceress, and that no one but the King's youngest daughter could release him from his enchantment and take him out of the well.

The next day a carriage drove up to the palace gates with eight white horses, having white feathers on their heads and golden reins. Behind it stood the servant of the young Prince, called the Faithful Henry. This Faithful Henry had been so grieved when his master was changed into a frog, that he had been compelled to have three iron bands fastened around his heart, lest it should break. Now the carriage came to convey the Prince to his kingdom, so the Faithful Henry lifted in the bride and bridegroom, and mounted behind, full of joy at his lord's release. But when they had gone a short distance, the Prince heard behind him a noise as if something was breaking. He turned around and cried out: " Henry, the carriage is breaking ! "

But Henry replied: " No, sir, it is not the carriage, but one of the bands from my heart with which I was forced to bind it up, or it would have broken with grief while you sat as a frog at the bottom of the well."

Twice again this happened, and the Prince always thought the carriage was breaking; but it was only the bands breaking off from the heart of the Faithful Henry, out of joy that his lord the Frog Prince was a frog no more.

The Goose Girl

*T*HE King of a great land died, and left his Queen
to take care of their only child. This child was a
daughter who was very beautiful, and her mother
loved her dearly and was very kind to her. And there was
a good fairy, too, who was fond of the Princess, and helped
her mother to watch over her. When she grew up she was
betrothed to a prince who lived a great way off; and as the
time drew near for her to be married she made ready to set
off on her journey to his country. Then the Queen, her
mother, packed up a great many costly things; jewels and
gold and silver; trinkets, fine dresses, and in short, everything
that became a royal bride. And she gave her a waiting maid
to ride with her, and give her into the bridegroom's hands;
and each had a horse for the journey. Now the Princess's
horse was the fairy's gift, and it was called Falada, and could
speak.

When the time came for them to set out the fairy went into
her bedchamber, and took a little knife and cut off a lock of
her hair and gave it to the Princess, and said: " Take care
of it, dear child; for it is a charm that may be of use to you
on the road." Then they all took a sorrowful leave of the
Princess; and she put the lock of hair into her bosom, got
upon her horse, and set off on her journey to her bridegroom's
kingdom.

One day, as they were riding along by a brook, the Princess
began to feel very thirsty, and she said to her maid: " Pray
get down and fetch me some water in my golden cup out of
yonder brook, for I want to drink." " Nay," said the maid,
" if you are thirsty, get off yourself and stoop down by the
water and drink; I shall not be your waiting maid any longer."
Then she was so thirsty that she got down and knelt over
the little brook and drank, for she was frightened, and dared
not bring out her golden cup; and she wept and said:

"Alas! what will become of me?" And the lock of hair answered her, and said:

> "Alas! alas! if thy mother knew it,
> Sadly, sadly would she rue it."

But the Princess was very gentle and meek, so she said nothing to her maid's ill behavior, but got upon her horse again.

Then all rode farther on their journey till the day grew so warm, and the sun so scorching that the bride began to feel very thirsty again; and at last, when they came to a river, she forgot her maid's rude speech, and said: "Pray get down and fetch me some water to drink in my golden cup." But the maid answered her, and spoke even more haughtily than before: "Drink if you will, but I shall not be your waiting maid." Then the Princess was so thirsty that she got off her horse and lay down, and held her head over the running stream and cried and said: "What will become of me?" And the lock of hair answered her again:

> "Alas! alas! if thy mother knew it,
> Sadly, sadly would she rue it."

And as she leaned down to drink, the lock of hair fell from her bosom and floated away with the water. Now she was so frightened that she did not see it; but her maid saw it and was very glad, for she knew the charm; and she saw that the poor bride would be in her power, now that she had lost the hair. So when the bride had done drinking, and would have got upon Falada again, the maid said: "I shall ride upon Falada, and you may have my horse instead." So she was forced to give up her horse, and soon afterwards to take off her royal clothes and put on her maid's shabby ones.

At last, as they drew near the end of their journey, this treacherous servant threatened to kill her mistress if she ever told anyone what had happened. But Falada saw it all and marked it well.

Then the waiting maid got upon Falada, and the real bride

rode upon the other horse, and they went on in this way till at last they came to the royal court. There was great joy at their coming, and the Prince flew to meet them, and lifted the maid from her horse, thinking she was the one who was to be his wife; and she was led upstairs to the royal chamber; but the true Princess was told to stay in the court below.

Now the old King happened just then to have nothing else to do, so he amused himself by sitting at his kitchen window, looking at what was going on, and he saw her in the courtyard. As she looked very pretty, and too delicate for a waiting maid, he went up into the royal chamber to ask the bride who it was she had brought with her, that was thus left standing in the court below. "I brought her with me for the sake of her company on the road," said she; "pray give the girl some work to do, that she may not be idle." The old King could not for some time think of any work for her to do, but at last he said: "I have a lad who takes care of my geese, she may go and help him." Now the name of this lad that the real bride was to help in watching the King's geese was Curdken.

But the false bride said to the Prince: "Dear husband, pray do me one act of kindness." "That I will," said the Prince. "Then tell one of your slaughterers to cut off the head of the horse I rode upon, for it was very unruly, and plagued me sadly on the road"; but the truth was, she was very much afraid lest Falada should some day or other speak and tell all she had done to the Princess. She carried her point, and the faithful Falada was killed; but when the true Princess heard of it she wept, and begged the man to nail up Falada's head against a large dark gate of the city, through which she had to pass every morning and evening, that there she might still see him sometimes. Then the slaughterer said he would do as she wished; and cut off the head, and nailed it up under the dark gate.

Early the next morning, as she and Curdken went out through the gate, she cried sorrowfully:

"Falada, Falada, there thou hangest!"

and the head answered:

"Bride, bride, there thou gangest!
Alas! alas! if thy mother knew it,
Sadly, sadly would she rue it."

Then they went out of the city and drove the geese on. And when she came to the meadow she sat down upon a bank there, and let down her waving locks of hair, which were all of pure silver; and when Curdken saw it glitter in the sun he ran up, and would have pulled some of the locks out, but she cried:

"Blow, breezes, blow!
Let Curdken's hat go!
Blow, breezes, blow!
Let him after it go!
O'er hills, dales, and rocks,
    Away be it whirl'd,
Till the silvery locks
    Are all comb'd and curl'd!"

Then there came a wind so strong that it blew off Curdken's hat, and away it flew over the hills, and he was forced to turn and run after it, till, by the time he came back, she had done combing and curling her hair, and had put it up safe again. Then he was very angry and sulky, and would not speak to her at all; but they watched the geese until it grew dark in the evening, and then drove them homeward.

The next morning, as they were going through the dark gate, the poor girl looked up at Falada's head, and cried:

"Falada, Falada, there thou hangest!"

and it answered:

"Bride, bride, there thou gangest!
Alas! alas! if thy mother knew it,
Sadly, sadly would she rue it."

"FALADA, FALADA, THERE THOU HANGEST!"
"BRIDE, BRIDE, THERE THOU GANGEST!"

Then she drove on the geese, and sat down again in the meadow, and began to comb out her hair as before; and Curdken ran up to her, and wanted to take hold of it, but she cried out quickly:

> " Blow, breezes, blow!
> Let Curdken's hat go!
> Blow, breezes, blow!
> Let him after it go!
> O'er hills, dales, and rocks,
>   Away be it whirl'd,
> Till the silvery locks
>   Are all comb'd and curl'd!"

Then a wind came and blew away his hat; and off it flew a great way, over the hills and far away, so that he had to run after it; and when he came back she had bound up her hair again, and all was safe. So they watched the geese till it grew dark.

In the evening, after they came home, Curdken went to the old King, and said: "I cannot have that strange girl to help me to keep the geese any longer." "Why?" said the King. "Because, instead of doing any good, she does nothing but tease me all day long." Then the King made him tell what had happened. And Curdken said: "When we go in the morning through the dark gate with our flock of geese, she cries and talks with the head of a horse that hangs upon the wall, and says:

> " Falada, Falada, there thou hangest!"

and the head answers:

> " Bride, bride, there thou gangest!
>   Alas! alas! if thy mother knew it,
>   Sadly, sadly would she rue it."

And Curdken went on telling the King what had happened upon the meadow where the geese fed; how his hat was blown away, and how he was forced to run after it, and to leave his

[365]

flock of geese to themselves. But the old King told the boy
to go out again the next day. And when morning came, he
placed himself behind the dark gate, and heard how she
spoke to Falada, and how Falada answered. Then he went
into the field, and hid himself in a bush by the meadow's side;
and he soon saw with his own eyes how they drove the flock
of geese; and how, after a little time, she let down her hair
that glittered in the sun. And then he heard her say:

> " Blow, breezes, blow!
> Let Curdken's hat go!
> Blow, breezes, blow!
> Let him after it go!
> O'er hills, dales, and rocks,
>   Away be it whirl'd,
> Till the silvery locks
>   Are all comb'd and curl'd!"

And soon came a gale of wind and carried away Curdken's
hat, and away went Curdken after it, while the girl went on
combing and curling her hair. All this the old King saw.
So he went home without being seen, and when the little
goose girl came back in the evening he called her aside, and
asked her why she did this; but she burst into tears, and said:
" That I must not tell you or any man, or I shall lose my life."
But the old King begged so hard that she had no peace till
she had told him all the tale, from beginning to end, word
for word. And it was very lucky for her that she did so,
for when she had done, the King ordered royal clothes to be
put upon her, and gazed on her with wonder, she was so
beautiful. Then he called his son, and told him that he had
only the false bride; for that she was merely a waiting maid
while the true bride stood by. And the young King rejoiced
when he saw her beauty, and heard how meek and patient she
had been; and without saying anything to the false bride, the
King ordered a great feast to be made ready for all his court.
The bridegroom sat at the head, with the false Princess on one
side, and the true one on the other; but nobody knew her
again, for her beauty was quite dazzling to their eyes, and

she did not seem at all like the little goose girl, now that she had her brilliant dress on.

When they had eaten and drunk, and were very merry, the old King said he would tell them a tale. So he began, and told all the story of the Princess, as if it was one that he had once heard; and he asked the true waiting maid what she thought ought to be done to anyone who would behave thus. "Nothing better," said this false bride, "than that she should be banished to the depths of the dark woods and live there forever." "Thou art she!" said the old King; "and as thou hast judged thyself, so shall it be done to thee." And the young King was then married to his true wife, and they reigned over the kingdom in peace and happiness all their lives; and the good fairy came to see them, and restored the faithful Falada to life again.

Briar Rose

A LONG time ago there lived a king and a queen, who said every day, "If only we had a child"; but for a long time they had none.

It fell out once, as the Queen was bathing, that a frog crept out of the water on to the land and said to her: "Your wish shall be fulfilled; before a year has passed you shall bring a daughter into the world."

The frog's words came true. The Queen had a little girl who was so beautiful that the King could not contain himself for joy, and prepared a great feast. He invited not only his relations, friends, and acquaintances, but the fairies, in order that they might be favorably and kindly disposed toward the child. There were thirteen of them in the kingdom, but as the King had only twelve golden plates for them to eat off, one of the fairies had to stay at home.

The feast was held with all splendor, and when it came to an end the fairies all presented the child with a magic gift.

One gave her virtue, another beauty, a third riches, and so on, with everything in the world that she could wish for.

When eleven of the fairies had said their say, the thirteenth suddenly appeared. She wanted to revenge herself for not having been invited. Without greeting anyone, or even glancing at the company, she called out in a loud voice, " The Princess shall prick herself with a distaff in her fifteenth year and shall fall down dead "; and without another word she turned and left the hall.

Everyone was terror-stricken, but the twelfth fairy, whose wish was still unspoken, stepped forward. She could not cancel the curse, but could only soften it, so she said: " It shall not be death, but a deep sleep lasting a hundred years, into which your daughter shall fall."

The King was so anxious to guard his dear child from the misfortune that he sent out a command that all the distaffs in the whole kingdom should be burned.

All the promises of the fairies came true.

The Princess grew up so beautiful, modest, kind, and clever that everyone who saw her could not but love her. Now it happened that on the very day when she was fifteen years old the King and Queen were away from home, and the Princess was left quite alone in the castle. She wandered about over the whole place, looking at rooms and halls as she pleased, and at last she came to an old tower. She ascended a narrow, winding staircase and reached a little door. A rusty key was sticking in the lock, and when she turned it the door flew open. In a little room sat an old woman with a spindle, busily spinning her flax.

" Good day, Granny," said the Princess; " what are you doing? "

" I am spinning," said the old woman, and nodded her head. " What is the thing that whirls round so merrily? " asked the Princess; and she took the spindle and tried to spin too.

But she had scarcely touched it before the curse was fulfilled, and she pricked her finger with the spindle. The instant she felt the prick she fell upon the bed which was standing near, and lay still in a deep sleep which spread over the whole castle.

The King and Queen, who had just come home and had stepped into the hall, went to sleep, and all their courtiers with them. The horses went to sleep in the stable, the dogs in the yard, the doves on the roof, the flies on the wall; yes, even the fire flickering on the hearth grew still and went to sleep, and the roast meat stopped crackling; and the cook, who was pulling the scullion's hair because he had made some mistake, let him go and went to sleep. And the wind dropped, and on the trees in front of the castle not a leaf stirred.

But round the castle a hedge of brier roses began to grow up; every year it grew higher, till at last it surrounded the whole castle so that nothing could be seen of it, not even the flags on the roof.

But there was a legend in the land about the lovely sleeping Brier Rose, as the King's daughter was called, and from time to time princes came and tried to force a way through the hedge into the castle. But they found it impossible, for the thorns, as though they had hands, held them fast, and the princes remained caught in them without being able to free themselves, and so died a miserable death.

After many, many years a prince came again to the country and heard an old man tell of the castle which stood behind the brier hedge, in which a most beautiful maiden called Brier Rose had been asleep for the last hundred years, and with her slept the King, Queen, and all her courtiers. He knew also, from his grandfather, that many princes had already come and sought to pierce through the brier hedge, and had remained caught in it and died a sad death.

Then the young Prince said: "I am not afraid; I am determined to go and look upon the lovely Brier Rose."

The good old man did all in his power to dissuade him, but the Prince would not listen to his words.

Now, however, the hundred years were just ended, and the day had come when Brier Rose was to wake up again. When the Prince approached the brier hedge it was in blossom, and was covered with beautiful large flowers which made way for him of their own accord and let him pass unharmed, and then closed up again into a hedge behind him.

In the courtyard he saw the horses and dappled hounds lying asleep, on the roof sat the doves with their heads under their wings, and when he went into the house the flies were asleep on the walls, and near the throne lay the King and Queen; in the kitchen was the cook, with his hand raised as though about to strike the scullion, and the maid sat with the black fowl before her which she was about to pluck.

He went on farther, and all was so still that he could hear his own breathing. At last he reached the tower, and opened the door into the little room where Brier Rose was asleep. There she lay, looking so beautiful that he could not take his eyes off her; he bent down and gave her a kiss. As he touched her, Brier Rose opened her eyes and looked quite sweetly at him. Then they went down together; and the King and the Queen and all the courtiers woke up, and looked at each other with astonished eyes. The horses in the stable stood up and shook themselves, the hounds leaped about and wagged their tails, the doves on the roof lifted their heads from under their wings, looked around, and flew into the fields; the flies on the walls began to crawl again, the fire in the kitchen roused itself and blazed up and cooked the food, the meat began to crackle, and the cook boxed the scullion's ears so soundly that he screamed aloud, while the maid finished plucking the fowl. Then the wedding of the Prince and Brier Rose was celebrated with all splendor, and they lived happily till they died.

The Iron Stove

ONCE upon a time when wishes came true there was a king's son who was enchanted by an old witch, so that he was obliged to sit in a large iron stove in a wood. There he lived for many years, and no one could free him.

"AT LAST HE REACHED THE TOWER . . . WHERE BRIER ROSE WAS ASLEEP"

THE FAIRY RING

At last a king's daughter came into the wood; she had lost her way and could not find her father's kingdom again. She had been wandering round and round for nine days, and she came at last to the iron stove. A voice came from within and asked her: "Where do you come from and where do you want to go?" She answered: "I have lost my way to my father's kingdom, and I shall never get home again." Then the voice from the iron stove said: "I will help you to find your home again, and that in a very short time, if you will promise to do what I ask you. I am a greater prince than you are a princess, and I will marry you." Then she grew frightened and thought: "What can a young lassie do with an iron stove?" But as she wanted very much to go home to her father, she promised to do what he wished. He said: "You must come again, and bring a knife with you to scrape a hole in the iron."

Then he gave her some one for a guide, who walked near her and said nothing, but he brought her in two hours to her house. There was great joy in the castle when the Princess came back, and the old King fell on her neck and kissed her. But she was very much troubled and said: "Dear father, listen to what has befallen me. I should never have come home again out of the great wildwood if I had not come to an iron stove, and I have had to promise that I will go back to free him and marry him!" The old King was so frightened that he nearly fainted, for she was his only daughter. So they consulted together and determined that the miller's daughter, who was very beautiful, should take her place. They took her there, gave her a knife, and said she must scrape at the iron stove. She scraped for twenty-four hours, but did not make the least impression. When the day broke a voice called from the iron stove: "It seems to me that it is day outside." Then she answered: "It seems so to me; I think I hear my father's mill rattling."

"So you are a miller's daughter! Then go away at once and tell the King's daughter to come."

Then she went away and told the old King that the thing

inside the iron stove would not have her, but wanted the Princess. The old King was frightened, and his daughter wept. But they had a swineherd's daughter who was even more beautiful than the miller's daughter, and they gave her a piece of gold to go to the iron stove instead of the Princess. Then she was taken there and made to scrape for twenty-four hours, but she could make no impression. As soon as the day broke the voice from the stove called out: " It seems to be daylight outside." Then she answered: " It seems so to me, too; I think I hear my father blowing his horn." " So you are a swineherd's daughter! Go away at once and let the King's daughter come. And say to her that what I foretell shall come to pass, and if she does not come everything in the kingdom shall fall into ruin, and not one stone shall be left upon another." When the Princess heard this she began to cry, but it was no good; she had to keep her word. She took leave of her father, put a knife in her belt, and went to the iron stove in the wood. As soon as she reached it she began to scrape and the iron gave way, and before two hours had passed she had made a little hole. Then she peeped in and saw such a beautiful youth all shining with gold and precious stones that she fell in love with him on the spot. So she scraped away harder than ever, and made the hole so large that he could get out. Then he said: " You are mine and I am thine; you are my bride and have set me free!" He wanted to take her with him to his kingdom, but she begged him just to let her go once more to her father; and the Prince let her go, but told her not to say more than three words to her father, then to come back again. So she went home, but, alas! she said more than three words; and immediately the iron stove vanished and went away over a mountain of glass and sharp swords. But the Prince was free and was no longer shut up in it. Then she said good-by to her father, and took a little money with her and went again into the great wood to look for the iron stove; but she could not find it. She sought it for nine days, and then her hunger became so great that she did not know how she could live any longer. And

THE FAIRY RING

When she had washed up the next evening she bit the second nut, and there was a still more beautiful dress inside. When the bride saw it she wanted to buy it also. But the maid did not want money and asked that she should sleep again by the Prince's door. The bride, however, gave him a sleeping draught, and he slept so soundly that he heard nothing. But the kitchen maid wept the whole night long and said: "I have freed you in a wood and from an iron stove; I sought you and have crossed a glassy mountain, three sharp swords, and a great lake to find you, and now you will not hear me!" The servants outside heard how she cried the whole night, and in the morning they told their master. And when she had washed up on the third night she bit the third nut, and there was a still more beautiful dress inside that was made of pure gold. When the bride saw it she wanted to have it, but the maid would only give it her on condition that she should sleep for the third time by the Prince's door. But the Prince took care not to drink the sleeping draught. When she began to weep and to say, "Dearest sweetheart, I freed you in the horrible wildwood and from an iron stove," he jumped up and said: "Thou art right. Thou art mine and I am thine." Though it was still night, he got into a carriage with her, and they took the false bride's clothes away, so that she could not follow them. When they came to the great lake they rowed across, and when they reached the three sharp swords they sat on the plow wheel, and on the glassy mountain they stuck the three needles in. So they arrived at last at the little old house, but when they stepped inside it turned into a large castle. The toads were all freed and were beautiful king's children running about for joy. There they were married, and they remained in the castle, which was much larger than that of the Princess's father. But because the old man did not like being left alone they went and fetched him. So they had two kingdoms and lived in great wealth.

> "A mouse has run,
> My story's done."

THE FAIRY RING

Rumpel-stilts-ken

BY the side of a wood, in a country a long way off, ran a fine stream of water, and upon the stream there stood a mill. The miller's house was close by, and the miller, you must know, had a very beautiful daughter. She was, moreover, very shrewd and clever; and the miller was so proud of her that he one day told the King of the land, who used to come and hunt in the wood, that his daughter could spin gold out of straw. Now this King was very fond of money, and when he heard the miller's boast his greediness was roused, and he sent for the girl to be brought before him. Then he led her to a chamber in his palace where there was a great heap of straw, and gave her a spinning wheel, and said: "All this must be spun into gold before morning, as you love your life." It was in vain that the poor maiden said that it was only a silly boast of her father, for that she could do no such thing as spin straw into gold. The chamber door was locked, and she was left alone.

She sat down in one corner of the room and began to bewail her hard fate, when on a sudden the door opened and a droll-looking little man hobbled in and said: "Good morrow to you, my good lass; what are you weeping for?" "Alas!" said she, "I must spin this straw into gold, and I know not how." "What will you give me," said the hobgoblin, "to do it for you?" "My necklace," replied the maiden. He took her at her word and sat himself down to the wheel, and whistled and sang:

"Round about, round about,
Lo and behold!
Reel away, reel away,
Straw into gold!"

And round about the wheel went merrily; the work was quickly done, and the straw was all spun into gold.

When the King came in and saw this he was greatly astonished and pleased, but his heart grew still more greedy of gain, and he shut up the poor miller's daughter again with a fresh task. Then she knew not what to do, and sat down once more to weep; but the dwarf soon opened the door and said: "What will you give me to do your task?" "The ring on my finger," said she. So her little friend took the ring, and began to work at the wheel again, and whistled and sang,

> "Round about, round about,
> Lo and behold!
> Reel away, reel away,
> Straw into gold!"

till, long before morning, all was done again.

The King was greatly delighted to see all this glittering treasure, but still he had not enough, so he took the miller's daughter to a yet larger heap and said: "All this must be spun to-night; and if it is, you shall be my Queen." As soon as she was alone the dwarf came in and said: "What will you give me to spin gold for you this third time?" "I have nothing left," said she. "Then say you will give me," said the little man, "the first little child that you may have when you are Queen. "That may never be," thought the miller's daughter, and as she knew no other way to get her task done she said she would do what he asked. Round went the wheel again to the old song, and the manikin once more spun the heap into gold. The King came in the morning, and, finding all he wanted, was forced to keep his word: so he married the miller's daughter, and she really became Queen.

At the birth of her first little child she was very glad, and forgot the dwarf and what she had promised. But one day he came into her room, where she was sitting playing with her baby, and put her in mind of it. Then she grieved sorely at her misfortune, and said she would give him all the wealth of the kingdom if he would let her off, but in vain; till at last her tears softened him and he said: "I will give you three days' grace, and, if during that time you tell me my name, you shall keep your child."

THE FAIRY RING

Now the Queen lay awake all night, thinking of all the odd names that she had ever heard, and she sent messengers all over the land to find out new ones. The next day the little man came, and she began with TIMOTHY, ICHABOD, BENJAMIN, JEREMIAH, and all the names she could remember; but to all and each of them he said: "Madam, that is not my name."

The second day she began with all the comical names she could hear of, BANDY LEGS, HUNCHBACK, CROOK SHANKS, and so on; but the little gentleman still said to every one of them: "Madam, that is not my name."

The third day one of the messengers came back and said: "I traveled two days without hearing of any other names; but yesterday, as I was climbing a high hill, among the trees of the forest where the fox and the hare bid each other good night, I saw a little hut; and before the hut burned a fire; and round about the fire a funny little dwarf was dancing upon one leg, and singing:

> "'Merrily the feast I'll make,
> To-day I'll brew, to-morrow bake;
> Merrily I'll dance and sing,
> For next day will a stranger bring.
> Little does my lady dream
> Rumpel-stilts-ken is my name!'"

When the Queen heard this she jumped for joy, and as soon as her little friend came she sat down upon her throne and called all her court around to enjoy the fun; and the nurse stood by her side with the baby in her arms, as if it was quite ready to be given up. Then the little man began to chuckle at the thoughts of having the poor child to take home with him to his hut in the woods, and he cried out: "Now, lady, what is my name?" "Is it JOHN?" asked she. "No, madam!" "Is it TOM?" "No, madam!" "Is it JEMMY?" "It is not." "Can your name be RUMPEL-STILTS-KEN?" said the lady slyly. "Some witch told you that!—some witch told you that!" cried the little man, and dashed his right

[378]

foot in a rage so deep into the floor, that he was forced to lay
hold of it with both hands to pull it out.

Then he made the best of his way off, while the nurse
laughed and the baby crowed; and all the court jeered at him
for having had so much trouble for nothing, and said: "We
wish you a very good morning, and a merry feast, Mr. RUM-
PEL-STILTS-KEN!"

Faithful John, the King's Servant

THE old King lay dying and was very much worried
in his mind because he was leaving behind him, as his
heir, his son, who was a headstrong and willful youth,
not yet come to years of wisdom. He called to his bedside
faithful John, who had been his servant ever since he was a
boy, and charged him thus:

"I am going to my last rest, and am sorrowful because my
boy is left alone in a high position, and will have no other
guidance but yours. Be his guardian and counselor, and serve
him faithfully even as you have served me, or I cannot die
happily."

"Master, I will," answered faithful John, "even if it cost
me my life."

"Now I can rest in peace," said the King. "When I am
dead you must lead him all over the castle, and show him the
halls and chambers and the vaults and the treasures therein.
But one room he must never enter, the last room in the long
corridor, for there hangs the portrait of the daughter of the
King of the Golden Palace, and she is so beautiful that whoever gazes on her picture will fall down in a swoon for love
of her, and will go through great perils for her sake. Therefore he must never enter that room."

The trusty servant pressed his master's hand and promised to do his commands, and soon afterwards the King laid
his head on the pillow and died.

THE FAIRY RING

After the old King was laid in his grave, the faithful John told the young King of the commands his father had laid upon him, and swore to serve him faithfully, even unto death.

When the days of mourning were over he told the young King that it was now time for him to see his inheritance; so they went all over the castle, up into the towers and down into the vaults, and saw all the great treasure the old King had collected; and they went into all the grand halls and splendid chambers, into all save one—the last room at the end of the long corridor, wherein hung the portrait.

The King noticed that they always passed this door, and asked John why.

"There is something there that it is dangerous to see," said John.

"But," answered the King, "I have seen everything else that I possess, and you must not imagine I am going away without seeing this."

Faithful John tried to argue him out of it, but it was of no use, and the obstinate King even made an effort to force the door open, and declared that he would not leave the spot till he had seen the contents of the chamber.

So John, seeing that there was nothing for it but to yield, sorrowfully took the key from the bunch and put it in the lock. He turned it suddenly and hurried in, hoping to cover over the portrait before the King saw it; but he was close on his heels, and John was too late to prevent the catastrophe, for no sooner had his master set eyes on the wonderful painting, which appeared to be living, breathing flesh, than he fell on the floor in a swoon.

Poor John carried him tenderly to his bed, deeply bewailing the misfortune that had come upon them, and by dint of forcing wine down his throat he brought him round again. The first words that he uttered were:

"Who is the lady of the beautiful picture?"

"She is the daughter of the King of the Golden Palace," replied John.

"Then," said the King, "we must seek her at once, for I

am filled with so great a love for her that if all the leaves on the trees had tongues they should not gainsay it."

Then trusty John thought for a long, long time as how to set about the matter, for it was very difficult to reach the presence of the beautiful Princess. At last he thought of a plan, and he said to the King:

"I have thought of a way by which you may achieve your end; all the things the Princess uses, and all the things about her, are gold—chairs, tables, dishes, pots and pans, all are fashioned of gold. There are five tons of gold bars in your cellars; you must have them wrought into articles of every kind, even into beasts and flowers, and then we will set out and seek her favor."

So the King sent for all the goldsmiths in the kingdom, and they worked day and night till all the gold was made into most wonderful and beautiful forms of the finest workmanship. Then they took them all aboard a great ship and set sail. They sailed for many days, till they came to the city where dwelt the daughter of the King of the Golden Palace.

The faithful John had decided that it was better for him to go ashore, so he told the King to remain on board and have all things in readiness, the treasures displayed and all in order, lest he should bring the Princess back with him. Then he tied up some of the smaller things in a handkerchief and rowed ashore.

When he entered the courtyard of the palace, he saw a beautiful girl filling two golden pails at the well. When they were full she turned, and, perceiving the stranger, demanded his business. So he untied the handkerchief and showed her the dainty trinkets. She was delighted with them, and at once said:

"The Princess must see these, for she has a passion for golden things, and will, no doubt, buy them all." So she took him by the hand and led him to the King's daughter. The Princess was even more beautiful than report had made her, and John was dazzled. The lady was very gracious to him and was charmed with his treasures, which she wished to purchase. But John said:

"I am only a servant. My master is a rich merchant who has even more beautiful things than these aboard his ship."

"Let them be brought hither," replied the Princess; but he said:

"That would take many days and nights, their number is so vast, and even if they were all brought hither there is no room in the palace large enough to show them to advantage."

The Princess's curiosity was very much excited by this time, and she said:

"Bring me to the ship, and I will see them there."

Faithful John was overjoyed at the success of his plans, and conducted her thither immediately. When the King saw her, he was so overcome with her beauty that he could hardly help her aboard, but he managed to control the violent beatings of his heart, and led her down into the cabin. John remained on deck, and commanded the helmsman to steer out to sea, and put on all the sail he could, so that they might leave the land far behind.

Down below the Princess was enjoying herself immensely, looking at all the beautiful and curious things, and several hours passed before she bethought her that it was time to go ashore. So she went on deck prepared to land immediately, and behold! no land was to be seen, nothing but the wide sea all around her.

"Ah!" she screamed, in sudden terror, " I am entrapped by a strange merchant. I would rather die than remain in his power!"

The King reassured her, and taking her hand he said: " I am no merchant, I am a king of royal blood like yourself. I have carried you off because my love for you is so great that I cannot live without you. You must know that when I saw your portrait, I was so stricken with love for you that I fell in a swoon before it."

When the King's daughter heard this her fear disappeared,

and love grew in its place and she was willing to be his bride.

One day, when John was sitting on deck piping sweet music, three crows flew over the ship, talking hard all the time. John understood every word they said, and this is what he heard:

"There he is, sailing home with the daughter of the King of the Golden Palace," said the first. "Ah! they are not home yet," said the second. "But she is with him in the ship," said the third. "What matters that?" began the first again; "when they land there will come a beautiful fox-colored horse, and he will spring upon it and the horse will bound away with him up into the air and he will never be seen again."

"But is there no way to save him?" the second one asked.

"Yes, if one springs up quickly behind him and seizes the pistols which are in the holsters and shoots the fox-colored horse, then the King will be saved. But nobody knows, and if one knew and told him, he would be turned into stone from toe to knee."

Then the second crow spoke again:

"I know still more, for even if the horse be shot he will not keep his lovely bride. When they arrive at the castle a bridal shirt will be brought to him on a dish, looking as though it were made of silver and gold, but it is only sulphur and pitch, and when he puts it on he will be burned to the marrow of his bones."

"Is there no way to save him?" asked the third crow.

"Oh, yes! if one were to take up the shirt with his gloves on and throw it on the fire before the King touches it, he will be saved. But what matter? for no one knows that, and if one knew and were to tell, he would be turned into stone from his knee to his heart."

Then the third crow spoke again:

"I know even more. Even if the shirt be burned the King will not keep his bride. After supper a dance will be held, and suddenly, when she is dancing, the Queen will turn pale

and fall in a faint; and if some one does not raise her up
and take three drops of blood from her little finger and throw
them away, she will die. But if anyone knows that and tells
it, he will be turned into stone from the crown of his head
to the toes of his feet."

Then the crows flew away, leaving John very quiet and
sad; for if he concealed what he knew, misfortune would fall
upon his master, and if he told, he must lose his own life; but
he decided that whatever happened to himself he must save
his master.

When they landed it happened just as the crows had said,
and a beautiful fox-colored horse appeared in front of the
King. He exclaimed with pleasure:

"Splendid! this shall carry us to the castle." And he
sprang into the saddle.

But John sprang up after him, and finding the pistols, shot
the horse dead. The other servants who were jealous of
John, began to grumble at this, and said:

"Shame to kill such a lovely animal, which was fit to bear
the King!"

But the King said:

"Peace; be silent. He is my faithful servant and I trust
him. Who knows what he has saved us from?"

Then they went on to the castle, and in the hall it happened
just as it had been foretold—a beautiful bridal shirt was
brought to the King. He was just about to pick it up and
put it on when John threw himself in front of him, and seizing the shirt, carried it to the fire and burned it.

Again the other servants set up a murmur:

"What is he about? See, he has burned the bridal shirt!"

But the King silenced them and said:

"He is my faithful John, and I trust him. Who knows
what danger he has averted?"

After the wedding supper a grand ball was given, and John
watched the Queen very carefully while she danced. Suddenly he saw her turn pale and fall in a faint. He hurried
toward her, and lifting her up he carried her away to her

chamber. Then he knelt down, and drawing three drops or blood from her little finger he threw them away. Soon the Queen stirred, and then sat up, quite herself again. But the King had watched all this, and this time he was furiously angry with faithful John, and ordered him to be thrown into prison. Next day he was brought to trial and condemned to be hanged at the gallows. When he was about to be executed he asked for the usual privilege of a condemned prisoner, to speak once what was in his mind. The King granted it, and faithful John began:

" I am innocent of any crime against you, and have always served you faithfully."

Then he told what he had heard the crows saying at sea; and how he had done all these things to save his master's life.

Then the King cried: " Pardon, pardon, my faithful friend; you are innocent!"

But at the last word he had spoken John had fallen down, turned into stone.

After this there was great sorrow and lamentation in the palace, and they had the statue raised and taken to their chamber and placed near the bed, and often the King looked at it and said:

" Ah! my trusty John, could I but bring you back to life again!"

Some time afterwards, to their great joy, twins were born to them, two healthy boys. One day the Queen was at church and the King was at home playing with his children, when he looked up at the statue and said:

" Ah, my poor faithful John, what would I not do to bring you back to life!"

To his surprise the statue answered him and said:

"If you will sacrifice what is dearest to you, you can restore my life to me."

" I will do anything in the world for you, only tell me what," answered the King.

Then the statue spoke again:

"Cut off the heads of your children, and sprinkle me with their blood, and I will be restored to life."

The poor King was horrified when he heard this, for how could he do such an awful deed as to kill his own children? But he thought of all John had done for him, and how much he had sacrificed, and, without flinching, he drew his sword to cut off their heads.

But as he was about to kill the little princes, faithful John became alive again, crying:

"Stop, stop, my master! Your faith in me is rewarded, and I am free."

The King was now as happy as he could be, and he thought to give his wife a pleasant surprise; so when he heard her coming he hid faithful John and the twins in a cupboard. When she came in he asked her if she had prayed for all her friends.

"Yes," she answered; "but I have been thinking of poor John, who is past our prayers."

Then the King said:

"We can restore him to life again, but we must sacrifice both our sons."

The Queen turned very pale at this and nearly fainted; but she thought of how it was their fault that John had suffered, and she said bravely that if it was to restore him to life it must be done.

The King was overjoyed to find that she thought as he did, and he threw open the cupboard door and disclosed, not only the twins, but faithful John also. Then they all rejoiced and were happy together to the end of their days.

Spindle, Shuttle, and Needle

ONCE upon a time there lived a girl who lost her father and mother when she was quite a tiny child. Her godmother lived all alone in a little cottage at the far end of the village, and there she earned her living by spinning, weaving, and sewing. The old woman took the little orphan home with her and brought her up in good, pious, industrious habits.

When the girl was fifteen years old her godmother fell ill, and calling the child to her bedside she said: " My dear daughter, I feel that my end is near. I leave you my cottage, which will, at least, shelter you, and also my spindle, my weaver's shuttle, and my needle, with which to earn your bread."

Then she laid her hands on the girl's head, blessed her, and added: " Mind and be good, and then all will go well with you." With that she closed her eyes for the last time, and when she was carried to her grave the girl walked behind her coffin weeping bitterly and paid her all the last honors.

After this the girl lived all alone in the little cottage. She worked hard, spinning, weaving, and sewing, and her old godmother's blessing seemed to prosper all she did. The flax seemed to spread and increase; and when she wove a carpet or a piece of linen, or made a shirt, she was sure to find a customer who paid her well, so that not only did she feel no want herself, but she was able to help those who did.

Now, it happened that about this time the King's son was making a tour through the entire country to look out for a bride. He could not marry a poor woman and he did not wish for a rich one.

" She shall be my wife," said he, " who is at once the poorest and the richest."

When he reached the village where the girl lived he inquired who was the richest and who the poorest woman in it. The richest was named first; the poorest, he was told, was a young girl who lived alone in a little cottage at the far end of the village.

The rich girl sat at her door dressed in all her best clothes, and when the King's son came near she got up, went to meet him, and made him a low courtesy. He looked well at her, said nothing, but rode on farther.

When he reached the poor girl's house he did not find her at her door, for she was at work in her room. The Prince

reined in his horse, looked in at the window through which
the sun was shining brightly, and saw the girl sitting at her
wheel busily spinning away.

She looked up, and when she saw the King's son gazing in
at her she blushed red all over, cast down her eyes, and spun
on. Whether the thread was quite as even as usual I really
cannot say, but she went on spinning till the King's son had
ridden off. Then she stepped to the window and opened the
lattice, saying, " The room is so hot," but she looked after him
as long as she could see the white plumes of his hat.

Then she sat down to her work once more and spun on, and
as she did so an old saying, which she had often heard her
godmother repeat while at work, came into her head, and she
began to sing:

> " Spindle, spindle, go and see
> If my love will come to me."

Lo and behold! the spindle leaped from her hand and rushed
out of the room, and when she had sufficiently recovered
from her surprise to look after it she saw it dancing merrily
through the fields, dragging a long golden thread after it, and
soon it was lost to sight.

The girl, having lost her spindle, took up the shuttle and,
seating herself at her loom, began to weave. Meantime the
spindle danced on and on, and just as it had come to the end
of the golden thread it reached the King's son.

" What do I see? " he cried. " This spindle seems to wish
to point out the way to me." So he turned his horse's head
and rode back beside the golden thread.

Meantime the girl sat weaving and sang:

> " Shuttle, weave both web and woof;
> Bring my love beneath my roof."

The shuttle instantly escaped from her hand and with one
bound was out at the door. On the threshold it began weaving the loveliest carpet that was ever seen. Roses and lilies

"JUST AS IT HAD COME TO THE END OF THE GOLDEN THREAD IT
REACHED THE KING'S SON"

"JUST AS IT HAD COME TO THE TOP OF THE CLOUGH TREAD IT KICKED THE KING'S SON"

bloomed on both sides, and in the center a thicket seemed to grow with rabbits and hares running through it, stags and fawns peeping through the branches, while on the topmost boughs sat birds of brilliant plumage and so lifelike one almost expected to hear them sing. The shuttle flew from side to side and the carpet seemed almost to grow of itself.

As the shuttle had run away the girl sat down to sew. She took her needle and sang:

> " Needle, needle, stitch away;
> Make my chamber bright and gay."

And the needle promptly slipped from her fingers and flew about the room like lightning. You would have thought invisible spirits were at work, for in next to no time the table and benches were covered with green cloth, the chairs with velvet, and elegant silk curtains hung before the windows. The needle had barely put in its last stitch when the girl, glancing at the window, spied the white-plumed hat of the King's son, who was being led back by the spindle with the golden thread.

He dismounted and walked over the carpet into the house, and when he entered the room there stood the girl blushing like any rose. "You are the poorest and yet the richest," said he. "Come with me—you shall be my bride."

She said nothing but she held out her hand. Then he kissed her and led her out, lifted her on his horse, and took her to his royal palace, where the wedding was celebrated with great rejoicings.

The spindle, the shuttle, and the needle were carefully placed in the treasury and were always held in the very highest honor.

THE FAIRY RING

The Magic Egg

THERE was once upon a time a lark who was the Czar among the birds, and he took unto himself as his Czaritsa a little shrew mouse. They had a field all to themselves, which they sowed with wheat, and when the wheat grew up they divided it between them. When they found that there was one grain over, the mouse said:

"Let me have it!"

But the lark said:

"No, let me have it!"

"What's to be done?" thought they.

They would have liked to take counsel of some one; but they had no parents or kinsmen—nobody at all to whom they could go and ask advice in the matter. At last the mouse said:

"At any rate, let me have the first nibble!"

The lark Czar agreed to this; but the little mouse fastened her teeth in it, and ran off into her hole with it, and there ate it all up. At this the lark Czar was wroth, and collected all the birds of the air to make war upon the mouse Czaritsa; but the Czaritsa called together all the beasts to defend her, and so the war began. Whenever the beasts came rushing out of the wood to tear the birds to pieces, the birds flew up into the trees; but the birds kept in the air, and hacked and pecked the beasts wherever they could. Thus they fought the whole day, and in the evening they lay down to rest. Now when the Czaritsa looked around upon her forces she saw that the ant was taking no part in the war. She immediately went and commanded the ant to be there by evening, and when the ant came the Czaritsa ordered her to climb up the trees with her kinsmen, and bite off the feathers around the birds' wings.

Next day, when there was light enough to see by, the mouse Czaritsa cried:

"Up, up, my warriors!"

Thereupon the birds also rose up, and immediately fell to the ground, where the beasts tore them to bits. So the Czar-

[390]

Itsa overcame the Czar. But there was one eagle who saw there was something wrong, so he did not try to fly, but remained sitting on the tree. And lo! there came an archer along that way, and seeing the eagle on the tree, he took aim at it; but the eagle besought him and said:

"Do not kill me, and I'll be of great service to thee!"

The archer aimed a second time, but the eagle besought him still more and said:

"Take me down rather and keep me, and thou shalt see that it will be to thy advantage."

The archer, however, took aim a third time, but the eagle began to beg of him most piteously:

"Nay, kill me not, but take me home with thee, and thou shalt see what great advantage it will be to thee!"

The archer believed the bird. He climbed up the tree, took the eagle down, and carried it home. Then the eagle said to him:

"Put me in a hut, and feed me with flesh till my wings have grown again."

Now this archer had two cows and a steer, and he at once killed and cut up one of the cows for the eagle. The eagle fed upon this cow for a full year, and then he said to the archer:

"Let me go, that I may fly. I see that my wings have already grown again!"

Then the archer let him loose from the hut. The eagle flew around and around, he flew about for half a day, and then he returned to the archer and said:

"I feel I have but little strength in me, slay me another cow!"

And the archer obeyed him, and slew the second cow, and the eagle lived upon that for yet another year. Again the eagle flew around and around in the air. He flew around and about the whole day till evening, when he returned to the archer and said:

"I am stronger than I was, but I have still but little strength in me, slay me the steer also!"

Then the man thought to himself:

"What shall I do? Shall I slay it, or shall I not slay it?" At last he said:

"Well! I've sacrificed more than this before, so let this go too!" and he took the steer and slaughtered it for the eagle.

Then the eagle lived upon this for another whole year longer, and after that he took to flight, and flew high up right to the very clouds. Then he flew down again to the man and said to him:

"I thank thee, brother, for that thou hast been the saving of me! come now and sit upon me!"

"Nay, but," said the man, "what if some evil befall me?"

"Sit on me, I say!" cried the eagle.

So the archer sat down upon the bird.

Then the eagle bore him nearly as high as the big clouds, and then let him fall. Down plumped the man; but the eagle did not let him fall to the earth, but swiftly flew beneath him and upheld him, and said to him:

"How dost thou feel now?"

"I feel," said the man, "as if I had no life in me."

Then the eagle replied:

"That was just how I felt when thou didst aim at me the first time."

Then he said to him:

"Sit on my back again!"

The man did not want to sit on him, but what could he do? Sit he must. Then the eagle flew with him quite as high as the big clouds, and shook him off, and down he fell headlong till he was about two fathoms from the ground, when the bird again flew beneath him and held him up. Again the eagle asked him:

"How dost thou feel?"

And the man replied:

"I feel just as if all my bones were already broken to bits!"

"That is just how I felt when thou didst take aim at me

the second time," replied the eagle. "But now sit on my back once more."

The man did so, and the eagle flew with him as high as the small fleecy clouds, and then he shook him off, and down he fell headlong; but when he was but a hand's breadth from the earth, the eagle again flew beneath him and held him up, and said to him:

"How dost thou feel now?"

And he replied:

"I feel as if I no longer belonged to this world!"

"That is just how I felt when thou didst aim at me the third time," replied the eagle. "But now," continued the bird, "thou art guilty no more. We are quits. I owe thee naught, and thou owest naught to me; so sit on my back again, and I'll take thee to my master."

They flew on and on, they flew till they came to the eagle's uncle. And the eagle said to the archer:

"Go to my house, and when they ask thee: 'Hast thou not seen our poor child?' reply, 'Give me the magic egg, and I'll bring him before your eyes!'"

So he went to the house, and there they said to him:

"Hast thou heard of our poor child with thine ears, or seen him with thine eyes, and hast thou come hither willingly or unwillingly?"

And he answered:

"I have come hither willingly!"

Then they asked:

"Hast thou smelt out anything of our poor youngster? for it is three years now since he went to the wars, and there's neither sight nor sound of him more!"

And he answered:

"Give me the magic egg, and I'll bring him straightway before your eyes!"

Then they replied:

"'Twere better we never saw him than that we should give thee the magic egg!"

Then he went back to the eagle and said to him:

"They said: ' 'Twere better we never saw him than that we should give thee the magic egg.' "

Then the eagle answered:

"Let us fly on farther!"

They flew on and on till they came to the eagle's brother, and the archer said just the same to him as he had said to the eagle's uncle, and still he didn't get the egg. Then they flew to the eagle's father, and the eagle said to him:

"Go up to the hut, and if they ask for me, say that thou hast seen me and will bring me before their eyes."

So he went up to the hut, and they said to him:

"O Czarevich, we hear thee with our ears and see thee with our eyes, but hast thou come hither of thine own free will or by the will of another?"

And the archer answered:

"I have come hither of my own free will!"

Then they asked him:

"Hast thou seen our son? Lo, these four years we have not had news of him. He went off to the wars, and perchance he has been slain there."

And he answered them:

"I have seen him, and if thou wilt give me the magic egg, I will bring him before your eyes."

And the eagle's father said to him:

"What good will such a thing do thee? We had better give thee the lucky penny!"

But he answered:

"I don't want the lucky penny, give me the magic egg!"

"Come hither, then!" said he, "and thou shalt have it."

So he went into the hut. Then the eagle's father rejoiced and gave him the egg, and said to him:

"Take heed thou dost not break it anywhere on the road, and when thou gettest home, hedge it around and build a strong fence about it, and it will do thee good."

So he went homeward. He went on and on till a great thirst came upon him. So he stopped at the first spring he came to, and as he stooped to drink he stumbled and the magic

THE FAIRY RING

egg was broken. Then he perceived that an ox had come out of the egg and was rolling away. He gave chase to the ox, but whenever he was getting close to one side of it, the other side of it got farther away from him. Then the poor fellow cried:

"I shall do nothing with it myself, I see."

At that moment an old she dragon came up to him and said:

"What wilt thou give me, O man, if I chase this ox back again into the egg for thee?"

And the archer replied:

"What can I give?"

The dragon said to him:

"Give me what thou hast at home without thy will and wit!"

"Done!" said the archer.

Then the dragon chased the ox nicely into the egg again, patched it up prettily, and gave it into the man's hand. Then the archer went home, and when he got home he found a son had been born to him there, and his son said to him:

"Why didst thou give me to the old she dragon, dad? But never mind, I'll manage to live in spite of her."

Then the father was very grieved for a time, but what could he do? Now the name of this son was Ivan.

So Ivan lost no time in going to the dragon, and the dragon said to him:

"Go to my house and do me three tasks, and if thou dost them not, I'll devour thee."

Now around the dragon's house was a large meadow stretching as far as the eye could reach. And the dragon said to him:

"Thou must in a single night weed out this field and sow wheat in it, and reap the wheat and store it, all in this very night; and thou must bake me a roll out of this selfsame wheat, and the roll must be lying ready for me on my table in the morning."

Then Ivan went and leaned over the fence, and his heart within him was sore troubled. Now near to him there was a

post, and on this post was the dragon's starveling daughter.
So when he came thither and fell a-weeping, she asked him:
"Wherefore dost thou weep?"

And he said: "How can I help weeping? The dragon has
bidden me do something I can never, never do; and what is
more, she has bidden me do it in a single night."

"What is it, pray?" asked the dragon's daughter. Then
he told her.

"Not every bush bears a berry!" cried she. "Promise to
take me to wife, and I'll do all she has bidden thee do."

He promised, and then she said to him again:

"Now go and lie down, but see that thou art up early in
the morning to bring her her roll."

Then she went to the field, and before one could whistle she
had cleaned it of weeds and harrowed it and sown it with
wheat, and by dawn she had reaped the wheat and cooked the
roll and brought it to him, and said:

"Now, take it to her hut and put it on her table."

Then the old she dragon awoke and came to the door, and
was amazed at the sight of the field, which was now all stubble,
for the corn had been cut. Then she said to Ivan:

"Yes, thou hast done the work well. But now, see that
thou doest my second task."

Then she gave him her second command:

"Dig up that mountain yonder and let the Dnieper flow
past the site of it, and there build a storehouse, and in the
storehouse stack the wheat that thou hast reaped, and sell this
wheat to the merchant barques that sail by, and everything
must be done by the time I get up early next morning!"

Then he again went to the fence and wept, and the maiden
said to him:

"Why dost thou weep?" and he told her all that the she
dragon had bidden him do.

"There are lots of bushes, but where are the berries? Go
and lie down, and I'll do it all for thee."

Then she whistled, and the mountain was leveled and the
Dnieper flowed over the site of it, and round about the

Dnieper, storehouses rose up, and then she came and woke him that he might go and sell the wheat to the merchant barques that sailed by that way, and when the she dragon rose up early in the morning she was amazed to see that everything had been done which she had commanded him.

Then she gave him her third command:

"This night thou must catch the golden hare, and bring it to me by the morning light."

Again he went to the fence and fell a-weeping. And the girl asked him:

"Why art thou weeping?"

He said to her: "She has ordered me to catch her the golden hare."

"Oh, oh!" cried the she dragon's daughter, "the berries are ripening now; only her father knows how to catch such a hare as that. Nevertheless, I'll go to a rocky place I know of, and there perchance we shall be able to catch it."

So they went to this rocky place together, and she said to him:

"Stand over that hole. I'll go in and chase him out of the hole, and thou catch him as he comes out; but mind, whatever comes out of the hole, seize it, for it will be the golden hare."

So she went and began beating up, and all at once out came a snake and hissed, and he let it go. Then she came out of the hole and said to him:

"What! has nothing come out?"

"Well," said he, "only a snake, and I was afraid it would bite me, so I let it go."

"What hast thou done?" said she; "that was the very hare itself. Look now!" said she, "I'll go in again, and if anyone comes out and tells you that the golden hare is not here, don't believe it, but hold him fast."

So she crept into the hole again and began to beat for game, and out came an old woman, who said to the youth:

"What art thou poking about there for?"

And he said to her: "For the golden hare."

She said to him: "It is not here, for this is a snake's hole," and when she had said this she went away. Presently the girl also came out and said to him:

"What! hast thou not got the hare? Did nothing come out, then?"

"No," said he, "nothing but an old woman who asked me what I was seeking, and I told her the golden hare, and she said, 'It is not here,' so I let her go."

Then the girl replied: "Why didst thou not lay hold of her? for she was the very golden hare itself, and now thou never wilt catch it unless I turn myself into a hare and thou take and lay me on the table, and give me into my mother's, the she dragon's hands, and go away, for if she find out all about it she will tear the pair of us to pieces."

So she changed herself into a hare, and he took and laid her on the table, and said to the she dragon:

"There's thy hare for thee, and now let me go away!"

She said to him: "Very well—be off!"

Then he set off running, and he ran and ran as hard as he could. Soon after the old she dragon discovered that it was not the golden hare, but her own daughter, so she set about chasing after them and destroying them both, for the daughter had made haste in the meantime to join Ivan. But as the she dragon couldn't run herself, she sent her husband, and he began chasing them and they knew he was coming, for they felt the earth trembling beneath his tread. Then the she dragon's daughter said to Ivan:

"I hear him running after us. I'll turn myself into standing wheat and thee into an old man guarding me, and if he ask thee, 'Hast thou seen a lad and a lass pass by this way?' say to him: 'Yes, they passed by this way while I was sowing this wheat!'"

A little while afterwards the she dragon's husband came flying up.

"Have a lad and a lass passed by this way?" said he.

"Yes," replied the old man, "they have."

"Was it long ago?" asked the she dragon's husband.

"It was while this wheat was being sown," replied the old man.

"Oh!" thought the serpent, "this wheat is ready for the sickle; they couldn't have been this way yesterday."

So he turned back. Then the she dragon's daughter turned herself back into a maiden and the old man into a youth, and off they set again. But the dragon returned home, and the she dragon asked him:

"What! hast thou not caught them or met them on the road?"

"Met them, no!" said he. "I did, indeed, pass on the road some standing wheat and an old man watching it, and I asked the old man if he had seen a lad and a lass pass by that way, and he said, 'Yes, while this wheat was being sown'; but the wheat was quite ripe for the sickle, so I knew it was a long while ago and turned back."

"Why didst thou not tear that old man and the wheat to pieces?" cried the she dragon; "it was they! Be off after them again, and mind, this time tear them to pieces without fail."

So the dragon set off after them again, and they heard him coming from afar, for the earth trembled beneath him. So the damsel said to Ivan:

"He's coming again; I hear him; now I'll change myself into a monastery, so old that it will be almost falling to pieces, and I'll change thee into an old black monk at the gate, and when he comes up and asks, 'Hast thou seen a lad and a lass pass this way?' say to him: 'Yes, they passed by this way when this monastery was being built.'"

Soon afterwards the dragon came flying past, and asked the monk: "Hast thou seen a lad and a lass pass by this way?"

"Yes," he replied, "I saw them what time the holy fathers began to build this monastery."

The dragon thought to himself: "That was not yesterday! This monastery has stood a hundred years if it has stood a day, and won't stand much longer either"; and with that he turned him back. When he got home he said to the she dragon, his wife: "I met a black monk who serves in a monastery and I asked him about them, and he told me that a lad and a lass had run past that way when the monastery was being built, but that was not yesterday, for the monastery is a hundred years old at the very least."

"Why didst thou not tear the black monk to pieces and pull down the monastery? for 'twas they. But I see I must go after them myself; thou art no good at all."

So off she set and ran and ran, and they knew she was coming, for the earth quaked and yawned beneath her. Then the damsel said to Ivan:

"I fear me 'tis all over, for she is coming herself! Look now, I'll change thee into a stream and myself into a fish—a perch."

Immediately after the she dragon came up and said to the perch:

"Oh, oh! so thou wouldst run away from me, eh!"

Then she turned herself into a pike and began chasing the perch, but every time she drew near to it the perch turned its prickly fins toward her, so that she could not catch hold of it. So she kept on chasing it and chasing it, but finding she could not catch it, she tried to drink up the stream, till she drank so much of it that she burst.

Then the maiden who had become a fish said to the youth who had become a river:

"Now that we are alive and not dead, go back to thy lord father and thy father's house and see them, and kiss them all except the daughter of thy uncle, for if thou kiss that damsel thou wilt forget me, and I shall go to the land of Nowhere."

So he went home and greeted them all, and as he did so he thought to himself:

"Why should I not greet my uncle's daughter like the rest of them? Why, they'll think me a mere pagan if I don't!"

So he kissed her, and the moment he did so he forgot all about the girl who had saved him.

So he remained there half a year, and then bethought him of taking to himself a wife. So they betrothed him to a very

THE FAIRY RING

pretty girl, and he accepted her and forgot all about the other girl who had saved him from the dragon, the one who herself was the she dragon's daughter. Now the evening before the wedding they heard a young damsel crying *shishki** in the streets. They called to the young damsel to go away, or say who she was, for nobody knew her. But the damsel answered never a word, but began to knead more cakes, and made a cock dove and a hen dove out of the dough and put them down on the ground, and they became alive. And the hen dove said to the cock dove:

"Hast thou forgotten how I cleared the field for thee, and sowed it with wheat, and thou mad'st a roll from the corn which thou gavest to the she dragon?"

But the cock dove answered:

"Forgotten! forgotten!"

Then she said to him again:

"And hast thou forgotten how I dug away the mountain for thee, and let the Dnieper flow by it that the merchant barques might come to thy storehouses, and that thou might'st sell thy wheat to the merchant barques?"

But the cock dove replied:

"Forgotten! forgotten!"

Then the hen dove said to him again:

"And hast thou forgotten how we two went together in search of the golden hare? Hast thou forgotten me then altogether?"

And the cock dove answered again:

"Forgotten! forgotten!"

Then the good youth Ivan bethought him who this damsel was that had made the doves, and he took her to his arms and made her his wife, and they lived happily ever afterwards.

* Wedding-cakes of the shape of pine cones.

The Sparrow and the Bush

A SPARROW once flew down upon a bush and said:
"Little bush, give good little sparrow a swing."
"I won't!" said the little bush. Then the sparrow
was angry, and went to the goat and said:

"Goat, goat, nibble bush, bush won't give good little sparrow a swing."

"I won't!" said the goat.

Then the sparrow went to the wolf and said:

"Wolf, wolf, eat goat, goat won't nibble bush, bush won't
give good little sparrow a swing."

"I won't!" said the wolf.

Then the sparrow went to the people and said:

"Good people, kill wolf, wolf won't eat goat, goat won't
nibble bush, bush won't give good little sparrow a swing."

"We won't!" said the people.

Then the sparrow went to the Tartars:

"Tartars, Tartars, slay people, people won't kill wolf, wolf
won't eat goat, goat won't nibble bush, bush won't give good
little sparrow a swing." But the Tartars said:

"We won't slay the people!" and the people said:

"We won't kill the wolf!" and the wolf said:

"I won't eat the goat!" and the goat said:

"I won't nibble the bush!" and the bush said:

"I won't give the good little sparrow a swing."

"Go!" said the bush, "to the fire, for the Tartars won't
slay the people, and the people won't kill the wolf, and the
wolf won't eat the goat, and the goat won't nibble the bush,
and the bush won't give the dear little sparrow a swing."

But the fire also said:

"I won't!" (they were all alike)—"go to the water," said
he.

So the sparrow went to the water and said:

"Come water, quench fire, fire won't burn Tartars, Tartars won't slay people, people won't kill wolf, wolf won't ea

goat, goat won't nibble bush, bush won't give good little sparrow a swing."

But the water also said:

" I won't!" So the sparrow went to the ox and said:

" Ox, ox, drink water, water won't quench fire, fire won't burn Tartars, Tartars won't slay people, people won't kill wolf, wolf won't eat goat, goat won't nibble bush, bush won't give little sparrow a swing."

" I won't!" said the ox.

Then the sparrow went to the poleax and said:

" Poleax, poleax, strike ox, ox won't drink water, water won't quench fire, fire won't burn Tartars, Tartars won't slay people, people won't kill wolf, wolf won't eat goat, goat won't nibble bush, bush won't give little sparrow a swing."

" I won't!" said the poleax.

So the sparrow went to the worms and said:

" Worms, worms, gnaw poleax, poleax won't strike ox, ox won't drink water, water won't quench fire, fire won't burn Tartars, Tartars won't slay people, people won't kill wolf, wolf won't eat goat, goat won't nibble bush, bush won't give little sparrow a swing."

" We won't!" said the worms.

Then the sparrow went to the hen and said:

" Hen, hen, peck worms, worms won't gnaw poleax, poleax won't strike ox, ox won't drink water, water won't quench fire, fire won't burn Tartars, Tartars won't slay people, people won't kill wolf, wolf won't eat goat, goat won't nibble bush, bush won't give little sparrow a swing."

" I won't!" said the hen, " but go to the sparrow hawk, he ought to give the first push, or why is he called the pusher!" *

So the sparrow went to the sparrow hawk and said:

" Come, pusher, seize hen, hen won't peck worms, worms won't gnaw poleax, poleax won't strike ox, ox won't drink water, water won't quench fire, fire won't burn Tartars, Tartars won't slay people, people won't kill wolf, wolf won't eat

* *Shulyak* means both *sparrow hawk* and *push.*

[403]

THE FAIRY RING

goat, goat won't nibble bush, bush won't give little sparrow a swing."

Then the sparrow hawk began to seize the hen, the hen began to peck the worms, the worms began to gnaw the poleax, the poleax began to hit the ox, the ox began to drink the water, the water began to quench the fire, the fire began to burn the Tartars, the Tartars began to slay the people, the people began to kill the wolf, the wolf began to eat the goat, the goat began to nibble the bush, and the bush cried out:

> "Swing away, swing away, swi-i-i-i-ing!
> Little daddy sparrow, have your fli-i-i-ing!"

The Iron Wolf

THERE was once upon a time a parson who had a servant and when this servant had served him faithfully for twelve years and upward, he came to the parson and said: "Let us now settle our accounts, master, and pay me what thou owest me. I have now served long enough, and would fain have a little place in the wide world all to myself."

"Good!" said the parson. "I'll tell thee now what wage I'll give thee for thy faithful service. I'll give thee this egg. Take it home, and when thou gettest there, make to thyself a cattle pen, and make it strong; then break the egg in the middle of thy cattle pen, and thou shalt see something. But whatever thou doest, don't break it on thy way home, or all thy luck will leave thee."

So the servant departed on his homeward way. He went on and on, and at last he thought to himself:

"Come now, I'll see what is inside this egg of mine!" So he broke it, and out of it came all sorts of cattle in such numbers that the open steppe became like a fair. The servant stood there in amazement, and he thought to himself:

[404]

THE FAIRY RING

"However in this world shall I be able to drive all these cattle back again?" He had scarcely uttered the words when the Iron Wolf came running up, and said to him:

"I'll collect and drive back all these cattle into the egg again, and I'll patch the egg up so that it will become quite whole. But in return for that," continued the Iron Wolf, "whenever thou dost sit down on the bridal bench,* I'll come and eat thee."

"Well," thought the servant to himself, "a lot of things may happen before I sit down on the bridal bench and he comes to eat me, and in the meantime I shall get all these cattle. Agreed, then," said he. So the Iron Wolf immediately collected all the cattle, and drove them back into the egg, and patched up the egg and made it whole just as it was before.

The servant went home to the village where he lived, made him a cattle pen stronger than strong, went inside it and broke the egg, and immediately that cattle pen was as full of cattle as it could hold. Then he took to farming and cattle-breeding, and he became so rich that in the whole wide world there was none richer than he. He kept to himself, and his goods increased and multiplied exceedingly; the only thing wanting to his happiness was a wife, but a wife he was afraid to take. Now near to where he lived was a general who had a lovely daughter, and this daughter fell in love with the rich man. So the general went and said to him:

"Come, why don't you marry? I'll give you my daughter and lots of money with her."

"How is it possible for me to marry?" replied the man; "as soon as ever I sit down on the bridal bench the Iron Wolf will come and eat me up." And he told the general all that had happened.

"Oh, nonsense!" said the general, "don't be afraid. I have a mighty host, and when the time comes for you to sit down

---

* *Posad*, or *posag*, a bench covered with white cloth on which the bride and bridegroom sat down together.

on the bridal bench we'll surround your house with three strong rows of soldiers, and they won't let the Iron Wolf get at you, I can tell you." So they talked the matter over till he let himself be persuaded, and then they began to make great preparations for the bridal banquet. Everything went off exceedingly well, and they made merry till the time came when bride and bridegroom were to sit down together on the bridal bench. Then the general placed his men in three strong rows all around the house so as not to let the Iron Wolf get in; and no sooner had the young people sat down upon the bridal bench than, sure enough, the Iron Wolf came running up. He saw the host standing around the house in three strong rows, but through all three rows he leaped and made straight for the house. But the man, as soon as he saw the Iron Wolf, leaped out of the window, mounted his horse, and galloped off with the wolf after him.

Away and away he galloped, and after him came the Wolf, but try as it would, it could not catch him up anyhow. At last, toward evening, the man stopped and looked about him, and saw that he was in a lone forest, and before him stood a hut. He went up to this hut, and saw an old man and an old woman sitting in front of it, and said to them:

"Would you let me rest a little while with you, good people?"

"By all means!" said they.

"There is one thing, however, good people," said he, "don't let the Iron Wolf catch me while I am resting with you."

"Have no fear of that!" replied the old couple. "We have a dog called Chutko * who can hear a wolf coming a mile off, and he'll be sure to let us know."

So he laid him down to sleep, and was just dropping off when Chutko began to bark. Then the old people awoke him, and said:

"Be off! be off! for the Iron Wolf is coming."

* Hearkener.

[406]

And they gave him the dog, and a wheaten hearth cake as provision by the way.

So he went on and on, and the dog followed after him till it began to grow dark, and then he perceived another hut in another forest. He went up to that hut, and in front of it were sitting an old man and an old woman. He asked them for a night's lodging.

"Only," said he, "take care that the Iron Wolf doesn't catch me."

"Have no fear of that," said they. "We have a dog here called Vazhko,* who can hear a wolf nine miles off."

So he laid him down and slept. Just before dawn Vazhko began to bark. Immediately they awoke him.

"Run!" cried they, "the Iron Wolf is coming!"

And they gave him the dog, and a barley hearth-cake as provision by the way. So he took the hearth cake, sat him on his horse and off he went, and his two dogs followed after him.

He went on and on. On and on he went till evening, when again he stopped and looked about him, and he saw that he was in another forest, and another little hut stood before him. He went into the hut, and there were sitting an old man and an old woman.

"Will you let me pass the night here, good people?" said he. "Only take care that the Iron Wolf does not get hold of me."

"Have no fear," said they, "we have a dog called Bary, who can hear a wolf coming twelve miles off. He'll let us know."

So he lay down to sleep, and early in the morning Bary let them know that the Iron Wolf was drawing nigh. Immediately they awoke him.

"'Tis high time for you to be off!" said they.

Then they gave him the dog, and a buckwheat hearth cake as provision by the way. He took the hearth cake, sat him

* Heavysides.

[407]

on his horse, and off he went. So now he had three dogs, and they all three followed him.

He went on and on, and toward evening he found himself in front of another hut. He went into it, and there was nobody there. He went and lay down, and his dogs lay down also—Chutko on the threshold of the room door, Vazhko at the threshold of the house door, and Bary at the threshold of the outer gate. Presently the Iron Wolf came trotting up. Immediately Chutko gave the alarm, Vazhko nailed him to the earth, and Bary tore him to pieces.

Then the man gathered his faithful dogs around him, mounted his horse, and went back to his own home.

The Grateful Cobra

ONCE upon a time there was a rajah and ranee who were much grieved because they had no children, and the little dog in the palace had also no puppies. At last the Rajah and Ranee had some children, and it also happened that the pet dog in the palace had some puppies; but, unfortunately, the Ranee's two children were two puppies and the dog's two puppies were two pretty little girls! This vexed her majesty very much; and sometimes when the dog had gone away to its dinner, the Ranee used to put the two puppies (her children) into the kennel, and carry away the dog's two little girls to the palace. Then the poor dog grew very unhappy, and said: "They never will leave my two little children alone. I must take them away into the jungle, or their lives will be worried out." So one night she took the little girls in her mouth and ran with them to the jungle, and there made them a home in a pretty cave in the rock, beside a clear stream; and every day she would go into the towns and carry away some nice currie and rice to give her little daughters; and if she found any pretty clothes or jewels that she could bring away in her mouth, she used to take them also for the children.

[408]

THE FAIRY RING

Now it happened some time after this, one day, when the dog had gone to fetch her daughters' dinner, two young princes (a rajah and his brother) came to hunt in the jungle, and they hunted all day and found nothing. It had been very hot, and they were thirsty; so they went to a tree which grew on a little piece of high ground, and sent their attendants to search all around for water; but no one could find any. At last one of the hunting dogs came to the foot of the tree, quite muddy, and the Rajah said: " Look, the dog is muddy: he must have found water; follow him, and see where he goes." The attendants followed the dog, and saw him go to the stream at the mouth of the cave where the two children were; and the two children also saw them, and were very much frightened and ran inside the cave. Then the attendants returned to the two princes and said: " We have found clear, sparkling water flowing past a cave, and, what is more, within the cave are two of the most lovely young ladies that eye ever beheld, clothed in fine dresses and covered with jewels; but when they saw us they were frightened and ran away." On hearing this the princes bade their servants lead them to the place; and when they saw the two young girls, they were quite charmed with them, and asked them to go to their kingdom and become their wives. The maidens were frightened; but at last the Rajah and his brother persuaded them, and they went, and the Rajah married the elder sister, and his brother married the younger.

When the dog returned, she was grieved to find her children gone, and for twelve long years the poor thing ran many, many miles to find them, but in vain. At last one day she came to the place where the two princesses lived. Now it chanced that the elder, the wife of the Rajah, was looking out of the window, and seeing the dog run down the street, she said: " That must be my dear, long-lost mother." So she ran into the street as fast as possible, and took the tired dog in her arms, and brought her into her own room, and made her a nice comfortable bed on the floor, and bathed her feet, and was very kind to her. Then the dog said to her:

"My daughter, you are good and kind, and it is a great joy to me to see you again, but I must not stay; I will first go and see your younger sister, and then return." The Ranee answered: "Do not do so, dear mother; rest here to-day; to-morrow I will send and let my sister know, and she, too, will come and see you." But the poor, silly dog would not stay, but ran to the house of her second daughter. Now the second daughter was looking out of the window when the unfortunate creature came to the door, and seeing the dog she said to herself: "That must be my mother. What will my husband think if he learns that this wretched, ugly, miserable-looking dog is my mother?" So she ordered her servants to go and throw stones at it, and drive it away, and they did so; and one large stone hit the dog's head, and she ran back, very much hurt, to her elder daughter's house. The Ranee saw her coming, and ran out into the street and brought her in in her arms, and did all she could to make her well, saying: "Ah, mother, mother! why did you ever leave my house?" But all her care was in vain: the poor dog died. Then the Ranee thought her husband might be vexed if he found a dead dog (an unclean animal) in the palace; so she put the body in a small room into which the Rajah hardly ever went, intending to have it reverently buried; and over it she placed a basket turned topsy-turvy.

It so happened, however, that when the Rajah came to visit his wife, as chance would have it, he went through this very room; and tripping over the upturned basket, called for a light to see what it was. Then, lo and behold! there lay the statue of a dog, life-size, composed entirely of diamonds, emeralds, and other precious stones, set in gold! So he called out to his wife, and said: "Where did you get this beautiful dog?" And when the Ranee saw the golden dog, she was very much frightened, and, I'm sorry to say, instead of telling her husband the truth, she told a story, and said, "Oh. it is only a present my parents sent me."

Now see what trouble she got into for not telling the truth.

"*Only!*" said the Rajah; "why this is valuable enough to

buy the whole of my kingdom. Your parents must be very rich people to be able to send you such presents as this. How is it you never told me of them? Where do they live?" Now she had to tell another story to cover the first. She said: "In the jungle." He replied: "I will go and see them; you must take me and show me where they live." Then the Ranee thought: "What will the Rajah say when he finds 1 have been telling him such stories? He will order my head to be cut off." So she said, "You must first give me a palanquin, and I will go into the jungle and tell them you are coming"; but really she had determined to kill herself, and so get out of her difficulties. Away she went; and when she had gone some distance in her palanquin, she saw a large white ants' nest, over which hung a cobra, with his mouth wide open; then the Ranee thought: "I will go to that cobra and put my finger in his mouth, that he may bite me, and so I shall die." So she ordered the palkee bearers to wait, and said she would be back in a while, and got out, and ran to the ants' nest, and put her finger in the cobra's mouth. Now a large thorn had run, a short time before, into the cobra's throat, and hurt him very much; and the Ranee, by putting her finger into his mouth, pushed out this thorn; then the cobra, feeling much better, turned to her, and said: "My dear daughter, you have done me a great kindness; what return can I make you?" The Ranee told him all her story, and begged him to bite her, that she might die. But the cobra said: "You certainly did very wrong to tell the Rajah that story; nevertheless, you have been very kind to me. I will help you in your difficulty. Send your husband here. I will provide you with a father and mother of whom you need not be ashamed." So the Ranee returned joyfully to the palace, and invited her husband to come and see her parents.

When they reached the spot near where the cobra was, what a wonderful sight awaited them! There, in the place which had before been thick jungle, stood a splendid palace, twenty-four miles long and twenty-four miles broad, with gardens and trees and fountains all around; and the light shining from it was to be seen a hundred miles off. The walls were made of gold and precious stones, and the carpets, cloth of gold. Hundreds of servants, in rich dresses, stood waiting in the long, lofty rooms; and in the last room of all, upon golden thrones, sat a magnificent old Rajah and Ranee, who introduced themselves to the young Rajah as his papa-and mamma-in-law. The Rajah and Ranee stayed at the palace six months, and were entertained the whole of that time with feasting and music; and they left for their own home loaded with presents. Before they started, however, the Ranee went to her friend, the cobra, and said: "You have conjured up all these beautiful things to get me out of my difficulties, but my husband, the Rajah has enjoyed his visit so much that he will certainly want to come here again. Then, if he returns and finds nothing at all, he will be very angry with me." The friendly cobra answered: "Do not fear. When you have gone twenty-four miles on your journey, look back, and see what you will see." So they started; and on looking back at the end of twenty-four miles, saw the whole of the splendid palace in flames, the fire reaching up to heaven. The Rajah returned to see if he could help any-body to escape, or invite them in their distress to his court; but he found that all was burned down—not a stone nor a living creature remained!

Then he grieved much over the sad fate of his parents-in-law.

When the party returned home, the Rajah's brother said to him: "Where did you get these magnificent presents?" He replied: "They are gifts from my father- and mother-in-law." At this news the Rajah's brother went home to his wife very discontented, and asked her why she had never told him of her parents, and taken him to see them, whereby he might have received rich gifts as well as his brother. His wife then went to her sister, and asked how she had managed to get all the things. But the Ranee said: "Go away, you wicked woman, I will not speak to you. You killed the poor dog, our mother."

But afterwards she told her all about it.

The sister then said: " I shall go and see the cobra, and get presents too." The Ranee then answered: " You can go if you like."

So the sister ordered her palanquin, and told her husband she was going to see her parents, and prepare them for a visit from him. When she reached the ants' nest she saw the cobra there, and she went and put her finger in his mouth, and the cobra bit her, and she died.

The Magic Ring

ONCE upon a time there lived an old couple who had one son called Martin. Now, when the old man's time had come he stretched himself out on his bed and died. Though all his life long he had toiled and moiled, he only left his widow and son two hundred florins. The old woman determined to put by the money for a rainy day, but, alas! the rainy day was close at hand, for their meal was all consumed, and who is prepared to face starvation with two hundred florins at their disposal? So the old woman counted out one hundred florins, and giving them to Martin, told him to go into the town and lay in a store of meal for a year.

So Martin started off for the town. When he reached the meat market he found the whole place in turmoil and a great noise of angry voices and barking of dogs. Mixing in the crowd, he noticed a stag hound which the butchers had caught and tied to a post, and which was being flogged in a merciless manner. Overcome with pity, Martin spoke to the butchers, saying:

" Friends, why are you beating the poor dog so cruelly? "

" We have every right to beat him," they replied. " He has just devoured a newly killed pig."

" Leave off beating him," said Martin, " and sell him to me instead."

" If you choose to buy him," answered the butchers de
risively; " but for such a treasure we won't take a penny less
than one hundred florins."

" A hundred!" exclaimed Martin. " Well, so be it, if you
will not take less"; and taking the money out of his pocket
he handed it over in exchange for the dog, whose name was
Schurka.

When Martin got home his mother met him with the
question:

" Well, what have you bought?"

" Schurka, the dog," replied Martin, pointing to his new
possession. Whereupon his mother became very angry and
abused him roundly. He ought to be ashamed of himself,
when there was scarcely a handful of meal in the house, to
have spent the money on a useless brute like that. On the
following day she sent him back to the town, saying: " Here,
take our last one hundred florins and buy provisions with
them. I have just emptied the last grains of meal out of
the chest and baked a bannock; but it won't last over to
morrow."

Just as Martin was entering the town he met a rough-
looking peasant who was dragging a cat after him by a string
which was fastened around the poor beast's neck.

" Stop!" cried Martin. " Where are you dragging that
poor cat?"

" I mean to drown it," was the answer.

" What harm has the poor beast done?" said Martin.

" It has just killed a goose," replied the peasant.

" Don't drown it—sell it to me instead," begged Martin.

" Not for one hundred florins," was the answer.

" Surely for one hundred florins you'll sell it?" said Martin. " See! here is the money." And so saying he handed
him the one hundred florins, which the peasant pocketed, and
Martin took possession of the cat, which was called Waska.

When he reached his home his mother greeted him with
the question:

" Well, what have you brought back?"

THE FAIRY RING

"I have brought this cat, Waska," answered Martin.

"And what besides?"

"I had no money over to buy anything else with," replied Martin.

"You useless ne'er-do-weel!" exclaimed his mother in a great passion. "Leave the house at once and go and beg your bread among strangers." And as Martin did not dare to contradict her, he called Schurka and Waska and started off with them to the nearest village in search of work. On the way he met a rich peasant, who asked him where he was going.

"I want to get work as a day laborer," he answered.

"Come along with me, then. But I must tell you I engage my laborers without wages. If you serve me faithfully for a year I promise you it shall be to your advantage."

So Martin consented, and for a year he worked diligently and served his master faithfully, not sparing himself in any way. When the day of reckoning had come the peasant led him into a barn, and pointing to two full sacks said: "Take whichever of these you choose."

Martin examined the contents of the sacks, and seeing that one was full of silver and the other of sand, he said to himself: "There must be some trick about this. I had better take the sand." And throwing the sack over his shoulders he started out into the world in search of fresh work. On and on he walked, and at last he reached a great gloomy wood. In the middle of the wood he came upon a meadow, where a fire was burning, and in the midst of the fire, surrounded by flames, was a lovely damsel, more beautiful than anything that Martin had ever seen, and when she saw him she called to him:

"Martin, if you would win happiness save my life. Extinguish the flames with the sand that you earned in payment of your faithful service."

"Truly," thought Martin to himself, "it would be more sensible to save a fellow-being's life with this sand than to drag it about on one's back, seeing what a weight it is." And forthwith he lowered the sack from his shoulders and emptied its contents on the flames, and instantly the fire was extinguished; but at the same moment lo and behold! the lovely damsel turned into a serpent and darting upon him coiled itself around his neck and whispered lovingly in his ear:

"Do not be afraid of me, Martin. I love you and will go with you through the world. But first you must follow me boldly into my father's kingdom, underneath the earth; and when we get there, remember this—he will offer you gold and silver and dazzling gems, but do not touch them. Ask him, instead, for the ring which he wears on his little finger, for in that ring lies a magic power. You have only to throw it from one hand to the other, and at once twelve young men will appear who will do your bidding, no matter how difficult it is, in a single night."

So they started on their way, and after much wandering they reached a spot where a great rock rose straight up in the middle of the road. Instantly the serpent uncoiled itself from his neck, and as it touched the damp earth it resumed the shape of the lovely damsel. Pointing to the rock, she showed him an opening just big enough for a man to wriggle through. Passing into it, they entered a long underground passage which led out on to a wide field above which spread a blue sky. In the middle of the field stood a magnificent castle built out of porphyry, with a roof of gold and with glittering battlements. And his beautiful guide told him that this was the palace in which her father lived and reigned over his kingdom in the underworld.

Together they entered the palace and were received by the King with great kindness. Turning to his daughter he said:

"My child, I had almost given up the hope of ever seeing you again. Where have you been all these years?"

"My father," she replied, "I owe my life to this youth, who saved me from a terrible death."

Upon which the King turned to Martin with a gracious smile, saying: "I will reward your courage by granting you whatever your heart desires. Take as much gold, silver, and precious stones as you choose."

"I thank you, mighty King, for your gracious offer," answered Martin, "but I do not covet either gold, silver, or precious stones; yet if you will grant me a favor, give me, I beg, the ring from off the little finger of your royal hand. Every time my eye falls on it I shall think of your gracious majesty, and when I marry I shall present it to my bride."

So the King took the ring from his finger and gave it to Martin, saying: "Take it, good youth; but with it I make one condition—you are never to confide to anyone that this is a magic ring. If you do, you will straightway bring misfortune on yourself."

Martin took the ring, and having thanked the King he set out on the same road by which he had come down into the underworld. When he had regained the upper air he started for his old home, and having found his mother still living in the old house where he had left her, they settled down together very happily. So uneventful was their life that it almost seemed as if it would go on in this way always without let or hindrance. But one day it suddenly came into his mind that he would like to get married, and, moreover, that he would choose a very grand wife—a king's daughter, in short. But as he did not trust himself as a wooer, he determined to send his old mother on the mission.

"You must go to the King," he said to her, "and demand the hand of his lovely daughter in marriage for me."

"What are you thinking of, my son?" answered the old woman, aghast at the idea. "Why cannot you marry some one in your own rank? That would be far more fitting than to send a poor old woman like me a-wooing to the King's court for the hand of a princess. Why, it is as much as our heads are worth. Neither my life nor yours would be worth anything if I went on such a fool's errand."

"Never fear, little mother," answered Martin. "Trust me; all will be well. But see that you do not come back without an answer of some kind."

And so, obedient to her son's behest, the old woman hobbled off to the palace, and without being hindered reached

the courtyard and began to mount the flight of steps leading
to the royal presence chamber. At the head of the landing
rows of courtiers were collected in magnificent attire, who
stared at the queer old figure, and called to her and explained
to her with every kind of sign that it was strictly forbidden
to mount those steps. But their stern words and forbidding
gestures made no impression whatever on the old woman, and
she resolutely continued to climb the stairs, bent on carrying
out her son's orders. Upon this some of the courtiers seized
her by the arms and held her back by sheer force, at which
she set up such a yell that the King himself heard it and
stepped out on to the balcony to see what was the matter.
When he beheld the old woman flinging her arms wildly about
and heard her scream that she would not leave the place till
she had laid her case before the King, he ordered that she
should be brought into his presence. And forthwith she was
conducted into the golden presence chamber, where, leaning
back among cushions of royal purple, the King sat, surrounded
by his counselors and courtiers. Courtesying low, the old
woman stood silent before him.

"Well, my good old dame, what can I do for you?" asked
the King.

"I have come," replied Martin's mother—"and your majesty must not be angry with me—I have come a-wooing."

"Is the woman out of her mind?" said the King, with an
angry frown.

But Martin's mother answered boldly: "If the King will
only listen patiently to me and give me a straightforward
answer, he will see that I am not out of my mind. You, O
King, have a lovely daughter to give in marriage. I have a
son—a wooer—as clever a youth and as good a son-in-law as
you will find in your whole kingdom. There is nothing that
he cannot do. Now tell me, O King, plump and plain, will
you give your daughter to my son as wife?"

The King listened to the end of the old woman's strange
request, but every moment his face grew blacker and his features sterner, till all at once he thought to himself: "Is it worth

[418]

while that I, the King, should be angry with this poor old
fool?" And all the courtiers and counselors were amazed
when they saw the hard lines around his mouth and the frown
on his brow grow smooth, and heard the mild but mocking
tones in which he answered the old woman, saying:

"If your son is as wonderfully clever as you say, and if
there is nothing in the world that he cannot do, let him build
a magnificent castle, just opposite my palace windows, in
twenty-four hours. The palaces must be joined together by a
bridge of pure crystal. On each side of the bridge there must
be growing trees, having golden and silver apples and with
birds of paradise among the branches. At the right of the
bridge there must be a church with five golden cupolas. In
this church your son shall be wedded to my daughter, and
we will keep the wedding festivities in the new castle. But
if he fails to execute this my royal command, then, as a just
but mild monarch, I shall give orders that you and he be
taken and first dipped in tar and then in feathers, and you
shall be executed in the market place for the entertainment of
my courtiers."

And a smile played around the King's lips as he finished
speaking, and his courtiers and counselors shook with laughter when they thought of the old woman's folly, and praised
the King's wise device and said to each other: "What a joke
it will be when we see the pair of them tarred and feathered!
The son is just as able to grow a beard on the palm of his
hand as to execute such a task in twenty-four hours."

Now, the poor old woman was mortally afraid, and in a
trembling voice she asked:

"Is that really your royal will, O King? Must I take this
order to my poor son?"

"Yes, old dame; such is my command. If your son carries
out my order he shall be rewarded with my daughter; but if
he fails, away to the tar barrel and the stake with you both!"

On her way home the poor old woman shed bitter tears,
and when she saw Martin she told him what the King had
said, and sobbed out:

"Didn't I tell you, my son, that you should marry some one of your own rank? It would have been better for us this day if you had. As I told you, my going to court has been as much as our lives are worth, and now we will both be tarred and feathered and burned in the public market place. It is terrible!" And she moaned and cried.

"Never fear, little mother," answered Martin. "Trust me, and you will see all will be well. You may go to sleep with a quiet mind."

And stepping to the front of the hut Martin threw his ring from the palm of one hand into the other, upon which twelve youths instantly appeared and demanded what he wanted them to do. Then he told them the King's commands, and they answered that by next morning all should be accomplished exactly as the King had ordered.

Next morning when the King awoke and looked out of his window, to his amazement he beheld a magnificent castle, just opposite his own palace, and joined to it by a bridge of pure crystal.

At each side of the bridge trees were growing, from whose branches hung golden and silver apples, among which birds of paradise perched. At the right, gleaming in the sun, were the five golden cupolas of a splendid church, whose bells rang out as if they would summon people from all corners of the earth to come and behold the wonder. Now, though the King would much rather have seen his future son-in-law tarred, feathered, and burned at the stake, he remembered his royal oath and had to make the best of a bad business. So he took heart of grace and made Martin a duke, and gave his daughter a rich dowry, and prepared the grandest wedding feast that had ever been seen, so that to this day the old people in the country still talk of it.

After the wedding Martin and his royal bride went to dwell in the magnificent new palace, and here Martin lived in the greatest comfort and luxury, such luxury as he had never imagined. But though he was as happy as the day was long and as merry as a grig, the King's daughter fretted all day, thinking of the indignity that had been done her in making her marry Martin, the poor widow's son, instead of a rich young prince from a foreign country. So unhappy was she that she spent all her time wondering how she should get rid of her undesirable husband. And first she determined to learn the secret of his power, and with flattering, caressing words she tried to coax him to tell her how he was so clever that there was nothing in the world that he could not do. At first he would tell her nothing; but once, when he was in a yielding mood, she approached him with a winning smile on her lovely face, and speaking flattering words to him she gave him a potion to drink, with a sweet, strong taste. And when he had drunk it Martin's lips were unsealed, and he told her that all his power lay in the magic ring that he wore on his finger, and he described to her how to use it, and still speaking he fell into a deep sleep. And when she saw that the potion had worked and that he was sound asleep, the Princess took the magic ring from his finger, and going into the courtyard she threw it from the palm of one hand into the other. On the instant the twelve youths appeared and asked her what she commanded them to do. Then she told them that by the next morning they were to do away with the castle and the bridge and the church, and put in their stead the humble hut in which Martin used to live with his mother, and that while he slept her husband was to be carried to his old lowly room; and that they were to bear her away to the utmost ends of the earth, where an old king lived who would make her welcome in his palace and surround her with the state that befitted a royal princess.

"You shall be obeyed," answered the twelve youths at the same moment. And lo and behold! the following morning when the King woke and looked out of his window he beheld to his amazement that the palace, bridge, church, and trees had all vanished, and there was nothing in their place but a bare, miserable-looking hut.

Immediately the King sent for his son-in-law and commanded him to explain what had happened. But Martin

looked at his royal father-in-law and answered never a word
Then the King was very angry, and calling a council together,
he charged Martin with having been guilty of witchcraft, and
of having deceived the King, and having made away with
the Princess; and he was condemned to imprisonment in a
high stone tower, with neither meat nor drink, till he should
die of starvation.

Then, in the hour of his dire necessity, his old friends
Schurka (the dog) and Waska (the cat) remembered how
Martin had once saved them from a cruel death; and they
took counsel together as to how they should help him. And
Schurka growled and was of opinion that he would like to
tear everyone in pieces; but Waska purred meditatively,
scratched the back of her ear with a velvet paw, and remained
lost in thought. At the end of a few minutes she had made
up her mind, and turning to Schurka, said: "Let us go together into the town, and the moment we meet a baker you
must make a rush between his legs and upset the tray from
off his head. I will lay hold of the rolls and will carry them
off to our master." No sooner said than done. Together
the two faithful creatures trotted off into the town, and very
soon they met a baker bearing a tray on his head and looking
around on all sides while he cried:

> " Fresh rolls, sweet cake,
> Fancy bread of every kind,
> Come and buy, come and take,
> Sure you'll find it to your mind."

At that moment Schurka made a rush between his legs—
the baker stumbled, the tray was upset, the rolls fell to the
ground, and while the man angrily pursued Schurka, Waska
managed to drag the rolls out of sight behind a bush. And
when a moment later Schurka joined her, they set off at full
tilt to the stone tower where Martin was a prisoner, taking
the rolls with them. Waska, being very agile, climbed up by
the outside to the grated window and called in an anxious
voice:

"Are you alive, master?"

"Scarcely alive—almost starved to death," answered Martin in a weak voice. "I little thought it would come to this, that I should die of hunger."

"Never fear, dear master. Schurka and I will look after you," said Waska. And in another moment she had climbed down and brought him back a roll, and then another and another till she had brought him the whole tray load. Upon which she said: "Dear master, Schurka and I are going off to a distant kingdom at the utmost ends of the earth to fetch you back your magic ring. You must be careful that the rolls last till our return."

And Waska took leave of her beloved master and set off with Schurka on their journey. On and on they traveled, looking always to right and left for traces of the Princess, following up every track, making inquiries of every cat and dog they met, listening to the talk of every wayfarer they passed; and at last they heard that the kingdom at the utmost ends of the earth, where the twelve youths had borne the Princess, was not very far off. And one day they reached that distant kingdom, and going at once to the palace they began to make friends with all the dogs and cats in the place and to question them about the Princess and the magic ring; but no one could tell them much about either. Now, one day it chanced that Waska had gone down to the palace cellar to hunt for mice and rats, and seeing an especially fat, well-fed mouse, she pounced upon it, buried her claws in its soft fur, and was just going to gobble it up when she was stopped by the pleading tones of the little creature, saying: "If you will only spare my life I will be of great service to you. I will do everything in my power for you; for I am the king of the mice, and if I perish the whole race will die out."

"So be it," said Waska. "I will spare your life, but in return you must do something for me. In this castle there lives a princess, the wicked wife of my dear master. She has stolen away his magic ring. You must get it away from her at whatever cost. Do you hear? Till you have done this I won't take my claws out of your fur."

"Good!" replied the mouse. "I will do what you ask." And so saying he summoned all the mice in his kingdom together. A countless number of mice, small and big, brown and gray, assembled and formed a circle around their king, who was a prisoner under Waska's claws. Turning to them he said: "Dear and faithful subjects, whoever among you will steal the magic ring from the strange Princess will release me from a cruel death, and I shall honor him above all the other mice in the kingdom."

Instantly a tiny mouse stepped forward and said: "I often creep about the Princess's bedroom at night, and I have noticed that she has a ring which she treasures as the apple of her eye. All day she wears it on her finger, and at night she keeps it in her mouth. I will undertake, sire, to steal away the ring for you."

And the tiny mouse tripped away into the bedroom of the Princess and waited for nightfall; then, when the Princess had fallen asleep, it crept up on to her bed and gnawed a hole in the pillow, through which it dragged, one by one, little down feathers and threw them under the Princess's nose. And the fluff flew into the Princess's nose and into her mouth, and starting up she sneezed and coughed, and the ring fell out of her mouth on to the coverlet. In a flash the tiny mouse had seized it and brought it to Waska as a ransom for the king of the mice. Thereupon Waska and Schurka started off and traveled night and day till they reached the stone tower where Martin was imprisoned; and the cat climbed up the window and called out to him:

"Martin, dear master, are you still alive?"

"Ah! Waska, my faithful little cat, is that you?" replied a weak voice. "I am dying of hunger. For three days I have not tasted food."

"Be of good heart, dear master," replied Waska. "From this day forth, you will know nothing but happiness and prosperity. If this were a moment to trouble you with riddles,

THE FAIRY RING

I would make you guess what Schurka and I have brought
you back. Only think, we have found you your ring!"

At these words Martin's joy knew no bounds, and he stroked
her fondly and she rubbed up against him and purred happily,
while below Schurka bounded in the air and barked joyfully.
Then Martin took the ring and threw it from one hand into the
other, and instantly the twelve youths appeared and asked
what they were to do.

"Fetch me first something to eat and drink as quickly as
possible; and after that bring musicians hither and let us have
music all day long."

Now, when the people in the town and palace heard music
coming from the tower they were filled with amazement, and
came to the King with the news that witchcraft must be going
on in Martin's tower, for instead of dying of starvation he
was seemingly making merry to the sound of music and to
the clatter of plates and glass and knives and forks; and the
music was so enchantingly sweet that all the passers-by stood
still to listen to it. On this the King sent at once a messenger
to Starvation Tower, and he was so astonished with what he
saw that he remained rooted to the spot. Then the King sent
his chief counselors, and they too were transfixed with wonder.
At last the King came himself, and he likewise was spell-
bound by the beauty of the music.

Then Martin summoned the twelve youths and said to
them: "Build up my castle again and join it to the King's
palace with a crystal bridge. Do not forget the trees with
the golden and silver apples and with the birds of paradise in
the branches, and put back the church with the five cupolas,
and let the bells ring out, summoning the people from the four
corners of the kingdom. And one thing more—bring back
my faithless wife and lead her into the women's chamber."

And it was all done as he commanded, and leaving Starvation Tower he took the King, his father-in-law, by the arm
and led him into the new palace, where the Princess sat in
fear and trembling awaiting her death. And Martin spoke to
the King, saying: "King and royal father, I have suffered

[425]

much at the hands of your daughter. What punishment shall be dealt to her?"

Then the mild King answered: "Beloved Prince and son-in-law, if you love me, let your anger be turned to grace—forgive my daughter and restore her to your heart and favor."

And Martin's heart was softened and he forgave his wife, and they lived happily together ever after. And his old mother came and lived with them, and he never parted with Schurka and Waska; and I need hardly tell you that he never again let the ring out of his possession.

Tit for Tat

THERE once lived a camel and a jackal who were great friends. One day the Jackal said to the Camel: "I know that there is a fine field of sugar cane on the other side of the river. If you will take me across, I'll show you the place. This plan will suit me as well as you. You will enjoy eating the sugar cane, and I am sure to find many crabs, bones, and bits of fish by the riverside, on which to make a good dinner."

The Camel consented and swam across the river, taking the Jackal, who could not swim, on his back. When they reached the other side, the Camel went to eating the sugar cane, and the Jackal ran up and down the river bank devouring all the crabs, bits of fish, and bones he could find.

But being so much smaller an animal, he had made an excellent meal before the Camel had eaten more than two or three mouthfuls; and no sooner had he finished his dinner than he ran round and round the sugar-cane field, yelping and howling with all his might.

The villagers heard him, and thought: "There is a jackal among the sugar canes; he will be scratching holes in the ground and spoiling the roots of the plants." And they all went down to the place to drive him away. But when they got there they found to their surprise not only a jackal, but a camel who was eating the sugar canes! This made them very angry, and they caught the poor Camel and drove him from the field and beat and beat him until he was nearly dead.

When they had gone, the Jackal said to the Camel, "We had better go home." And the Camel said: "Very well; then jump upon my back as you did before."

So the Jackal jumped upon the Camel's back, and the Camel began to recross the river. When they had got well into the water the Camel said: "This is a pretty way in which you have treated me, friend Jackal. No sooner had you finished your own dinner than you must go yelping about the place loud enough to arouse the whole village, and bring all the villagers down to beat me black and blue, and turn me out of the field before I had eaten two mouthfuls! What in the world did you make such a noise for?"

"I don't know," said the Jackal. "It is a habit I have. I always like to sing a little after dinner."

The Camel waded on through the river. The water reached up to his knees—then above them—up, up, up, higher and higher, until he was obliged to swim. Then turning to the Jackal he said, "I feel very anxious to roll." "Oh, pray don't; why do you wish to do so?" asked the Jackal. "I don't know," answered the Camel. "It is a habit I have. I always like to have a little roll after dinner." So saying, he rolled over in the water, shaking the Jackal off as he did so. And the Jackal was drowned, but the Camel swam safely ashore.

The Brahman, the Tiger, and the Six Judges

ONCE upon a time a Brahman, who was walking along the road, came upon an iron cage, in which a great tiger had been shut up by the villagers who caught him.

As the Brahman passed by, the Tiger called out and said to him: "Brother Brahman, brother Brahman, have pity on me, and let me out of this cage for one minute only to drink a little water, for I am dying of thirst." The Brahman answered: "No, I will not; for if I let you out of the cage you will eat me."

"Oh, father of mercy," answered the Tiger, "in truth that I will not. I will never be so ungrateful; only let me out, that I may drink some water and return." Then the Brahman took pity on him and opened the cage door; but no sooner had he done so than the Tiger, jumping out, said: "Now, I will eat you first and drink the water afterwards." But the Brahman said: "Only do not kill me hastily. Let us first ask the opinion of six, and if all of them say it is just and fair that you should put me to death, then I am willing to die."

"Very well," answered the Tiger, "it shall be as you say; we will first ask the opinion of six."

So the Brahman and the Tiger walked on till they came to a Banyan tree; and the Brahman said to it: "Banyan Tree, Banyan Tree, hear and give judgment." "On what must I give judgment?" asked the Banyan Tree. "This Tiger," said the Brahman, "begged me to let him out of his cage to drink a little water, and he promised not to hurt me if I did so; but now, that I have let him out, he wishes to eat me. Is it just that he should do so or no?"

The Banyan Tree answered: "Men often come to take shelter in the cool shade under my boughs from the scorching rays of the sun; but when they have rested, they cut and break my pretty branches and wantonly scatter my leaves. Let the Tiger eat the man, for men are an ungrateful race."

At these words the Tiger would have instantly killed the Brahman, but the Brahman said: "Tiger, Tiger, you must not kill me yet, for you promised that we should first hear the judgment of six." "Very well," said the Tiger, and they went on their way. After a little while they met a camel. "Sir Camel, Sir Camel," cried the Brahman, "hear and give judgment." "On what shall I give judgment?" asked the Camel. And the Brahman related how the Tiger had begged him to open the cage door, and promised not to eat him if he did so; and how he had afterwards determined to break his word, and asked if that were just or not. The Camel replied: "When I was young and strong, and could do much work, my master took care of me and gave me good food; but now that I am old, and have lost all my strength in his service, he overloads me and starves me and beats me without mercy. Let the Tiger eat the man, for men are an unjust and cruel race."

The Tiger would then have killed the Brahman, but the latter said: "Stop, Tiger, for we must first hear the judgment of six."

So they both went again on their way. At a little distance they found a bullock lying by the roadside. The Brahman said to him: "Brother Bullock, brother Bullock, hear and give judgment." "On what must I give judgment?" asked the Bullock. The Brahman answered: "I found this Tiger in a cage, and he prayed me to open the door and let him out to drink a little water, and promised not to kill me if I did so; but when I had let him out he resolved to put me to death. Is it fair that he should do so or not?" The Bullock said: "When I was able to work my master fed me well and tended me carefully, but now I am old he has forgotten all I did for him, and left me by the roadside to die. Let the Tiger eat the man, for men have no pity."

Three out of the six had given judgment against the Brahman, but still he did not lose all hope and determined to ask the other three.

They next met an eagle flying through the air, to whom the Brahman cried, "O Eagle, great Eagle, hear and give judgment." "On what must I give judgment?" asked the Eagle. The Brahman stated the case, and the Eagle answered: "Whenever men see me they try to shoot me; they climb the rocks and steal away my little ones. Let the Tiger eat the man, for men are the persecutors of the earth."

Then the Tiger began to roar and said: "The judgment of all is against you, O Brahman!" But the Brahman answered: "Stay yet a little longer, for two others must first be asked."

After this they saw an alligator, and the Brahman related the matter to him, hoping for a more favorable verdict. But the Alligator said: "Whenever I put my nose out of the water men torment me and try to kill me. Let the Tiger eat the man, for as long as men live we shall have no rest."

The Brahman gave himself up as lost; but again he prayed the Tiger to have patience and let him ask the opinion of the sixth judge. Now the sixth was a jackal. The Brahman told his story, and said to him: "Uncle Jackal, Uncle Jackal, say what is your judgment?" The Jackal answered: "It is impossible for me to decide who is in the right and who in the wrong unless I see the exact position in which you were when the dispute began. Show me the place." So the Brahman and the Tiger returned to the place where they first met, and the Jackal went with them. When they got there, the Jackal said: "Now Brahman, show me exactly where you stood." "Here," said the Brahman, standing by the iron tiger cage. "Exactly there, was it?" asked the Jackal. "Exactly here," replied the Brahman. "Where was the Tiger, then?" asked the Jackal. "In the cage," answered the Tiger. "How do you mean?" said the Jackal; "how were you within the cage? which way were you looking?" "Why, I stood so," said the Tiger, jumping into the cage, "and my head was on this side." "Very good," said the Jackal, "but I cannot judge without understanding the whole matter exactly. Was the cage door open or shut?" "Shut and bolted," said the Brahman. "Then shut and bolt it," said the Jackal.

When the Brahman had done this, the Jackal said: "Oh, you wicked and ungrateful Tiger! when the good Brahman opened your cage door, is to eat him the only return you would make? Stay there, then, for the rest of your days, for no one will ever let you out again. Proceed on your journey, friend Brahman. Your road lies that way and mine this."

So saying, the Jackal ran off in one direction, and the Brahman went rejoicing on his way in the other.

THE FAIRY RING

Muchie Lal

ONCE upon a time there were a rajah and ranee who had no children. Long had they wished and prayed that the gods would send them a son, but it was all in vain —their prayers were not granted. One day a number of fish were brought into the royal kitchen to be cooked for the Rajah's dinner, and among them was one little fish that was not dead, though all the rest were dead. One of the palace maid servants seeing this, took the little fish and put him in a basin of water. Shortly afterwards the Ranee saw him, and, thinking him very pretty, kept him as a pet; and because she had no children she lavished all her affection on the fish and loved him as a son; and the people called him Muchie Rajah (the Fish Prince). In a little while Muchie Rajah had grown too long to live in the small basin, so they put him in a larger one, and then when he grew too long for that, into a big tub. In time, however, Muchie Rajah became too large for even the big tub to hold him, so the Ranee had a tank made for him in which he lived very happily; and twice a day she fed him with boiled rice. Now, though the people fancied Muchie Rajah was only a fish, this was not the case. He was, in truth, a young rajah who had angered the gods, and been turned by them into a fish and thrown into the river as a punishment.

One morning, when the Ranee brought him his daily meal of boiled rice, Muchie Rajah called out to her and said: "Queen Mother, Queen Mother, I am so lonely here all by myself! Cannot you get me a wife?" The Ranee promised to try, and sent messengers to all the people she knew to ask if they would allow one of their children to marry her son, the Fish Prince. But they all answered: "We cannot give one of our dear little daughters to be devoured by a great fish, even though he is the Muchie Rajah and so high in your majesty's favor."

At news of this the Ranee did not know what to do. She

[431]

was so foolishly fond of Muchie Rajah, however, that she resolved to get him a wife at any cost. Again she sent out messengers, but this time she gave them a great bag containing a lac of gold mohurs,* and said to them: "Go into every land until you find a wife for my Muchie Rajah, and to whoever will give you a child to be the Muchie Ranee you shall give this bag of gold mohurs." The messengers started on their search, but for some time they were unsuccessful. Not even the beggars were to be tempted to sell their children, fearing the great fish would devour them. At last one day the messengers came to a village where there lived a fakir, who had lost his first wife and married again. His first wife had had one little daughter, and his second wife also had a daughter. As it happened, the Fakir's second wife hated her little stepdaughter, always gave her the hardest work to do and the least food to eat, and tried by every means in her power to get her out of the way in order that the child might not rival her own daughter. When she heard of the errand on which the messengers had come, she sent for them when the Fakir was out, and said to them: "Give me the bag of gold mohurs, and you shall take my little daughter to marry the Muchie Rajah." ("For," she thought to herself, "the great fish will certainly eat the girl, and she will thus trouble us no more.") Then, turning to her stepdaughter, she said: "Go down to the river and wash your saree, that you may be fit to go with these people, who will take you to the Ranee's court." At these words the poor girl went down to the river very sorrowful, for she saw no hope of escape, as her father was from home. As she knelt by the riverside, washing her saree and crying bitterly, some of her tears fell into the hole of an old seven-headed cobra, who lived on the river bank. This Cobra was a very wise animal, and seeing the maiden, he put his head out of his hole and said to her, "Little girl, why do you cry?" "Oh, sir," she answered, "I am very unhappy, for my father is from home, and my stepmother has sold me to the Ranee's people to be the wife

* A lac of gold mohurs is equal to about $750,000.

[432]

of the Muchie Rajah, that great fish, and I know he will eat me up." "Do not be afraid, my daughter," said the Cobra; "but take with you these three stones and tie them up in the corner of your saree"; and so saying he gave her three little round pebbles. "The Muchie Rajah, whose wife you are to be, is not really a fish, but a rajah who has been enchanted. Your home will be a little room which the Ranee has had built in the tank wall. When you are taken there, wait and be sure you don't go to sleep or the Muchie Rajah will certainly come and eat you up. But as you hear him coming rushing through the water, be prepared, and as soon as you see him throw this first stone at him; he will then sink to the bottom of the tank. The second time he comes, throw the second stone, when the same thing will happen. The third time he comes, throw this third stone, and he will immediately resume his human shape." So saying, the old Cobra dived down again into his hole. The Fakir's daughter took the stones and determined to do as the Cobra had told her, though she hardly believed it would have the desired effect.

When she reached the palace the Ranee spoke kindly to her, and said to the messengers: "You have done your errand well; this is a dear little girl." Then she ordered that she should be let down the side of the tank in a basket to a little room which had been prepared for her. When the Fakir's daughter got there, she thought she had never seen such a pretty place in her life, for the Ranee had caused the little room to be very nicely decorated for the wife of her favorite; and she would have felt very happy away from her cruel stepmother and all the hard work she had been made to do, had it not been for the dark water that lay black and unfathomable below the door, and the fear of the terrible Muchie Rajah.

After waiting some time she heard a rushing sound, and little waves came dashing against the threshold; faster they came and faster, and the noise got louder and louder, until she saw a great fish's head above the water—Muchie Rajah

[433]

was coming toward her open-mouthed. The Fakir's daughter seized one of the stones that the Cobra had given her and threw it at him, and down he sank to the bottom of the tank; a second time he rose and came toward her, and she threw the second stone at him, and he again sank down; a third time he came more fiercely than before, when, seizing the third stone, she threw it with all her force. No sooner did it touch him than the spell was broken, and there, instead of a fish, stood a handsome young prince. The poor little Fakir's daughter was so startled that she began to cry. But the Prince said to her: "Pretty maiden, do not be frightened. You have rescued me from a horrible thraldom, and I can never thank you enough; but if you will be the Muchie Ranee, we will be married to-morrow." Then he sat down on the doorstep, thinking over his strange fate and watching for the dawn.

Next morning early several inquisitive people came to see if the Muchie Rajah had eaten up his poor little wife, as they feared he would; what was their astonishment, on looking over the tank wall, to see, not the Muchie Rajah, but a magnificent prince! The news soon spread to the palace. Down came the Rajah, down came the Ranee, down came all their attendants and dragged Muchie Rajah and the Fakir's daughter up the side of the tank in a basket; and when they heard their story there were great and unparalleled rejoicings. The Ranee said: "So I have indeed found a son at last!" And the people were so delighted, so happy and so proud of the new Prince and Princess that they covered all their path with damask from the tank to the palace, and cried to their fellows: "Come and see our new Prince and Princess. Were ever any so divinely beautiful? Come see a right royal couple—a pair of mortals like the gods!" And when they reached the palace the Prince was married to the Fakir's daughter.

There they lived very happily for some time. The Muchie Ranee's stepmother, hearing what had happened, came often to see her stepdaughter, and pretended to be delighted at her

"THE RANEE SAID, 'THIS IS A DEAR LITTLE GIRL'"

"THE FAIRY-BOOK, THERE'S A DEAR LITTLE GIRL"

good fortune; and the Ranee was so good that she quite forgave all her stepmother's former cruelty, and always received her very kindly. At last, one day, the Muchie Ranee said to her husband: "It is a weary while since I saw my father. If you will give me leave, I should much like to visit my native village and see him again." "Very well," he replied, "you may go. But do not stay away long, for there can be no happiness for me till you return." So she went, and her father was delighted to see her; but her stepmother, though she pretended to be very kind, was, in reality, only glad to think she had got the Ranee into her power, and determined, if possible, never to allow her to return to the palace again. One day therefore she said to her own daughter: "It is hard that your stepsister should have become Ranee of all the land instead of being eaten up by the great fish, while we gained no more than a lac of gold mohurs. Do now as I bid you, that you may become ranee in her stead." She then went on to instruct her how she must invite the Ranee down to the river bank, and there beg her to let her try on her jewels, and while putting them on give her a push and drown her in the river.

The girl consented, and standing by the river bank, said to her stepsister: "Sister, may I try on your jewels? How pretty they are!" "Yes," said the Ranee, "and we shall be able to see in the river how they look." So, undoing her necklaces, she clasped them around the other's neck. But while she was doing so her stepsister gave her a push, and she fell backward into the water. The girl watched to see that the body did not rise, and then, running back, said to her mother: "Mother, here are all the jewels, and she will trouble us no more." But it happened that just when her stepsister pushed the Ranee into the river her old friend the Seven-headed Cobra chanced to be swimming across it, and seeing the little Ranee likely to be drowned, he carried her on his back until they reached his hole, into which he took her safely. Now this hole, in which the Cobra and his wife and all his little ones lived had two entrances—the one under the water

THE FAIRY RING

and leading to the river, and the other above water, leading out into the open fields. To this upper end of his hole the Cobra took the Muchie Ranee, where he and his wife took care of her; and there she lived with them for some time. Meanwhile, the wicked Fakir's wife, having dressed up her own daughter in all the Ranee's jewels, took her to the palace, and said to the Muchie Rajah: "See, I have brought your wife, my dear daughter, back safe and well." The Rajah looked at her, and thought, "This does not look like my wife." However, the room was dark and the girl was cleverly disguised, and he thought he might be mistaken. Next day he said again: "My wife must be sadly changed or this cannot be she, for she was always bright and cheerful. She had pretty loving ways and merry words, while this woman never opens her lips." Still, he did not like to seem to mistrust his wife, and comforted himself by saying, "Perhaps she is tired with the long journey." On the third day, however, he could bear the uncertainty no longer, and tearing off her jewels saw, not the face of his own little wife, but another woman. Then he was very angry and turned her out of doors, saying: "Begone! since you are but the wretched tool of others, I spare your life." But of the Fakir's wife he said to his guards: "Fetch that woman here instantly, for unless she can tell me where my wife is, I will have her hanged." It chanced, however, that the Fakir's wife had heard of the Muchie Rajah having turned her daughter out of doors; so, fearing his anger, she hid herself, and was not to be found.

Meantime, the Muchie Ranee, not knowing how to get home, continued to live in the great Seven-headed Cobra's hole, and he and his wife and all his family were very kind to her, and loved her as if she had been one of them; and there her little son was born, and she called him Muchie Lal,* after the Muchie Rajah, his father. Muchie Lal was a lovely child, merry and brave, and his playmates all day long were the young cobras. When he was about three years old a bangle seller came by that way, and the Muchie Ranee bought

* Little Ruby Fish.

[436]

some bangles from him and put them on her boy's wrists and
ankles; but by the next day, in playing, he had broken them all.
Then, seeing the bangle seller, the Ranee called him again and
bought some more, and so on every day until the bangle seller
got quite rich from selling so many bangles for the Muchie
Lal—for the Cobra's hole was full of treasure, and he gave the
Muchie Ranee as much money to spend every day as she liked.
There was nothing she wished for he did not give her, only
he would not let her try to get home to her husband, which
she wished more than all. When she asked him he would
say: " No, I will not let you go. If your husband comes here
and fetches you, it is well; but I will not allow you to wander
in search of him through the land alone."

And so she was obliged to stay where she was.

All this time the poor Muchie Rajah was hunting in every
part of the country for his wife, but he could learn no tidings
of her. For grief and sorrow at losing her he had gone well-
nigh distracted, and did nothing but wander from place to
place, crying, " She is gone! she is gone! " Then, when he
had long inquired without avail of all the people in her native
village about her, he one day met a bangle seller, and said to
him, " Whence do you come? " The bangle seller answered:
" I have just been selling bangles to some people who live in
a cobra's hole in the river bank." " People! What people? "
asked the Rajah. " Why," answered the bangle seller, " a
woman and a child. The child is the most beautiful I ever
saw. He is about three years old, and of course, running
about, is always breaking his bangles, and his mother buys
him new ones every day." " Do you know what the child's
name is? " said the Rajah. " Yes," answered the bangle
seller carelessly, " for the lady always calls him her Muchie
Lal." " Ah," thought the Muchie Rajah, " this must be my
wife." Then he said to him again: " Good bangle seller, I
would see these strange people of whom you speak; cannot
you take me there? " " Not to-night," replied the bangle
seller; " daylight has gone, and we should only frighten them;
but I shall be going there again to-morrow, and then you may

come too. Meanwhile, come and rest at my house for the night, for you look faint and weary." The Rajah consented. Next morning, however, very early, he woke the bangle seller, saying: "Pray let us go now and see the people you spoke about yesterday." "Stay," said the bangle seller; "it is much too early. I never go till after breakfast." So the Rajah had to wait till the bangle seller was ready to go. At last they started off, and when they reached the Cobra's hole the first thing the Rajah saw was a fine little boy playing with the young cobras.

As the bangle seller came along, jingling his bangles, a gentle voice from inside the hole called out: "Come here, my Muchie Lal, and try on your bangles." Then the Muchie Rajah, kneeling down at the mouth of the hole, said, "O lady, show your beautiful face to me." At the sound of his voice the Ranee ran out, crying, "Husband, husband! have you found me again!" And she told him how her sister had tried to drown her, and how the good Cobra had saved her life and taken care of her and her child. Then he said, "And will you now come home with me?" And she told him how the Cobra would never let her go, and said: "I will first tell him of your coming; for he has been as a father to me." So she called out: "Father Cobra, father Cobra, my husband has come to fetch me; will you let me go?" "Yes," he said, "if your husband has come to fetch you, you may go." And his wife said: "Farewell, dear lady, we are loth to lose you, for we have loved you as a daughter." And all the little cobras were very sorrowful to think that they must lose their playfellow, the young Prince. Then the Cobra gave the Muchie Rajah and the Muchie Ranee and Muchie Lal all the most costly gifts he could find in his treasure-house, and so they went home, where they lived very happy ever after.

The Valiant Chatteemaker

ONCE upon a time, in a violent storm of thunder, lightning, wind, and rain, a tiger crept for shelter close to
the wall of an old woman's hut. This old woman was
very poor, and her hut was but a tumble-down place, through
the roof of which the rain came drip, drip, drip, on more sides
than one. This troubled her much, and she went running
about from side to side, dragging first one thing and then
another out of the way of the leaky places in the roof, and as
she did so she kept saying to herself: " Oh, dear! oh, dear! how
tiresome this is! I'm sure the roof will come down! If an
elephant, or a lion, or a tiger were to walk in, he wouldn't
frighten me half so much as this perpetual dripping." And
then she would begin dragging the bed and all the other things
in the room about again, to get them out of the way of the
wet. The tiger, who was crouching down just outside,
heard all that she said, and thought to himself: " This old
woman says she would not be afraid of an elephant, or a lion,
or a tiger, but that this perpetual dripping frightens her more
than all. What can this ' perpetual dripping ' be?—it must be
something very dreadful." And hearing her immediately afterwards dragging all the things about the room again, he said
to himself: " What a terrible noise! Surely that must be the
' perpetual dripping.' "

At this moment a Chatteemaker,* who was in search of his
donkey, which had strayed away, came down the road. The
night being very cold, he had, truth to say, taken a little more
toddy than was good for him, and seeing, by the glare of a
flash of lightning, a large animal lying down close to the old
woman's hut, he mistook it for the donkey he was looking for.

So, running up to the tiger, he seized hold of it by one ear,
and commenced beating, kicking, and abusing it with all his
might and main. " You wretched creature!" he cried, " is
this the way you serve me, obliging me to come out and look

* Potter.

[439]

for you in such pouring rain and on such a dark night as this? Get up instantly or I'll break every bone in your body"; so he went on scolding and thumping the tiger with his utmost power, for he had worked himself up into a terrible rage. The tiger did not know what to make of it all, but he began to feel quite frightened, and said to himself: "Why, this must be the 'perpetual dripping'; no wonder the old woman said she was more afraid of it than of an elephant, a lion, or a tiger, for it gives most dreadfully hard blows."

The Chatteemaker, having made the tiger get up, got on his back and forced him to carry him home, kicking and beating him the whole way, for all this time he fancied he was on his donkey; and then he tied his forefeet and his head firmly together, and fastened him to a post in front of his house, and when he had done this he went to bed.

Next morning, when the Chatteemaker's wife got up and looked out of the window, what did she see but a great big tiger tied up, in front of their house, to the post to which they usually fastened the donkey. She was very much surprised, and running to her husband, awoke him, saying: "Do you know what animal you fetched home last night?" "Yes, the donkey, to be sure," he answered. "Come and see," said she, and she showed him the great tiger tied to the post. The Chatteemaker at this was no less astonished than his wife, and felt himself all over to find if the tiger had not wounded him. But, no, he was safe and sound, and there was the tiger tied to the post, just as he had fastened it up the night before.

News of the Chatteemaker's exploit soon spread through the village, and all the people came to see him and hear him tell how he had caught the tiger and tied it to the post; and this they thought so wonderful that they sent a deputation to the Rajah, with a letter to tell him how a man of their village had, alone and unarmed, caught a great tiger and tied it to a post.

When the Rajah read the letter he also was much surprised, and determined to go in person and see this astonishing sight. So he sent for his horses and carriages, his lords and attendants, and they all set off together to look at the Chatteemaker and the tiger he had caught.

Now the tiger was a very large one, and had long been the terror of the whole country around, which made the whole matter still more extraordinary; and all this being represented to the Rajah, he determined to confer all possible honor on the valiant Chatteemaker. So he gave him houses and lands, and as much money as would fill a well, made him a lord of his court, and conferred on him the command of ten thousand horse.

It came to pass, shortly after this, that a neighboring rajah, who had long had a quarrel with this one, sent to announce his intention of going instantly to war with him; and tidings were brought at the same time that the Rajah who sent the challenge had gathered a great army together on the borders, and was prepared at a moment's notice to invade the country.

In this dilemma no one knew what to do. The Rajah sent for all his generals, and inquired of them which would be willing to take command of his forces and oppose the enemy. They all replied that the country was so ill prepared for the emergency, and the case was apparently so hopeless, that they would rather not take the responsibility of the chief command. The Rajah knew not whom to appoint in their stead. Then some of his people said to him: "You have lately given the command of ten thousand horse to the valiant Chatteemaker who caught the tiger. Why not make him commander-in-chief? A man who could catch a tiger and tie him to a post, must surely be more courageous and clever than most." "Very well," said the Rajah, "I will make him commander-in-chief." So he sent for the Chatteemaker and said to him: "In your hands I place all the power of the kingdom; you must put our enemies to flight for us." "So be it," answered the Chatteemaker; "but, before I lead the whole army against the enemy, suffer me to go by myself and examine their position, and, if possible, find out their numbers and strength."

[441]

The Rajah consented, and the Chatteemaker returned home to his wife and said: "They have made me commander-in-chief, which is a very difficult post for me to fill, because I shall have to ride at the head of all the army, and you know I never was on a horse in my life. But I have succeeded in gaining a little delay, as the Rajah has given me permission to go first alone and reconnoiter the enemy's camp. Do you therefore provide a very quiet pony, for you know I cannot ride, and I will start to-morrow morning."

But, before the Chatteemaker had started, the Rajah sent over to him a most magnificent charger richly caparisoned, which he begged he would ride when going to see the enemy's camp. The Chatteemaker was frightened almost out of his life, for the charger that the Rajah had sent him was very powerful and spirited, and he felt sure that even if he ever got on it, he should very soon tumble off; however, he did not dare to refuse it, for fear of offending the Rajah by not accepting his present. So he sent back to him a message of thanks, and said to his wife: "I cannot go on the pony, now that the Rajah has sent me this fine horse; but how am I ever to ride it?" "Oh, don't be frightened," she answered; "you've only to get upon it, and I will tie you firmly on so that you cannot tumble off, and if you start at night no one will see that you are tied on." "Very well," he said.

So that night his wife brought the horse that the Rajah had sent him to the door. "Indeed," said the Chatteemaker, "I can never get into that saddle, it is so high up." "You must jump," said his wife. So he tried to jump several times, but each time he jumped he tumbled down again. "I always forget when I am jumping," said he, "which way I ought to turn." "Your face must be toward the horse's head," she answered. "To be sure, of course," he cried, and giving one great jump he jumped into the saddle, but with his face toward the horse's tail. "This won't do at all," said his wife as she helped him down again; "try getting on without jumping." "I never can remember," he continued, "when I have got my left foot in the stirrup, what to do with my right foot or where to put it." "That must go in the other stirrup," she answered; "let me help you." So after many trials in which he tumbled down very often, for the horse was fresh and did not like standing still, the Chatteemaker got into the saddle; but no sooner had he got there than he cried: "Oh, wife, wife! tie me very firmly as quickly as possible, for I know I shall jump down if I can." Then she fetched some strong rope and tied his feet firmly into the stirrups, fastened one stirrup to the other, and put another rope around his waist and another around his neck, and fastened them to the horse's body and neck and tail.

When the horse felt all these ropes about him he could not imagine what queer creature had got upon his back, and he began rearing and kicking and prancing, and at last set off full gallop, as fast as he could tear, right across country. "Wife, wife!" cried the Chatteemaker, "you forgot to tie my hands." "Never mind," said she, "hold on by the mane." So he caught hold of the horse's mane as firmly as he could. Then away went horse, away went Chatteemaker — away, away, away over hedges, over ditches, over rivers, over plains —away, away like a flash of lightning—now this way, now that—on, on, on, gallop, gallop, gallop—until they came in sight of the enemy's camp.

The Chatteemaker did not like his ride at all, and when he saw where it was leading him he liked it still less, for he thought the enemy would catch him and very likely kill him. So he determined to make one desperate effort to be free, and stretching out his hand as the horse shot past a young banyan tree, seized hold of it with all his might, hoping that the resistance it offered might cause the ropes that tied him to break. But the horse was going at his utmost speed, and the soil in which the banyan tree grew was loose, so that when the Chatteemaker caught hold of it and gave it such a violent pull it came up by the roots, and on he rode as fast as before, with the tree in his hand.

All the soldiers in the camp saw him coming, and, having heard that an army was to be sent against them, made sure that the Chatteemaker was one of the vanguard. "See," cried they, " here comes a man of gigantic stature on a mighty horse! He rides at full speed across the country, tearing up the very trees in his rage! He is one of the opposing force; the whole army must be close at hand. If they are such as he, we are all dead men." Then, running to their Rajah, some of them cried again: "Here comes the whole force of the enemy" (for the story had by this time become exaggerated); "they are men of gigantic stature, mounted on mighty horses; as they come they tear up the very trees in their rage; we can oppose men, but not monsters such as these." These were followed by others, who said: "It is all true," for by this time the Chatteemaker had got pretty near the camp; they're coming! they're coming! let us fly! let us fly—fly, fly for your lives!" And the whole panic-stricken multitude fled from the camp, those who had seen no cause for alarm going because the others did, or because they did not care to stay by themselves, after having obliged their Rajah to write a letter to the one whose country he was about to invade, to say that he would not do so, and to propose terms of peace, and to sign it and seal it with his seal. Scarcely had all the people fled from the camp when the horse on which the Chatteemaker was came galloping into it, and on his back rode the Chatteemaker, almost dead from fatigue, with the banyan tree in his hand. Just as he reached the camp the ropes by which he was tied broke, and he fell to the ground. The horse stood still, too tired with his long run to go farther. On recovering his senses, the Chatteemaker found, to his surprise, that the whole camp, full of rich arms, clothes, and trappings, was entirely deserted. In the principal tent, moreover, he found a letter addressed to his Rajah, announcing the retreat of the invading army and proposing terms of peace.

So he took the letter and returned home with it as fast as he could, leading his horse all the way, for he was afraid to mount him again. It did not take him long to reach his house by the direct road, for while riding he had gone a more circuitous journey than was necessary, and he reached there just at nightfall. His wife ran out to meet him, overjoyed at his speedy return. As soon as he saw her, he said: " Ah, wife, since I saw you last I've been all around the world, and had many wonderful and terrible adventures. But never mind that now: send this letter quickly to the Rajah by a messenger, and send the horse also that he sent for me to ride. He will then see, by the horse looking so tired, what a long ride I've had; and if he is sent on beforehand, I shall not be obliged to ride him up to the palace door to-morrow morning, as I otherwise should, and that would be very tiresome, for most likely I should tumble off." So his wife sent the horse and the letter to the Rajah, and a message that her husband would be at the palace early next morning, as it was then late at night. And next day he went down there, as he had said he would; and when the people saw him coming, they said: " This man is as modest as he is brave; after having put our enemies to flight, he walks quite simply to the door, instead of riding here in state, as another man would." For they did not know that the Chatteemaker walked because he was afraid to ride.

The Rajah came to the palace door to meet him, and paid him all possible honor. Terms of peace were agreed upon between the two countries, and the Chatteemaker was rewarded for all he had done, by being given twice as much rank and wealth as he had before, and he lived very happily all the rest of his life.

THE END